BEAUTIFUL BRUTE

A COURT UNIVERSITY NOVEL

EDEN O'NEILL

BEAUTIFUL BRUTE: Court University Book 3

Copyright © 2020 by Eden O'Neill

This book is a work of fiction and any resemblance to any person, living or dead, any place, events or occurrences, is purely coincidental and not intended by the author.

Cover Art: RBA Designs
Editing: Straight on till Morningside

Table of Contents

Chapter One

Cleo

A massive chest rose and fell with heavy breath beside me.

I slept… with a *boy*.

A giggle suppressed as I hunkered down, peeking at him from my pillow. He was beautiful in ways that weren't right, hard body filling half my bed and long.

Holy crap, was he long.

His actual ankles hung off my full bed, sliding out of the sheets when he tugged them up and tucked them above his hips. A perfect V-shape lingered below chiseled ab muscles, his chest broad and golden.

I bit back a snicker at his dick hair. He gave me full-on dick cleavage, a smattering of dark hair at the base of his dick. I couldn't see *all* of said dick currently, but his morning wood outlined my rainbow bedding like nothing else.

Oh my gosh.

A sigh in his sleep and he turned, perfection from his chiseled jaw line to his full lips. He had a deep cavity near his right eye, like an old scar from something. Outside of that tiny imperfection, he stunned with hallowed cheekbones cut from the gods and a pair of deep-set eyes that glistened when he laughed. He had green eyes when they weren't closed, and though I'd only seen him in a dark club and my bedroom last night, they'd been awesome. They were like see-through marbles.

Clear.

Lush.

Utterly gorgeous.

I tried not to breath now for fear he'd wake up and see me ogle. And my *God* his laugh. He had such a rich tone, the lines around his mouth revealing he liked to do this often. He liked to laugh, a kidder and a jokester. He kept trying to find ways to bring it out of me last night, to poke and touch me.

He'd been perfect.

He *was* perfect from his body, to his smile, to his laugh. He had the looks of Chris Pine, his shaggy brown hair that curled and feathered only adding to his features. With the fun-loving personality of Chris Pratt and the height of a Hemsworth, he was absolutely all the Chrises.

All the boxes checked.

All goals met.

All virginity lost.

A reminder of that burn, that soreness, quaked between my legs, and I *hoped* I hadn't come across as much of a virgin now as I did last night. I mean, I couldn't have been a great lover, it being my first time and all that, but I hoped he hadn't noticed.

He'd been *good*, slow, and it didn't hurt once we picked up. In fact, I'd been so overwhelmed by sensory overload and the fact I'd come so quick last night, the discomfort hadn't even bothered me.

This guy had made it easy, all golden and glistening with sweat. He'd enveloped me in a way that made me feel small but not in a bad way, his name, Brett.

Cleo Erikson-Fairchild had a conquest dadgummit.

The huzzah I kept internal. It was all I could do not to leave this bed and doodle his name surrounded by hearts in a notebook. He'd just been really sweet, and I definitely wanted to go out with him again. That was if he hadn't picked up I'd been a virgin. I'd heard it could be a turn off for guys so I hadn't mentioned it.

I need to call Kit!

My friend would want to know how I fared last night. We hadn't gone to the club with intentions to lose my virginity, but I sure had been open to it. I'd wanted to head into my senior year of college a new woman, ready for the world and go beyond my comfort zone. I always stayed in that tight little box a lot.

I didn't want to be in that box anymore.

Meeting Brett last night had come with opportunity, and though I started to reach for my phone to call my roommate and best friend since freshman year, I stopped when a hand came to settle around my hips. Brett hugged me to him, and I found a nice place there, his body heated and warm.

Lacing my fingers across his chest, I stared up at him, full well *knowing* I was all googly-eyed.

"So, um, I'm awake," he drummed, a lid peeking open. He revealed one of those glistening green marbles. He grinned. "Just FYI in case you were wondering."

Holy crap.

Stiffening, I tried to play the fact off. "Oh, okay. Cool."

"Cool." A chuckle when he peeled both eyes open, a translucent, sea foam green rounding his irises. He was an aquatic prince sans the trident, his arms stretched wide before he brought them around me again. "I just felt bad. You know, since you were staring and all that."

My face heated. "I wasn't staring."

"Hmm." An ass pinch before his big hand hugged my cheeks. "How does that lie go again?"

He pressed his mouth into my neck, and I thought I'd come right there, the burn tingling my lower lips. He jiggled my bottom, and when he got anywhere close to touching me *down there*, I giggled.

He pulled back, the grin sexy on his full lips. "You're cute, you know? Sexy."

A foreign term to me, but I drank it in as hard biceps surrounded me. Brett tipped my chin, kissing my mouth open, and immediate warmth settled in my tummy. Deep, his tongue dueled with mine, hot lava in his touch as he tugged the sheets off my body.

"So goddamn sexy," he crooned, sliding his hand between my legs. I jumped, accidentally kneeing him, and he smiled. "You okay?"

Stop being such a virgin.

Okay, so I wasn't a virgin anymore, but I still felt like one. All this was new, but I closed my eyes, trying to stay out of my head. This was all good until Brett explored with his thick fingers, thumb and forefinger brushing my sex. I jumped again on instinct, wriggling, but froze entirely as he entered my raw core.

His fingers retreated immediately, of course, lashes fanning up, and I nearly face-palmed myself.

I nudged his arms. "Don't stop."

"You sure?"

I cupped the sharp blades of his back for emphasis, bringing him down on me. A sexy grin and his lips returned to mine, my hands bracing his shoulders. He took us right back to where things left off, easing my legs apart. He actually got his entire digit in before my body protested and froze up again. I was just so sore, *badly* since it had been my first experience last night, and this time, Brett ignored my urge to keep going.

"Yeah, you're not, okay." He fell to his side, concern on his perfect Chris Pine lips. "What's up? You're not into this?"

So I was definitely into this.

But how did one tell this perfect fusion of, simply put, *the best* Chrises that she'd only been touched like once and that was by him?

"Er, um," I started, and when his eyebrow raised, I sighed. "I'm just inexperienced."

"Right." Another grin before he pressed his mouth to mine, that big Hemsworth body all over me. "You're funny."

I wished I was. I wished it didn't still hurt because he was fucking sexy and I wanted him inside me right now like I wanted ice cream sundaes. Like I wanted lava cake and snickerdoodles. Like I *loved* caramel corn.

Jesus, he makes me insatiable.

"This tight, little body isn't inexperienced," he said, moving a hand over my breast. He pinched a nipple, and I moaned. He breathed heat over it. "It's sexy as fuck."

Again, foreign to me, which was why I'd been so forthright at the club last night. I was tired of being the soft, inexperienced virgin. I wanted to have some fun and finally get out of my head. I let life hold me back a lot, and Kit amping me up last night only helped me out. *She'd* been having sex since high school, and my college roommate couldn't believe I hadn't had the same experiences yet. She'd called me sexy too before, I guess, but that was so not me in my shorts past my knees and calf-length skirts. I was mission trips and Netflix, not sexy woman of the

5

world. That'd just never been me.

But Brett had made me feel that way last night, adventurous. He'd made me laugh, so hard I thought I'd barf a lung. His experience in the bedroom only added to the perfection he was. He'd made me feel so deeply, knew pleasure. Just like now.

Tweaking my nipple, he positioned a knee between my legs. He rubbed my sex, just a brush, but it tickled, and I squeaked.

I actually *squeaked*.

A slow eyebrow lift in my direction, and I literally did palm my face.

You suck, Cleo Erikson-Fairchild. You totally suck!

My fingers peeled away. "Okay, I have a confession."

"All right." A smirk before he played with my fingers, and I was glad he found this funny because I sure didn't.

I bit my lip, completely embarrassed. "Uh, last night was my first time."

"First time for what?"

I gave him a look, an obvious one, and his eyebrows jumped so far up his face I thought they'd shoot into his Chris Pine hairline.

Our fingers stopped the dance when he removed one. He twirled it in front of me. "So what we did last night…"

"My first time."

"You're serious?"

"As a heart attack."

Reality moved over his face then, and when he lay back, looking completely freaking stunned, I knew I lost him.

Brett's thick fingers shoved into his hair in silence, his sight dancing on my star-coated ceiling. I'd put up those corny, glow-in-the-dark stars when I'd been like twelve, but had been too lazy to take them down. We'd had to come to my childhood home last night since I was on break from school, but I didn't expect my parents back until later today since they were out of town on business. My adoptive father—well, technically, my stepdad—was a congressman and my mom worked for him. I thought them being out of town gave me an opportunity.

But now, I was only embarrassed.

My heart beat like a jackrabbit during Brett's silence, and I thought he'd literally run from my bed like I had a contagious disease.

Say something please.

Too many moments passed, too many of him staring at the ceiling. Wide-eyed, he looked like one of those memes were the guy is trying to calculate the most intricate problem. His throat jumped. "All right."

"All right?" I asked, hopeful. I hoped it would be all right.

I really wanted to see him again.

He was nice, and though he was probably local, I was sure I could work something out to see him again. I was supposed to be going back to school tomorrow, but my university was only like an hour away. A long distance thing could work if…

Totally ahead of myself, I deflated. Especially when something hardened Brett's features.

His eyebrows drew in, his stare calculated, cold. It was the opposite of how I'd seen him before.

"Brett?"

He said nothing, the swallow hard in his

throat. Turning, he schooled whatever that was before. He picked up my hand, lacing my fingers. "A virgin... all right."

"All right?"

He nodded, but this time, he smiled. "I can be about that. No big deal."

"Really?"

"Really." No hesitation with his chuckle, that wonderful laughter that forced heat instantly into my belly. He'd gotten me drunk off that sound without a lick of alcohol last night. There'd been a reason I'd taken this guy home with me. He'd been so nice, easygoing.

He'd been gentle.

Perfect.

He was perfect now, wrapping a thick arm around me. He tugged at my chin. "Really, it's not a thing. I'm okay with it."

He was okay with it.

Tipping my chin, he kissed me, and suddenly, my vision was filled with wedding bells and "Here Comes the Bride."

A growl and he had our fingers laced, dragging them up and above my head. He pressed his whole big body on me, and when I ground my hips into him, he blessed me with that deep laughter again.

"You sure you were a virgin, gorgeous?" he asked, biting my lips. I believed I'd been, but with him all hot and hard on top of me I wasn't sure.

Turning the tides, I shifted, forcing him on his back. He let me be myself with him, be... sexy. He let me take control and when he gathered my hair, I bit back a moan.

"Hon! We're home. Where are you?"

Holy fucking shit!

I fell off the bed, like literally rolled off the bed with a thud.

Brett scrambled to the side, eyes wide. "Shit. You okay?"

"Cleo?"

Mom's voice traveled from somewhere in the house again. Meanwhile, I was on the floor flopping around on my purple shag rug. My childhood bedroom was literally like *My Little Pony* threw up in it, a fascination I had from my pony figurines on my desk to the artist renderings I bought from the internet and put on my walls.

It was a phase, okay?

"Honey?" My adoptive father, Rick, called from within the house as well. "Darling? Is everything all right? We heard something. Should we come up?"

Shit, he's home too!

Neither one was supposed to be, obviously, since I brought a boy into their house and screwed him.

Oh my Goddd.

"Everything's fine!" I called, hoping to God they didn't come up. Scrambling, I got my naked butt off the floor, and I shot to the door. I locked it. "Everything's good. I swear!"

"You're sure?"

"Positive!" Panicked, I listened through the door, and when I heard nothing, I turned around, facing Brett. He'd gotten up from the bed.

And was gloriously naked.

His length hung heavy, thick and veiny. I'd been intimidated as hell by him last night, and his dick had been a huge part of that.

But then the rest of him.

Golden perfection, hard and chiseled everywhere he needed to be. A pair of thick thighs pulsed with muscular definition. This guy obviously worked out and frequently. He literally looked like Thor without the hammer, his fingers coming up and curling in his feathered hair. "Your, um… parents, I'm guessing."

"Parents?" My lips parted in a daze with my sight on that body in front of me.

His smile righted. "Yeah. Downstairs." He pointed a finger in that direction. "Should we do something…"

Oh, fuck!

Groaning, I gathered all his things. Like all his stuff from his shoes and shirt to his jeans. I threw the lot at him, but couldn't find his boxers.

Where the hell are his boxers?

"Er, um." Like he knew, he tugged them off my *My Little Pony* lamp.

If I could physically die in that moment, I would have.

A smile and he was bunching them up with the rest of his stuff. "I'm assuming I need to leave now."

God, did I not want him to, but gathering a sleep shirt and a pair of shorts I'd worn the other night, I knew he needed to. I found my sports bra too and tugged all three on. "Yeah, and I'm so sorry."

"It's cool. So, um…" He gazed around, but when I pointed toward the window his eyes widened. "Wait. The window?"

I mean, I hadn't tried it, but I figured it was possible. Mom liked to do gardening work out there when she was actually home. There should be some vines up the wall he could climb down…

A hand grappled my waist, like nearly my entire waist with how big it was. A cool smile and Brett was pressing his naked body up against me. He still hadn't put his clothing on so I felt basically every inch of him.

"Cleo, I haven't climbed out of a girl's window since high school," he said, so tempting. He buried his face in my hair. I hadn't cut it in a while and the soft brown waves basically sat at my butt. He bunched it. "Can we do a little better than that?"

Oh, we could do way better, and that consisted of us hopping back in that bed while he made me melt. In fact, he dropped the clothes between us, his stuff hitting the floor, and when he brought both arms around me, I thought that's exactly where we were headed.

That was until steps hit the hallway.

A heavy cadence, *my dad*, before a fist tapped on the other side of my door.

"Honey, you coming down?" Another tap. "We've obviously ruined the surprise, but we came home early." A light chuckle. "We wanted to see you."

Well, I was definitely surprised, and under any normal circumstances, I would have wanted to see them. Since Dad was a congressman, they were basically never home, my mom the same since she worked for him. That's how they'd met, inseparable since. It'd been a surprise when they told me they were getting married but a happy one.

"We brought danishes for you too, sweetheart."

My heart would warm had I not had a naked boy up against me, a boy whose gaze shot toward the door the moment my dad's voice drifted inside.

And what a simmer it held.

Brett's hand literally curled around my waist at the presence of my dad, his entire body stiff and rigid. The appearance of my father obviously bothered him, as it should because *that was my dad* on the other side of the door. My adoptive father had always been pretty laid-back, but at the end of the day, the man raised me, had been in my life since I was eleven, and I was his little girl. I was still that even at twenty-two and about to be a senior in college. Dad wouldn't be happy Brett was in here *at all*, and I shoved Brett out of his stupor.

"You have to go," I whisper-growled, picking up his stuff and nudging him toward the window. He stood solid, an impenetrable landmass, and my heart raced inside my chest. "What are you doing?"

"Actually, I think I've changed my mind." His look peeled away from the door and settled on me. If my dad bothered him before, there was no tell of that now, his hands gathering my waist and tugging me to him. His nose graced my cheek. "Don't make me leave, Cleo. I want you."

Good fucking God.

Internally groaning, I obviously had a weakness for guys who gave off Chris energy. A kiss to my neck and I knew I was letting him stay. What I didn't know was how I'd make that happen with *my dad* on the other side of the door. I patted his chest. "Okay. Just… get in the closet or something."

He smirked. "The closet?"

"Yes, I'll make up an excuse or something. Get them to run to the store real quick."

It'd buy us more time if anything else.

He didn't move, still holding me, but him hiding was *not* negotiable this time. I pushed him toward the closet, and by the grace of God, he moved his gargantuan-sized legs. I opened the walk-in, pushing him inside and when I stepped back to close the door, he smiled at me ever so innocently. He also kept his clothes strategically placed over his johnson, looking freaking cute as hell, and I seriously thought I'd melt.

"Hon?" Dad called.

Gah!

I shut the door on his cute smile, knowing I'd have to do some fast talking to get my parents out.

I'd only been thanking the heavens above Brett hadn't driven over here. We'd both taken ride shares out to the club, so when we left, we did the same back here. No way would I be able to explain a guy's car in my driveway.

I was seriously screwed, something I knew because getting my parents out, even to go to the store, when they'd just arrived wouldn't be easy. They'd come home early to spend time with me, and they hadn't just come into town to see me off to school, but my stepbrother too. He was due to arrive later today and was my adoptive father's kid from his previous marriage.

A long story, but I hadn't actually met my stepbrother, Jaxen Ambrose, even though our parents had been married since we were both eleven. Jaxen'd chosen to stay in the Midwest with his mom while his dad obviously lived with my mom and me. I'd remembered being really sad about that when I was a kid, learning I had a step-sibling only later to find out I wouldn't be seeing him. I guessed Rick and Jaxen's mom had a rough divorce. I didn't know the details, but hadn't questioned it and definitely respected Jaxen's decision to stick with his mom. Mine had been my rock since my own dad left.

It took me a real long time to get over that, my dad abandoning my mom and me. In fact, I still wasn't completely over it, but I had moved on. That was made easier by the man who adopted me at the age of thirteen. Rick Fairchild had been the cornerstone of this family for a long time, and I knew he was really looking forward to Jaxen coming down here. Jaxen'd decided to come here to finish up his senior year, in college like me. We already had so much in common, and I was looking forward to meeting him.

I hadn't had siblings in a long time.

My crap together and some clothes put on, I made it to the door, opening it up and seeing my dad's face. He had his suit on, well partially. He hadn't worn the jacket, but still presented as a congressman through and through. His tie was navy, an American flag pinned to it. A wide smile, and he gave me the biggest hug.

"I was starting to think something was wrong," he said, pulling away. He had dark hair, naturally curly but always moused it back for work. The man I called my father never had a single hair out of place, nor a five o' clock shadow on his jaw. Not even during Christmas when he and Mom didn't have to work. He just always had things together, which had been so important for me and my mom. We needed that a long time ago, thrived on it.

I hugged him again, super tight. I missed him whenever he and Mom were away.

"Nothing's wrong." *Much.* I only had a boy in my closet. A boy I had no idea how I'd let go. I released Dad. "Sorry. Just woke up."

This obviously surprising him, his head tilted.

"My daughter sleeping past ten? Wow, are you sure you're my Cleo?"

Chuckling, I told him I was. He threw an arm around me in response, my dress definitely lazy today. He asked about that too as I usually came out of my room in workout clothes in the morning. I liked to run before five generally.

"Late start," I said on our way down the hallway. I'd have to send them to the store for *something*, but if I led with that, he'd probably push and find that weird. After all, he'd just gotten here and that would be weird. I always liked to see both him and Mom when they arrived.

For now, I decided to let him lead me downstairs. "Kit took me out, so yeah, I was up pretty late."

Dad and Mom knew all about Kit. We'd been roommates since freshman year, and funny enough, we grew up in the same town but didn't know about each other until we'd been assigned our living arrangements. We'd been joined at the hip ever since, the girl my best friend. Like most people, I didn't see many of my old friends anymore when we all parted ways after high school to go to college. We still kept up with each other in one way or the other, but for the most part, we didn't talk a whole lot. A big reason for that was me. I wasn't really about social media so much. I was more into activism and volunteering on campus. I'd even done a mission trip earlier this summer abroad, the time of my life.

Dad and I found my mom in the kitchen reading the paper. She was in a pleated skirt and white blouse, the perfect pairing to my dad. He'd just had his dress slacks and white shirt on, but his blazer rested across the kitchen island.

"Look who I found," Dad proclaimed, kissing the top of my head. "Sleeping in past ten."

"Who are you and where is my first born?" she asked, still saying that. It'd been years since my brother and she still called me her first born.

The first like there were others now.

Mom's thoughts obviously hadn't traveled where mine had. Her brown eyes warmed, same tone as mine. We shared a bright hazel as well as our brunette hair. Mom kept hers in a bun most days. She grinned. "Should I take your temperature?"

"Mom," I groaned. Dad dropped his arm and I wandered over to my mom's waiting arms. "Stop. I slept in. So what."

"So what?" she eyed Dad behind me. "I've only been telling her that for years."

Dad flashed nothing but his teeth. "I'm telling you, *Invasion of the Body Snatchers*. This isn't our child."

"Clearly." She jostled me. "How have you been? You had a late night or something?"

Something like that.

My gaze drifted toward the ceiling, but with a nudge, my mom had me sitting on a barstool beside her.

My parents had a wide kitchen in our suburban home, the multi-level within only two miles of the beach. I grew up within a short drive of the Miami coast, but could count how many times I'd actually been to Miami on one hand. I loved the sun, but preferred our more modest-sized town and the childhood home I grew up in. When we were all here, my parents and I, the place was always full. Mom and Dad constantly had events, both family gatherings and business. I remember being a teen while they hosted dinner parties for the neighborhood, but no matter how busy they got, they always made sure to tuck me in. I had more than one nanny growing up, but never, not once, did my mom and dad make me feel like they didn't care, like they weren't there for me. They were off changing the world, my role models whom I respected and loved. Our house was such a family place, welcoming with its feel, which was why Mom and Dad said they'd bought it.

"We wanted a place for you to bring back your babies."

Mom always said that, the home reserved to be filled up with grandchildren. Of course, I'd never slowed down enough to even think about that. I'd been ultra-focused on school and my volunteer work. I did orchestra for a time too before I got too busy.

Mom's hand came to tug at my waist-length hair, the haircut definitely needed on my end. My mousy brown hair nearly hit my butt, and though it was completely unmanageable, I only liked to cut it after it was long enough to donate. I supposed with my parents' work in politics and helping people, I'd always gravitated toward that too. I couldn't do much in school, but always actively tried to help out where I could. My mission trip had been to Haiti.

Mom immediately started asking about that. I hadn't seen them except for a drop-in here and there all summer, and they really did only come home now to see me off before going back to school. That and, of course, to be here when my stepbrother Jaxen arrived. From what I understood, his plane was scheduled to come in sometime this evening.

I might have asked them about that.

Had I not heard movement on the stairs.

Literally creeks and cracks, stopping all conversation.

Stopping me.

A glance and my family's gazes made a beeline in that direction. Mom lowered her arm. "Is someone here?"

Oh no.

Dad actually started to go in that direction, but there was no need.

Because he walked right in the room.

Brett waltzed into the kitchen like he'd been frequenting it for years, his eyes following mine. He walked right up to the kitchen island. Joined my family.

What the fuck did he think he was doing?

My heart catapulting into my throat, I thought I'd pass out. There was no explanation for this. Absolutely no explanation that would excuse the fact that the boy I slept with was now downstairs and very much standing in front of my parents. I could explain all I wanted, and my parents still wouldn't be about this.

Oh my God. Oh my God. Oh my God.

This had to be akin to dying, this feeling inside. Complete and utter dread filled me as my parents' eyes twitched wide and my mom got completely off her barstool. Dad had come around from the bar at this point, maybe a foot away from Brett.

Holy fuck, he's going to kill him.

It was like Dad *knew* what I did in his house, approaching him, but Brett... well, Brett was the only one in this situation who didn't appear to be totally floored by the turn of events in front of him. He stood there, cool as a cucumber in front of my dad.

18

My mouth parted. "Dad…"

"Jaxen," came out of my Dad's mouth first, *my eyes* twitching wide.

What…

But that's what Dad had called him when he approached him, Jaxen. Dad put a hand out.

But Brett hugged him instead.

It'd been a sudden hug and one, clearly, my adoptive father hadn't anticipated.

Dad froze, his arms slowly coming down around the hugger. "Son?"

Son…

My blinks rapid, the guy who hugged him merely brought an arm farther around my dad. The pair shifted, and I found nothing but green eyes in my direction.

They accompanied his smile.

"Hey, Dad," the boy with the beautiful green eyes said, his words shocking me still. He hugged my father harder. "Good to see you."

Chapter Two

Jax

Golden… absolutely fucking gold.

The hug had been an even better touch.

Stomaching it, nothing but pure and utter bliss rolled through me, my gaze on my stepsister. She stood there, stunned in her fucking *My Little Pony* shorts.

Because yes, she had those too.

Her bedroom looked like the pony exploded in it, and had she not been such a good lay, it might have bothered me a little.

She was a gangly thing, tall. I considered myself a tall guy at six foot two, but this girl came up to my chin.

And what a little priss she'd been.

I hadn't known I'd popped her cherry, but that'd been a win for me. I hoped one of many.

But she didn't fool me… this girl chewing her lip and staring at me from behind my dad's shoulder. Girls like her, model-esque with a cup size that held the highest percentage of their body weight liked to play the sweet, innocent thing. They feigned not to know how sexy they were just to get compliments, and though they may keep their virginity in check, they just as easily let guys pound every hole but their pussy to hold on to the title. My stepsister was one of those girls.

Sexy.

Shallow as fuck.

Mine to end.

She'd be an easy one to break, almost not even a challenge. She'd been all over my dick last night like the little entitled whore she was, wrestling with her hands now while my bio dad fawned all over me. What I wouldn't give to be in her head right now.

I was about to be.

"Jaxen..." my sperm donor of a father said in my ear, grappling my shoulder. He'd been surprised I'd hugged him. *Clearly*.

Because in any other circumstances, I wouldn't have.

I wouldn't have granted him the satisfaction, but today, I would.

Today was different.

A sigh actually racked the fucker's shoulders, and again, I had to stomach it. That was why I was here, for this.

Boning my stepsister had just been a bonus.

She looked about two seconds away from freaking out, wrestling with that ass-length hair of hers. She was pale as fuck considering how close she lived to the beach, but maybe, just maybe I might have had something to do with that. She truly hadn't known who I was to her, and had I not stalked the hell out of my father and his create-a-family on social media, I might not have known who she was either. Oddly enough, the chick hadn't been on social media, but my father was. A politician, his handles were filled with pictures of her and my stepmom.

I tried not to growl at the woman he cheated on my mother with, the one who ultimately ripped my family apart. My father was a slimeball, point-blank, but now, he hugged me like time hadn't passed.

Like he hadn't left my ass when I was eleven.

I pulled back with a smile now, making myself. He held me out, just looking at me, and I was well aware I was basically this guy's clone. We had the same jawline, strong and with an intensity to his eyes that contrasted his relaxed expression. He liked to smile a lot, just like me.

Usually.

He tapped my neck. "Why didn't you tell us you got here?" he asked, then passed a look over to stepsis. "Cleo?"

Nothing from her direction, and honestly, she hadn't known. I didn't tell her. That had been a delight of my own the minute I'd realized my stepsister and I had been at the same club last night. I had flown in early, stopped by to see a friend. My buddy LJ was attending a wedding in Miami, and after stopping and catching up with him, I left with a couple of bridesmaids. They'd been local so we checked out the scene, headed to the club.

Cleo tugged on her hair like Rapunzel, literally that long. "I, um…"

Tell them. I dare you.

I wished she would blow this shit right out of the water, tell them what went down and how I'd fucked her into an oblivion last night. Honestly, she may have been just figuring it out herself. That she'd slept with her stepbrother.

And that she'd enjoyed it.

I had her ass wriggling last night, like a true virgin, and how easy she'd let me take it.

Hair fell from her fingers. She started to say something, but bio dad had more of his focus on me. He started saying a bunch of shit completely lost on me, a mantra of "when did you arrive" and "how good it is to see you." Nodding with a smile, I told him the same.

Too easy.

He made it so, wanting it to be easy. He wanted me standing here and forgetting about the past. He wanted his second chance with me, and I was giving him that by being here.

But that didn't mean it wouldn't be without cost.

My pockets were a little empty from his payout, but I wasn't talking about money. I was talking about time and need for payment from the past. My biological father, Rick, dropped his arm around me. "Well, I'm just glad you're here. Maggie?"

He waved stepmother bitch over, basically Cleo's clone. They had the same height, same body type and everything. I had to admit my father's family was hot, and since he wasn't a hopeless case, after all, half my looks unfortunately did come from him, I supposed that'd been the reason why he'd been able to nab them.

"I want you to meet your stepmom," he said, but didn't look nervous. He looked almost proud to introduce me to the woman he'd ruined our family for. He grinned. "My Maggie."

His Maggie.

She came over to me, taking my hand and I had another moment. One where I had to slowly check myself. I could end all this right now.

Don't be fucking stupid.

"Good to meet you, Jaxen."

"Good to meet you," I forced and good as hell at it. I'd prepared for this.

I was ready for this.

But stepmom didn't let go of my hand, beaming a hundred watt smile at me. If Mary Sunshine had a whore sister, this woman would be it, blinging her pearly whites at me. She had my father's money and his arm, something I or my mother never needed. My mom had been successful in her own right, didn't need his shit.

Unlike this bitch.

She obviously relished in it, their fancy-ass house and that big fucking diamond on her finger. Stepmom grinned. "Oh my goodness, Rick. He looks nothing like those old pictures you've shown us. Wow, I never would have recognized you. You've obviously grown up and so handsome."

Rick shook my shoulders. "Of course, he is. He's my son, isn't he?"

Another pulse in my stomach that I had any biological connection at all to this man. I checked myself again. "Genetics are something, huh?"

"I mean, I'd say that. You two look so much alike. It's uncanny really. Wow."

My jaw worked, but Maggie smiled, finally letting go of me. Noticing her daughter was mysteriously absent from the conversation, she waved at Cleo. "Darling, why didn't you call us? I'm sure your father would have wanted to know Jaxen got here early."

I fought the cringe. Obviously, I knew stepsis and Rick were close. He had been in her life for a long time.

He was her dad.

I heard her even call him that, listening for a while before I made my appearance. It just made what I planned to do to this girl that much easier.

Cleo slid under her mother's arm, but I wouldn't look at her, letting my dad talk and go on and on about how good it was to see me. It was a friendly enough exchange, but all the while, I felt the younger whore's eyes on me. She obviously had questions for me.

This was going to be fun.

"Well, now. How about breakfast then?" Maggie suggested. "We'll all go out and—"

"Actually, if you have the stuff, I can get something together," I said, stealing the attention. I smiled. "I don't mind. Used to cook a lot at home."

I'd learned from the best, no thanks to my dad. He hadn't been there to show me anything. Let alone how to cook. Even still, he flashed a wide smile in my direction after what I'd said. He shook my shoulder. "Bet you've learned a lot from your mom, haven't you?"

I noticed he left out Mama in that sentence, *both* my mothers celebrity chefs. Perhaps, it bothered him that after *him* my mom had moved on from asshole to something better. I forced my grin. "Right. Learned a lot from both of them."

Rick kept his own smile, rubbing my shoulders. He asked if I needed help after that, help getting things together or if I needed anything. Like the good son I was, I told him I didn't need a thing. And actually urged him and my stepmom to relax. I heard they'd just got home.

They should rest their feet.

I swear to God, I should have gotten an Academy Award for that shit. Because not only had they left with grins of delight, they left me with my stepsister. Told her she should stay and get to know me.

Yeah, she should.

She needed to know *all* about me. The room clear, though, I gave her my back, rooting around the kitchen for the eggs. I was well aware her attention was on nothing but me the whole time.

She just didn't say anything.

She didn't dare and not for a long time. Eventually, she eased her little self over to my side of the bar, and once there, she played with her T-shirt.

I dragged my gaze up the length of her, how scared and intimated she appeared to be. Again, she didn't fool anyone. I knew how this girl was.

I knew what she took.

I knew what she *thought* was hers, and that alone let me know all about her. Her lips parted. "Jaxen…"

"Jax," I said, eyeing her down to her Pony shorts. Such a waste. This girl's tits were gorgeous, but she dressed like she rolled out of kid's donation bin. Even last night her dress had basically been down to her ankles, part of that whole "innocence" thing she obviously tried to pull off. Again, I gave her my back, cracking some eggs before whipping them up. She came toward me again, her soft breaths pants behind me.

"But…" she started, and I slowed, whisking slowly. She blew out a breath. "You told me your name was Brett."

I did tell her that, told her a lot of things. But that was just the beginning of all this for her.

I grinned.

"My name is Brett," I said, nearly laughing. "My middle name that is."

It'd been really so easy. It was like she'd gone to that club to get laid and maybe she had. I wouldn't put it past her.

I mean, she was her mother's daughter.

She started to say something else, but I walked up on her.

And how those double-Ds shook.

They trembled right beneath her tee, and I was glad.

She was about to know *exactly* where we stood.

Putting the bowl of eggs down, I crowded her, her soft heat under my tongue. She smelled like cherries and whore.

Probably, since she hadn't showered.

I'd sweated all over this girl last night, my cum probably still inside her. We'd manage to break a condom last night, but I hadn't worried too much since she had said she'd been on the pill. She'd even looked excited that it'd happened.

Little slut.

I brushed her chin with my knuckles, her breath hiking. The chrome ring on my fourth finger touched her chin, and she quivered. Right down to those double-Ds under her T-shirt. I smirked. "Probably should go take a shower before breakfast, sis," I stated, tapping her chin. "After all, my cum's still inside you."

Shock rattled her stiff, her face flushed. Her lips shook apart, but before she could open her mouth, I pressed a finger to her lips.

"Better hurry now," I said. "Don't want to be late for family breakfast."

Another touch of her jaw, my ring brushing it before pulling away. This ring on my finger meant something where I came from, and all bowed down to it.

She would too.

Cleo's eyes coated in tears I refused to look at. I had no time for it. Quickly, she left my sight, and I did nothing but smile as I whisked up the eggs. I

was going to make this girl burn.
And I'd laugh all the way there.

Chapter Three

Cleo

I blew chunks into the toilet. Literal chunks until there was nothing left but stomach acid.

I quivered by the end.

I ached.

My knees hit cold tiles, my fingers uncurling from the toilet seat. The shower was on and the room filled with choking steam, but I didn't turn it off.

It concealed my sobs.

And I did sob, violently. I shook like a torrential storm, in a horror film of my own. It'd been a horror film he'd created.

He'd been so cruel to me.

There'd been almost... hatred in Jax's eyes when he spoke to me, and I didn't understand.

I didn't understand.

I'd *never* in my entire life been treated in such a way. I was no saint, but not ever had someone just been completely mean to me when I'd done nothing to them. Jaxen had targeted me. He'd gone for me, clearly.

He'd taken my virginity.

The sobs grew and grew, the steam from the shower clogging the room. I'd turned it on to drown out the tears but hadn't even made it in there.

Flushing the toilet with shaking limbs, I forced myself to stand, to commence with my day. Before I came up here, I told Mom and Dad I wanted to take a quick shower, needing to do so before breakfast.

"Probably should go take a shower before breakfast... my cum's still inside you."

I stumbled inside the running water, clothes still on. I hit the shower tiles, then fell to my knees. My hair and clothing soaked, I retched again over the drain.

I didn't stop until I heaved a shuddered breath.

Eventually, I got myself together enough to strip off my clothes and scrub up, being extra careful. I was still so sore, but I had to scrub. Jax's voice was in my head.

God.

My stomach rolled the entire time, but I managed not to throw up again. I tried to make it as quick as I could, knowing Mom, Dad, and Jaxen were waiting for me. I didn't know what he'd do if I took too long. Tell them?

Do worse?

I didn't know what any of this was, nor why he tried to hurt me. I just knew he had, and I was shaking when I finally did turn off the shower. Moving quick, I grabbed a towel, wrapping it around myself. I stepped out and immediately went for my toiletry bag.

I wiped the mirror before opening it up, then brushed my teeth. I gurgled in the shower, but still, my mouth tasted awful.

A heavy breath and I stared at dead eyes in the mirror. They'd been eyes filled with life and excitement just last night. Jaxen had managed to steal that away.

But... why?

How could someone who didn't even know me be so cruel to me? He'd had to have known who I was last night, right? I mean, I told him my name.

He had to know.

I just summed up that he had to have been crazy, a complete lunatic. It was the only explanation. Normal people didn't just do things like that to people they didn't know, and I'd never met the guy before last night.

Yeah, he just must be crazy.

All well and good until I realized he was my stepbrother and I did have to be around him. Heck, we even were taking a road trip tomorrow. I was supposed to drive us both back to campus. Me to start my senior year and him to start his own.

Immense fear racked my shoulders at what that trip may contain, but before I could ralph again, I padded for my birth control pills. I usually took them first thing in the morning. Obviously, I hadn't been having sex, but I had such bad periods I'd been taking them since high school.

I pulled the pack out, then filled up my rinse cup on the sink. After, I fingered the pack but dropped the whole thing at the sight of extra pills.

Oh my God.

I counted one, then two missed, something I never did, but my routine had been off being home and not at school.

"...my cum's still inside you."

Holding my mouth, I ran, then dry heaved over the toilet, remembering how Jaxen and I had broken a condom last night. I hadn't thought much about it at the time because I'd *believed* I had been on birth control. It'd even felt good with him inside me, the unrestricted heat of him. I'd actually felt molten inside after I realized.

Only to find out he was my stepbrother.

I let a crazy person come inside me, someone related to the man I called father. There was obviously no blood relation, but still.

But still…

Immediately, I took the pill for today, then sprinted from the bathroom, rushing to my bedroom. I threw on the first thing I could find, a sundress and sandals before towel drying my hair as well as I could. I grabbed my purse, phone, then rushed down the stairs.

The laughter stopped me at the base.

Three voices, my adoptive father, my mom… and Jax. They seemed to be having the time of their life without me somewhere in the house, but I couldn't let them see me.

I needed to go to the drugstore.

With careful steps, I toed out of the house, then ran for my bicycle. My long-handled Schwinn rested against the tree in our front yard so I took that, knowing if I opened the garage door and got my car, the house would hear. The drugstore was also only a couple blocks away, and I preferred riding instead of driving whenever I could anyway, better for the environment.

I didn't turn back, peddling as hard as I could. I tried not to think about the fact I could definitely have my stepbrother's baby for being stupid. Because if I thought about it, even an iota of the thought, I may be sick to my stomach again. He'd screwed me definitely knowing who I was, did that when I hadn't even done anything wrong to him. Imagine what he'd do if I actually did something to cross him.

Something like get pregnant.

Chapter Four

Cleo

I made up some excuse once at the drugstore, texting Mom that I ran out of tampons and had to go out and get reinforcements. Part of the lie was true, the part about reinforcements. Mom sent me a quick text back, and even though she'd been bummed about me waltzing out, she understood.

Mom: Want us to wait for you? Jaxen made omelets!

I couldn't eat anything now, let alone anything made by my crazier-than-hell stepbrother. I told her no, but to enjoy herself. Meanwhile, I was mustering up the courage to ask the pharmacist for the morning after pill. This had to be some kind of nightmare, needing such a thing after only having sex once.

I am in my own nightmare.

A horror film filled with green eyes that looked like marble glass and a stepbrother crafted from the same gods who made hot Chrises. My stepbrother Jaxen was gorgeous. Crazy as fuck, but gorgeous. That couldn't be denied, and if he hadn't been my stepbrother and, I don't know, been a decent human being to me and we'd been in a committed relationship, I could do worse than him to procreate with. That obviously wasn't the scenario I was given so, forcing courage, I walked up to the drugstore counter. I lived in a pretty moderately sized town, but we mostly only had mom and pop stores on this end. Drugstores included.

I held my breath, hoping I didn't know someone behind the counter. It'd been known to happen. Especially since my dad was a politician. I didn't recognize the old man coming over though and smiling, I mumbled what I needed.

"I'm sorry. You're going to have to say that again, young lady," he said, cuffing his ear. "These old ears have been known to go on the fritz."

I thought I'd literally die, but managed to grit out, "The morning after pill, please."

He raised a finger, saying, "Just one moment," before he walked away and left my face dying in heat. My phone buzzed while I waited, and I picked it up, seeing a text from Kit. Turned out I had a few, and I wasn't surprised since I hadn't gotten back to her last night after leaving the club with Jaxen.

Kit: So tell me you got laid. Because that is the only reason and I mean ONLY reason you're excused for not texting me after leaving the club to get your mack on!

I cringed. Kit herself had been preoccupied most of the night. In fact, she'd had several guys all over her and when I texted her I was leaving with a guy myself she'd been floored. Jaxen and I left so quick in fact Kit hadn't even gotten to meet him. Jaxen and I just connected so we left.

How had I gotten myself into this?

I knew. Because I was trying to be adventurous, get myself out of my comfort zone.

Me: We slept together, yes.

Kit: OMG! Virgin no more! Ah! I told you this year was going to be great! You're walking with no fear in life now, lady! You got this!

Her excitement I could actually feel, Kit one of those who always walked before she could run. She was adventurous and did live life without fear.

I'd always admired her for that since I consistently lived in my tight little box.

My fingers hovered over the text message, needing to tell her the truth. Fact of the matter was, I had more fear than ever.

I was pretty much worse than when I started.

"Okay, one morning after pill. Will that be all… Cleo?"

My gaze shot up, the old man no longer behind the counter, but a set of smoky brown eyes and a dashing grin.

And he held my morning after pill in his hands.

The Greek god literally lifted a finger, a slow dread as I took in his swept-back hair and chiseled jawline. I knew him too, and he clearly knew me.

We'd gone to high school together.

"Cleo Erikson-Fairchild," the guy said, freaking *Lawson Richards*. This guy had been everything in school.

And I mean, everything.

Captain of the football team…

Check.

Hotter than hell…

Check. Check.

Official ruiner of my entire existence?

Ultra check.

The sickness brewed to epic proportions, this guy holding my, erm, um, reinforcements. Bagging them, he looked at me with a soft smile, and I probably would have died right there had I thought it wouldn't raise a commotion. The last thing I needed was an ambulance whisking through here and announcing to the entire block that a girl passed out in the drugstore trying to buy the morning after pill in front of her childhood crush. Lawson had been a senior when I'd been a sophomore, and honestly, he shouldn't even know who the hell I was.

But he did, that grin widening at me. He placed hands on the counter. "That is you. How the hell are you? How was your summer?"

I had to admit it'd been better. Tugging on my purse, I shrugged. "It was fun, I guess." Though not as exciting as his from what I'd heard. He'd graduated at this point, but I knew he'd gone overseas as well. Our parents were friends, my mom and his pretty active in our school when we'd both been going, and since she kept up with Lawson's mom, I knew he'd not only gone backpacking through Europe after he graduated from college but also stopped for a beat to build schools somewhere in the Southern hemisphere. This guy was a legend with his volunteer work and definitely shouldn't be at this drugstore holding my morning after pill.

Good freaking gravy.

With a nervous chuckle, I asked how his summer was, but he passed it off, another smile at me.

"Good, good," he'd said, *still* holding my pill. "But I'm sure yours was real fun. You went to Haiti, right?"

My brow twitched up, a chuckle on his end.

"Mom," he said. "She keeps up with yours. Heard all about your work down there. Super cool."

Really? My face flushing, I attempted to pass it off. I rubbed my arm. "It was exciting. Fulfilling."

"No doubt. How long were you down there?"

"Just the beginning of summer. Feels like a lifetime ago." I honestly hadn't wanted to leave. I really loved helping people and coming back home to

Netflix all summer on the couch hadn't been nearly as eventful. I put a hand out. "But what I did was nothing like you. I heard you were building schools. Backpacking?"

A neck rub before he cuffed his arms, like huge arms. The guy was nearly as big as my stepbrother.

Quit thinking about him…

Hard not to considering what I came here for and what Lawson had on the counter just south of his chin. He smiled. "Yeah, it was a good time. Wish I was there now. Didn't want to come home."

"Me either."

"Yeah." A twinkle in his eyes as he fell back. "Think you'll do it again next year?"

"I'll try. Not sure. I want to teach so I'll probably be looking for jobs, I can imagine." Teaching was what I was going to school for, elementary education my track. "What are you doing here anyway?"

"Killing time and I guess getting experience." He pushed the bag my way. "I'm actually going back to Bay Cove to get my pharmaceutical degree. This past summer was just as much about self-exploration as it was about helping people. I wasn't sure what I wanted to do, and while I was there I decided graduate school was for me. You go there too, right? Bay Cove-U?"

The fact that this guy knew anything about me at all blew me away. After all, he was literally everything when I'd been in school and not just to me. I knew our moms knew each other, but he maybe said a word or two to me, and that'd been because I was in the way of his group while they'd been walking down the hallway. He'd never been mean about it, just passive.

That didn't seem to be the case now as he looked at me and smiled. My face immediately heated and I played with my hair. "I do. Maybe I'll see you."

"Maybe." Another dashing smile before he went to ring me up. "This all for you or…"

I literally forgot about what I came in here for.

I chewed my lip, letting Lawson know that was all I needed. He finished bagging me up, then handed it off.

"Thanks."

"No problem," he said. "I'll see you around then?"

"Yeah, hopefully," I returned, hugging the bag to my body. His gorgeous eyes flickered to it before finding mine, and I wrestled with my hair again. I shrugged. "I don't normally buy things like this. I mean…"

I didn't know *what* I meant or why I felt the need to explain to him. I guessed since our parents knew each other?

I wanted to die again. Especially when he chuckled. Palming the counter, he leaned forward. "You're not the first to come in here. And even if you were, so what? People have sex. Not a big deal and nothing to be embarrassed about."

But still, I was *here* and in front of him.

He winked. "See you around. At school?"

"For sure."

He backed away, and I was chewing my lip by the time I got out of the store. Kit kept texting, but I could only deal with one thing at a time right now. I decided to take a sidewalk corner behind the store and after buying a bottle of water from the vending machine, I read the box. Might as well get this done now.

*

I rushed home, but even still, the hour had long passed breakfast. I'd obviously missed the gathering, and I knew the moment I rode up the driveway past dad's silver Mercedes. Someone was behind the vehicle in the yard. He was pulling weeds.

And was shirtless.

My stepbrother Jaxen was down to the jeans he'd worn last night, tugging and pulling at ragweed in my mom's flower garden. She had people who came and did this, of course, but for whatever reason, my stepbrother was on his knees and doing it himself. His chiseled back muscles roved and strained while he dug in the dirt between flower bushes, his muscled frame glistening with sweat. The squeak of my bicycle gave him pause.

He shifted in seconds.

On his feet before me, growing like a beautiful monster. He tugged off gloves too small for his big hands, my mom's. Tossing them, he came over, and I thought I'd vomit right where I stood.

What does he want? What does he...

He appraised me, just once before his hand slammed on my bicycle handle. A strong grip and his eyes danced, his body smelling of sweat and raw heat. Truth be told, he smelled *really* good, and I may have had thoughts to enjoy that.

Had he not been my stepbrother.

Oh, and the fact that he scared the ever-loving shit out of me.

A growl in his voice as he dragged his gaze up from my sundress to my eyes. A small smirk. "You missed breakfast, sis."

So he noticed, obviously having a good time with my parents. I heard them laughing together. I swallowed. "Had to go get something."

"Right." Liquid glass eyes dragged back to my bike. "And on this. What the fuck is this?"

He tugged at my bike, but I held on, pushing back from him. "What the hell is your deal?"

"What do you mean?" He feigned innocence, leaning back on my dad's car. His feathered brown locks fluttered in the wind. "Do I seem like I have a deal?"

Only totally, and he wasn't fooling anyone. I saw how he'd looked at me before. There'd been basically hatred there. Add to the fact that he'd screwed me *definitely* knowing who I was, he had a deal.

I just couldn't figure out what it was.

I couldn't figure out why it was warranted. He either had a bone to pick or was seriously screwed up in the head.

I picked the later, starting to pedal off but his hand slammed down on the bike again. "Let me go."

"No." He straddled my wheel with his big thighs, a god atop *my* bicycle. He was almost playful about it, jovial as he tugged my handlebars closer with a grin. "Where did you go?"

"Out."

"Obviously, but where, and why the fuck on this?" He angled a look. "You don't have a car or something?"

"I do, but where I went is close and riding my bike is better for the environment."

"Riding my bike is better for the environment," he parroted, seriously whacked out in the head. Puffing up, he cuffed his big biceps with a head shake. "Jesus, Rick really outdid himself with you lot. I mean, could you be more of a Girl Scout?"

"Could you be more of an asshole?"

The words escaped so quickly, *too* quickly, and I couldn't stop them. I'd been on fire.

He'd made me mad.

I *never* said things like that to people. I may have thought them once or twice, but never did I actually say things like that. It just wasn't in my character, but he was driving me crazy.

His eyes went crazier.

Hands grappling my handlebars, he jutted my bike forward and attempted to throw me off it.

"Stop!"

He didn't stop, tugging on my handlebars and with a strong push, I pedaled off and darted in the other direction. I thought I was free, getting to the backyard.

The rake handle came out of nowhere.

It intercepted my spokes, stopping my wheel, and I flew forward.

My scream hit the air as I bypassed my handlebars completely, literally flying over them. The ground came quickly.

But I hit a chest first, a firm one when my stepbrother tackled me up and got me flush against his hard body.

"Let go, psycho!" I slapped at his chest, fighting him, but he was too strong. My arms gathered, he pinned them at my sides, dragging me up his body.

He grinned. "Oh, please struggle," he said,

pulling me close.

His actual cock probed at my tummy, and a quake hit the entirety of my limbs that he was actually getting *off* on this.

My stepbrother was truly a psychopath, the devil masked as a beautiful god, and I started to scream, until his gaze past over my shoulder. He let go of me quickly, so quick I actually fell to my knees on the dirt.

"And what's this?" came from behind me, Jaxen's eyes on the small volcanic eruption that had been my purse. It launched off into the yard when I flew over my bike handles.

And my purchase had been inside.

I'd taken the pill, but still had the box it came in. I should have thrown it away behind the pharmacy when I'd had the chance.

I should have thrown it all away.

I knew that the moment my stepbrother got the box in his hands. He studied it for what felt like forever, and every second that passed, a slow dread moved through me. If he looked deranged before.

Nothing but pure evil faced me now.

He didn't even look upset, merely smiling in response. "So the Girl Scout isn't so perfect. What? You miss a birth control pill?"

"Give that back." I reached for it, but he grabbed me again—hard. He jerked my arm behind my back, and I called out.

His nose brushed mine. "Or did you lie to me?" he growled, tugging my arm harder. "You a liar? You're not on the pill?"

"I am, but I missed a couple."

"You missed a couple." A dark chuckle, his lips pulling apart against the bridge of my nose. He bit down on it a little. "I think you lied, sis. I think you never were on birth control."

"I was. I am. I swear. I just missed a couple. That's why I took the pill. I wasn't trying to trap you or anything. Jaxen…"

"*Jax.*" He mouthed my neck and the harsh heat stalled my breath, my entire body swimming in fear. I felt my heart race in my neck, my tummy quivering. He smiled his crazed smile. "I think stepmommy dearest and Rick need to know exactly what you are. A lying whore who goes around trying to trap guys."

"I didn't." I pleaded. "Why would I have gotten the pill in the first place? You see I already took it."

The packaging was all there, right there in front of him.

A deep chuckle and I realized he was playing with me, just more of this madness. More getting *off* on this.

"Even still, I think I'll tell them," he stated, dragging his finger down my neck. "They need to know what we did. Who you are?"

Tears pricked my eyes, my hand on his bicep. "Jax, please don't."

His hand found my mouth, forcing my lips apart. His eyes twitched crazy again, his smile a dark one. "You don't get any rights here. *Not* with me."

"Why are you doing this?" I pleaded, shaking. "Why are you treating me like this? What did I do?"

"What did you do?" Another smile. He let me go, and I fell to my knees, my shins completely covered in dirt.

I dragged my head up.

"Try existing, Girl Scout," he said, tossing the

box at me. It hit my shoulder and he smirked. "The fact that you're a whore just like your mother makes it more fun for me."

My chest heaved, my insides threatening to explode outside my body again. Heavy steps and he sauntered back over to the rake that had tossed me over my bicycle handles. He'd obviously pushed it into my spokes.

His hand rested on the top. "Probably should get yourself inside. Clean yourself up?" A wide grin. "You look like you're about to cry."

I wouldn't and definitely *not* in front of him.

Getting to my feet, I brushed myself off, grabbing my things.

I heard nothing but his dark chuckles as I headed inside.

I'd hear them in my nightmares.

Chapter Five

Cleo

Jaxen obviously had a bone to pick with my mom and me. He didn't even know us, yet hated us, but I refused to try and figure out his crazy. Outside had been the musings of an obvious psychopath, but something I could do about it was alert my dad. This news would most certainly crush him. He'd really wanted Jax to come down here and get to know us, to know me. He'd been so thrilled he was coming he even got Jaxen into my university. Something kind of hard to do considering Jaxen was a senior like me and entrance into Bay Cove was very competitive. He'd wanted someone there for Jax to connect with, me there.

He'd wanted us to be a family.

He'd shared this more than once, constant talks over the dinner table and how thrilled he was that his son had not only agreed to come down, but go to school here. Jaxen did come, but clearly with some kind of delusional chip on his shoulder. Maybe he hated me because his dad hadn't been around. Maybe he was angry and that made him ruthless.

Either way, I didn't care.

I just knew my dad would want to know about this. He wanted us to be a family, but he *never* would have wanted this. Jaxen had been peaches and cream in front of my parents, but it had to be a front. Didn't it?

Maybe he just hates you.

Again, I couldn't care, the guy totally dangerous. He'd gone from so kind last night, gentle. I'd met him and hadn't even wanted to leave him, his hands so big and strong and his personality completely inviting. He'd been, in a word, perfect.

And nothing but a lie.

He didn't care about me. He just wanted to crush me, and Dad needed to know. I found him in his office, tapping on the door frame. He was surrounded by papers and, as per usual, working when he'd come home to relax and be with family. I was well aware he and Mom would be off and back to business first thing tomorrow after Jaxen and I were supposed to go to school.

His eyes flickered up. "Oh, come in, sweetheart. Come in. I'm almost done here."

By done, he must have been referring to a break. My adoptive father never stopped being busy. His work in politics kept him always preoccupied.

It was one of the things I admired about him.

Constantly in the trenches, Dad fought policies and the men and women above them to make things better for so many people over the years. And that'd been only in the years since he'd married my mom. The pair may have met in politics, but he'd worked as an active player in government long before my mom and I came along. He'd been the saving grace for our family. The rock for both my mom and me. We'd had some trying times before he'd come along.

Heartbreak.

Struggle.

And he'd been there for the aftermath, still fighting but with a different struggle. He picked up the pieces of a shattered family broken by pain and suffering. He'd mended us and put me completely back together with my mom. I honestly didn't remember life before Rick Fairchild came into our lives.

At least, I tried not to.

Dad waved me in around his stacks of papers, probably in here since after breakfast. He grinned. "Come. Come. I'll make room for you."

He'd always said that, could make room however tight. It only made the reason I came to him that much harder.

But I needed the strength.

His son was crazy, point-blank. I didn't want to come in here, bust everything up but I felt like I had no choice. What Jaxen had done last night and today was completely unacceptable. He'd been cruel, evil and malicious. People got locked up for lesser things they'd done.

And he did it right in my adoptive father's house.

Jax was a guest in this house and he hurt me, my strides quiet into my dad's study. Dad had his MacBook open, but closed it after striking a few keys.

He sat back with laced fingers. "What's up? Missed you at breakfast this morning." His eyebrows drew in deeply. "Mom said you were having feminine worries."

As awesome as my dad was he was still a guy at the end of the day. I rolled my eyes. "It's called a period, Dad."

"Yes, er, um, period." Rick Fairchild's cheeks colored, a man who gave speeches in front of hundreds, thousands. He patted his desk. "Anyway, you doing all right?"

I took him up on the seat he offered, lounging back against his desk. I shook my head. "Not exactly. I wanted to talk to you about that."

His brow jumped. "Your, um…" A neck scratch. "Period, honey? I have to say, I think your mom is better suited."

Dear God.

"No, not the period."

Appearing relieved, he chuckled. "Then what then?"

How could I say his son was a freak? How could I tell him the son he was trying to reconnect with, unite our families together with, was crazy and had it out for me? This house was well aware of my dad and Jaxen's history.

There was a reason I'd never met my stepbrother before.

My mom, Rick, and I were a family built on pain, struggle. The three of us came from divided households, from heartache, and through the ashes, we'd been able to find each other. We *healed* but that couldn't deny what each of us had come from.

Dad had his own woes back in the Midwest, his own mangled history. That past divided his previous family, and though I didn't quite know the details, I did know not once had it'd ever been in the cards for me *or* Mom to meet Jaxen. Every time I'd bring it up, I was given words like "it's complicated" or "it just can't happen." Jaxen, I guessed, had been adamant about staying with his mom after the divorce, and it had to have destroyed my father inside.

I knew because of how he was with me.

I'd gotten so much love from this man that I called father. He'd *been* my father, and we weren't even related. If something had divided him from his family, a messy divorce or whatever, it would have broken him.

Even if he never showed it.

He'd been strong, but I caught him more than once looking at photos. Pictures of Jaxen and the ones of him as a little kid. He had so many, stopping at age eleven, the age I guess when they'd been separated.

Thinking about all that now, I had nothing but a lack of words. What I had to say would literally break my dad's heart.

I just knew it would.

"Honey?" He tilted his head at me. "What's going on?"

I had to be brave. I had to tell the truth. Even with the potential damage, I had to.

I wet my lips. "I guess I wanted to talk to you about Jaxen."

"Oh?" So much pride on his face, a strong smile. Broad smile. It brightened his whole expression, his eyes warm. "He's great, isn't he?" he stated turning. Flicking open the blinds, I was well aware of who he could see in the front yard.

I saw him too, *Jax* revving up the lawnmower and using it. He'd pulled Dad's out right from the garage, the one usually only our gardening staff used.

Just as half naked, Jaxen mowed away, glistening in the warm heat outside. He rubbed his brow, and catching Dad's eye, he lifted a hand.

Dad returned, another smile on his lips. "Can you believe he *volunteered* to do that? And right after breakfast. A breakfast *he made*." Dad chuckled. "I told him we had people to do that, but he insisted."

He did?

I watched him, Jax's head going down as he continued to push the mower. His biceps shifted, his broad shoulders and abs working over every bump

51

and rocky surface in the yard.

Dad flicked the blinds, and he gratefully cut me off from the sight of my stepbrother.

My stepbrother I *slept* with. I dragged my eyes up. "Dad—"

"He called me that too," he said, staring at the blinds though they were closed. He rubbed his mouth. "I just… I never thought he would. At least, not so soon. Not again."

Not again…

Dad's lashes flickered in my direction, emotion in his eyes I'd definitely heard in his voice. Use of the title had made him emotional, a word I used for him every day.

A word I took for granted.

As far as I knew, Jaxen had no father. He had two mothers, his mom remarrying. I didn't know his moms, but I was sure he felt complete fulfillment in his life. But still, the chance to reconnect with your father…

Perhaps, he did just hate me. Perhaps, he really did want to know Rick, *his* dad.

I came out of my stupor when my adoptive father held my hand, squeezing. He would technically always be that. He'd been around for me, but we'd never have what he and Jax had. Jaxen was his, completely.

Dad smiled. "I'm so happy for you and your mom. That you were open to this, welcoming him." Dad passed a look over to the closed blinds. "He's had it rough and… I know he's suffered. He had to because I wasn't there."

But why wasn't he? It didn't make sense. Rick Fairchild just wasn't the type to not be there.

I knew because he was for me.

"He didn't even keep my last name after the divorce," he said, making my chest squeeze. "I guess I don't blame him. I wasn't there."

Something had to have been really bad, something maybe my mom knew about but not me during that time period in question. It hadn't been my business. I had always been the kid, the child, and it wasn't my place. I'd just selfishly taken Rick for my own.

"You're happy he's here?" I asked, knowing the answer. I shook my head. "I mean, of course you are. It's… it's so good."

"It is." He held my shoulders. "And I appreciate you so much. For being there. *Driving him* tomorrow to school." He chuckled. "I guess you'll really get to know each other soon. Makes me so happy."

It truly did, didn't it?

"Anyway, what did you want to talk to me about?" He leaned in. "Again, honey. If it's women's worries—"

"It's nothing." I laughed, forcing myself to smile through my emotion. I had to, physically unable to break this man's heart. I shook my head. "I just wanted to say I'm looking forward to getting to know him."

He squeezed my arm, the grin overtaking his entire face. It was in that moment I knew something deeply. I literally could do nothing about this situation, my stepbrother being here. I couldn't hurt this man.

Even if his biological son truly was a monster.

Chapter Six

Cleo

A sleep-deprived body greeted me the next day, not looking forward at all for the drive I had to take with my stepbrother in tow. It'd be a quick one, only an hour or so to campus, but with Jaxen so close in the front seat...

He'd literally stared me *down* last night at dinner, pinned me in place with a shared understanding between us. It was a look that he had all the cards.

It was a look that he could destroy me.

He could, this entire family dynamic, with our secret hookup, but for now, at least last night, he'd kept our drama to the cuff. He'd been the perfect son, chatting with both Dad and Mom and appearing to have a good time doing it. He seemed to really want to be here, even with me.

That's what scared me the most.

He was so good at the show, the life of the party. He had jokes for days, smiles. At one point, he even showed my parents the latest dance craze on TikTok, showing them his feed before giving an example of himself in the dining room. It'd been a riot.

For everyone but me.

I'd tugged my comforter close that night, needed it close and that security, but every time I did, I smelled him. Drew in his harsh heat and undying warmth. It'd felt so good to be in his arms just last night, but sickened me now.

He did sicken me. With every one of his smiles. His jokes. I kept trying to figure out if he was the real deal.

Or simply playing us all.

I couldn't blow any of this out of the water, though, threading my fingers at dinner. I chimed in when I was needed to, but for the most part, I gauged my time playing with my hair or staring at the clock. When it was acceptable, I went to bed, and this morning, I skipped breakfast entirely. Eventually, Mom walked it up to my room, and when she found me in my closet packing up the last of my stuff for school, she hadn't given me a hard time. She figured that's what I'd been doing all morning. Packing.

Not suffering in silence.

My gas tank was full when I got out to my car, not surprising since I found my parents there too. Dad had packed all the stuff I'd brought to the door earlier, and now, they held each other, waiting for me. This was a routine with us. They always came home, no matter where they were on the globe, to see me off, and we almost always did it early. I liked to get to school before the hallways of my dorm started to crowd, and they had a busy day of activities as per usual. The time generally just worked out for us both, so that's what we did.

Currently, Dad wore loose-fitting pants and Mom, Lycra leggings and a sports top. They were perfect outfits for playing singles at the country club, which they liked to do whenever they were in town.

I got a big hug between them both when I got out to my station wagon. The old 1970s vehicle was my baby and exactly what I'd asked for when my parents said they'd give me a car for high school graduation. It was a classic, completely restored and shined like it just drove off the lot. It was also my thing and matched my personality. I tended to go for vintage flare, wearing secondhand boots, high-waisted shorts and a top tied at my tummy for move-in day.

"You got everything, baby?" Mom asked, holding me out. "If not, we can always send someone out to get something to you."

My parents were busy, my dad very important, and even though I had the nannies and caretakers growing up, not once did I feel swept under the rug. Not once did I feel like I was a bother or not loved. They always took care of me, in their special ways, but they always did. I loved them an awful lot for it, and with the separation, I was very independent. There wasn't a thing that came at me that I couldn't handle myself.

At least, generally.

My stepbrother was absent from this party, but hell, if I was going to ask about him. I didn't even want to see him and would have enough of him on the road. I knew he and Dad went out late afternoon yesterday to get his things. I guessed he'd dropped all his stuff off at a hotel when he'd arrived, intending to stay there. Well, when Dad had heard that they'd immediately left to go get his stuff. I'd seen them leave, and when they returned, they came back with a big rolling bag.

Currently, said bag was being dragged outside the house, my stepbrother with a fist on it. He lifted a hand from the front door, and Dad left, going to him.

And hell, if Jaxen couldn't stop looking gorgeous.

I really *hated* my eyes. Because every time I looked at him, I noticed all these little things. Like how the wind perfectly captured and tousled his hair, more curly than feathered.

I didn't want to notice his hair or how his eyes captured the sun in the light. I didn't want to know how he truly looked like a Hemsworth in all the shirts he strained or the jeans he filled out. Currently, his behemoth thighs hugged a pair of low-rider jeans, sagging perfectly below his tapered waist. He wore a polo, the collar popped and the material hitting his big honking shoulders. I saw every ounce of him, every muscled and perfect inch. I was well aware of what he looked like naked.

And that definitely didn't help.

Dad got to him, and of course, he helped him with his bag. Mom hugged me, and though I told her I didn't need anything, answering her previous question, her gaze had been on anything but me. She watched my dad and Jaxen, the pair of them chatting as they headed from the house to the street with us.

Mom pulled me close. "Your dad's just shining, isn't he?" she said, so happy too. They both were.

Everyone but me.

"I'm so happy for him," she continued nodding, then looked at me. "You'll take good care of your stepbrother, won't you?"

My stepbrother.

I wanted to gag where I stood, but I told her I would. Of course, I would. I'd do it for Dad. He was happy. I knew that.

Even still, I couldn't stop the nausea. Especially when Jaxen made it into my airspace. I caught a whiff of him, and he was only at the back of the car, Dad helping him load his bag. The distinct smells of tea tree and various spices, a bodywash or an aftershave, and I remembered it well.

I'd bathed in it when he'd fucked me.

Unable to even get close, I stayed on my side of the car. Dad and Jaxen exchanged a few words at the back, and whatever they were caused Dad to smile. Immediately, Dad reached for him, a hug. They'd done that when Jaxen arrived so I hadn't been surprised.

But Jaxen hadn't cringed the first time.

Just a glimmer of it, a clear and visual shift of his features. It'd been like he was pained with the touch, but just as quickly, he schooled his features. The hug had been brief, but right after, Jaxen was putting on the aviator shades he had clipped to his shirt. Suddenly, those green eyes were gone and any evidence of what I'd seen wiped away.

But I'd definitely seen it.

I didn't know what to make of that, but said nothing, my mom giving me a hug, then my dad. Dad let go. "Safe trip then. Okay, sweetheart?"

I nodded, noticing Jaxen head to the *other* side of the car. He kept distance, placing his thick arms on the top. He smiled. "I can drive too if you wanna relax, Cleo. I don't mind."

He kept doing that, *offering* things either to me or anyone else there to listen. I obviously didn't trust him and no way in hell would he be driving my baby.

"I'm good," I said, schooling *my* features. I faced my dad. "And we'll be safe."

"How I'll miss you, baby." Another hug from Mom. Letting go, she lifted a hand to Jax. "And it was so nice meeting you, Jaxen."

"Likewise, Mrs. Fairchild," he said, nothing but a cool smile on his lips. He hiked it higher. "And Cleo and I will be perfectly safe. I'll look out for her."

I was sure he would…

The bastard.

He really had me turning into someone I wasn't, thinking so negatively. I just kept getting the feeling like he was waiting, absolutely simmering to do something and cause chaos. He had ample opportunity to during our drive, and I hoped he wouldn't try something since I'd be driving a two-ton vehicle with him in the passenger seat. This could be wishful thinking, of course, but the hope was all I had.

It really was.

This was my reality, and I had to get used to the fact that I had an insane person for a stepbrother. Dad opened the car for me, and after getting in, I gave him another hug through the window.

"Thank you again," he said before giving me a kiss atop the head. He pulled back. "And let me know if you need anything, all right?"

"Okay."

"And you too, son," Dad said, Jaxen getting in the car too. His huge form filled up the whole right side, and I was choking on his scent by the time he closed the door. He smelled like boy, *male*.

God.

Jax hunkered to see Dad. "Will do. I promise you won't have to worry about me."

God, he really was good at that. Putting on the charm and probably just as good at something else.

That something being breaking promises.

*

"Think we can change the station to something a little more, um, secular?" Jax stated on the road.

I'd been driving all of five minutes.

On the highway, the wind cut through Jax's hair, sending those tousled locks flying. Cinnamon spice and his male essence flew through the wind every second we traveled, my windows down, and I grumbled.

"It's not Christian music," I stated, knowing he was making fun of my music now like he'd done my bike. Was nothing safe from this guy? I sat up. "It's folk."

A slow eyebrow lifted. "Okay, well. I'm changing it."

The music switched to hip-hop before I could protest, and after, Jax stretched that large body of his back into my seat. He tucked his hands under his arms. The aviators still covered his eyes, but I was still well aware of the fact that he circulated that gaze of his around my ride. His head angled up. "And what the fuck is this car?"

And *now,* he was going for my baby. My jaw shifted. "What of it?"

"What of it?" Sitting up, he flicked my fuzzy dice. "Will this bucket of bolts actually make it to campus? The last time I've seen one of these was in *The Brady Bunch.*"

Since that was one of my favorite shows, I said nothing, then *got nothing* but his arrogant smirk. He dropped an arm on the dash, looking at me. "What's your deal?"

"Deal?"

A nod before he was flashing me those stunning greens. They literally looped his pupils like druzy quartz when he popped his aviators into his hair. "The whole perfect politician's daughter bullshit. Between you and your mother, I swear to

God I'm choking on that shit. You both for real with that?"

Stiffening, I rubbed my hands on the wheel, my heart beating its drum in my entire chest. I had no idea if he was speaking to me this way because he truly wondered or he was just mean.

Something told me it was the latter.

My stepbrother obviously wanted to test me, but I wouldn't let him speak that way about my mom. He'd also called her a whore before, which continued to travel along the line of this guy and his psychoticism.

"Don't say that about my mom," I said, leveling my voice. It was all I could do not to lash out at him or drive us off the road. "We're not perfect, and I'm definitely not."

I wished I was. Because if I did, my life would be completely different right now. For starters, I wouldn't have him in my life.

But I guessed, I wouldn't have Rick Fairchild either.

Life was a toss up, wasn't it? A cruel game of give and take. Had I been perfect, I wouldn't have my adoptive father.

I guess basically over me and my response Jaxen crossed his aviators back over his eyes. He no longer stared at me, as he tossed his head back and bumped it to hip-hop. But considering we had at least an hour drive and maybe even an interaction or two when we did get to school, I wanted to squash this. I didn't want to be his friend.

But I didn't have to be his enemy either.

"Can we talk?" I asked, braving myself. I gripped the wheel. "About the other day."

"What about it?" The guy hadn't even looked

at me, head back like he was going to sleep.

I huffed. "Look. We obviously didn't get off to the right start."

A slow smile lifted. "Oh, I got off just fine, Girl Scout," he paused, tilting his face toward me. "And last I checked, you did too."

A heart race, a slam as it worked its way up into my throat. That was what I was talking about, exactly what I was talking about. He was Dr. Jekyll and Mr. Hyde. Sickeningly sweet to my family, doing chores and crap, then the next thing I knew, verbally assaulting me. Not to mention, how he'd physically attacked me, forcing me off my bike and…

Making love to me.

It'd been so nice when he'd been that way. When he'd been Brett and so sweet.

It was all a lie, Cleo. A lie.

"I don't know what I did to you." Silence on his end. I swallowed. "And we don't have to be friends, but we can get along. At least, for my dad."

"Your dad," he mocked me, his voice cold. "You want us to get along for *your* dad."

So much spite in his voice when he said that. I shook my head. "Our dad then."

A laugh, Joker-esque. He was like Deadpool, charming, dashing even, yet lethal. That was what made him so scary. How inviting his personality could be when he put on the show, only to find out he had a blade behind his back.

One aimed straight for the heart.

At least, for mine, and shifting, he gave me his eyes again when he pushed his sunglasses up. Such beauty, such hypnotic darkness. He was the Pied Piper in denim jeans with rock hard abs.

"You wanna know why we can't be friends?"

he asked, his eyes actually twinkling at me. He lifted
a hand. "Why we can't just get along and be perfect
stepsiblings for our perfect parents?"

So he really didn't like them… he'd said it.
Right there, he'd said it, sarcasm completely dripping
from his voice. He was putting on a show.

A more than dark one.

A curled finger and he was brushing my chin,
dragging it down my chest.

"Jaxen…"

My breath trembled as he tucked his finger
between my breasts, uncurling and tracing the swell.
It took all I had to keep us straight on the road, my
swallow hard.

He smiled.

"Because of that," he said, pulling my top
slightly away. His rough digit against my skin caused
my back to rise, my breath to intake. He grinned.
"Because of this. Because of what I do to you."

He pulled his finger out, actually tasting it. He
wet his two fingers, then his digits went right for my
top again.

"Stop…"

But a moan as he pinched my nipple through
my shirt and bra. I was only wearing a bralette so I
felt *everything*. It was like he knew, my chest
trembling.

"We fucked, Girl Scout," he said, an actual
growl in his voice. His dark chuckle followed. "And
you want to do it again."

"I don't," I bit, but my body betrayed me. My
breast trembling in his hand. He massaged the whole
thing at this point, my foot accelerating the wheel.
We weren't on the highway yet, but had we been,
we'd have crashed into the fast lane. "Get your hands

of me."

Surprisingly, he did, a quick let go. Returning to his seat, he had a smile that'd make the Cheshire cat jealous, both arrogant and lovely.

It matched his eyes.

Those bright pools of mischief and beauty. The line was so thin between heaven and chaos in them, between light and darkness. He shielded me from them again when he put his shades down.

"I will fuck you again, stepsis," he threatened, his voice passive. He didn't even look at me, his stare on the road. "And when I do, you'll know who I am. You will. But you'll *still* want it."

My eyes laced, glassed in something akin to emotion. I wouldn't give in to him, refused as I gathered myself together and looked at the road. No, I wouldn't sleep with him again, but there was no telling him that. My stepbrother drew the line in the sand and no truce would be had. He really did hate me, wanted to break me.

But that didn't mean I couldn't fight back.

Chapter Seven

Jax

I fell asleep beneath my aviators. I lifted them, and Girl Scout was right where I left her.

Stiff as a motherfucker.

I had her all worked up like I had that night I tasted her body, tight and hands white-knuckled on the wheel. Those pink polished fingernails left track marks on my body.

I'd driven her fucking insane.

I'd felt bad, at first, that I'd been the one to pop her cherry.

But then she'd opened her goddamn mouth.

Calling me an asshole yesterday hadn't been smart for her and put things in a hell of freaking perspective for me. I was down here for one purpose and one purpose only.

Dad's arrival that first day had only cemented it.

The asswipe had actually tried to *engage* with me, speak to me like we had been for years. Since I'd arrived, it'd been "son" this and "my boy" that.

I'd fuckin' cringed every time.

I had hidden it away, of course, good at that. But every time Rick Fairchild had taken my hand or hugged me, it'd taken everything in me not to knock his goddamn lights out. He actually acted like he had been glad to see me. Like he'd been around or tried at all to contact me before eighteen. Because that's when he'd first reached out, *high school* and his contact had been few and far between since. That man was a goddamn liar and so good at the show.

I supposed that was because he was a

politician.

I guessed I had gotten something from my sperm donor father at the end of the day. I was a hell of a good fucking actor because not only had I popped his stepkid's cherry, I'd gotten dear old stepmom to trust me too. I had the whole family eating out of the palm of my hands.

This academic term was going to be fun.

I'd done pretty well in school, kept up on my grades so my shit transferred pretty good. I'd gotten into my new university, Bay Cove-U, with flying colors, and my politician sperm donor hadn't even had to make any calls for me. He'd offered to, but I turned him down in the end. I didn't need him, his resources *or* his influence. Like always, I did just fine.

And how good it'd feel to fuck with his stepkid while I was there.

Cleo was the closest access I had to my father, the one I could hurt the most, and by hurting her, I'd get to him. I'd ruin his fucking life like he ruined mine.

The car slowed.

I rose up, squeezing my eyes a bit. Girl Scout had pulled us off the highway, our route scenic and slower by the coast. I wasn't in the Midwest anymore, crystal clear water to my left and half naked bodies at the beach. I saw several clusters of bouncing tits playing volleyball.

As there were no complaints by me, I eased back, enjoying the view.

Stepsis's tits sweated.

A constant drip between her double-Ds. It was something I'd noticed quite often behind my shades. Though, I'd tried not to.

Fuck, I need to taste her again.

She drove me wild already, and I had to admit, it'd be hard to play this cat and mouse game with her for long. My stepsister was fucking hot with her legs for days and thick thighs I could die between. A mere taste of her sweet pussy hardly had me in my right mind when I had her.

And then her smell.

Sweet, *innocent.* She played quite a show for me, acting all shy and shit. Her goddamn taste in hillbilly music only added to it, all eclectic like her sense of style and dress. She wore brown lace up boots and cargo shorts now like Dora the Explorer.

And what the fuck was up with her hair?

A dark braid draped long across her tits, one she twisted nervously between her fingers as she drove mile after mile. I could climb that thing like fucking Prince Charming to Rapunzel, but I was no goddamn prince. I hoped to be this girl's fucking nightmare.

My phone buzzed.

Royal: Hey, cocksucker. You make it to campus yet?

Knight: Yeah, show us some palm trees and shit.

LJ: Just no tits. I got a girl now, you know. *wink emoji*

Yeah, I knew. My buddies back home *all* had women in their lives. Pretty goddamn awesome women, but women nonetheless. I liked them all, but currently, I was the only one of my brothers from other mothers who was single.

Royal: Jesus. Yeah, no fucking tits, please.

Knight: Right? SMDH. This ain't fucking grade school no more. You always send tits. No tits.

Did I?

I smirked.

Me: Fuck, when did you guys get to be so goddamn lame?

Royal: You call it lame. I call it growing the fuck up. December handed me my ass last time she got a hold of my phone. She'd been playing Candy Crush or some shit, then you start sending me titties and shit. I don't need them, bro. I got the real thing. *grin emoji*

LJ: Yeah, no titties, man.

Me: Okay, Jesus. No goddamn tits.

I snapped a pick of the beach to my left. We'd been driving for a little while, and it seemed my new campus might be directly off the coast. I sent it to my boys.

Me: Paradise.

LJ: I'll say. And who's the girl, bro? *wink emoji*

What the fuck?

I clicked the photo I sent, immediately noticing my error.

Cleo had her hand on the wheel in the photo, and though I'd snapped the shot of the beach behind her, I caught a perfect angle of her glow. The sun glistened behind her like she was a goddamn Disney princess.

I dragged my gaze up, and she was looking at me, a long but shy stare.

A blink and her lashes shifted back to the road, but not fast enough.

I snapped another picture of her, on purpose this time. I send it to my friends with the text, "My fucking stepsister *eye lift emoji*," before sitting back.

"Why did you do that?"

I didn't glance over at her, angling my arm out the window. "Call it commemorating the moment." I swung my gaze to her, and her mouth parted. I tipped my chin. "Your mouth was hanging open just right. Wanted to let my buddies know what I was going to have around my cock later."

I stamped my legs out for emphasis, instantly hard when she gazed right between them. I expected her to tell me off, which she did when she mumbled, "In your dreams," before placing her gaze back to the road. What I *hadn't* expected was for her to bite her little lip.

Goddamn.

Images immediately in my head, that perfect fucking mouth giving me head while she worked my balls, and right away, the asshole in my jeans took note. I thought I'd literally bust a nut through my fly, my cock steel. My phone buzzed in the next moment, and I picked it up, pretending I didn't notice her little mouth action a minute ago.

Knight: That's your stepsister? Holy fuck, man. What you gonna do?

Royal: Right. WTF?

LJ: Be careful.

I hadn't expected this reaction from my friends.

And then that last text….

LJ's "be careful" I didn't get and when I started to text back, the car slowed again. Pretty Pretty Princess navigated her old-ass station wagon off to the side of the road by the guard rails with views of the beach.

I sat up, the girl unstrapping. She got out of the car, like completely out, then snapped the door shut behind her.

My eyes twitched wide.

What the fuck's she doing?

I unstrapped.

Getting out, I rested my arms on the top of the car. "What's going on?"

"We're here," she said simply. She tossed a hand in the direction of the guardrail, a sign posted there.

Bay Cove University.

I saw the sign, but I saw no campus. My mouth twitched. "We're *here*?"

I circulated my gaze. Outside of the school sign, there was nothing but beach, then of course, the road to our right.

Cleo propped her fists tight on her adventure shorts. "Campus starts here. The marine biology students do their work out here by the beach."

"So why the fuck are we here?"

She wasn't listening to me, and before I knew it, she was opening the truck.

I followed her with my gaze and my eyes expanded when she took out my bag...

And tossed it in the street.

It literally flew like she'd gone for a shot put medal at the Olympics, and shooting off her car, I dashed into the street after it.

Traffic didn't see me, a Beamer honking and skidding. This was followed by a minivan, dance moms clearly on one hundred in this place when the woman threw her finger out the window and tossed me the bird.

I gave it right back, holding my other hand out for traffic like a cop. I heard horns *and my heart* in my goddamn ears, but eventually, I was able to

72

work my way into the middle of the street. Traffic had gratefully slowed, then moved around me, and getting my bag handle, I dragged it back.

I ran while horns sounded and people tossed obscenities my way and only stopped to catch my breath after I got my bag out of the street.

Huffing, I grabbed my knees, my head jerking up just in time to see. Cleo was already back in her car.

And she was pulling away.

No, *pulling* was an understatement, wheels spinning as she darted off the side of the road. Her old station wagon went into overdrive, and I saw nothing but the butt of it as she merged into traffic.

A buzz in my pocket, I ripped my phone out of my jeans in a fury, and heat crept up my neck at the sight of a text.

I got you to campus. Enjoy the rest of your year.

We'd exchanged numbers at the club, but I hadn't even programmed her name into my phone. She hadn't been worth it and still wasn't.

I grinned, not even bothering to text her back. I'd see her again and soon. So stepsis wanted to play, huh?

Funny, how she actually thought she was in the goddamn game.

Chapter Eight

Cleo

My ears rang by the time I'd arrived at Bay Cove's main campus. Nestled off the shore, palm trees and students lined its winding paths, and I released a harsh breath.

Don't go back. Don't go back. Don't go back.

I already had—twice, the last of which I'd gone all the way to where I'd dropped Jax off only to find him not there. He'd either hitchhiked, caught a ride share, or something else.

Either way, he was on the move.

One hundred percent, my stepbrother would be pissed. Three hundred percent, I'd be fried if he managed to get a hold of me.

I *never* did things like that. I never lost my temper so bad that I'd just been cruel and left someone on their own like that. He simply brought out the worst in me, but between him joking about putting things in my mouth and promising I'd come back to him in any type of capacity, I'd lost my mind. He had to be joking if he thought I'd ever touch him again, let alone have sex with him. He was disgusting and filthy and just…

Don't you dare go back.

If anything, for my own personal safety at this point. I'd merely called him an asshole and he'd manhandled me in my own backyard with our parents within feet of us. Jaxen Ambrose was dangerous, cruel.

I gripped the wheel in a harsh panic, trying to navigate the road like some shaking psychopath. Campus was fairly busy considering the early hour, truly the best place to go to school. Most picked the university on location alone.

Constant refurbishments made buildings donated by aristocrats and scholars shine, the campus glistening and radiating off the beach. Most considered Bay Cove a party school, but I'd gone here because it was equal parts academics and progressiveness. The campus had many student programs in which its students' voices could be heard. It was a great place for activism, growth, and had many ways in which I could and did get involved. I shared a lot with my parents in that way and was always looking for ways I could do more for the world.

Add to the fact campus was simply beautiful with its lush landscapes and sparkling shoreline, Bay Cove was a vision beyond any student's dreams. It'd been a place I got to call home for the past three years.

It was also extremely large and I hoped to easily blend into it this year. I had to disappear, the only way I could avoid Jax and whatever recourse I may receive from leaving him alone and throwing his bag out into traffic.

I palmed my temple, actually quivering. I had to get out of my head a little when I noticed people I knew. People from classes and whatever during the previous three years. I waved at them, dragging their bags and stuff along the walks. Many people knew me before I even came here because of my stepdad, and yeah, I also stood out like a sore thumb in this place because of my car. I could only thank God the bus system was pretty good here. I could use that instead of drive to class.

Because if Jax saw this car, I knew, just *knew*

there'd be trouble. The guy was quite literally outside of his mind, and my panic brewing, I slowed my car.

I had to.

Feeling literally on the cusp of hyperventilation, I parked on some random street. I needed to collect myself and quickly unstrapped.

I had to scream.

I mean, I made sure there were no other people around, of course. No one around to think I was crazy, but tossing my head back, I let it roar. I even balled my fists, jumping on terra ferma like a kid having a hissy fit. If anyone saw me, they *would* think I'd lost my mind.

I think I had a little.

I kicked at my tire, shaking my baby before hunkering down and hugging my legs. I was angry, frustrated.

But mostly, I was scared.

Jaxen *scared* me, and though I couldn't see his reaction much when he'd leaped into traffic to get his bag—after all, I'd been trying to get the hell out of Dodge myself—he had to be pissed.

I mean, I would have been.

I buried my face in my hands, elbowing back against my wheel. A quick sprint and someone was jogging up on me. Jumping, I nearly peed myself until I realized it wasn't Jaxen.

But he was kind of beautiful too.

Hell, if Mr. USA was a thing, Lawson Richards would win by a landslide. Like every time and he'd wear the hell out of the sash. He cruised up to me in a set of basketball shorts and tank that hung so low it gave him man cleavage. The guy seriously had pecs for days.

Almost as hard looking as…

Shaking myself out of that thought like a Tiny Toon, I watched as he hunkered down, his eyes wild. He had a pair of earbuds in his ears he took out at seeing me. "You okay? I heard you scream or... something."

Oh, fuck. Maybe this street wasn't as quiet as I thought, and getting up, I let him help me. I dusted myself off. "I'm fine. Just having a panic attack."

"A panic attack?" Shock ripped through his timeless features. He was like seriously one of those earls out of a Jane Austen novel. His hair sweated back, he still appeared perfect, flawless. He brushed a tanned arm across his brow. "You all right now?"

"Yeah." Just not so casually losing my mind. "Ever just need to scream?"

Of course, he didn't. He was perfect. This guy spent his summers backpacking through Europe and probably would join the Peace Corps at some point in his lifetime. No, he didn't have a psycho stepsibling set out to ruin his life, but he laughed, laughed with me instead of at me when I joined too.

He tucked his hands under his arms. "Not lately, but it's been known to happen, yeah."

Yeah? "Yeah?"

His eyes twinkled. "Yeah. That's kind of where I was at when I was in Europe and didn't know what to do with my life. Eventually, it brought me back here. Slowly starting to figure it out now."

"Well, can I get some of that ability to solve problems *efficiently* instead of screaming?" I shook my head. "I could use some of that."

"Tell you what? Once I bottle it, I'll give you a cut for the idea. I'd make a fucking fortune."

I'd laughed, seriously laughing *hard* and not just at myself this time. It felt good, and finally, I realized I wasn't panicking.

Lawson smiled. "You okay now? I was jogging, happened to see you. I just moved into an apartment about a block over."

Hence, why I'd seen him. I nodded since I actually did feel okay. "Thanks for stopping. Checking on me."

"Thanks for not actually dying. I was about two seconds away from calling the cops until I saw it was you. Figured I'd check first."

"Well, thank you for that." Because *that* would have been more embarrassing than it already was. I shook my head. "But yeah, I'm okay. Sorry I scared you."

"No problem." A chuckle before he popped the earbud back in his ear. His arm flexed and everything, his smile wide. "Maybe next time scream *inside* your car. Works for me."

A nudge and he had me laughing again and burning where his elbow touched me. Seriously, I was a mess and so shouldn't be thinking about boys. My judgment was obviously off.

He looked at me. "Or you know sometimes coffee helps. Conversation?" He winked. "I could offer that if you're interested and need an ear."

Wait. Was he asking me out?

Elicit small freak-out inside.

I twisted my braid. "Might be good. And way healthier than just me screaming by myself."

"For sure." Another deep laugh as he tugged out his phone. "Can I get your number or..."

"Yeah." He ended up giving me his and I called him. He got it, smiling before ending the call.

"Cleo Erikson-Fairchild," he said as he typed, flashing his dimples. He pocketed his phone. "I'll see you around then. And again, maybe keep the screams in your ride next time."

Another grin before he was jogging away and leaving *me,* smiling like a complete loon. Immediately, I took out my phone, texting Kit. She tended to not arrive until later in the day, but she'd definitely want to hear about this.

Me: Girl, you will not believe what just happened! My childhood crush just like asked me out. It was so random.

I hadn't told her anything about Jaxen or anything else since I expected to see her today. Needless to say, I had a lot to dish, and I expected a text right back after what I sent. She was always up in my social life since I barely had one.

Silence on her end and since I was almost to our dorm, I figured I better finish the drive. I'd see her today anyway.

I was still reeling from everything by the time I got to Tempest Hall. Kit and I had lived here since freshman year, but it was a great setup and I found I liked the efficiency of a coed dorm more than living on my own in an apartment. Shared living was better for the environment, and it also saved my parents money. They didn't mind the cost, of course, but I never liked to overspend with them if I could help it. It was just being considerate, considering the money was theirs and not technically mine.

Kit stayed with me over the years because it was cheaper for her too and, of course, because she was my bestie. We only had one more year and we wanted to enjoy it together before our lives started. We may have lived close to one another, but who knew where life would take us once we got separate jobs. We were just going to relish what we had now.

Seize the day.

Still no text from her as I made my way upstairs. I only tugged one of my bags, figuring I'd get the rest on several trips. Honestly, I just wanted to lie on my bed for a second and come down from my freaking out. I hadn't heard from Jaxen either after my sole text to him and figured I'd have to block him actually. I fully expected a freak-out of explicit text messages on my phone.

"Hello? Kit?" I dropped my keys on the end table we had by the door once inside. This was a shared living space for three so we'd have a new roommate coming in too. We had a new one every year and things always turned out pretty well with whoever they ended up being.

No sounds in the place, but I noticed Kit's pink duffel by the door. I left my rolling bag there too, then wandered through the common area down to the bedrooms. Kit usually took one of the ones down there and I took the third connected to the kitchen. "Kit?"

Muffled sounds from down the hall, and I figured she just hadn't heard me. I started to knock on the door, but it was partially open, so I pushed.

"Kit…"

Grunts and moans… pants, as my best friend slammed her hand against a headboard. Naked from the waist down, she had a guy behind her, the dude drilling her pussy to the point the bed beneath them skidded across the floor. He fucked her so wildly neither heard my gasp.

I backed up. "Oh my gosh. I'm so sorry! I'm mean…" I handled the door, completely flustered. "Jesus, close the door or something."

Face flushed and giggling like a little girl, I

attempted to back up but all I did was hit the door so loud the two jumped off each other. Immediately, Kit grabbed a blanket to cover herself, a wash of her blond curls all over the place, but this guy didn't move. He stared at me.

What. The. Fuckkkk.

Beautiful green eyes danced at me, Jax pulling a wave of his feathering hair out of his eyes. He too was naked from the waist down and didn't even bother to hide his junk. He sat there in the open air.

He even widened his legs.

A dick, erect and perfect, glistened between his huge thighs, a wide grin on his face "Hey, stepsis. Crazy, I got here before you. What took you so long?"

Jaw dropped… to the friggin' *floor*.

"*Step*sis?" Kit scrambled, her bright blue eyes going from Jaxen to me. "Cleo?"

I couldn't speak. I couldn't breathe. I swallowed. "Why is he here?"

Kit's attention shifted to Jaxen before back to me. A slow dread. "Cleo—"

"Why the *hell* is he here, Kit? Here in this dorm with *you* like…" I waved a hand at all the nakedness, sheer panic in my veins.

Kit launched herself from the bed at me, but by then, I backed out of the door.

She grabbed my arm in the hall, the sheets pressed to her chest. She attempted to burrito herself in, but since she had my arm, I saw *all* her lower bits. She tugged me. "Cleo, what's going on? Why did Jaxen call you his…"

"Stepsister?" I wriggled away from her hand. "Because he is, Kit, and why is he here? With you like this?"

She frowned. "He's not your stepbrother, Cleo. He's…" She turned around, and at this point, Jax sat on the bed. *Her* bed. He still hadn't covered up, simply sitting there.

And looking cocky as hell.

That cool smirk was reserved for nothing but me, his beefy arms leaning back on the bed as he flashed his abs and dick at me. "Didn't you hear, stepsis?" he asked, head tilted. "I'm your third roommate."

Third roommate…

But then it all made sense, him. Him *here* with her. He'd done it on purpose.

He'd done *this* on purpose.

My lips trembled apart. "What are you talking about?"

Jaxen said nothing, but Kit did, waving her arms in front of me and cutting me off from the devil himself. He stared on from behind her, nothing but a coy smile on his lips.

"Cleo… He's your stepbrother?" Kit swallowed, that dread in her eyes up ten knots. "What? He said he was our roommate."

Of course, he did. He just walked in here, a life ruiner. He was here to ruin my life.

I ran, all I could do. I went to the first place I could think of.

My bedroom had a locked door.

I screamed, but this time it wasn't in the open air. It was in a pillow, and I did that while my best friend pounded on the door. I ripped my vocal cords raw.

Even then, it hadn't been enough.

Chapter Nine

Jax

Girl Scout had locked herself in her room, completely dramatic.

Smirking, I texted my moms to let them know I made it to campus, as well as the guys since they all cared about that shit. I got a "cool" from my friends and a "call me later" from Mama on my group text with my moms. She liked to hear my voice so I hadn't been surprised about that.

Mom: Everything went okay?

Mama Bear: I can't believe you're so far away. *sad emoji*

The woman who adopted me, Mama, came from a house full of children but couldn't have her own. I supposed I'd been a blessing for her when she came into my biological mom's and my life. Even though Mama and I didn't share biology, that didn't matter. That was my *mom* just as much as my own biological mother.

They were my everything.

I hated being this far away too, but it was necessary.

I let them rest easy knowing I was good, but left out a few of the more... colorful details about how I'd arrived on campus. I'd been on the side of the road for about five minutes before a Jeep full of brunettes had come into my view. They'd been on the *other* side of the guardrail, just wrapping up after some surfing on the beach.

Needless to say they'd been more than accommodating to help me out with my plight. I told them the gist of my situation, that I needed a ride.

I'd even gotten a few digits in the process.

Mom: Glad to know you're okay. You let us know if you need anything.

Mama Bear: Like a plane ride back home *grin emoji*

I rolled my eyes. Odds were both my parents were in another country now. They constantly traveled for work with their jobs, cooked for people all over the goddamn world. When they weren't doing that, they were managing the half a dozen or so restaurants they owned and operated together.

I personally couldn't cook much for shit compared to them, and was actually going for my business degree just to help them out with that side. They'd laughed when I told them, never thinking I could take shit serious.

If only they knew.

I was taking shit as serious as a heart attack down here, the victory of that in my ear for the last hour or so. I'd *heard it* from Kit for screwing her and not telling her I was Cleo's stepbrother. Honestly, when I walked in here and saw a leggy, blue-eyed goddess, I'd had nothing but revenge on the brain. I just got done basically hitchhiking, so screwing Cleo's roommate and rubbing it in her face later seemed like a hell of a good plan. Now, *had I'd known* Kit and the Girl Scout were actually friends and not just a roommate placement, I would have recorded that shit. If anything, just so I could play it back and drive the dagger deeper. My stepsister was making this shit too easy here.

She'd shown that with her temper tantrum.

Kit honestly hadn't known who I was, not that the Girl Scout would let her get a word in edgewise. I'd heard it all outside my door, Kit pleading, Cleo ignoring. After Kit had given up, that's when she came for me, but it wasn't my fault she had her hands all over me after I arrived. I'd barely introduced myself before we were in her room, and though I had opened that door for us to hook up, the choice had all been hers in the end. She wanted a screw, and I gave it to her.

So that had been my first hour at Bay Cove, eventful to say the least.

Me: I'm not coming home, Mama. At least, not now.

I wanted to, God did I, but it wasn't happening. I had an opportunity here. A way to kill old wounds, and I was fucking taking it. Neither of my moms knew why I'd actually come here and they wouldn't.

I'd carry that shit to my grave.

Me being here was as much for them as it was for me. Especially for Mom. I'd always been the one to protect her. I owed her that for doing that for me my entire goddamn life.

Mom: Of course he's not and stop trying to make him, honey. Jax, I'm so happy that you're trying to do this. I know this is hard for you.

My hand squeezed my phone, the one part in all this difficult for me. I had to turn on a lot of shit inside myself, do a lot of shit, but lying to the woman who gave birth to me I'd never wanted to be a part of the equation.

Mama Bear: I'm sorry, baby. I support you. You know I'm soft. *wink emoji*

I put away the feelings inside, at least tried to. *Fuck.*

Mama Bear: Anyway, we both love and miss you already.

Me: I miss you both too. Don't worry about me.

The only person who needed to worry was my stepsister, and tossing my phone, I started unpacking my stuff. I didn't have a whole lot so it didn't take me long. I got my computer and stuff set up when my phone buzzed again.

Rick Fairchild: Hey, bud. You make it in?

Even his *name* grated me, but I forced myself to interact with bio dad.

Me: I did and thanks for that phone call you made. About the dorm?

Turned out my sperm donor was good for something besides abandoning his son. He'd managed to make the very call that got me into the dormitory to live with his daughter in the first place.

He just hadn't known.

Honest to fuck, I'd never wanted to live in a dormitory. Even on a nice ass campus like this. I was a senior and over that shit, liked my privacy.

But then dear old dad mentioned that his daughter was staying at Tempest Hall, and well, I figured why the fuck not? He made the call to get me into Tempest last minute, and I'd done the rest. The space was coed so that made a specific placement even easier. I got right into her space, literally down the hall from her.

Rick Fairchild: Oh, good. So you're settled in okay?

Me: Yep.

Rick Fairchild: All unpacked.

Me: Yep.

Just because I had to be nice to the guy didn't mean I had to carry on conversation with the motherfucker, but he still attempted. His text message bubble came and dropped quite a few times. Like he was thinking, trying to find the right words to say.

He never would.

He couldn't possibly, which was the reason I was even down here in the first place. I'd speak the words for the both of us. He knew what I'd have to say by the time I was done.

And it'd be oh so sweet when he got the message.

Rick Fairchild: Good. Good. Well, I'm happy and very happy you're down here.

Nothing on my end.

Rick Fairchild: Any chance you've spoken to Cleo? I mean, since she dropped you off? She's not responding to texts from her mom and me, and we just wondered if she got in okay too.

Oh, that's right. He didn't know I wiggled my way into her dorm suite. He'd just made the call to get me into the building.

Me: Nope, but she sounded fine.

If screaming down the hallway was fine. I heard enough outside my door. Eventually, Kit did get out of my face, then headed back to Cleo. It was more pleading, more back and forth. It ultimately all resulted in Kit giving up and leaving the dorm entirely. Who knew where she went after that. Maybe to give Cleo space.

Hell, if I fucking cared.

Rick Fairchild: Good. That's great.

More text message bubbles and I had a moment of, *Don't you fucking dare.* If this fuck of an absent father said anything else besides "good day and have a great year" I was going to throw my phone through the goddamn wall.

Rick Fairchild: Well, I got to let you go.

Work, you know, but I'll check in.

Me: Thanks.

That issue in my life sorted, I tossed my phone on the bed, then changed my T-shirt and jeans. I'd walked for a few minutes out in that hot sun before getting picked up by the girls, and after getting my dick wet with Kit, I wanted to freshen up.

The dorm was still quiet when I finally left my room around dinner time. A big rolling bag was at the door and with Cleo's door still closed down the hall, I figured she was still holed up in there.

You have to come out of the bedroom sometime, Girl Scout.

Rather than wait for her, I decided to get some food. They had a food court downstairs, so I left quietly to get fries and chicken wings before coming back. Stepsis's door was still closed and Kit's was too, at that point, so she'd come back.

I retired to my room for the rest of the night to get my campus email and stuff set up. I was going through my class schedule when I heard the squeak of a door on the other side of mine, muted steps right after.

I dashed off the bed in half a second, easing the door open to catch darling stepsis grabbing her stuff. The lights were off in the dorm, but that ass was unmistakable.

Such a goddamn waste.

She really was hot as hell, full ass and ultra tight... goddamn. Again, it was dark but her slender curves couldn't be confused with Kit's. Cleo's friend was a lot shorter than her.

I eased against my door frame, careful not to move or make a single noise. A tug and Cleo was rolling her bag down the hall. She had at least two more in the car so I knew that wasn't all of it. She disappeared inside her room, and I started to push off the wall until she came right back out.

A towel wrapped around her trim body, her dark hair cloaked her face. The girl had nothing but that and her shower caddy before escaping the dorm and quietly shutting the door behind her. Perhaps, stepsis believed she was safe to shower since it was so late.

She was never safe from me.

I grabbed my own towel, then stalked her all the way to the showers.

And how delightful to find them just as coed as the dorms.

Not much movement inside when I stalked my way in. It was after goddamn 3 a.m., so I easily spotted my stepsis as she made her way to the communal showers. There were private, individual stalls, but it being so late, maybe the Girl Scout wanted to stretch out.

My johnson steel in my shorts, I gripped my length through the material, watching as Cleo dropped the towel, then proceeded to turn on the water.

Heavy current fell down her naked back, hitting her glorious peach just right. Her cheeks flushed, I wanted to fill my hands with them. Cleo tugged her hair free and when she did, a sheet of dark silk teased her asscheeks.

I jerked my shirt off.

"Hello?" She turned right away, then gasped when she saw me. Immediately, she aimed her naked body for the wall.

I blocked her only exit.

"Jax... What the fuck?" She flailed like a

fucking fish, flattening herself against the wall in an attempt to shield herself, but there was no shielding. She's fully exposed from her pink nipples to her unshaven snatch, completely natural, which was how I preferred it anyway. She looked like a woman down there, and I was all about that.

A chuckle rolled from me as I tossed my shirt. "Why are you freaking? It's not like I haven't seen it."

"I don't *care* if you've seen it." She attempted to whisper-shout, but it was all screeches and eeks. She had a loofah in front of her pussy at this point, which was hilarious. It covered absolutely nothing and her arm over her tits, basically less. There was no hiding those. Her right spilled through her fingers with the weight.

I wet my mouth.

"Stop that," she growled, obviously noticing. She worked her shoulder in the direction of the exit. "Get out."

"No." A wink before I kicked off my shoes. They joined the shirt and I went for my belt. "If you wanted privacy, you shouldn't have gotten into a communal shower, stepsister."

A groan as she watched me, but an immediate intake of breath when I shoved both my shorts and boxers down.

I hung real heavy, clearly after seeing her naked.

Dampening my mouth again, I pretended not to notice her jaw hanging slack in my direction. I turned on a shower head.

"Besides, I need a shower too," I said, reaching down and grabbing *her* bodywash out of her caddy. I rose, lathering up really good in the jets.

"I'm sure you already know this, but my stepsister left me on the side of the road today. I'm fine by the way. Thanks for asking."

I masked the growl in my voice, but I think she saw the heat in my eyes. She'd almost gotten me goddamn killed in traffic, and I think the only reason I hadn't done anything immediately about it was because she'd caught me with her friend. The reaction had been so sweet at the time I'd given her allowances for earlier offenses.

Well, no longer.

Her mouth parted, her eyes scanning my hands lathering my chest. "I…"

"You what?" I passed into her space, cherry candies and floral scents array. I had no idea if the flowers were from her bodywash or from her. My eyebrows narrowed. "You're sorry?"

"Fuck no," she growled, her large chest bouncing. "You deserved it."

She didn't know *what the fuck* she deserved and hand to her throat, I cut off more of her lip.

She gasped, trembling. Her hazel eyes I could see myself in, the soft tone completely swimming in fear. She clawed at my hand. "Stop it."

I only squeezed, panic making that fear blaze in her eyes. She was scared of me.

I was glad.

She needed to know who the fuck I was, that I wasn't fucking around. I edged closer. "Tell me I deserve that shit again. I fucking dare you."

A quiver before her hands left mine, the fear transforming in her eyes. There was hate there, something I woke up. Her expression hardened. "You deserved it. And *more*. You're an asshole, Jaxen Ambrose. You're a complete ass who treats people like shit."

This girl obviously had a death wish. She obviously wanted to *test me* and was stupid as fuck. I had her in the shower, vulnerable, and yet, she completely talked back to me.

And was currently staring at my dick.

A quick flash, but I'd seen it, a heat in her eyes I couldn't mistake. I'd seen it the day I fucked her.

My thumb brushed her pulse point. "See something that interests you, Girl Scout?" I asked, causing her to gasp again. My cock was about three inches away from her pussy. I nudged it. "You want me inside you?"

I gave her a promise in her old-ass car. *She'd* want me and not only that, she'd ask for me fully knowing who I was. There'd be no games this time. No bullshit about who I was. She'd *want me* inside her. Her stepbrother. Her enemy.

Her bully.

I'd make her quiver to her toes, and that would be my ultimate revenge. That'd she would choose this and prove who she was to me.

Nothing but a whore like her mother.

I wanted to break all this perfect bullshit she put off, this girl giving a show just like I was. I knew who she was.

I was just waiting for her to show it.

Cleo

He had me in the worst place to be, naked and trembling in his arms. A part of me hated that he might be right. That I did maybe want him to touch me.

That I remembered what it felt like.

I think in that moment I truly did hate him, but not because he had me cornered in this shower. But because of what he gave me and took away. To what he'd allowed me to feel only to end up being a psychopath in the end. He was crazy. He was psycho.

I bared teeth. "You're nothing but a cruel psychopath, and I'll never want you. You'll *never* touch me again. Ever."

A smirk before a dark gleam appeared in his eyes. He was a beautiful demon with nothing but mischief in his eyes. He squeezed my throat, and I quivered, his big body crowding me in the corner.

"You give yourself away, stepsister," he hummed, smelling harshly of male. He was dizzying, the cruel taste of him on my tongue. He grinned. "Oh, how you fucking want me…"

"I don't want you!"

His arms caged me in an instant, the soar of a wingspan around me. He was like a dark bird, a vicious crow with nothing but hate in his eyes. He still had that hate, a disgust that physically made his lips curl. He eyed me. "I can smell it on you."

I shoved at him and he got my hands in one tight fist. He ripped them above my head, extending me out and I screeched. His hand got my mouth, his lips to my ear. "Should I check? *See* how wet you are for me?"

I bucked, my thighs slapping his. I could feel him, *all over me* I could feel him, his body hard everywhere I was so soft. "Jaxen, *please*."

"Jax," he growled, such vicious delight in his eyes. He touched our noses. "Is that a yes, then?"

"It's a hell no."

He squeezed my jaw until the point where it

hurt. I wanted to scream, but honestly, I was scared of what he'd do. If he'd physically bring harm to me, touch me in ways I didn't want to be touched. He said he'd check out how wet I was for him.

But if he did, he'd see the truth.

He'd see how much I trembled for him, see how much I hated that he did bring things out in me. It was as confusing as it was heartbreaking.

Tears in my eyes he'd obviously seen, something in his eyes twitching. The end result was him grabbing my face harder.

And pulling in closer.

"I'll be waiting for you, Girl Scout," he said, nose brushing my ear. He bit my lobe. "And if you know what's good for you, you won't make me wait long."

"It'll never happen," I charged, more confidence in the statement than I felt. I had to. I couldn't back down.

Because I didn't know what he'd do if I did.

Nothing but a smirk as he let go, his eyes playful with his stare. "You're making this so fun for me. You know that?"

He reached for my chin, and I smacked his hand away.

A chuckle. "So much bite." He bit his own lip. "Keep that. It only adds to what you are."

He touched my jaw, a ring on his finger. I'd seen it before, but as he wore it in the shower too, I found that odd. In fact, he never took it off, some kind of animal on it.

The gorilla had its teeth bared, dark and evil just like the guy who wore it. Tapping my nose, Jax let me go, only taking the seconds to rinse himself off before turning off the shower.

"You know where I'll be," he said, taking his towel and cinching it around his chiseled waist. He winked. "And make sure to thank Rick for me."

"Thank him?"

Another wink. "After all, I wouldn't have gotten into your dorm room at all without him. The call he made?"

My lips parted as he stalked away, his feet slapping the tiles. The door slammed shut after he left and I stood under jets until the water went cold. He had my adoptive father wrapped around his finger.

And once again, I was at a loss for what to do about that.

Chapter Ten

Jax

A group text woke me up a few days later, an ungodly hour at 8 a.m., but as my buddies started classes this week, I wasn't surprised they were up. It was only move-in week for me, and I didn't start classes until next week.

Royal: What do you guys think of this?

His next text was a picture of sparkling jewelry, the sapphire jewel in the velvet lined box like something out of that movie *Titanic*. Fuck, it was big enough. It took up the whole box he'd had it in and was surrounded by little white diamonds.

I smirked.

Jax: It's nice, man, but I have to say, the color doesn't bring out your eyes much. ;)

Royal: It's not for me, asshole. It's for Em. A wedding present?

Not like I could forget since I was a groomsman. Royal had asked all us guys to be in his wedding later this term. He and his fiancee, December, were supposed to wait until we all graduated to get married, but the pair must have gotten antsy because over the summer Royal'd sat down and asked Knight, LJ, and myself to be in his wedding. Royal said he and December were planning a wedding back home in Maywood Heights during the holidays, and my first thought, as well as the rest of the guys, was what December's dad thought about that. Her dad had been more than vocal about wanting the two to wait when they got engaged our junior year. Royal had assured us her dad was cool with it, though, and I guessed I wasn't surprised.

Anytime I saw December's dad with him, they seemed to be hitting it off.

Good for Royal since December's dad was truly fucking scary.

Us guys got to know him a lot since December's dad was also our friend Paige's father. We'd lost her far too soon, but since that loss, Mr. Lindquist had softened quite a bit. The dude had been prickly as fuck, but once December came around, things started changing. I think Paige's death put things into perspective for the guy. He was super protective of December, and Royal had had to prove himself a lot over the years since Paige's death.

He must have accomplished that feat since Mr. Lindquist was finally allowing his daughter's hand to go to Royal. My buddy and his girl were their own happy little fairy tale, and I was happy for him. It was hard not to love December, just like her sister Paige.

Jax: Obviously, I was just giving you a hard time.

Royal: Right. Any other opinions? Maybe from someone who actually has a girl?

I lifted my eyes to the air but allowed that one. I didn't have a girl, but didn't want one. These motherfuckers were totally weighed down since they got women in their lives.

No, thanks.

I had my own battles at the present to deal with, particularly a stepsister down the hall I wanted to wake up from her sleep and hound. I wasn't done with her, not by a long shot. I'd gotten her right where I wanted the other night, let her know her place.

The tears only let me know I had.

100

I'd been surprised to see them, unexpected, but I passed them off as more of her head games. She'd wanted me to stop by giving emotion, but I called bullshit on that. The girl was full of shit, but her faux tears let me know how desperate she was. That I was getting to her.

And once that happened, my bio dad would know where I stood. He'd know who I was and wouldn't be able to fuck with me, my mom, or our family anymore. The asshole needed to pay for his sins, and I'd be the Grim fucking Reaper. My stepsister would be a casualty for *his sins*. The girl was mine to have.

Mine to shatter.

Knight: Anyway, let a master take a look.

LJ: Right. And, Jax, how the hell are you even up before noon?

Me: I'm up because of you motherfuckers.

Royal: Then go back to fucking sleep. God. Guys?

LJ: I like it, R.

Knight: Yeah, it's cool, but is it a little impersonal?

Royal: What do you mean?

Knight: I mean, it seems really flashy for Em, right?

I decided to chime in since I agreed. December was casual. A lot like Paige had been in that way.

Me: Yeah, not really her style.

Royal: Fuck, I was afraid of that. She told me earlier at breakfast she just ordered my groom's gift and I got fucking panicked. Next, thing I knew I was at Prinzes' Jewelry.

His family's company, I supposed Royal

could have any fine merchandise he wanted—at any hour. Outside of the jewelry store, the Prinze legacy owned half the banks in town as well as many other small businesses.

Royal: I guess I'll have to think more about this.

Knight: Well, when you do, lend me some help for something for Greer. Our anniversary is coming up, and I don't know what the fuck I'm doing.

I nearly howled in laughter in my bed.

Me: Anniversary? Seriously? Y'all been dating, what? Like five seconds and you're getting her something already?

Knight: Try a goddamn year, fucker. This fall? Anyway, enough from your single ass.

LJ: Yeah, enough, bro.

Well, Jesus if they didn't want my fucking help, then they didn't have to get it.

I tossed my phone and the device started buzzing moments later. I saw Royal's dumbass face flash across it, a picture of us both at the lake when we were kids. We used to fish all the time, neighbors for life and my first best friend. I loved all my brothers, but Royal and I had been day one bros being neighbors our whole lives. He'd stayed at my house countless times when his father had beaten the shit out of him growing up, my moms going to bat for him whenever Mr. Prinze decided to show his sorry ass to come and get him. My moms would never let him go, protecting him. Eventually, Royal got stubborn, and my moms couldn't step in as much as we got older. Royal was his own man and had his own battles to fight. Pops got his just desserts in the end, though. That fucker was gratefully behind bars, more than one of us happy about that. He'd deserved that shit, and free of him, Royal finally got to live his life, be happy.

Didn't mean I couldn't be pissed at him and the other guys for talking shit to me, though.

Removing my attention from my buzzing device, I decided to pick up my computer. Since I was up, might as well go over my email. To my surprise, I had quite a few things in my campus box. Some of the professors let us know they sent the syllabus already and the class could check it out online. I wasn't trying to get into my school shit right now, but it was something to do.

But then the video chat notification.

It came right up on the corner of my screen, Royal's face again. The dude was relentless. I turned that shit off, but no sooner than I had, the call sounded once more.

He's not going to give up.

I wouldn't if I wanted to talk to him. That's just what we fucking did. We hounded, all of us, until we got our way.

Sighing, I opened the chat only to find not one but three faces appear.

No, this fucker did not pull me into a group video chat.

But there they were, all three of my best friends. Royal sat back in his executive chair like the boss and future CEO he was. He inherited all of his father's companies after the man landed his ass in prison, but currently, Royal had shareholders running things while he was in school. He must still be at home in his castle, because his location was clearly his dad's office.

Fully dressed, Royal sat back in his Pembroke

University sweatshirt, his blond hair wet like he'd just gotten out of the shower. He sat at the desk with his finger to his lips and our buddies Knight and LJ looked about the same. They too were wearing university gear, but only Knight's ass looked like a grandmother. He had a set of black rimmed glasses on, yelling at the camera with no sound.

I lifted my eyes. "Knight, bro. Your sound isn't fucking on."

More yelling on his end, and LJ had his head tossed back in laughter. He had that mane of his tied up, chuckling hard. Meanwhile, Royal appeared to be over this shit already.

Royal put a hand to his face. "Knight?"

"I got it. Fuck," Knight gritted, the screen shaking when he tapped it. "This is Greer's computer. Leave me the fuck alone."

"Right, Grandpa Reed," I smirked, which got me the bird right in my screen. Knight actually held it there, tapping at the camera before sitting back in what appeared to be his frat. He was the only one out of the four of us who decided to join a fraternity when we all went off to school.

"Say that shit again," Knight growled, but then a shot of a blond bombshell with nothing but a set of boy shorts and a tiny top on angled into the sideview of his screen. His girlfriend Greer was goddamn gorgeous, and if I didn't think I'd get my ass annihilated, I might whistle or say some shit about that.

She casually strode through the shot, and almost immediately, Knight tilted the screen almost closed. "Baby, I'm on a call with the guys. Can you not for like a second? They can see like your full ass."

A shriek after that, obviously her since she realized we'd seen. By this time, even Royal was roaring, and lifting his screen, Knight sneered at us.

"Enough from the fucking peanut gallery," he grunted. "She's not used to me making video calls."

"Neither are you, Grandpa," I chided with a wink.

Another flip off in my screen, and chuckling, I lay back, lacing my fingers across my chest.

"So, Jax, did we say we were fucking done with you?" Royal asked, eyeing me. "Jax leaves the chat, and you just thought we were going to fucking let you?"

He said this, but his eyes danced, clearly just giving me a hard time here. I rolled my eyes. "Nah, I was just over the handling. Plus, I don't want to hear all your shit."

I was single, so fucking what?

"Well, maybe you should fucking hear it." A eyebrow lift on Royal's end. "You might not be such an asshole."

Why the *fuck* did people keep calling me an asshole lately? Cleo may have me on that, but it was so not deserved this last fucking time. I scratched into my hair.

"Right, man." Knight fixed his screen. "Not to mention, you really haven't been acting like yourself. We barely saw you over the summer, and when we did, you looked like you had the fucking world on your shoulders. What's your deal?"

My deal had nothing to do with them, silence on my end, but then LJ had to lean in front of the screen.

"This have to do with your grand master plan?" he asked, tilting his head. "The one to fuck with your dad's family?"

My lashes blinked, eyes fucking wide, and it took me a second to get my thoughts back. I'd seen LJ over the summer, but not once had I mentioned some grand master plan to fuck with my dad's family. I may have alluded to some things when I'd last seen him, but I'd never put it all completely out there.

I guessed he'd figured it out.

LJ smirked. "That's it, isn't it? I'm right, aren't I?"

"Wait a goddamn second." Royal raised a hand. "What master plan?"

"Yeah, what plan?" Despite wearing glasses, Knight leaned it. He normally wore contacts, so I couldn't remember the last time I'd actually seen him in glasses. Maybe middle school? He scratched his head. "I think I'm missing something."

"Me, too," Royal chimed in, and when LJ started to open his fucking mouth again, I lifted my hands.

"There's no goddamn plan."

"Like hell there isn't," LJ cut me off, leaning back in his own bed. "Dude was going on about how he had some kind of shit in store for his dad and stepsister. R, remember how I told you Jax and I had a weird-ass conversation when I went down to Miami for that wedding for Billie's dad?"

Billie was his girl, and though I had seen him at the wedding, I thought the conversation would be between the pair of us. I mean, I'd said nothing incriminating and may have told him more if not for how he'd reacted. He'd been completely judgmental when I only sorta talked about some of what I'd planned to do.

"Yeah, but nowhere in that conversation was there mention of fucking plans." Royal's blond eyebrows narrowed.

LJ folded his long arms. "That's because I hoped there wouldn't be. That's because I *hoped* after talking to him he'd get some sense in that thick-ass scull."

"Hold up." Knight propped his glasses up into his dark hair, really looking like a fucking grandpa now. "Is that why you went running off to Florida the way you did?"

Royal's eyes twitched wide. "Holy fuck. Is that why?" But then a sigh. "Jax…"

"Don't fucking 'Jax' me." I wanted to toss my computer, goddamn *destroy* it. "And none of you have fucking anything to do with this."

"No, dude. But when it comes to you, we have every fucking right." Royal again, his expression serious. "We care about you, man, and this shit sounds dangerous. Not physically, but mentally."

"Yeah, you shouldn't give a shit about your dad and definitely not about his family."

That last bit came from Knight, *Knight* who'd do anything to protect, *avenge* his family. We all would. That's how we operated, brotherhood, *family* the most important thing.

That's what our chrome rings meant, and we all had them. We'd gotten them in high school, a unity that ensnared us for life. Recently, the three had given what we called king rings to their girls, but the sentiment was still there. We were family, tight-knit as hell, and we'd do anything to protect our house.

My family, my *moms* were my house, and my boys should be supporting that.

My jaw fucking tight, I braced my screen. "That fucker, my father, *destroyed* my family. That fucker left…"

I didn't have to finish because they knew. They knew *everything*. My dad hadn't just left us, left me. No, he destroyed us. And sent my mother in and out of therapy for years to deal with it. Thank God she had Mama. Thank God she had support and me to help bring her back from it. It'd been some dark times back then, and it had been up to me to step up and keep everyone sane. I kept everyone happy.

I made things all right.

Well, now that I was older and had access, I could do more. A golden opportunity had come around when, out of the ether, my dad had wanted me to come down here. He'd been preaching about reconnecting with me, and I jumped on it. I wanted to see this new family he created. The one he left us for. I wanted to see the woman he'd *cheated on my mom* with.

And I wanted to see the daughter he'd replaced me with.

My buddies… they'd never be able to understand that. All of us shared our trauma, but mine was my own. It was *mine* to fix. Not theirs.

Silence through the screen, like they knew I was mulling so much shit over. I hated the pity, the remorse on all their faces as they looked at me.

At this point, Knight had peeled his gaze away, and though LJ looked on, he wasn't saying anything.

Royal gripped his hands, leaning in. "I know you've been hurt."

"Do you?" Emotion in my voice. Emotion I fucking *hated*. I wet my lips. "Do you know what it's like to pick up your whole family after that shit? To be the one with the humor and the laughter…"

I'd spoken too much, knew that. But Jax, me, wasn't the one people took seriously. Jaxen Ambrose was always the one with the laughs. I *was* always laughing but not any-fucking-more.

Now, I was making shit right *finally*, and my buddies, as much as I loved them, weren't going to take that away from me.

LJ started to say something, but Royal waved a hand. It was like a silent exchange was going on I wasn't a part of.

Royal cradled his arms. "We want you to be happy. We want that, so how can we do that for you?"

A nod from the others in the screen, and I fought from pinching my eyes. Instead, I tapped my keyboard. "Just let me do what I have to do."

A jaw clench from Royal, then another nod from the others. Royal sat back and eventually did move the conversation on to other things. Things like December, things like his wedding. The others popped in too, when appropriate, and I did as well. Happy for that.

They were things that, gratefully, had nothing to do with me.

Chapter Eleven

Cleo

A week or so of classes passed, but I'd begged housing for a new living placement. I spent the majority of my time outside of my living space and the other, locked up in it. Between avoiding Jax and hiding out from Kit, it'd been a necessity. My friend had been incessant on trying to hash things out with me, texting me, calling me. I avoided her at all costs and thought, with a new placement, I might be able to talk to her again—eventually. She'd said things weren't her fault, that she'd been misled and I believed her, but I was just so embarrassed about the whole thing. Embarrassed about *my place* in the whole thing. I was naked and pressed up against my stepbrother only days later and all the countless times before with him and me simply made me sick. Add to the fact I'd found the pair of them screwing?

I just couldn't talk to her. Not yet.

Housing hadn't budged following my request, not with the term already starting and placements solid. I'd been told the best they could do for me was something for next term, but I couldn't wait until next term. Not with how awkward as hell things had been. Kit was basically stalking me.

Then there was Jax.

He lingered, always there. I barely left my room, but I didn't have to. I *felt him* down the hall from me. Just silently waiting.

I'll be waiting for you, Girl Scout… And if you know what's good for you, you won't make me wait long."

He actually said that to me, said that like I'd

ever touch him again. Jaxen Ambrose was dangerous, absolute filth and the scum of the earth. As it turned out, he had gotten Dad to assist with a placement in Tempest Hall. But unbeknownst to my adoptive father, Jax had wiggled his way into *my* dorm specifically. Neither Dad nor Mom knew anything about my stepbrother actually living with me, and how did I know? Because of the way the conversation went.

"Have you run into your stepbrother yet?" Dad'd asked me, simply giddy. Both he and Mom had been blowing up my phone since I hadn't checked in as soon as I'd arrived to school. I always did so I had more than a few text messages and missed phone calls before I finally answered. Dad had laughed light. *"I hoped for it to be a surprise, but I got him into Tempest Hall with you. I'm sure he's nearby. You should look for him."*

Because he hadn't known. He hadn't known *at all* that Jax was in the same living space as me. If he did, he would have told me.

And yes, I was definitely surprised.

"It'll be so nice to have him nearby," Mom had said too, a video call. *"You can help him, and you both can get to know each other."*

Dad had simply appeared ecstatic on the line, agreeing. He really wanted this situation to work out between Jax and me.

But how could it? I had a psychopath for a stepbrother, one out to get me at the first strike. I was so frustrated and depressed about my situation I didn't even go to classes for the first week. Just stayed in my room. I kept thinking the ball was about to drop, that Jax would strike. But worse...

That I would succumb to it.

I had no idea how an interaction would be between us if I let it happen, and what had started as a daring act to put me out of my comfort zone and lose my virginity turned into a tried and true nightmare. I'd just wanted to be free for once, not be bound by my head, and someone had taken advantage of that. Someone with perfect green eyes and a handsome grin. Someone who's laughter had elicited nothing but tingles when I'd met him.

But now haunted my dreams.

Eventually, I had to come to terms with my current reality. This was my life, a mess, but my life nonetheless. My parents, God love them, really wanted this to work between Jax and me, and though *I knew* that was a hopeless case, I just couldn't disappoint them. Doing that would crush my dad's heart. I knew that Jax really didn't care about any of this. He obviously had issues with me, Mom, *and* my adoptive father. Truth be told, he might even hate Rick Fairchild as much as he hated me, but at the end of the day, *my dad* didn't know that. *My dad* never mentioned any hate or issues that Jax had with him because every time we talked and he talked about Jax, it was only good things. They were still checking in with each other, getting along.

So how could I ruin that?

It'd be selfish so I refused. Instead, I put my big girl panties on and went to class. I went on with my life. I proceeded in the typical college experience, getting coffee before my classes.

That's when I spotted Kit.

She'd been at the Bean Brewery, the hottest spot to go for coffee on campus, which was why I went there. It was always busy, but they were fast. Especially when you used the app to put your order in.

Kit had been behind the counter, a barista apron on and since the place had been so busy, I hadn't noticed her until I was too late. I stared at my best friend since freshman year in the face, her blond curls tied back and looking so petite before me. Since I was so tall, I could literally lay my head on top of hers in photos.

She'd stopped, of course, mid-call-out and clearly surprised to see me too. We were about three weeks into classes at this point, and she'd pretty much given up on trying to talk to me. She hadn't even been texting anymore, just coming and going. That last day she'd stood outside my door she'd said she would back off, that she'd wait for me to come to her when I was ready.

How ironic as that was exactly what ended up happening here today.

She rubbed her hands on her apron, sliding in front of the cash register. She opened her mouth to say something to me, but I stepped back.

"Cleo!"

I walked off, darted around the other patrons in line, but her hand looped around my arm.

"Just let me get you a coffee. Jesus, stop please!"

I was ashamed and couldn't even look at her, and definitely didn't want to stop. I tugged my arm free, but she got it again. I faced her. "I don't want to talk."

"I know." She raised her hands as if I were a small child she may scare off.

She just might.

A sweep of her blond curls she pulled out of her face. Some had fallen from her ponytail, a

114

crushed tone to her cheeks from her mad dash after me. She huffed. "Just let me get you your coffee order, okay? Did you use the app?"

I nodded, and before I could protest, she walked off. She sprinted back behind the counter, and though I could have darted off, I stayed. She came back in like three seconds, but was very much sans coffee.

She chewed her lip. "We have to make it over. One of the new people misread the—"

"Forget about it."

"Please, Cleo. God." Hands on my arm, she squeezed. "Please, just let me remake it. After I do, you can leave. Just let me please."

A slow pain seared my insides at the harsh plea in her eyes. She wasn't to blame in this situation. I knew that.

It was just so hard.

I just kept *seeing her*, seeing her with him, and it brought everything back with him and *me*. Stomaching my pride, I slid my arm out of her hands, folding them. "Okay, that's fine."

One would have thought I granted her dearest wish with the sudden light in her eyes, and that made me feel even worse. She told me, "Two seconds," before she was off, and huffing, I decided to take a seat while I waited. I ended up over by the windows since the place was so busy, staring out at the beach. I watched the waves for a while before I had to turn away, feeling a little sick again. I was usually okay by the water.

But not always.

That was excruciatingly hard since I lived by water my whole life, but usually, I was pretty good about it. I didn't have anxiety attacks anymore and funny enough, large bodies of water didn't freak me out as much as other things. Sometimes I just got these triggers I couldn't handle. Storms too hard on my windshield for example.

Swimming pools…

My gaze pulled up at the appearance of my friend, her grin too wide with a coffee in her hands. "Medium mocha latte with almond milk and no whipped cream."

I thanked her, truly thanked her. Coffee sounded very good right now and always helped as it was something comforting. I took those comforts where I could these days, and she used to be one of them.

Kit rubbed her hands, then eventually, took it upon her self to sit at my table. She must have been working, but she seemed not to care.

"Cleo," she started, wrestling so hard with her hands. This was killing her, *killing me* and I knew that, but… "You have to know how sorry I am. I really didn't know Jaxen was your stepbrother, and had I known, I definitely wouldn't have hooked up with him. Fuck, knowing what I know now about him, I totally wouldn't have. That guy's a total asshole."

A chuckle, light but it did sound. It was a relief to hear it, feel it. I felt so alone in the fact that I did know who Jaxen was. He had both my parents wrapped around his finger. Meanwhile, I was off on this island by myself.

Seeing my laughter, Kit's eyes shined. She took my hands. "I mean, he totally is, right? What kind of guy doesn't share that he's your friend's stepbrother?"

"That one," I said, totally knowing that. "He's

awful."

"I can see that. Jesus." Another lip bite as she looked at me. "I really didn't know. He honestly just said he was our new roommate. And dude, I never do stuff like that but he's like… seriously hot and oh my God so charming it's scary. I mean, it was like he hypnotized the panties off me or something."

God, did I know how he worked. That charm. That evil.

The guy had some kind of crazy darkness inside him, but what was awful was, clearly it was reserved mostly for me. Kit had been a victim in all this, another one of his cruel games to get to me. He hadn't said this.

It'd just been obvious.

"You forgive me?" Kit asked, so much hope in her eyes, but I couldn't in good faith accept her apology. I couldn't because that meant she did something wrong.

And I definitely couldn't without giving my own first.

I did as words spilled out of my mouth like a raging river, a current of the chaos and evil that was Jaxen Ambrose. I told Kit everything. How he was the one I'd met at the club that night, how he'd told me his name was Brett only for me to later find out he was my stepbrother. I told her how kind he'd been to me.

Until he wasn't.

I'd told her everything and ended with how he'd promised I'd come back to him. How he'd called both my mom *and me* a whore when the only person I'd ever slept with was him in my whole life. Kit sat awed, a fair amount of disgust on her face the whole time. At one point, I actually thought she'd be sick.

That had been the part where I walked in on them together.

"And I slept with him?" Complete dread overtook her face, large breaths from her lips. "Oh my God."

I'd grabbed her hands then. She really hadn't known, and I had understood that. I really did, but was sick over this all myself. "I'm not mad at you."

"Well, you should be. Fuck." She tugged her hands into her lap, staring at the beach. "He's a psychopath."

"I know."

"What are you going to do?"

"I don't know. It's complicated."

"What's complicated about an asshole?"she asked, head tilted. "Do your parents know about this?"

"No, and that's why it's so complicated."

Obviously, none of this made sense to my friend. I gnawed my lip. "My dad… *both* my parents just want us to get along. Jaxen and my dad specifically have a really rough history, and though I don't know the details, I do know that Rick Fairchild raised me when he had a biological son back in the Midwest."

She frowned. "You think all this… you and him is about that?"

"I don't know." I shook my head. "I just know my dad wants this to work. He… craves it almost. I just don't want to disappoint him, Kit. This whole thing would crush him."

"Yeah, which is why you need to tell him." She hugged her arms. "He'd want to know about this."

"But what if Jaxen does really want to get to know him?" My greatest fear, that maybe *he did* have issues with my adoptive father but was here to legitimately try and fix them. "I can't be the reason my dad doesn't get to reconnect with his son."

"You wouldn't be the reason. Babe, that dickwad dug his own grave with what he did and continues to do to you. Don't you see that? You have to tell your—"

"I said I can't be the reason!"

Her eyes twitched wide, the clanking of coffee cups and various conversations filling the air between us.

I heard my heart in my head after that, felt it and was visibly shaking by the time my friend took my hands. She said nothing, of course, waiting. She knew a lot of my issues, God love her.

Which was why she *didn't* say anything.

She knew what I felt, the guilt I had. We'd only been friends for a few years, but she was my ride or die. She knew stuff.

She knew a lot of stuff.

"What are you going to do then?" she asked, rubbing my hands, and like I told her, I didn't know. I just knew what I *wasn't* going to do.

And that was break up my family again.

Chapter Twelve

Cleo

About the only good thing to come from the situation with Jax was, now that Kit was in the know, we could hate him together. We loathed him as a united front, and over the course of the next few weeks, he made that easy. Jax wasn't only an asshole. He was *a guy* and one who didn't pick up after himself. We found his school books and random trash all over the dorm's common area quite often. He also ate everything, like literally everything. If Kit and I left something in the fridge, it was apparently free rein for the human garbage disposal.

Then there'd been the girls.

He moved his way through them, our dorm basically a revolving door. And Jax didn't discriminate. Women from all walks of life waltzed through our dormitory, then right into his bedroom. They never stayed, though. He always walked them out before it got too late.

A perfect gentlemen.

It was during one of these nightly exits he happened to come across Kit and myself. We'd been sitting on the floor, studying. We hadn't made it completely known we weren't at odds anymore, but we hadn't tried to hide it either. We were just both extremely busy with the last year of our college education, and I assumed Jax was too. We actually didn't see or hear him a lot.

Not that we wanted to.

The moans could be heard clear into our rooms, at least mine, and seeing Kit and me together that night, he smirked. He sauntered into the room in his normal fair, shirtless from his previous tryst. His ripped pecs and massive biceps were especially golden these days since he was out in the sun like the locals now that he was living here. It gave him a glow and streaked his chestnut-colored locks in a way that annoyed me that I actually noticed.

His board shorts hanging low, he worked a shirt over his tight abs, his eyes dancing on Kit and me. "So you two kiss and makeup then?"

We ignored him conjointly, and lifting his eyes, Jax decided to take it amongst himself to reach for the bag of popcorn between us. I might have let him, choosing to ignore his entire existence when I could, but Kit sure didn't. Before he could reach, she picked up the bag.

Then threw it swiftly across the room.

She'd made sure to roll up the front first so it didn't spill, but she did. The bag cut clear across Jaxen's gorgeous face, nearly hitting him had he not dodged, and shocked, my lips parted.

Jaxen's eyes blazed. Like literally transformed into green fire. "The fuck?"

"Go fetch," Kit said, not even bothering to look up at him. He basically loomed over her, a simmering force, but not only had she pretended not to notice, she turned the page in her textbook. "That's what dogs do, don't they?"

I actually had to physically contain my laughter, my teeth biting down on my lip. If Jax's gaze was heated before, a volcanic eruption encircled his irises now. I braced myself for retaliation, and he didn't disappoint when he swiped Kit's textbook from underneath her.

"Hey—"

He ripped it in half without another thought,

like legit tore it in half like some kind of strong man. After, he tossed it with the popcorn. It hit the wall, landing on top of the popcorn bag.

He smirked. "You first," he said, then winked at me. "But I'll take you second, stepsis."

Absolute chills as he crossed over me, tugging my hair before leaving the room. He left the dorm with a click of the door, and groaning, Kit tossed her head back.

"He's literally the worst," she said, shaking her head, but I admired her so much. She'd been able to stand up to him. I wanted to as well, but he honestly wasn't worth it. That and I was reminded of the fact that he continued to have me blocked in a corner when it came to our parents. It seemed every call I got from either of them surrounded him. They wanted to know how he was doing, if he was good and we were getting along okay together.

"...if you know what's good for you, you won't make me wait long."

Another reason I wasn't trying to test my stepbrother. He really hadn't been messing with me. I think because he was waiting.

Instead, I just endured, and this was made a lot easier by Kit. It was so nice to have her back, and I'd missed her like freaking crazy.

At first, of course, she'd pestered me about talking to my parents about Jax. More than once, especially since now he was driving her crazy with his lack of housekeeping and harem of women who came calling for him. Eventually, though, she accepted where I stood.

I didn't want to create chaos in my life, *for my family*, and wouldn't do anything I didn't need to do. Anyway, Jax, at least to me, was basically furniture at this point. Besides that night in the shower, he hadn't hassled me. He'd made good on his promise. He *was* waiting.

He'd be waiting well into his grave.

Anyway, things weren't completely tense in my life. For starters, I'd heard from Lawson, and Kit could kick me for being in my feelings as long as I was about my stepbrother and not telling her more about my childhood crush. He hadn't officially asked me out yet for coffee, but we had been texting back and forth. He was really busy with his pharmacy school program, and since I was focused on my last year too, I wasn't trying to bug him too much for a date. We'd talked mostly about school, classes and how the term was going. Of course, Kit constantly saw me over my phone and nudged me more than once to make a move.

"You can call him, you know," she'd said one night. *"Ask him out?"*

And then, no joke my phone buzzed.

We'd both screeched seeing Lawson's name, and after a few texts back and forth came the question.

Lawson: How about that coffee Saturday night? Or dinner?

The fact I'd gotten a dinner request more than meant something, but my stomach dropped at the fact I actually had plans.

Me: I'm actually going out of town with my mom. A last-minute thing. Rain check?

Mom had called earlier in the week to let me know she wanted to do a girls trip since I had a three-day weekend from school. There was a national holiday on Monday so she surprised me with an impromptu invite for a spa weekend. She'd invited

Kit too, and since we'd both wanted out of this dorm and away from the stepbrother bastard, we'd jumped on it. I'd asked if Dad would be around, but she said he was busy with his own plans for the weekend.

Lawson: This wouldn't be you teaching me a lesson, would it? Since it took me so long to ask? *wink emoji*

I laughed as my phone buzzed again.

Lawson: Grad school has been hell, but I'm really regretting my prioritizing now if you say no. Really want to go out with you. *smile emoji*

So, um, yeah totally the most perfect thing he could have said.

Me: Oh, it's so not a brush off. I really do have plans, but let's do the weekend after. I'd get out of this, but my mom wants to do a girls weekend and I like never see her.

Lawson: Totally get it, but couldn't help giving you a hard time. Haha. You have fun. I'll get at you when you get back.

I told Kit about the response, and we both squealed. We came from the same town and though we'd gone to rival schools, even *she'd* heard of the golden boy who was captain of like all the sports back then.

"Such a hot piece of ass," she'd said, which was totally a Kit answer.

The week breezed by pretty fast after that, and even being around Jax hadn't bothered me knowing I'd see my mom soon. I missed her, and any chance I got to take my mind off this whole thing with the step sibling from hell was one I'd jump on.

Mom sent a car for both Kit and me on Saturday morning, real early so we could make the most of our day at the spa.

I'd locked up our dorm, and besides a few glares and some eye rolls a couple days before, I had managed not to see Jaxen. He'd been out most of the week, doing God only knew what he did. Probably getting laid or making someone else's life hell.

Since he wasn't ruining mine at the present, I went on my merry little way, Kit clearly pumped by this whole extended weekend.

She'd packed like four bags and wore nothing but a bikini top and shorts for the day. She had a really cute body and flaunted it whenever she could. I stayed more modest in my off-the-shoulder peasant top and high-waisted shorts. I paired it with a set of lace-up sandals, and where I was more vintage chic, my best friend was spring break at the Hamptons. She was yin to my yang, and I loved her for it.

We'd fallen a sleep on each other in the black town car. It'd come really early so we got caught up on our Zs then. About an hour or two later, we woke up to find we'd arrived to a fancy resort off the Florida coast. My parents and I had vacationed to this one before with its beautiful views of the beach and its seaside cabanas. I was well aware the place wasn't cheap, but Mom spared no expense when she was in her treating mood. She'd even sprinkled a little more of her fairy dust when the door was opened and champagne flutes with raspberries were passed Kit's and my way.

Kit chugged hers, hugging me over to her. "Have I mentioned how much I *adore* your mom?"

I merely laughed at her since she always brought stuff like that up, how my parents were quote unquote "loaded" and I should take advantage of it more. Again, that was their money, and when I made my own, I intended to treat myself. I was well aware that school teachers didn't make much, but my parents also taught me about investments and I had several mutual funds that had been growing for years now from my own savings. My adoptive father had also put a trust in my name, but like the mutual funds, I'd been growing it since I'd gained access at eighteen. I wouldn't squander the gifts life had given me and hadn't been born with money. Before Rick Fairchild had come into our lives, Mom and I had been a middle income household. I was well aware what was given could be taken away, so no, I didn't throw around money.

I let Kit be her Kit self, though, sipping my champagne while we were led into the ritzy resort. This place was like Disney World for adults, and I looked forward to pedicures and hot stone massages. They even had yoga classes in the morning, so I could imagine the three of us would be doing that too. Mom and I always took advantage of that option when we stayed here.

"Oh, darling. Woohoo!"

And speak of the devil, in came my mother, already ready and raring to go the moment Kit and I crossed the threshold of the resort. She had her terry cloth robe on, basically dancing her way over to us in her flip-flops.

"Hey, Mom," I said, hugging her so tight. She smelled warm, like home. Her dark hair up, she had a relaxed flush to her cheeks, and I wondered if she'd already had a rubdown before we arrived.

She smacked a kiss on my cheek. "Oh, honey. I'm so happy you're here. Good trip? Not too bumpy on the road?"

"Just fine."

"Mmm. Fabulous. And Kit!" She grabbed her,

making my best friend giggle. "So happy you could come."

"Me too, Ms. Fairchild. Me too." Kit pulled back. "And thank you so much for inviting me."

"Of course. It's going to be fabulous, and you both look outstanding! School going well?"

We gave her a little mini update as she looped arms between ours, but I made sure to leave out anything having to do with my stepbrother. Kit did too as she'd *been warned*. This weekend wasn't the time or place, and what did my grumpy ole stepbrother have to do with anything anyway now that we were here? This place was simply paradise, and I was ready for a good time.

"So I'm thinking mani and pedicures first," Mom immediately came in with after our updates. "Then lunch on the beach? That sound good?"

Kit shared a glance with me like she thought my mom was joking, and laughing, I let Mom know that was fine. All that sounded simply like heaven.

And a whole weekend away from Jax?

Even better.

He couldn't affect me here, not with the sun, the beach, my mom, and my bestie. No, here was safe, easy.

Mom secured a room for Kit and me connected to hers, a massive suite with an actual living room and kitchen area. There, Kit and I quickly got changed, then we were off for the first leg of our relaxing weekend. Mom met us down at the nail salon, and we ate hors d'oeuves and sipped more champagne. We got the all-star treatment the whole time, and by the end, I literally hadn't thought about anything stressful, hard to any other way. This place was literally paradise, and the nail salon actually opened out to the beach with extraordinary views. I got a hot stone massage while they did my pedicure so I was completely limber by the time our nail appointment finished. Mom mentioned a beachside restaurant for lunch, and we were just heading there when Mom suddenly let go of me, waving her hand.

"Oh, you're here!" she said, flailing her arms. She sprinted across the resort lobby in her sundress. We'd all gotten dressed before lunch.

It took me a second to realize exactly where she was going and to whom she was going to. But when I saw my adoptive father, Rick, in a powder blue golf polo and trousers the smile immediately overtook my face. Mom mentioned he'd been busy, so I obviously hadn't expected him.

Kit hooked my arm. "Your dad? I thought he was busy."

I did too and started to go toward them.

Until I saw him.

My stepbrother followed up from behind my adoptive father, and he was flanked by like three, to put it bluntly, ridiculously hot dudes.

Coming up on Jaxen's sides appeared to be cover models who muscled their way off *GQ*'s latest issue, all of them wearing golf polos and pressed pants that hemmed perfectly above their golf shoes. The one with the dark hair had thighs that looked like as big as my waist while the blonds stalked massive in height. Especially the one with the man bun. He towered above the rest like a building. Meanwhile, in the center, my stepbrother Jaxen sauntered like a point to their hot guy flying V. He too had a golf polo on that flashed his golden chest and hugged smoothly over every hard curve he had. A golf club in his hands, he had his hair swept back today too. Like he tried to look good.

I hated that he didn't have to.

I hated that my breath actually stalled for reasons only partially of fear. Meanwhile, on my side, was Kit who'd said nothing but *"Damn"* in my ear at the sight of the lot, but when I jerked her arm in the direction of my stepbrother, she froze too.

"Shit. What's he doing here?" she edged out, but maintained her smile when my parents brought the group over. It appeared Dad had found my mother because currently, he had his arm wrapped around her while she hugged his waist. Dad grinned. "Told you she'd be surprised, honey."

Oh God. More surprises.

My smile no doubt looked fake as hell as my dad left my mother to hug me, but not because I didn't want to see him. I was too busy trying to mask the complete and utter dread at seeing Jaxen, my tormentor and relentless nightmare, during the very weekend that was supposed to be free of him.

He studied me from behind my dad's shoulder, but normally, where he'd appear smug at getting one over me, the look was replaced with something far darker.

Nothing but anger blazed from behind my dad, tried and true. In fact, it was so harsh I think even whoever he was with had noticed.

The blond with the short hair placed a hand on his shoulder, but Jaxen didn't twitch or even flinch.

It was like he hadn't noticed the touch at all.

Jax just stared at me, me with my adoptive father and the expression only loosened a little when my mom came over to greet him. He put on a little smile for her as he took her hand, but nothing could remove the red that crept up from his golf shirt. The entire side of his neck raised in color, his temple pulsing and stiff despite his smile. Mom opened her hands up to the guys beside him, and Jaxen backed up.

"My friends," he said, "LJ, Knight." He pointed to the guy with the man bun, then the guy with the massive legs. Like legit, that last guy looked like he lifted semis for a living. Jaxen worked his chin to the last guy. "And my buddy Royal."

The one who'd touched him, his smile wide, legitimately, when he lifted a hand to my mom.

"This is my stepmother Maggie," Jaxen said to his friends, a slight flare of his nostrils. He pointed the golf club he had at me. "And my stepsister Cleo and her friend Kit."

I and my lot got the golf club in our direction and barely even a smile. It was like he didn't even want to try.

Like he was over the whole thing.

The madness inside clearly teetered a line, and he looked away as each one of his friends waved a hand at me. I was only able to ignore that, what happened when Dad dropped an arm over my shoulder.

"My girl," he said, then looped another around mom's waist. "Both of them."

"Nice to meet you all," Royal said, his attention shifted between us and his friend, who currently looked like he wanted to punch a hole in something. Jaxen had his fist clenched despite his smile, white knuckled on his golf club and I wasn't the only one to notice.

The big, tall guy, LJ, leaned over, whispering something to him. Whatever it was made Jax loosen up, but obviously something was going on here. Oblivious to it all, though, my dad merely grinned, so proud of his girls. Only after he noticed Kit too did he let go of us.

"Mr. Fairchild, good to see you," Kit said, shaking his hand when he gave it and backing me up, my friend returned to my side. She looped my arm. "Didn't know you'd be here this weekend."

"Oh, I'm not. Not officially." He air quoted, his smile nothing but wide. He really didn't notice this, Jaxen between his friends, simmering, while his buddies radiated smiles in our direction. It was like his friends were trying to compensate for Jax's lack thereof.

I mean, the expression barely touched his eyes.

My stepbrother's charisma was truly faltering here, and honestly, it pissed me off that he was still doing this with his show. He clearly was upset that I was here, clearly *hated* me, but he continued with the bullshit.

"Just wanted to see my girls before us guys started our weekend," Dad said, then nudged me. "And don't be mad at your mother. I told her not to tell you we'd be here. Even Jaxen didn't know. He just found out like an hour ago."

I saw that now, *hence* his reaction. He really didn't know I'd be here.

Well, I guessed it all made sense now.

He really hadn't been able to keep his shit together upon seeing me either.

And now that he did see…

I fully expected the worst out of this guy. Especially if we were staying in the same resort for an entire extended weekend.

Dad hugged Mom. "I invited Jaxen and he invited some of his friends, but don't worry, C. We'll do our best to stay out of your hair."

Dad passed me a wink, laughter in his voice. I forced a laugh too, as did Kit beside me, but she had to feel the shake in my arms. My mouth dried like the freaking Sahara at what vicious delights this guy would do to me now, knowing I was here. It *angered* me. Frustrated me to hell.

And I was tired of playing too.

I didn't want to pretend anymore, completely over all this.

"We won't even eat lunch with you today," Dad said, letting go of Mom. He headed over to Jax. "Really just wanted to say hi. We're all headed over to the golf course now. Right, son?"

So stiff at the words, a dark glint in his eyes before my stepbrother schooled it—he really was so good at that—and clearly got his sanity back. He shined my adoptive father the brightest of smiles and gave his hand to my mom when she offered it in farewell too. Kit rubbed mine while I watched it all, and eventually, Mom nudged Dad away so we could get back to our girls' weekend.

"Okay. Okay," Dad said, giving me a hug. "I'll see you later. I'm sharing the room with your mom so I'll be around."

That sounded good to see him, that he'd be around, but it sucked that his devil spawn had to be too. He probably wouldn't be in the same suite, but he'd be nearby.

Our parties separated, Jax and his friends going one way with my dad while Mom, Kit, and I went the other. I asked Kit to hang with Mom a second because I needed to go back to the room for something.

The pair ended up saying they'd go to the gift shop to wait for me. Meanwhile, I stalked back to the lobby, hoping to find Jax, and surprisingly, he, his friends, and my dad were still there. They headed to the pro shop, but I waved down Jax, asking to speak to him for a second.

Dad immediately noticed, his smile wide, but without making a deal of it, he pointed toward the pro shop.

Jax's friends started to hang back too until Jax waved them on. I got lingering looks from all of them, but the longest was definitely that guy Royal. It was like he was trying to figure me out, like he was cautious and didn't want to leave the two of us alone.

"We'll be fine," Jax said to him like he picked up on that too, and nodding, Royal left and went with the other guys.

I got right to it.

"Look, I know you don't want to be here knowing that I'm here," I started, and he didn't even grant me with his attention. He stared off. Like he was done with this, done *with me.* I crossed in front of him. "I know you don't like me and that the last place you want to be is *here* with *me,* but I'll stay out of your way. I'll do that if you do the same."

I didn't want to be around him either. *The last place* I wanted to be, and since I was over this conversation too, I started to leave.

He wouldn't let me.

In fact, he grabbed me up so quick I basically got whiplash, my braid hitting my chest. His irises flared to an ultra green, his lips pursing.

"You ever think for once," he stated, his fingers biting hard into my flesh, "that not every goddamn thing in my life is about you?"

He made it seem that way, like his driving force in life was about me. Ruining my life.

He let go of me so fast I nearly fell, having to actually catch myself on my sandals. He shook his head. "You stay the fuck out of *my* way, because no. Not everything is about the goddamn Girl Scout all the time."

His voice cracked on the end there, like literally cracked as he looked at me.

He stalked away without another word, and I followed his back all the way to the pro shop. His friends had been waiting there, right at the entrance. He passed them with a shake of the head, and they didn't wait before going after him. They went with him like large sweeps of the ocean. He moved, and they moved.

I guessed I needed to do the same on my end.

Chapter Thirteen

Jax

Around the third hole, I'd managed to keep my mouth shut. My buddies had gratefully done all the talking during lunch, and that kept up on the course. But then Rick spoke directly to my friends.

He spoke about me.

"So you boys have been friends with Jaxen long then?" he asked, casually because he honestly didn't know. He didn't remember. He didn't *care* and asked the question like he'd never met any of them before. These guys had been friends with me basically my whole life.

He didn't remember.

He was too busy with his sickeningly perfect family, in his sickeningly perfect house, and with his sickeningly perfect job. I knew this whole weekend would be bullshit. I *fucking knew*, which was why I didn't even want to go. I had to admit, Rick talked a good game, wanting to hang out with *just me* for three whole days…

I *knew* that shit was fucked, and instead of going with my instincts, my gut, I allowed my friends to convince me to go. Even then, I refused. It was only after they'd offered to come down here too and back me up I even entertained the weekend at all. I let them get in my head. I let them *push*.

When I should have listened to number one.

I knew the real man here on the golf course today, the liar. The cheat. I'd only been foolish for a half a second to think something else.

Well, he checked my ass in the end, didn't he?

I started to open my mouth, respond to his idiot-ass question myself, but like a pro, Royal peeled in. He'd been doing that, *they all* had. My friends didn't even give me the seconds to think about interacting with my biological father.

Mostly, because they knew what would happen.

Royal's arm came around my shoulders, the one who did the most talking today. I wasn't surprised, I supposed. He was always the cool and calm one whenever any of us were in our feelings. He patted my chest. "Uh, yes, sir. Since elementary school. Right, buddy?"

So many things in Royal's eyes, so many unspoken words. I got the same from both LJ and Knight on the other side of my father. They were speaking to me without really speaking.

They were warning me.

But all this, today, was all their goddamn fault anyway. I let them get in my head, let them allow me to believe for even a second that this man...

That this man cared.

I was nothing but a show to this motherfucker, a way to add to his perfect family unit. He wanted me to be a part of the act.

And fuck did he play my ass.

"Sure," I said, shouldering away. Getting my club, I putted the green. I tapped the ball right into the hole, having done this more than once. "Something he'd know if he remembered."

The words came out, and I didn't even try to stop them, seeing them all over everyone's faces when I stood. I got the telltale disappointment from my friends, the biggest supporters in my corner. That's why they'd come, to support me, but only I knew there was nothing to support. This sick fuck didn't want anything to do with me.

If he did, I would have been enough.

A neck rub from my buddy Knight, and LJ, well, his eyes had flickered away entirely. It was only Royal that stared on, shaking his head, and Rick, *my father's* jaw shifted a little. It was like he was finally starting to see the brevity of what he'd done, his absence.

And how I truly felt about it.

This whole thing had been a lie from the jump, and I'd failed when I let this guy get into my head. He'd called me last week at school, preaching about a weekend away, and I wanted nothing to do with it. I figured, what was the fucking point? I hated this guy.

But then my friends.

They'd been able to convince me of something else, show me the opportunity in the time. If my busy congressman of an absent father was taking an entire weekend away, taking the time to be with just me, then that meant something. It was something none of them ever had due to crap and fucked up happenstance with their own fathers. They said it would be worth it to spend time with him, but not for him, for me. They said to give it a chance and that they, my good friends, would come too. They'd even brought their girls, made it a whole trip. They'd literally dragged their ladies down and put a stop to their entire lives to be here with me, root for me.

What they hadn't known was this was a losing game from the jump.

And I think everyone could see that now.

This cause with me and my bio dad was a lost one. A pointless one I should have never entertained.

My friends had labored for nothing, brought their women down for nothing. Currently, all their girlfriends and Royal's fiancee, December, were living it up at the resort. My boys had sacrificed time *with them* for this.

For this fucker.

A throat jump in Rick's direction and a throat clear from Royal. He was trying to appease things, even now with the tension. Royal braced the back of my neck. "I'm sure he just forgot, Jax. It was a really long time ago," he started, then frowned at me. "And we all look different. *Are* different."

We weren't that goddamn different, and the fact I had not one but three best friends? Yeah, that shit was hard to fucking forget. I went everywhere with these guys, and Royal himself was our goddamn neighbor when my dad had literally been living in our house. My mom and I hadn't moved.

He should have remembered.

Hands slid into Rick's pockets, his smile a faint one. "Yes, I must have forgotten. I'm sorry, son. This old memory of mine."

He passed it off with laughter, but there were no jokes here and since he obviously didn't know what to say, he tapped the air. "My apologies. To all you fellas. Really."

"Completely not a big deal." LJ raised his hand, his look passed to me. "Right, Jax. Not a big deal?"

"Of course, it's not." Knight on my other side. He slapped my shoulders. "Jax has always been the kidder."

The *wrong* thing to say, completely. Especially when my dad did laugh, given the permission to, an out. He was given allowances once

140

again to not know shit about me and my life, and I was tired of giving them.

I'd given him more than ten years.

Knight squeezed my shoulders as I checked myself once again, and Royal took the opportunity during my check to putt his own ball. Knight and LJ left to join him and Rick fucking Fairchild took the opportunity to come over to me.

He edged in, his smile still small. "I'm really sorry, son. I didn't mean—"

"You don't ever, do you?" I asked, point-blank. I got up in his face. "So tell me. What did you actually mean, *Rick*?"

"Jax."

Royal hadn't actually bent down to putt, standing there, and both LJ and Knight the same. They stood there, stood on watching my father and me.

I'd like to say Rick looked shocked by what I said, that it completely surprised him that I called him anything else but Dad. After all, that's what I'd been calling him the entire time he'd been back in my life.

Yeah, I can lie too motherfucker.

Learned from the best, how to act like you care about someone when you really didn't. God, he was so good.

And I was such an idiot.

I started to walk away, but he got my arm— fucking dangerous. I ripped it away, and that's when my buddies stepped in.

"Cool the fuck off," Royal growled, tugging me back and away. "Don't do this. *Don't* say something you'll regret."

But I wouldn't, and oh, how sweet it would be

to tell this guy off. I'd been tasting it, *for years* tasting it on my tongue. I pressed my chest to Royal's. "Get out of my way before I go through you."

Unfazed, he stared at me, nostrils flaring.

And behind us we had an audience.

My other buddies stood in the wings, crowding me. They *all* shielded me, a protective conclave, but I didn't need their protection.

"Fellas?"

From behind them came my father, bio dad with his golf club in his hands. He waited on, seeing what my friends were doing.

Which was keeping me from killing him.

It seems he didn't care for the courtesy, coming forward. A heavy sigh and he was passing a look between us all. "Can I talk to my son for a moment? Just the two of us?"

I had absolutely nothing to say to this man. Not a goddamn thing. He knew where we stood now obviously. I had a bone to pick with him and always would, why I was here.

I just wished I would have held tight to my guns.

I should have told him hell no to this fucking weekend from the jump, not entertained all this bullshit, and my friends looked like they wanted to do anything but leave.

My dad stood tall, though. Stood his ground and after looking at me, maybe even gauging the situation, my buddies eventually backed off.

"We'll go get some drinks," Royal suggested, and both Knight and LJ reluctantly nodded. All three had given me the eye, though, a silent plea. They wanted to know if I'd be okay.

But I wasn't sure.

I didn't know what I'd do if left alone with this man, but I allowed it. Royal waved the group on, and they took a golf cart to go get those drinks. Meanwhile, my biological father and myself stood on in the hot sun.

Another sigh on his end, a deep one as he fisted his club. "Do you have something to say to me then? You want to say something to me?"

Well, where did I fucking start?

I said nothing, though, unable to give him the satisfaction. Instead, I peeled around him, but Rick got my arm. "Come on, Jaxen—"

"It's Jax, which you'd know if you knew anything about me, my life, or my friends."

His hand left, complete and all brightness evaporating from his eyes. He'd been nothing but shines and smiles since we'd been reunited, a false sense of security I'd given him. It'd been on purpose. His lips dampened. "I know you've been dealt a shitty hand. That I dealt it to you."

"Do you?" Up in his face again. I smiled. "Tell me. How shitty was it? Tell me how I'm *supposed* to feel about you."

"You can feel any way you want. And I get your anger."

This fucker didn't know the half. I shot a finger. "You don't get to try and figure me out."

"No, but I'd like to. I'd like to know how you feel and…" A hand raised and dropped. "Is this how you've felt the whole time? Is this how you *feel*?" I started to walk away but he grabbed me again. "Jaxen—Jax," he corrected, sighing as he let me go. "I want to understand. I want us to talk. If this is how you've felt the whole time, why didn't you just tell me?"

I shouldn't have to.

And I had so much more in store.

I was going to *ruin* what he had. What he built.

And it'd start with his ho of a stepdaughter.

How easy it would be for me to crush this fucker where he stood? To tell him exactly what me and his precious little stepdaughter had been up to. How she was all over me?

And how she was just as much of a slut as his wife.

"I think we should call it a day, *Dad*," I stated, completely mocking him before wetting my lips. "I'm sure you got some girls to get back to."

After all, he'd brought them, hadn't he? Made sure they were here with us during a weekend to get to know me. That's what he'd actually said.

And I'd fallen for that shit.

Rick's eyes twitched wide at that last statement, but as I didn't feel like expanding on it, I left his ass on the green. I took the last golf cart, getting in.

"Jax… Jax, can we talk?"

I peeled away, not even giving this guy another thought.

He could walk his ass back to the resort.

Chapter Fourteen

Cleo

Kit had to ditch me for tennis the following morning. She had a tendency of eating dairy when her body definitely didn't agree with it and had been up half the night with the most epic case of diarrhea. I knew because I'd *heard it*, and rather than make her get up this morning, I let her sleep. Mom told me she'd meet me at the courts as she and Dad had been talking about something before I left. I hadn't heard much, but I had heard Jaxen's name.

It hadn't been the first time.

They'd gone to bed talking about him, whispers in their room. I'd walked in to say goodnight to them last night. I'd been with Mom and Kit all day. We'd had a fun-filled day with the spa, shopping, and then the beach, but I hadn't seen Dad all day. He'd made good on his promise, doing his own thing. I assumed with Jaxen and those other boys.

He'd appeared more than tense when I came in, his smile forced. Mom had had her hand on his shoulder.

"Goodnight, baby," Mom had said, but something told me I wasn't supposed to be there. It'd been the way she looked at me.

And the way my adoptive father barely did.

I'd received a hug from him, both of them before heading off to my area of the suite, but something had definitely felt weird about the exchange, off. I started to close the door, and that's when I heard Jaxen's name. There'd been no context really. Just his name.

In any sense, their exchange really hadn't been any of my business. But the fact that they'd been speaking again about him this morning did set a worry in my gut. I wanted to know what was going on, but then, I kept hearing Jax's voice in my head.

"Not everything is about the goddamn Girl Scout all the time."

I was well aware not everything in his life was about me, but if he'd done something, something regarding my family, I wanted to know. I was basically on autopilot by the time I got down to the tennis courts. Several people were already there, a few girls around my age and an older couple. The girls played at the first set of courts, and I studied my phone, waiting to hear something from my mom.

Mom: Baby, it's going to take a little longer than anticipated for me to come down. Why don't you see if someone needs a player for doubles or something?

It'd been known to happen, and though I wasn't shy about approaching a group, I did wonder what was up.

Was this still about Jax?

I started to text her back before a shrieked and startled, "Watch out!" shot from my right. Next thing I knew, a tennis ball had sideswiped my face.

I jumped, stumbling back, and a girl with a dark ponytail and wide eyes approached me. She wore a black tennis outfit that exposed her navel, her hair almost as dark and coal-toned as her outfit. She also had pretty pale skin, definitely not a local and obviously on vacation. The thing was, her hair and skin tone made her look like some kind of majestic princess, a freaking-the-hell-out princess as she dropped her tennis racket and sprinted over to me in

146

her white tennis shoes.

"Oh my fucking *God*. I am so sorry," she said, cringing as she made it over. "Are you okay? I told them not to let me play."

"Them" being two other girls, the rest of the group I noticed when I came in, who were currently rushing over to me as well. The redhead made it first, freckled and classic-looking with her high-waisted skirt and perfect skin. She seriously looked like some on-screen goddess, then the other girl, little and with hair so blond it looked white. I honestly questioned if she was some kind of anime character or something out of *Final Fantasy*. She had the big eyes and everything, ultra cute and chibi-like.

Between the three, they were definitely a sight to be had and were all definitely freaking out that I just got sideswiped by a tennis ball. Well, almost sideswiped. I was fine, though, and actually started to laugh at them freaking out and fawning over me.

"Oh my gosh, girl. Are you okay?" Redhead, not freaking out *as much*. But still freaking out. "We can call someone."

"Yeah, do you need water? An ambulance?" The dark-haired princess this time, the one who had nearly hit me. She bit her lip, then wrestled to get her phone. She had it propped right in the front of her skirt. "I'll get an ambulance."

"December, I don't think it's that serious." Redhead screen goddess started to laugh now, waving her down. She looked at me, appearing a little older than the others. She didn't necessarily look older, but the way she carried herself was definitely different. Her smile was warm. "You don't need one, right? Maybe just some water?"

"I can get that!" The little one, blond girl and so chipper. She rushed off to the court coolers while the others hovered over me. I didn't actually need water, was fine, but I took it when she came back. After all, she made the effort.

"Thanks," I said, recapping it. "I'm fine, though. I swear."

"How could you be? Christ, I nearly knocked your fucking nose off." The dark-haired girl tapped her head. "Okay, I'm so not playing anymore. I almost killed someone."

"No, it's cool." I chuckled, but she frowned.

"Are you sure? I've like never done this before. Billie tried to teach me, but I suck."

"You don't suck," the redhead, Billie I guess, said. She grinned. "You're just inexperienced. I wish I didn't know as much as I did about tennis. I grew up around country clubs."

The dark-haired girl bit her lip. I recalled Billie calling her December. December tugged at her ponytail. "Well, I'm a hopeless case. You and Greer go."

"Oh, I haven't played either." The blond, Greer, chuckled. "You don't play I'll *really* look bad."

"Gee thanks," December said, but did laugh, which was good. She'd literally been freaking out up to this point, and I really was okay. She faced me. "You're good, though?"

"I'm good."

"Good." Elation took on a new form with her smile, the girl truly gorgeous. *All of them* were. Honestly, I got up this morning, put on some workout pants and a sports bra to come play, but these three looked literally Instagram-ready. Even the chibi blond looked cute in her silver workout outfit. We'd essentially worn the same thing today, but she appeared ready for an aerobics video.

After assuring them I was good, *again*, I let them go, but December refused to play again.

"I don't want to hit anyone. Anyway, we have an uneven number of players," she said, waving the other girls. "You guys go on ahead."

"Oh my *God*, you won't hit anybody. You just need to work on your swing," Billie assured her. "You're hitting it now like you're hitting a baseball. You just need to relax into it."

December didn't look convinced. She groaned. "Doesn't matter. Like I said, we don't have enough players."

"Sure, we do." But then, Billie looked at me. She waved her racket. "Wanna play or are you waiting for someone?"

Since I was, but had been advised to seek others for a match, her request did sound like a good idea. "Actually, I am waiting for someone, but she told me if I could find a group that needed a player to go ahead. She said she'd be a while."

"Oh, perfect. See, December, now you can play." Billie nudged her with her racket, but December looked anything but thrilled.

"Joy-gasm," she stated, more than sarcasm in her voice, but she laughed. She swung her ponytail at me. "You don't mind playing with the human destructo machine do you?"

I laughed. "Of course not." But then, I stopped. "But *maybe* we should be on the same team just in case."

That actually made them all laugh and surprised me too. This morning had been more than stressful. Hell, this whole weekend so far.

Dark-haired princess put out her hand. "I'm December," she said, shaking my hand. "And this is Billie and Greer."

She pointed to the redhead and blond respectively. I shook both. "Cleo. Nice to meet you guys."

And it was really nice. With Kit being sick, I wasn't sure how today was going to go at all. I mean, my parents were upstairs going over something that had to do with my nightmare of a stepbrother.

So yeah, this was nice.

We got right into it after I texted my parents and ended up telling Mom she didn't have to rush. I'd obviously found a party who needed a fourth, and since I filled that slot, I was good for a while. She'd gotten back right away, apologizing profusely. She said some stuff came up with Dad and it was probably a good idea for them to have a quiet breakfast in the suite anyway. I didn't ask what was wrong, but when Mom took it upon herself to *say* nothing was wrong I didn't feel the need. She literally texted, "Nothing is wrong. Don't worry," with a smile emoji. She also told me to have fun so I decided to.

I played on December's side, the pair of us pretty good as I too had experience on the court and was able to help her. With Billie helping Greer on the other side of the net, we were pretty evenly matched. We got an amazing work out in between the four of us, and they all literally had me laughing by the workout's end. December was a riot, and oh my God, she cursed like a sailor. It was hilarious, and she definitely didn't take herself too seriously. I think, honestly, the Billie girl took things serious enough for all three of them. She was obviously older, not much but older. She had a maturity to her easily seen, but was also kind and had a nurturing sense about her. That was clearly observed in the way she helped both the girls, even me at some points in the game. She may have taken herself seriously, but she was really nice, and the cute girl, Greer, I took for the youngest. She just had a sweetness about her. Ironic as she cussed nearly as much as December.

I think we *really* worked out December, because by the time we were done, she was sprawled out on the court with her face up in the sun.

"Oh my God. I'm going to die," she huffed, Greer joining her. She sat a slightly bit more proper with crossed legs, but looked wiped nonetheless.

I was too, handing them all waters from the cooler. I chugged down mine. "You did really good today."

"Oh, you're real generous." December grinned. She literally was laid out on her back, her hand on her chest. "You and Billie did good."

Screen goddess had her shades on, smiling at us all. I swear, the girl didn't even sweat, barely a glisten on her brow. She shrugged. "Eh. I had a good day."

"A good day?" December propped up on her elbows. "You and Greer annihilated us."

"More like Billie annihilated." Greer chuckled. "I was just along for the ride."

We all laughed at that, and after, December and Greer got back up on their feet, we all walked to gather our gear up.

"A day of sailing and sun will be welcome after that," December said, shouldering her bag. "And, Cleo, you should come with us. We're heading out after the girls meet up with their boyfriends and I do with my fiancé."

Oh, that sounded fun, me being seventh wheel. I shook my head. "Probably shouldn't. I'm supposed to be doing stuff with my mom this weekend." Though she hadn't made it down currently, I probably should be around for when she was free. Then with Kit being sick, I obviously needed to be around for her. I'd texted her earlier, but she hadn't answered so I assumed she was still asleep. "Besides, you girls are going to be enjoying things with your guys. I wouldn't want to intrude."

"Oh, girl, you totally wouldn't be." December passed off with a grin. She shielded her eyes with her shades. "Anyway, you wouldn't be the only single. One of my guy friends, Jax, is going to be there too."

The name obviously gave me pause.

As well as the next person I saw.

The guy came out of nowhere, which was freaking hilarious since he was built like a small Mac truck.

Knight, *Jax's friend*, Knight came charging onto the tennis courts with one goal in mind. Clearly, as he not only tackle-hugged one of the girls I'd been playing with, Greer, but completely whisked her off her feet.

She squealed, but *not* with delight. She charged her little fists at Knight as he swung her around, nothing but a deep chuckle eliciting from his behemoth-sized frame. He was basically half naked in a pair of basketball shorts and a tank that showed *all* the abs. I recalled Lawson wearing something similar—it barely covered any of the guy's body it hung so low at the neck and sides. It gave complete way for *this guy's* big arms and massive chest.

"Knight! What the fuck!" Greer shot, Knight hugging her close. He got her on the ground, and with their size difference, I'd be freaking terrified.

"I missed you, baby," was all he said, laughing while the other girls, December and Billie, shook their heads. Eventually, Greer got Knight off her enough to breathe, but if she was upset before, she clearly wasn't now.

She melted before him, the guy hugging her into his body as he kissed her deeply. The pair were in their own little world until December strode by and groaned at the sight.

"God, you oof," she stated, rolling her eyes. "Needy much? She doesn't want your ass all the time. Jesus."

A darkness hit Knight's eyes. He slowly let go of Greer. Next thing we all knew, Knight darted off after December.

She shrieked and he chased her all the way to the net until the appearance of another stopped him mid-chase.

"Calm the fuck down," Royal barked, another friend Jax had introduced to us yesterday. He was dressed more in the average fair, a T-shirt that hugged his firm biceps and big chest. He'd sweated basically through it, though, glistening in the sun, and his blond hair was tousled. He gathered an arm around December, kissing her cheek before growling at Knight. "And no, I did *not* just see you chasing my girl."

"Chill, bro. She can handle herself." Knight chuckled, his arm around Greer now. It seemed she really had forgiven him for scaring her before, because she currently had her arms looped around his thick waist like a little girl and her huge teddy. He squeezed her. "And *I* should be scared. You know your girl."

"I do." He pressed a kiss on the top of her head, nothing but complete adoration in his eyes as he looked at her. He pinched her chin. "Don't have to worry anything about that. Hey, princess."

"Hey, Mr. Prinze." She crooned, completely giddy for this guy. He cradled the back of her neck when he kissed her until a whack above his head from a walking man tower passed him. This guy was also half naked, nothing but a pair of sweatpants on that cuffed at his ankles and hung low on his chiseled hips. He also sported a gold cross around his neck and I recalled him being introduced as LJ.

He received nothing but a growl from Royal's direction for the hit, and December had to physically tug Royal back when he started to stalk the guy's way.

She patted Royal's chest. "Easy, babe."

Still, Royal didn't let up as his friend, LJ, winked at him before finding Billie. He too picked her up, but was a bit more civilized about it. He got her right around her waist, lifting her up in the air while he kissed her. This took her easily three feet off the ground, her petite body sliding down his as he returned her to her feet.

"Eew. Sweaty!" Billie groaned, all LJ's glistening and muscled man-parts all over her. She smacked at his chest. "You don't touch me until you have a shower."

"That shit *ain't* gonna happen." He pretty much tongued her into submission after that, which got more than one towel thrown in their direction. They all hit his Fabio-like locks, which hung down on his shoulders today instead of being tied behind.

He threw one or two towels back at the group.

"You deserve that shit, asshole." Royal snarled, his teeth actually bared. Considering he wasn't the biggest nor the tallest guy, he intimated the most out of all of them. It was just the way he carried himself, completely intense, but I watched the mold shatter at just a pinch at his clothes. He found December's eyes then, his smile on her as he kissed her. He brushed her chin. "You girls ready to go? We just got done at the courts."

"Yeah," she said, but then panned. "Where's Jax?"

"Pardon me, if I'm not as eager to get here as the rest of these fuck—"

A bounce of a basketball before I found my stepbrother's eyes, his speech completely cut off. He'd been laughing... smiling when he said the words. I knew because all the joy, all his complete humor wiped away...

At seeing me.

It was like he'd completely transformed, the light completely evaporating from his eyes. It shifted to a deep internal darkness I'd always seen, but this time?

It made me sad.

I'd never seen my stepbrother, in all these weeks I'd known him, genuinely happy. When he put on smiles before it'd always been false, but this time, it was real. *This time* it was genuine because he was with his friends. He hadn't expected to see me.

I guessed I'd crashed up his plans again.

Another bounce of the ball as he came over, his feathered curls tousled and damp. He too only wore a pair of sweats. Well, shorts as they cut off right below his knees, his toned calves shifting and flexing with every step and bounce of the basketball. He had a shirt, but he chose not to wear it, the thing hanging slack on his big shoulder. He had a mole on his right pec near his nipple, something I remembered as I stared at it while he slept.

I'd studied *everything* about him that night we were together, every beautiful flaw and tiny detail. I just remembered recalling how I couldn't fathom being so close to something so wildly perfect.

And wild had been right.

My stepbrother was completely untamed, a fiery inferno concealed in the frame of a beautiful male. He'd studied me too when he came over, passing each and every one of his friends. He stopped right in front of me, his jaw stiff and temple pulsing. He jerked his chin at me. "What the fuck you doing here?"

Silence, absolute in that moment. Before those seconds, everyone had been laughing.

But no more.

His friends, LJ, Knight, and Royal finally realized I was standing there. I hadn't been surprised. I mean, they'd been with their girls, so why would they have noticed me?

They sure did now, studying me. LJ and Knight's eyes flashed open, but Royal, well, he looked away. He rubbed his jaw in the seconds and started to swing his gaze back to Jax.

Until December launched a towel at him.

She literally picked it up, throwing it right at Jax's head. With Jax's sight on me, he obviously wasn't paying attention. It hit him right in the forehead, and when he ripped it away, he growled at her. "What the fuck was that for?"

"What the fuck is wrong with you?" she

blazed, then shot a finger at me. "Apologize to my new friend."

"You're new *friend*?" If Jax could physically transform, he would. I mean, he honestly appeared to grow three sizes like right in front of me. "Fuck that. My stepsister isn't your friend."

"Your stepsister?" December's eyes twitched wide. She passed a look to me. "Wait. Cleo? You're *that* Cleo?"

That Cleo.

I wanted to be sick, feeling about a million sizes small. He'd obviously talked to them about me, all of them about me.

And they probably hated me too now.

Whatever venom my stepbrother spewed was, clearly, about to be the opinions of these girls I'd had a pretty good time with today. My next thought was to dart for the hills until December literally came over.

And put her arm around me.

I froze, not knowing what to do. She stood there, completely confident with my stepbrother in both our faces.

What the...

The sudden stance flared Jax's eyes like nothing else, his jaw clenching. "What the *hell*, Em?"

She jerked her chin in my direction. "This girl is my new friend. The girls and I hung out with her today."

Obviously flummoxed, Jax's lips opened and closed like a fish. He started to say something else until December pulled me closer.

"We had a good time with her, and she's great. We've also invited her to go sailing with us."

"Sailing?" Eyes heated pools, Jax's fists

physically paled as they clenched at his sides. "Like hell she's going sailing with us."

"Well, that's up to her, isn't it?" December stated, dropping her arm from my shoulder. "Now, you don't have to like it. Hell, I don't care if you like it. She's my friend. *Not yours* and you will respect my friends."

I'd never seen my stepbrother so maddened, like he literally looked liked Bruce Banner before he changes into the Hulk. He grabbed a handful of his hair before swinging his gaze over to his boys' direction. He launched a finger at December. "Royal, come get your girl."

And come he did, but I noticed he didn't pull her away. He stood between them, stood between *us*. He encircled an arm around December's waist, fingers clasping her waist. "Jax…"

"I don't fucking believe this." Jax actually chuckled, but there was no humor there. "You're joking, right?"

"I'm going to ask you *nicely* not to do this. Not to make me make a choice between…" Royal shook his head. "Just don't put me in that kind of predicament. With you and Em? It's not right, and you know it's not."

"What about the predicament you're putting *me in*, bro?" he asked, getting up in his face. "You don't know what you're doing."

"Well, do you?" Royal questioned, sighing. "Because in all honesty, Jax, I think we're all kind of confused what you're trying to do here."

The other guys said nothing, their girls standing beside them, but there was an understanding there from Jax's friends. Knight and LJ both stared at Jax, nodding slightly, which only made Jax's jaw clench more.

"I don't have to explain anything to you guys," he said.

"You're right. You don't." Royal slid hands into his pockets. "But today was supposed to be an easy day. Just let it be. We can *all* go sailing. Hang out?" Royal folded fingers behind Jax's neck. "Just be easy."

I had no idea *who* this guy was to think he could talk to Jax in the way he did. He couldn't possibly have seen the man I'd endured, the bastard. The brute. My stepbrother had made my life nothing but hell.

Jax's attention flickered in my direction, and the craziest thing happened when Royal let go of him.

He backed off.

Like literally backed away, bouncing his basketball. He caught it, shaking his head.

"Whatever," he said, then looked at Royal. "Just keep her the fuck out of my way."

My lips parted as he bounced that ball again, another sigh on Royal's lips as he watched his friend walk away. Royal jerked his head in the direction of Knight and LJ and like soldiers, they took their girls and headed off after Jax. Royal did too, but not before passing a look at December.

She said nothing, frowning, and though he did too, eventually he let all that exchange be.

"I'll meet you in the room to change," he said. "Don't take too long. I don't need to hear any more from him."

December nodded, hugging her arms, and even though the majority of the party left, that didn't put me any more at ease. December bent down for her bag, but before she could go, I sprinted over.

"I don't think I should go," I urged. "Besides, I already got stuff planned anyway."

Not a lie. I was supposed to be hanging out with my mom and Kit this weekend. Not to mention, me and water didn't necessarily get along. It just wasn't my favorite thing *at all.*

Jaxen being there only made it worse.

I believed his friends would genuinely keep him in check, but what would happen after this was all over? Just the thought of it made me sick, and even if I had a good reason to put myself into the ring of fire, I'd be hard-pressed to say this was it. My stepbrother was a psycho, mad. He absolutely hated my guts.

And the feeling definitely wasn't far off from mine.

He wasn't my favorite person, and being stuck on a boat with him? I wouldn't put my enemies through that if I had any.

December ripped that dark hair of hers down, and picking up her bag, she threw it on her shoulder. "If you do already have plans, that's fine, and you really don't have to go. In fact, I get it if you don't want to, but I think you should. It'll be good for him."

"How so?"

"I'm not sure actually," she said, peering off in that direction. "I just know Jaxen Ambrose is one of my closest friends. He's a good guy, but he hasn't been so great since we've come down here. You obviously scare him."

"*I* scare *him*?" I shook my head. "I think you're wrong about that."

"I don't." She smiled at me. "And you should

come. It'll be a good time, and Jax will get over that you're there."

Again, I think she was wrong about that. I huffed. "He hates me."

"That's the thing, I don't think he does," she said, surprising the hell out of me. She smiled again. "I just think *he thinks* he does."

Chapter Fifteen

Cleo

"Have you lost your mind?" Kit blasted into the phone. Apparently, she was up and going because now she yelled at me. "Cleo... you *hate* water, and now, you're stuck in the middle of the ocean with your stepbrother and his hotter than shit friends?"

Okay, she was being slightly melodramatic.

I mean, I wasn't in the middle of the ocean.

Jax and his friends had sailed us just off the coastline. We were currently in the harbor, and I felt safe enough.

Enough.

Huffing, I believed maybe I had lost my mind in taking December up on her offer. I guessed... I didn't know. I allowed her to get into my head a little.

"He thinks he does..."

I mean, what did that even mean? How did someone only kinda sorta hate you in their mind? There was hate or there wasn't. No gray and Jax definitely ebbed more toward the "hate me" category.

I'd met the gang at the dock after they all left, and not only had my stepbrother *not* looked at me the whole boat trip thus far, he'd made sure enough space was between the pair of us that a small planet could probably be inserted into it.

That was saying something considering we weren't on a huge vessel.

Jax's friends had secured us something moderately sized. Not in the yacht category at all, but easily the largest sailboat in the harbor. As it turned out, all the guys had sailing experience and took turns. Knight took the majority of the time. But I think he only did that so he could cuddle with Greer around the ship's wheel. He also let her wear his hat, which I found cute. He'd worn an actual captain's hat after the boys had gone back to their rooms and changed, and Jax's buddies *and* their girls had given him a huge hard time about that. I'd enjoyed watching their comradery. Enjoyed being a part of their good time. The only downside had been my stepbrother, who currently treated me as if I had an incurable disease. His friends had been doing well by him.

They kept me away from him.

The girls had literally swept me off to the one side of the boat while the boys played cards on the other after we'd anchored. Eventually, I grew tired of the deliberate separation and came down here below deck.

Kit hadn't been awake when I came to ask her to go with me. She'd still been sleeping off her epic night of diarrhea, but I needed a buffer. It was either that or a way out of my situation. I thought maybe my mom would help out in that department.

"*I actually think it's a good idea,*" she'd said when I had asked, hoping, praying for a way out. She'd touched my arm. "*Your stepbrother needs a good time.*"

Dad had been working at the time, also unusual. He was supposed to be hanging out with Jax all weekend, but not only had he been in the suite under a ton of work, he'd advised the same.

"*You kids should have fun,*" he'd said, the smile barely touching his eyes. "*Anyway, it'll help me make it up to Jax for all the work I have to do this weekend. It snuck up on me as you can see.*"

I could see, his entire workload completely in front of him like we were at his office. It was so unlike him, to work when he'd put a priority out there. When my adoptive father scheduled time, he made sure to stick to it. No matter how busy he always was.

He hadn't even been able to look at me when I'd left, and I'd noticed my mom had gone over to him. She'd said something to me without actually saying something to me when I left. That I should leave. That the two needed space.

There were still so many questions going on here, still so many things up in the air that I didn't know what to make of them. I just knew my stepbrother kind of sort of didn't hate me but *didn't know he didn't* and my best friend was currently yelling at me on a nice ass boat. Turned out, she couldn't have gone on the trip today even if she wanted to. She'd only called me after being in the bathroom again for an hour.

"I think I am losing my mind," I said, twisting my hair. I'd pulled it out of the braid in my restlessness. Currently, I sat on the majority of it in my one-piece bathing suit. I'd had it since high school and just never replaced it. I probably should, though, since I'd filled out a lot since senior year. My boobs barely fit in the hunter green suit, but I couldn't seem to let go of the thing since there was technically nothing wrong with it. I huffed. "I must be a glutton for torture."

"Must be," Kit said, but then a moan. She sounded completely exhausted, and I felt terrible. I mean, I knew her being sick wasn't my fault, but I had dragged her along this weekend.

"You should get some sleep," I told her. "I'll

be fine. His friends are doing a pretty good job of keeping me away from him."

More than. I really hadn't seen him since we'd boarded. He'd stayed on his side of the boat, and I'd been staying on mine.

Kit sighed. "Are you sure? Outside of all that with your crazier-than-shit stepsibling, I really don't like you being out there. I mean… you know why."

The same reason both my parents had been surprised when I'd mentioned sailing in the first place. Quite honestly, they'd appeared taken aback, which I think also contributed to another reason they ultimately wanted me to go sailing today.

Water and me… well, we were complicated, but I was okay. I felt safe and since there were plenty of guardrails, I'd been good. Big water really wasn't a huge issue for me.

I stared out through the boat's windows, the ocean waxing and waning behind the glass. I could still see the shore, which helped as well, and I could technically swim. It was something Mom had made sure I knew how to do years ago, and I'd done it despite my fear of water. It took a lot out of me, but yes, I did know how to swim, and if something happened, I'd be okay.

I'd be okay.

My concerns laid more with my stepbrother, and after assuring Kit I would be okay, I let her go and placed my phone on my beach bag. Everyone had placed their bags down here in the boat's lounge area. The boat had several couches as well as a couple bedrooms down the hall. I hadn't been in those, but I noticed one of them was occupied when I came down here. Considering I hadn't seen Knight or Greer in a while since we anchored, I assumed why.

166

I guessed I wasn't the only one hunkered away, but after a few moments of playing on my phone, I did decided to brave the hell up and go upstairs.

That door connected to the bedroom was still closed as I passed it, and I had a laugh at the few grunts and groans behind it. The room was definitely occupied, and shielding my eyes, I let the sun hit me when I graced the top of the boat. It seemed the party had moved to this side, because I noticed Billie and December lying out in their bikinis. They'd been chatting at the boat's stern before I'd gone down.

December rose upon seeing my head pop up, waving me down in a navy two-piece with sunglasses on that covered half her face. They were big and white and very similar to Billie's, who had a round set on her face. Billie really looked like a 1950s beach bunny in her high-waisted polka dot bikini, the epitome of Marilyn Monroe as she sunbathed next to December. Seeing me, Billie waved me over as well, and I started to go that way until my shoulder was clipped.

Jax stalked his way below deck, but his journey was cut off by me.

And hell, was he completely beautiful.

He was wearing a Hawaiian shirt he'd left half open, his golden chest stunning and perfect. He had dark hair chasing down his ab line until it disappeared completely into his shorts, and noticing *I noticed*, he smirked.

"Up here, Girl Scout," he stated, his body completely crowding me in. There wasn't a lot of space in the stairwell, and I shifted to come around him.

He didn't let me.

Arms extended, he caged me, thick arms toned and hugging me between them.

"Back off," I said, but he refused, his gaze dragging across my entire body. It lingered on my breasts, which were entirely too big for this bathing suit. I pressed a hand to his chest. "Jax..."

He took my hand, looping our digits. Then, with force, he grabbed me, mashing me up against his hard body. My heart rocked so hard against my chest, it hit his. He tugged me close. "I warned you about staying the fuck away from me, stepsister," he said, pinching my jaw. He forced it up. "Just remember that."

He let go so forcefully I almost fell, his flip-flops smacking the wooden stairwell on his way down. He disappeared below deck, and I tried not to appear as flush as I felt when I finally got my crap together and headed over toward the other girls. Without even stating, I was well aware they'd seen the whole thing.

I mean, they were both still looking in that direction.

As it turned out, they weren't the only ones, LJ and Royal were drinking beers on deck only several feet away. They too had been looking in that direction, but it was Royal who shook his head before going back to his conversation with LJ. Greer and Knight weren't in sight so I assumed, once again, that was them below deck. They'd been the smart ones, staying out of this drama.

I popped a squat on a beach towel by Billie and December. They had several out, and I took advantage. At this point, December had her sunglasses completely propped into her hair, her dark tresses still released and flowing freely off the tops of her fair shoulders. She raised her knees. "What did he say to you now?"

Since I really didn't want to talk about it, I shook my head, and Billie, she rose up too. She, at this point, hugged her knees, staring away at the ocean. But December... well, she didn't let this go.

Crossing her legs, December did nothing but sigh. "Can I offer you some advice, Cleo?"

Since I could use some, I sat up. "I'll take it, but I feel like this situation is beyond it."

I mean, even they didn't know what his deal was and they'd basically said that.

December frowned. "I've known Jax for a long time. Well, not super long, but long enough. Right now, he's acting out. He's pushing you on purpose to see how far he can take it."

That wasn't unknown to me. He'd pretty much said that. I shrugged. "What do I do about it?"

"Well, for starters, don't let him win." She tilted her head. "These boys can be beasts when they're up in their heads. But that's all this is. He's going to see he's wrong about this. Wrong about you?"

Did she know something? I thought to ask, but before I could, Jax reappeared, Knight and Greer in tow. Well, more like Knight was chasing Jax. Jax's friend currently had nothing on but a sheet around his waist. I assumed nothing since he was covering himself. He had it cinched tight in his thick fist, the top curve of his ass hanging out while he stumbled over himself to chase after Jax. "I'm going to fucking *kill you*, you asshole!"

That's when I realized Jax had something in his hands, what appeared to be clothes as he shook his hips at his friend. He chuckled. "Come get it, *big daddy*."

Knight's eyes shot open, and Greer palmed her face. She, at least, had her bathing suit on. Completely flushed, she attempted to tie her other bikini strap. "Knight, let it go. I'm sure one of the other guys have something you can wear or something."

He wasn't listening, snarling as he stomped around deck in a sheet while Jax darted away from him like a jackrabbit. Knight would get close, but Jax would jut out of reach in quick time. In another dash of escape, Jax climbed up on the boat's rails, holding onto part of the boat to steady himself. "Not until you call me daddy too, big guy."

Jax fanned his eyelashes at Knight, and I might have smiled had I not been internally freaking out about where he stood. He was quite literally on top of the guardrails. This wasn't a high jump, but he could stumble and fall or something. Maybe even hurt himself if he hit the water wrong.

The boys' other friends, on the other hand, were roaring. Especially LJ who was completely losing it in laughter. He slapped his leg, and even Royal was chuckling behind his hand. Royal waved Jax's down. "Come on, Jax. Quit playing and give him back his shit."

Some debate appeared in Jax's eyes. "I don't know. I feel like he should apologize for calling me an asshole."

Knight snarled. "Fuck you."

To which Jax quickly danced Knight's clothes over the edge. Knight's jaw dropped open and started to rush Jax again before Royal pulled him back. Royal eyed Jax. "Jax…"

"I'm still waiting for my apology." He

smirked. "I was merely passing by and—"

"Like fucking hell you were!" Knight grunted. "This fucker kicked the door open while Greer and I were getting dressed, and had my girl *been naked*, we wouldn't even be talking right now."

"Still waiting for that apology." Jax cuffed his ear, and rather than continue playing the game, Royal came over. He took the clothes from Jax, then tossed them back at Knight.

"There," Royal said. "You have your clothes. Now squash this shit."

"You better sleep with one eye open, fucker," Knight growled, but did retreat when he stalked away. Greer had made it over to the circus at this point, and he took her, the pair charging below deck. Meanwhile, LJ finally calmed down enough to speak, wiping the tears out of his eyes.

LJ smirked. "I think you just stopped World War Three, bro."

"Right." Royal rolled his eyes, then passed a look at Jax. "And get the fuck down before you do something stupid and kill yourself."

"Yes, father," Jax stated, and when he did appear to get down, I discovered the current state of my breath.

And how I hadn't realized I'd been holding it.

I literally couldn't breathe until my stepbrother started to make his way down, and with the excitement over, LJ and Royal left him to it. The two headed back to their girls who were now up with me. I think the events in question brought great humor to both December and Billie. They were still laughing and talking about it when LJ and Royal made their way over to them.

"Always got to be the center of attention,"

Royal stated, grabbing December. He tipped his beer back. "I swear, we can't go anywhere."

He really did sound like a father, like he cared, and I might have listened to the group's conversation had I not had my eyes still on Jax. It appeared he'd stopped his descent from the rails because he currently was standing on them watching me.

He had his smirk on me, his smile nothing but wide. Standing, he closed his eyes.

Then let himself fall.

Now, in the back of my mind, I knew nothing was wrong. The water was deep enough to swim. He'd be fine, but in that moment, I didn't see him anymore.

I saw someone else.

Memories from my past grappled their fearful hold on me, and I couldn't help rushing over to the rails to check and see if my stepbrother, of all people, was okay. This was so terribly, terribly stupid. Of course, he was okay.

Of course, he could swim.

My panic didn't allow for reasonable thoughts, though, nothing but my past in full swing in my mind. I got to the side of the boat and peered over, searching the water, searching for *anything*, but all I came up with was empty water. No one was there.

Until there was.

A body, still and belly down floated several feet away in the sun. The ocean carried him, my stepbrother spread eagle and facedown in the middle of deep blue water. I must have screamed, but I didn't remember.

I was too busy climbing over the rails myself.

I hit current almost instantly and completely flailed, my body forgetting... everything. It was like I couldn't remember anything. Not my swim lessons or the years of therapy I'd had to remove my fear of water. It was like the terror wasn't completely erased.

And never could be.

I knew that now, kicking beneath the steady waves. My vision clouded, all I saw was a weighted little body, one who'd sunk clear down to the bottom of the pool. His eyes were closed.

He was already dead.

My little brother Nathan had drowned, and now, I was about to drown too, my gasping lungs filling deeply with water. I choked, struggling for some kind of air or breath.

Instead, I got hands.

Strong hands lifted me, later, cradling me. I hit a hard chest, pressed close, and kicking legs darted us to the surface.

My lungs filled with air the moment I breached the surface, hacking as I gripped my arms around a neck and my legs around a thick waist.

"It's okay, Cleo. It's okay."

A voice, deep and strong kept saying that. Over and over kept saying that. Despite, my fear lingered on, absolutely terrified. I held on for dear life, holding tight and not wanting to let go. I smelled spices and aftershave.

I smelled *him*.

I knew it was Jax without even looking at him, holding him close while others shouted in the distance. Royal was in the water too. I saw him swimming out to us, yelling at us. "Is she okay?" he asked, complete horror in his eyes. "Is she alive?"

Jax said nothing, only holding on to me and

swimming right past him. He swam so fast I couldn't measure the time between almost drowning and getting back to the boat. He wouldn't let go of me until we got completely there, and even then, he pushed LJ off me after the tall guy had pulled us both back onto the boat.

The whole gang was there. Even Knight and Greer had surfaced, their eyes wide in utter terror, but Jax, he pushed everyone away from me.

"Back the fuck off her!" he bit out, then hovered over my face. He had water droplets gathered thickly in brown eyelashes, his unruly hair wet and incredibly curled. He caged my face. "Girl Scout? Look at me. Can you breathe?"

I gasped, still coughing. Royal had made it up out of the ocean too at this point, and he'd gone in completely clothed. He still had his flip-flops on. "Jax…"

But Jax's attention was only on me, his fingers pulling my hair out of my face. It'd completely gathered around my neck, so long.

"Cleo?" he gasped, his thumbs completely trembling on my cheeks. That's when I realized he was just as shaky as me, his cool, green eyes completely unfurled with terror. I'd scared him.

But he'd scared me first.

One of those thumbs brushed the corner of my lips, words on his own lips. I never got to hear them.

Because I was too busy hitting him.

A punch to his stupid chest before a slap to his cheek sent his beautiful face flying in another direction. It came back surprised, enraged as his eyes shifted from worry to intense fire. I'd surprised him, caught him off guard.

Especially when I slapped him again.

He caught it this time, his big hand completely encircling my wrist. I had another hand and used it, my stepbrother catching it again.

"Cleo. What the hell—"

"You're not dead!" I cried, kneeing at him since he had my hands. He got on top of those too. Like his full huge body on mine, and I bucked. "You're not dead. You stupid fucking asshole!"

I couldn't see… blind myself with rage. Blinded with visions, memories. I was blinded by everything I'd fought so hard to overcome. It had taken me *years* to be right after I'd watched my little brother, merely a child, drown before my very eyes. He'd been three years old. Just a baby.

And the whole thing had been my fault.

I knew that just as well as Jax pinned me down. No more anger in his eyes.

Just confusion.

He was confused why I was hitting him, fighting him. He locked my wrists to the deck. "What the *hell* is your problem? It was just a joke, Girl Scout."

Well, a joke to him, wasn't a joke to me, and before he could make me the fool more, I wrestled from underneath him. I think I only got out from under him because he let me in the end. He outweighed me by probably close to a hundred pounds.

I didn't care, barely able to walk when I did get to my feet. That's how much I shook, completely unstable down to the toes on my bare feet. I swung around at the grip of my wrist.

Jax tugged me back.

"What is your deal? I didn't," he started,

175

shoving a hand in his dripping locks. He still wore all his clothes, of course, too, his sandals on. "I didn't…"

But the thing was, he did. He knew exactly what he was doing. He'd wanted to scare me, get his revenge for earlier today.

I guessed he gained what he wanted in the end.

"Get your fucking hands off me," I charged, ripping my arm away. Tears clouded my eyes. "And *never* again."

I think we both knew what never meant. Never in my life did I want anything more to do with him.

Never in my life would he *ever* touch me again.

I'd promised him that before, but I think, in the past, I'd only partially meant it. I hated that about myself, but it was true. Some of me, deep down, still had wanted him in the past. Wanted him to want me, to be like how things were that first night we met.

The day built completely on lies.

Jax's lips parted, his friends materializing behind him. They all stood off in the wings, but he didn't look at them. He was too busy watching me escape below deck and I was very proud of myself when I got down there. Slamming one of the bedroom doors, I put my face in my hands.

And managed not to cry until I was behind closed doors.

Chapter Sixteen

Jax

I'd never forget the look on her face. It was like I'd traumatized her.

It was like I'd destroyed her.

I shouldn't care, but for some reason, the moment we docked I was chasing after her. Cleo'd locked herself below deck, and I'd only had access to her after we *had* docked. She'd kept herself locked away that whole time, ignoring me when she'd finally opened the door to leave. She'd pushed me away from her, and blocking my path, my friends were the only thing standing in my way from getting to my stepsister.

Royal had grabbed my arm before I could even hit the dock, and the other guys got in my way so I *couldn't* touch the dock. The girls were already off the boat, scowling while they stood idle with their beach bags. I'd heard the most from December after all this. That'd been what I got to hear while I was trying to get my stepsister to talk to me through a freaking door. December had been livid, the guys equally pissed. I'd heard nothing from Billie and Greer.

Probably only because I didn't know them as well.

My friends were taking this way more seriously than they probably should. I mean, what should they care? My drama was my drama. The whole thing had also been *a joke*, and had I realized the reaction I'd get, I may have reconsidered it. I'd only been trying to get a rise out of my stepsister, which I guessed I'd been able to accomplish...

My only confusion rose with her reaction and why, if she didn't fucking know how to swim, she went into the ocean after me like Flipper. It was beyond stupid, and I more so wanted to scold her for that. She'd obviously just been trying to play the hero since she hated me.

The decision had almost gotten her goddamn killed.

My buddy with his *hand on me* was seriously pissing me off, and working it away, I stalked my way over to my other asshole friends blocking my path. I couldn't even see Cleo from behind LJ and Knight, the girl long gone. I growled. "Get the hell out of my way."

I got a push instead, *Knight* like he had a freaking right. I shot out a finger. "Touch me again."

He didn't want to test me right now, any of them. None of this had anything to do with them.

Knight got up in my face in response, and rather than allow a brawl to go on right here and now, LJ surprisingly shot an arm out.

He placed it right between us, more so on Knight.

"Let him go," he said, Royal appearing at his right. He didn't say anything, and I guessed he agreed. LJ jerked his head in the direction of the dock. "You deserve anything you get when it comes to that girl. Just know that."

But what did *he* know?

He knew nothing, none of them did, and rather than put up with their eyes of judgment, I hopped off the boat and onto the dock. I got three more sets of eyes and further judgments along the way, the last of which was December herself. She had her arms folded, but she didn't look angry.

She just looked sad.

By the time I got to the resort, I'd had no visual on Cleo, which let me know right away she wasn't in the immediate vicinity. My stepsister was hard to miss between her extended height and breasts for days. She'd actually tried to hide them behind a pair of coveralls before she left the boat. Like they could be covered and conceal the fact that the swimsuit she'd worn made her look like a goddamn wet dream. The thing was about two sizes two small and had her tits spilling out the sides like she was Pamela Anderson in her prime.

It was one of the things that pissed me off even more about her. How she dressed like a complete and total reject, but still managed to look sexy as hell. I'd believed for a long time she'd been playing me with that. But as I knew her longer and longer, caught her staring at her feet more than the world when she strode casually through campus, I wondered how much of it was actually an act. She never saw me when I noticed her walking. I made sure of that, but still, she did it.

Every time she did it.

She appeared to lack confidence, like she wanted to hide or blend in. It made me wonder how much all of that was just *her* and that she actually didn't know how hot she was. In the past, I hadn't allowed myself to frequent the thoughts.

Maybe it was just easier that way.

Easier than now as I looked for a girl I'd been trying to do nothing but break since I'd gotten down here. She hadn't made it easy. Still *around* and though I had backed off from her, she hadn't met my challenge. She hadn't come to me, and that had floored me. I knew she was attracted to me, still was.

I saw that in spades today when I'd had her fine ass pressed up against the boat. Still, she hadn't come back for me. She'd been harder than I thought to unravel, stronger.

I darted my gaze around long enough to look like a fool, and eventually, I got my head out of my ass enough to try her room. I knew where she, Rick, her mom, and Kit were staying. Rick had even given me a room key. That'd been before we had it out on the golf course, though.

I hadn't known what was up with Cleo's friend Kit or where she'd been. And honestly didn't care. Especially at the present. Getting to the room in question, I tapped on the door out of formality. But when it didn't open, I went for my room key. The green light clicked, and I reached for the handle, but didn't have a chance to tug it. The door opened right away.

And my father came out.

My bio dad in all his glory waltzed into the hall, looking pissed the fuck to hell. He wasn't even dressed for vacation, a dress shirt and slacks on like he was at the office. I'd turned him down for hanging out today. Turned him down for *all* the days. I wanted nothing more to do with him this weekend.

The sentiment seemed to be shared now.

He had his arms cuffed, puffed up like he actually was pissed at me. It took me all of half a second to realize Cleo was either very much here or had called him. She'd had ample time to do both. She'd spent the rest of our sailing trip by herself with access to her cellphone. She'd also been on the shore long enough to tell my father everything about what happened.

But would she dare?

She just might, my hand scrubbing my hair. "Hey, uh. Is Cleo in there?"

I had no idea what the fuck I was doing. Why was I even here?

And why had my heart felt like it did?

It literally thudded to the point where I could hear it in my goddamn head, reminiscent of how it'd been out there in the water. The rush of letting myself fall off the boat had been one thing, but it'd been entirely another to hear Cleo's screams, then later, see her struggling amongst the waves. She'd gone in after me, tried to save me.

But then she hadn't come up.

That's what my heart felt like now, like I *couldn't breathe*, and though I physically didn't get that, I did want to talk to her. I just... I wet my lips. "Cleo. Is she—"

"She is." Dad made himself bigger now, confirming my fear. She'd told him, probably everything, but that didn't mean he knew it all.

My jaw shifted. "Look. I don't know what she said," I started, a loss for words. I scrubbed my hair again. "Can I just talk to her please? There was a misunderstanding."

That sounded about right, a misunderstanding.

My father merely allowed those words to hang in the air and I noticed something. Something pretty big.

He didn't move. Not a goddamn inch.

If anything, he worked himself completely out of the door, closing it behind him. He cuffed his sleeves again, and I felt that heartbeat in my head once more. I really shouldn't care about that, his judgment. But for some reason when it came to this? He sighed. "Jax, it's one thing to be upset with me.

It's one thing to pull that kind of shit with me."

Never in my life had I ever heard this man use such language. He was always perfect, sickeningly perfect.

Always.

Rick Fairchild never broke his holier-than-thou persona, a politician through and through. He kept his nose clean. No, he never used such words.

But he had on me, staring at me in this empty hallway. Eventually, in our silence, we weren't alone, and the couple that passed, he gave them his perfect signature smile. They went into their room, and no sooner had their door clicked closed than he was pulling his hand down his face.

"Do you hate me that much?" he asked, the words croaking in this throat. "That much to do something so cruel and…" His throat bobbed. "So vile to her?"

He swung his gaze in my direction, pinning me down. I didn't know what all this shit was about. But at the end of the day, what happened was a goddamn *joke*.

"I told you it was a misunderstanding," I said, my voice incredibly even. I wouldn't give this dude any of my emotion. *Never.* "And I don't know what she said to you, but it really all was just a joke. Teasing between me and her."

And nothing to get this upset about. If anything, she should be apologizing to me. *She* was the one who jumped into the water and didn't know how to swim.

And had I not gotten to her…

Working my hands, I let those thoughts fall. I had gotten to her. I had saved her so no harm done.

Rick obviously didn't feel that way. If

anything, what I said made him only looked more and more pissed. He scrubbed into his hair too. As I just had and I wondered if that'd been how I looked not a second ago. I was well aware how much I looked liked this guy.

And how I hated him for it.

I did hate him, hated him so much I couldn't see straight most days, but me being here and checking on Cleo had nothing to do with that. It wasn't about *him*. Sometimes, just once? It was about me, and I didn't know why I was still out here even talking to this guy.

I started to shoulder around him, but he grabbed me, not hard but he did stop me. He put his hand right on my shoulder.

"You won't go in there, Jax," he said. He shook his head. "I'm sorry, but I can't let you."

I shouldered from under his hand. This guy wouldn't touch me. "Just let me fucking talk to her. Apologize? It's the least you can do."

"The least I could do." A nod as he parroted. His eyes flicked in my direction. "And what you call teasing was *damaging*, son. Do you know anything about your stepsister? This family?"

More than I wanted to, but apparently not enough when he sighed. He made it sound like it was out there to find, though. That it could have been if I'd looked.

I must have missed something.

"Cleo," he started. "Cleo and her mother dealt with some heavy stuff before I came around. Maggie had a son before we got married. Cleo had a brother. His name was Nathan."

Frowning, I didn't understand. I'd never heard about another kid, never seen him.

But then he'd said… *had?*

The tick of the word flicked a switch on in my brain, my mouth drying. "What happened to him?"

But it was like I knew. Before he even said, I knew. I saw that all over his face.

He didn't have to say a word.

"Drowned," he said, *drowned.* He pocketed his hands. "The boy was a toddler. Happened in their family pool when Maggie was still married to Cleo's father."

My head lifted, but for some reason, the story didn't stop there. I saw that too all over his face, pain like he'd experienced it himself. Maybe he had in a way, being in their lives and all that. "Cleo wasn't even ten and she was watching him. She tried to save him," he paused, his words sobering. "Nearly drowned herself."

Nearly drowned herself…

I needed to talk to her. Explain or… I don't know. I just had to do something, but again, he wouldn't let me past. *Again,* he stood in my way. I pushed my father, but he shouldered me back. "Let me in there *now.*"

"Why, Jax?" he asked, shocking me. "So you can hurt her more? Hurt *this family* more?"

This family…

The words actually had me smirking. I shouldn't be surprised hearing them, and truly, I wasn't.

After all, he'd chosen them before.

Lifting my hands, I backed off, and when Rick started to come my way, I shook my head.

"Go back to your family, Rick," I said, making his face fall. "That's what you want, right? What you always wanted?"

The words hurt to say, and I wanted to knock a hole literally into my chest with my fist. Somehow, I felt the cavity would hurt less.

It had to. Impossible any other way.

Rick's throat shifted, what appeared to be sting and anguish twisting his face, but he wasn't fooling me. He didn't care, never had.

I left before he could say anything, but as I hit the elevators, I still heard his voice down the hallway.

"I've always wanted *you*," he said. "Always."

I didn't turn after I heard them; even with the words ricocheting down the hallway, I didn't. I physically couldn't look that way until the elevator doors pinged open and the door to his room clicked closed. He'd gone back inside. Gone back to his family, and I escaped onto the elevator for part of mine. My friends were somewhere in this resort. My brothers.

I held my shit together and got into the elevator, letting the door close. I hit no buttons, just standing there. I needed a goddamn second before I did anything, and I was wrong about that earlier hurt. Something did hurt worse in the end, and I let myself feel it. For two seconds, I let that man hurt me again. I absorbed his words.

But then, I let them go like the horseshit they were.

Chapter Seventeen

Cleo

Jax didn't come back to school. At least, not back to the dorm anyway. He kept his door locked, but neither Kit nor I had seen him return to the dormitory after the three-day weekend. We hadn't seen him the rest of the trip either. Like he was gone without a trace.

Not like I cared.

He could jump off a cliff as far as I was concerned and maybe he had. I didn't know. He very well still could be attending classes. After all, Bay Cove was huge. Odds were my stepbrother was meddling in with the many undergrads and trying to dodge me just as much as I had him. I hadn't heard that conversation he had outside the suite with my adoptive father, but I had heard both my dad's voice and Jaxen's. Dad was angry, something he never got, and he didn't tend to lose his patience.

He'd said nothing after he got back inside the suite, his expression considerably sad. He'd tried to hide it, of course, but couldn't mask the disappointment. These antics with Jax had done that to him. That was something I knew and felt incredibly guilty about.

I'd only told Dad and Mom about Jax pretending to drown and hadn't even wanted to spill that. I'd been crying when I came in, a mess, and they'd tugged it out of me. I wasn't trying to protect my stepbrother by concealing everything else he'd done. Honestly, I hadn't cared anymore, but what I didn't want was for him to win. He'd done enough damage in my life. I knew Jax pulling that last little stunt he had wasn't my fault. My stepbrother was a jerk, point-blank, but I couldn't help thinking had I not inserted myself amongst his friend circle, he wouldn't have gone off the way he had. He literally jumped off the deep end.

I supposed that was neither here nor there now.

I'd also become the sudden recipient of frequent check-ins with both Mom and Dad. No sooner had I stepped foot in the dorm had they been calling me, texting me. The next couple days, I'd heard from them no less than a half a dozen times, and just like that, it was like that time after it all happened.

When we'd lost Nathan.

I couldn't get my mom off me after his passing, and even worse after my biological dad finally up and left. It was statistically proven that marriages tended to fall apart after the loss of a child.

And so I was responsible for yet one more thing.

It'd been *my fault* Nathan had drowned because I was supposed to be watching him. I'd only been nine, but it'd been my responsibility. I'd told him to shove off that day, let go of his hand because he always wanted to play. He'd only been three. Of course, he'd wanted to play.

Of course, he wanted to play…

All that trauma had played back in a mad dash when I saw Jax's limp body in the water. I was that little kid again.

Powerless.

He'd played me for a fool, and I really was one. Actually longing after someone like him. I had for a time.

A stupid fool.

Jaxen Brett Ambrose was a bully, and I loathed him, pure evil down to his rotten core. He was dead to me. Gone completely from my life in every way he needed to be. He wouldn't touch any part of me anymore, and I couldn't afford to let him.

It'd almost killed me the first time.

I forced myself to charge on after returning to school. This was made harder with Mom and Dad's sudden worry, but I managed. When they weren't calling, Kit was popping her head in too and checking on me. She'd said she could kick herself for getting sick.

"*I should have been there*," she'd said, but I didn't think she could have helped. The result would have been the same. I knew I would have gone into the water after Jax. I would have labored over nothing, the guy incredibly selfish.

I had made her promise me we wouldn't talk about him again. Almost a full week of classes went by and he hadn't shown up, so there really wasn't a point in talking about him or to him unless we had to do so. And if he did come back, I'd cross that bridge when I got there.

Lawson: So how about that date then? You still want to hang out? I'm free Saturday.

I had to smile at the text from Lawson. I'd expected to hear from him after the weekend from hell, but he was also a guy, so I wasn't surprised he let almost a week pass before getting back to me about our date. I really probably shouldn't be dating, but at the present, I definitely needed a way to get out of my head.

Me: Of course! Do I have to wear anything special?

Lawson: Just bring yourself and that smile *smile emoji*

Of course, the text nearly had me squealing in my bedroom. This guy was a huge deal back home, and though he told me not to wear anything special, I instantly was out of my room and in Kit's. She had a way better closet than me and dressed me in something chic yet comfortable for the evening.

The pink dress flared out at my hips and stopped about mid-thigh. All my other dresses were basically church-going length and used for when I made speeches at charity events or attended press schedulings for Dad.

Kit also gave me a pair of brown booties that made my legs look really long. Especially in a dress cut for my petite friend. I wanted to wear my hair up, but my friend urged me to sport it at length. I'd be sitting on it all night, but she said it'd be worth it.

"It complements your pretty eyes," she said, hugging me in front of her vanity mirror. She wanted me to go out just like that and bare shouldered, but nights had been chillier recently. I convinced her to let me wear my white knit sweater, and after doing my makeup, she released me to my date. Lawson texted when he arrived, and rather than make him come up and try to navigate my dorm, I decided to come downstairs.

When I got outside, he sat behind the wheel of a black Mercedes, but got out upon seeing me. He had a red rose in his hands, and though he'd told me not to dress up, he looked incredibly stylish in his black dress shirt and twill pants. They hugged his firm thighs heavily, his dark hair swept and styled. He presented the rose to me with a handsome grin, taking the initiative by brushing a kiss on my cheek.

His lips warm, I leaned into them and definitely hoped to feel more than I had. The chaste kiss left nothing but a subtle warmth in my cheek at the brush, but I figured that may just be because he only kissed me on the cheek.

Don't compare him to him.

I didn't, refused as Lawson pulled away and gathered my arm. I didn't want this guy to be like my stepbrother. If I did, I'd be setting myself up for nothing but disappointment.

I was well aware of that fact, smiling at Lawson as he led me to his pretty car. It was sleek and expensive and just so happened to be a slightly newer model than one of my parents' cars. I wasn't surprised. Most of the people in my neighborhood growing up were either politicians or businessmen. I knew Lawson's father himself was an alderman, his mom on the PTA of our prep school.

"You look lovely," he said upon getting inside, and I tried not to let the fact I noticed his gaze drag well over my body in this too tight dress.

Actual heat graced my cheeks. I'd never been good with compliments, never put myself in a position to get them really. I was too busy with school and my volunteer work typically.

Instead, I buried my hot face in the rose and asked him where we were going. He'd been elusive about that, though, saying the location was a surprise. Flashing his deep dimples, he merely put his car in drive and cruised us off into the night.

The sun was starting to set on campus, making it completely beautiful and lush with its bright tones. Lawson kept us on the highway, driving along the beach until we came up to a pier about four or five miles away from campus. The location was known for its exquisite restaurants with oceanic views and definitely required more than my smile to eat inside. The place was completely posh, and not only did Lawson get us reservations, he had us at one of the best tables with amazing views of the shoreline.

"Just bring my smile tonight, huh?" I asked, admiring the scenic landscape. I worked off my sweater into Lawson's hands and he placed it on the back of my chair. I grinned back at him. "This place is pretty fancy."

"Is it?" Lawson passed that off, pulling out my chair and letting me sit. He pushed me in. "Didn't notice."

Right. He totally noticed because he looked damn good himself, his dress shirt tugging across his muscles when he worked himself into his chair. I eyed him, and he merely chuckled.

"I figured you'd prepare anyway," he said, his eyes dancing with candlelight. The flame flickered on our table, waving in the calmly lit room. His dimples deepened. "Girls always do. Guys always say that kind of thing. That their dates don't have to try, but somehow they always turn up beautiful. Doesn't seem to matter what we say."

His gaze lingered on me like it had in the car, and at yet another compliment, I truly did feel that heat in my cheeks. Lawson relieved it a little to order us drinks, but then after, his attention was right back on me. He smiled. "You really do look beautiful, and I thank you for even coming out tonight after I made you wait so long."

It truly wasn't a big deal, and I was floored he was even interested in me. Guys like him and girls like me were miles apart.

He braced his hands behind the candlelight, but before either one of us could say anything more, the waiter returned with our drinks. We'd had our menus, but I failed to even look at mine. I started to open it, but Lawson faced the waiter.

"Steak tartare to start," he stated, taking the initiative. "Then for our entrees, I'll have the blackened chicken Parmesan and the lady will have the salmon with avocado salsa."

My menu falling, I'd never had anything ordered for me. But then again, I didn't go out on many dates. This was probably commonplace, and since I liked salmon, I went with it, smiling as he looked at me.

"You'll love it," Lawson said, replacing our menus with my hand. He'd taken it right away, aggressive but assertive. He was clearly a guy who knew what he wanted. He looped our digits to the side of the flickering light. "Now, tell me about your weekend. You hung out with your mom, right?"

Since I had, I told him about it. I thought I'd leave some details out. But in the end, it erupted like word vomit. I told him all about my stepbrother from hell and how he'd turned up out of the blue. I even mentioned him pretending to drown and me almost drowning trying to save him. By the end, our entrees had arrived, and I quickly realized I'd gone on so long about my stepbrother that the sun had completely set outside and our meals had actually arrived.

I cringed upon seeing my salmon and his blackened chicken arrive between us, that I had drudged on for so long and about topics I really didn't want to talk about. My stepbrother was a complete asshole, and here I was doing the opposite of what I wanted to do tonight—forget about him.

I chewed my lip. "I'm sorry. You asked me about my weekend and…"

I made a gagging noise like I thew up words at him. Which I basically had, but calm and cool, Lawson merely shook his head. He finally let go of my hand at his point, something I realized he hadn't done the whole time during my word vomit. He'd listened to the whole thing, taken it in. "You have nothing to apologize for. The guy sounds like a total ass."

"Oh, he is, but I definitely shouldn't be giving him this much power." I sighed. "He's already taken enough of it."

A chuckle before Lawson picked up his wine glass, and when he gestured to mine, I picked up my glass as well.

"To your stepbrother then," he said, serious as he clinked my glass. "Because that's the last second he'll take of your energy."

I liked the sound of that, sipping my wine. I realized in all my spiel, I'd already downed half of it, and Lawson was completely on that too. He gestured the waiter to us right away, and it was nice not to think about things. He had all the boxes checked, taking care of everything. All too quickly, my top off arrived, and we relaxed into deep conversation.

As we finished our dinner and just talked, I discovered I liked just listening to him. It was easy with him, no pressure, and since he took care of everything, I could just *be*. Before I knew it, I was sitting there with my third glass of wine, and though I didn't normally drink that much, I found I didn't want to leave right away. He'd done what I wanted in the end, gotten me out of my head.

I think I might have done that a little bit for him too. He had my hand again, seeming like he enjoyed listening to me too.

"Well, I'm full," he said, sitting back. Our hands still together, he stared at our digits, toying with them before staring warmly at me. "Ready to go?"

Since I was, I let him pay the check, and though I thought we'd go to his car, we ended up on the pier. We just talked some more, strolling along the dock. Eventually, we made it to his car, but once we were there, Lawson suggested we take the scenic route back to campus. It was the long way, but he said there was a place he wanted to show me that had awesome views of the ocean.

Honestly, I was really tired. I'd also been drinking more than I should have, which made me drowsier. I hadn't wanted to disappoint him, though, so I agreed under the caveat we'd return to campus before it got too late. He promised we would, and as we drove, I really did enjoy spending time with him. He was easy to talk to, no pressure, and did appear to get just as much joy out of spending time with me.

Our nighttime cruise ended up being on the top of a hill with a large expanse of the sky as it met dark ocean. As it turned out, the place was a hiking trail, and Lawson's hand never left mine.

His fingers traced down my palms, constant little touches. Sometimes he'd get my wrist or even my arm when he put his around me after we parked. The whole experience was terribly romantic, and since I was a hopeless one, I was here for the whole thing.

I just wanted to feel protected, to feel safe and cared about. Laying my head on his chest, he talked to me about random facts involving the history of the trail and the ocean. Pretty soon, my eyes started to drift closed, and that's when he pinched my chin.

And kissed me.

It was soft, warm, and I wanted to imprint him into my entire being. I wanted *this kiss* and him to be important. I wanted it to have the most feeling out of every other kiss I'd ever had. I wanted to remember him above all else and beyond anyone else. I wanted this to be it.

I wanted him to be someone else.

I fought for this feeling with him to cover the lasting impression of another, to be priority in my memory of kisses. In fact, I tried so hard it took me a second to realize when things got *too* hot and Lawson's hands ventured to places I wasn't ready to go. Gripping my thigh, he pushed my legs apart, and as Lawson's fingers graced my panties, I shoved them away.

So many questions in his eyes when I pulled back, and I felt bad. I gripped his shirt. "Sorry."

"No. It's okay," he said, his finger tracing underneath my chin. "Just too much?"

I nodded, a small smile on his lips before he kissed me again. There was less pressure than before, which I liked. He kept things really chill, easy as his tongue tasted mine. He tasted like wine, and though hints of his cologne were a little overwhelming, I didn't mind since he was such a good kisser. His big hand eased behind the nape of my neck, and kissing harder, he moved it down. He got one good squeeze of my breast before I pushed him away again.

"Lawson…"

He let me go, completely this time, but he also worked his hand down his jaw. He pulled back completely, staring out the window, but *this time*, he looked pissed, and I didn't understand.

I sat back to my own side of the car, adjusting my skirt.

"So I can't touch you either?" he asked, coming so far out of left field my eyes twitched wide. With a sigh, he wrestled dark hair. "I'm just saying. I thought…"

"What did you think?" Completely closed off now, I felt suffocation in his nice car.

He put his head back. "I thought you were casual. That this wouldn't be a thing."

"What made you think that?"

He lifted a hand. "I mean, I saw you that day at the pharmacy. I don't know. With what you bought and everything—"

"So that gave you license to try and get into my pants?"

Another hand raise, this time to pat the air. "Just relax. It's just seeing that I assumed sex wasn't a thing for you. That you weren't one of those closed-off chicks."

Chicks, huh?

Suddenly disgusted with him and the fact I'd fallen for his Don Juan crap, I got out of the car. I didn't know where I was going to go out in the middle of nowhere.

I must not have, because after I got out with my purse, slamming the door, I stood there. I placed my back to his ride, huffing after being basically fondled.

His window pulled down.

"What are you doing, Cleo?"

Silence.

"You gonna get back in the car? I can take

you home. Is that what you'd like?"

Again, I said nothing. Needing a moment to cool the hell off before speaking to him.

He gave me more than that.

Before I knew it, he was starting the car, and I whipped around to find him backing away. "Hey!"

Nothing but headlights in my eyes as he backed off the overlook, then onto the road. He peeled away after that, leaving me stunned, and screaming, I got out my phone. I barely could find the buttons to call Kit, let alone speak to her. I was shaking, unable to breathe. I actually had to squat just to relieve my panic.

I heard her voice, and it took me a second to realize my predicament. I was alone. Alone out in the middle of nowhere.

And I'd let myself get played yet again.

Chapter Eighteen

Jax

My phone buzzed with a number I didn't recognize, and when I answered, a voice I didn't really feel like hearing shouted at me.

"Is this that asshole Jaxen Ambrose?" Kit, Cleo's friend and roommate, blared into the line. She barked over chatter and whirling machines, and my eyebrow lifted.

"Yeah, how'd you get this number, Kit?" I didn't recall giving it to her, thought I'd remember.

"You gave to it to me, you asshole. *Before* we slept together?"

Oh, yeah. That was right. What started out as me trying to get her digits turned into us rolling around in her bed. I lounged back against my headboard. "What do you want? I'm trying to do homework."

Honest for fucking once, and frankly, all I could do being stuck down here in Florida. I had to at least ride out the semester if I even wanted a chance of graduating from college in the spring. Even still, the possibility of transferring in the middle of my senior year to anywhere would be difficult. It was already hard enough coming in as a senior so trying to transfer second semester? Yeah, it'd be a son of a bitch.

Odds were, I'd ultimately be stuck at Bay Cove University. But at least, I'd be able to take advantage of the time. I'd gotten my own place on the *other* side of campus from her and Cleo. I'd found a nice apartment complex, and though I'd had to completely abandon my shit at the other place, it'd been worth it. I wasn't trying to walk back up in that bitch.

Not that any of them would want to see me either.

I didn't care so much about that part. Stepping back, for me, had just been easier. I hadn't heard from either of the girls at this point, so I had a feeling the notion was shared. Truth be told, outside of my friends, I'd been lying pretty low on the social circuit. I'd finished out the weekend with them, a long, drawn-out weekend with awkward silences and judgmental eyes. After I'd come back and seen them, they'd allowed the ragging to go for the most part. What was done was done and what was said was said. I didn't need to hear any more from them and they knew that.

Rick had been even more quiet, not that I cared. In fact, the only people I was personally related to who had reached out to me were my moms, and since they'd only asked how I was doing, I knew at least Rick wasn't running his mouth to them. I wasn't surprised. My biological mother, Sherry, had had zero contact with my dad after the divorce. Too much tension there.

That came with the territory when your husband cheated on you.

This had been widely known in my house growing up. That infidelity had come and pulled them apart. They may not have spoken to me about it personally, but they'd known I knew. I'd *heard* it, nothing but arguments in my house toward the end there. I'd heard the truth. I'd even walked in on that last one.

It'd been the last night my father stayed at the house.

He'd been gone the next day, disappearing completely from our lives. The next thing I'd known, the only contact I'd had with my dad was through the family courts. The judge had asked me who I wanted to stay with, my father pleading with his eyes across the court room. It was like he'd wanted me to choose him.

But why would I choose him when he hadn't even chosen me?

He'd completely abandoned us, gone for nearly a year without contact. The next time I had seen him had been in the court and that'd been laughable that he could ever fathom I'd want anything to do with him. Because of him, I'd gotten to see my mother's looks changed. How she used to smile, but suddenly was in her room crying for hours on end. I'd had to make dinner for her, take care of her, for what felt like months before she'd finally been able to get up and out of the bed. She hadn't even been able to look at me most days, like the mere sight of my face reminded her of him. In the back of my mind, I think I'd known it did. Something akin to shame on her face every time she'd realized she had allowed those tears to spill in front of me.

Things had gotten a lot better when Mama came into our lives. She'd been able to pick Mom up, help her, help *me* help her. I'd just been a kid, and she'd been our saving grace. This family had healed because of her.

And how high and mighty my bio dad thought he was. Coming in and trying to be a dad to me now. I was in my fucking twenties, didn't need a "dad" anymore, and when I had, he'd been nowhere insight.

Just like now.

Things got hard, and he bolted, but this time, I

didn't let it affect me. I enjoyed his radio silence and was biding my time. The semester would be over soon, then I could get the fuck out of this bitch.

"Right. You're doing homework," Kit said, calling me for some goddamn reason. "Anyway, you got a car?"

Another eyebrow lift, and I moved my textbook off my lap. "Why?"

"Obviously, need a ride."

I smirked, lying back. "And you're calling me? Go get yourself a ride share."

"I would, but Cleo is out in the middle of fucking nowhere, and it's just a lot easier if—"

"Wait. Wait. Hold up." *Cleo?* I sat up. "What about Cleo and why is she out in the middle of nowhere needing a ride?"

"Because some asshole she went out with tonight left her there and I'd go get her myself but my car died. I'm also at work now and stuck. I tried all our other friends, but no one is answering their phones."

"Where is she?" I was already up and out of the bed, jerking my shirt on. "Address *now*."

If this girl couldn't keep herself out of trouble for a fucking night. First she hopped into the ocean not knowing how to swim and then this.

"Wait. You're going to help her?"

Fuck me, if I couldn't help myself and in my frenzy to get pants and shoes on, I passed it off as guilt. I felt guilty for what happened over the weekend. I'd wanted to fuck with her, piss her off, but I hadn't known about her brother. That had changed things a little. I'd wanted to break her.

But that shit…

Yeah, that was deep shit, and rather than go

on with her friend about this, I urged Kit for a fucking address so I could go pick Cleo up. She gave it to me, someplace literally out in the middle of goddamn nowhere. Kit could only give me landmarks outside of the road Cleo was on, and finally getting to my car, an electric blue Madza, I revved it up. I'd bought the thing new shortly after the semester began. Fuck, if I was trying to bus it to and from classes while I'd been down here.

"You're really going to get her?" Kit asked as I pulled out of my complex's garage. "This isn't a trick? Because seriously, Jax, this isn't a joke. Cleo's all alone out there."

Exactly why I was in my car trying to get to her. The only thing keeping my mind off the prick who'd left her out there was because *I was* trying to get to her. I grunted. "You hear me in my fucking car, don't you? Does it sound like I'm messing around?"

An air of relief in her voice, but the sigh that followed didn't sound convinced. "I guess I just thought you'd need more convincing. I called you in desperation. Really couldn't get a hold of anyone else."

Well, I didn't need convincing, already on the road and tapping the location into my phone. Without street numbers it couldn't get me anything solid, but close enough when Kit mentioned a trail.

God, this fucking Girl Scout.

Kit was apparently spot on with Cleo's location. Because not only was Cleo exactly where Kit said she'd be when I got there, the Girl Scout was in the dark using her cell phone for light. There were no streetlights out here, the place completely pitch black. I saw nothing but a little glow as I revved closer, pulling onto a dirt car park.

My lights on, Cleo shielded her eyes from them, backing away a little so I could park. She was also half dressed in an outfit that barely covered her ass and a sweater that fell off her shoulders, exposing the flushed state of her neck and arms.

I saw fucking red.

Getting out the car, I slammed the door, stalking up to her, and seeing me, her eyes flashed wide.

"What the hell are you doing here?" she hissed, gripping her little cell phone like she was about to throw a goddamn tantrum. She stomped her little brown boot and everything.

Cute.

She was completely cute, and I'd have noticed it more if I wasn't so pissed. I growled. "Who the *fuck* left you out here in the middle of nowhere?" It was *freezing*, and working my coat off, I attempted to put it around her basically bare shoulders.

She shrugged away from me, doing nothing to help the current state of my rage.

I shot a hand out with the jacket. "Fine. But it's cold out here, and you need to put this on."

"I want nothing from you," she huffed, but her knees… clattered. Folding her arms, she pretended not to notice. "Anyway, I called Kit."

"Well, Kit's car doesn't fucking work. She's also stuck at work so she called me."

She made a face like she sucked a lemon. "Why would she do that?"

"I was a last resort." And even though she fought me this time, I made her put the jacket on. Eventually, she took it, sliding her arms through the holes, and I put out of my mind what a vision it was

204

to see my stepsister swallowed up by my coat. It swam on her, making her all petite looking as it swallowed her up.

Channeling my senses back to my aggression, I folded fingers over my eyes. "Who the hell left you out here? Tell me."

"No," she bit out. "No, I won't. And why should I tell you anything?"

I stalked into her space, breathing the same air, *tasting* her. Her scent hinted of wine and that same soft sweetness I'd been trying to force out of my head. I'd been trying to sever this girl from my memory like a violent disease since last weekend. Especially since she'd left such an impression the last time.

I'd had her all over me, her trembling limbs looped around me when I'd saved her. She'd held onto me for dear life, like I'd been her life-force and she wanted to fuse herself into me. It'd been like she needed me beyond the immediate sense. I'd obviously saved her...

But that'd been all it was, her need for survival. Even still, she'd gotten so deep inside my head.

And it drove me goddamn crazy.

"Fine," I growled, then shot a finger toward my ride. "Get in the car then. I'll take you home—"

Shock riddled me frozen when she squatted in her boots. She quite literally hunkered down, nothing but defiance in her eyes as she hugged her arms *in my* jacket. She lifted her chin. "I'm not going anywhere with you."

Son of a...

"Hey!"

Hands at her thighs, then her ass when I

tossed her over my shoulder. Her curtain of long hair fell down my back as she kicked and flailed her skinny legs.

"What are you doing!" A slap to my back, a punch to my arms. "Put me down this instant!"

Chuckling, and I couldn't even help myself. She was even cute *mad* and certainly not threatening.

"No." I swung around with her in my arms, making her squeal. I chuckled again. "The way I see it, you got two options…"

"What?" She growled, punching my back again.

Good. I had her attention.

I grinned. "Option A." I thrust out a finger, though she couldn't see. "I leave you here, then track down this fucker who left you. Then proceed to chop his balls off and force-feed them to him."

Her legs stopped. Good, really listening now.

"Or option B." I paused, and getting a firm hold of her, I returned her to her feet. She slid the entire length down my body, every soft and supple curve in my hands. I felt every quiver, every shake trembling within her.

I even felt her heartbeat.

It thudded against my chest, and once I got her to the ground, she didn't move. In fact, she held on to my shirt so tight her little fists paled.

I braced her shoulders. "You let me take you home. Get you safe," I finished. I wanted her to take that option and was beyond questioning it at this point. I just wanted to help her, save her.

I guessed we were both fucking crazy.

She was for jumping in water after me despite being deathly afraid of it. I supposed I was now jumping into my own tremulous waters.

"Option B," came from her pretty lips, though a bit struggled. Clearly, she labored over the decision and was maybe even conflicted by it.

My hands fell away from her, making myself. "Good choice."

I jerked my head in the direction of the car, and she followed me to it. I got inside after she did and hoped to God I was making the right decision here. I hoped to God I wasn't fucking myself over. I was letting her do this shit again.

I was letting myself do this shit again.

Chapter Nineteen

Cleo

"Where'd you get the car?" Silence had been between us for quite some time before that. My stepbrother was like a raging bull coming down off something. His hand grappling the wheel, he looked intense, no doubt pissed at having to come and get me.

So why had he then?

I didn't understand why he bothered since he hated me, his hands ghost white on the wheel most of the drive. It was a long drive. Lawson had basically taken us out in the middle of nowhere for our scenic look of the ocean. Looking back, it really hadn't been a smart decision to come out here. I didn't really know the guy despite going to school with him and had probably had too much wine to make the right decisions tonight.

He probably knew that, Cleo.

His objective was obviously clear, get the girl alone after getting a few drinks in her. He thought I was an easy lay just because of the way I'd been reintroduced into his life.

Asshole.

My asshole radar must have been broken. How else could I explain being in the current presence of basically my enemy, my stepbrother? He saved me again, but so what? He had more than one offense to make up for, his list a mile long.

With a sigh, Jax swept his hair back, dusky brown curls flopping into his face. He appeared to have just gotten out of the shower, his hair still wet and darker than usual. The fact that I noticed annoyed me, how hot he looked in his bucket seat while he drove. His black T-shirt strained across his hard chest, the lean muscles beneath his golden skin shifting at even a subtle turn of the wheel. He wet his lips. "Bought the car at the beginning of the year. Needed a way to get around."

That new car smell definitely surrounded me, and the guy probably paid cash for it. I knew his moms did pretty well, were celebrity chefs and had some restaurants. He didn't talk about them at all, really nothing about his life before he'd invaded mine. I shrugged. "It's nice."

A smirk. "What would be nice is if you could stay out of trouble. Who the fuck was that guy who——"

"Oh, don't act like you care," I shot, watching the red heat creep up his neck. I huffed. "You don't. So don't pretend."

Silence as he drew his hand down his chiseled jaw. He didn't protest so I assumed he didn't care.

I gripped my arms, staring out my window at a dark beach. "Where have you been anyway?"

"And like you care about that?"

I swung my gaze over, clashing immediately with his. His friends had made it sound like he was pretty laid-back, happy-go-lucky even. I mean, I'd seen a hint of that, I guess, but he was so different around me. So intense, and that's when he wasn't angry. He seemed to constantly straddle the line, anger or nothing but serious.

After a beat, the road found his attention. "Found an apartment off Lake Shore. Been staying there."

Lake Shore was very nice, the best really. I might be staying there too had I wanted to bleed my parents out of their cash—which I didn't. Just because I could live lavishly didn't mean I took every opportunity to do so. "Why?"

Another smirk. "Don't even."

"Don't even what?"

His green eyes flashed in my direction. "Look. You hate me. I get that. But you don't have to make small talk just because I'm giving you a ride home."

But the thing was, I wasn't. I *wanted* to know more about him.

In fact, I always had.

He'd been the one to throw down the gauntlet and remove the desire. I hugged myself within his jacket, the thing smelling so good. Smelling like him. "I'm not just making small talk."

"Well, aren't you?"

I shook my head. "I want to know."

Those words were thick in the air, another sigh on his end.

"I guess I thought I was making it easier," he said. "Easier for the both of us."

He thought about... me in that decision? I found that hard to believe.

His jaw shifted. "Anyway, it was easier, right?" he asked, swinging a glance in my direction. He faced the road. "Easier without me?"

I supposed it had been.

I played with the sleeves of his jacket in silence. The thing swallowed me up and was incredibly warm. I shrugged. "Maybe."

"Maybe?"

I nodded. "You just make things hard."

The understatement of the year, and though he may have expected that, I observed a noticeable shift of his jaw, like he actually cared what I thought about him.

Of all things.

"And hate is a strong word," I said, catching his gaze again. "I'm not sure about that either."

Because I wasn't, hard for me to actually hate someone. I mean, I'd thought it more than a few times when it came to him, but that didn't make it true. I supposed I wanted it to be true.

I really wanted it to be.

Like I said, he made things hard, and I found I couldn't keep his attention. I drifted my sight outside the window, easier to study the dark waves along the passing beach. Time traveled by, and soon enough, Jax got us back on campus. We cruised to the dormitory in his sleek ride, and no one was more surprised than me to show up to the place in one vehicle when I'd left in another. The fact the second car belonged to my stepbrother? Well, yeah, I wouldn't have bet on those odds.

Jax parked right outside the doors, the soft purr of his engine running. The car was a stick shift, so even idle, it sounded ready.

"So you're really not going to tell me who this dipshit is you went out with?" He'd asked more than once so I wasn't surprised by another. He'd been steamed when he got me, like he really would go for Lawson if I let him. The whole thing was terribly confusing. Why he came to get me. Why he cared now... He frowned. "The fucker needs to know that shit isn't okay."

"You going to go hurt him now?" I asked, curious. I slipped off his jacket. "There are worse ways to hurt people, you know."

Like completely owning their heart for an

entire night only to crush it, to betray their trust in the worst possible way. He'd done that. He did that. He'd done worse than that. I handed him the jacket, and though he took it, he said nothing.

"Thanks for coming to get me," I said, suddenly very cold now. I wasn't completely sure it was the absence of the jacket either. There was so much space between us, something more than physical distance. I felt like I was finally letting go of him.

And he was letting me.

He took the jacket back, placing it in his lap. I started to open the door before his throat cleared.

"You okay, then?" he asked, so quiet in his purring car. I turned, and he was bunching his hair a little. He shrugged. "I mean, are you all right now? Okay?"

I didn't know exactly what he was asking. If I was okay about tonight or okay *after* him. I didn't know if I would ever be okay.

I mean, I still felt him in my skin.

Part of that was the jacket, yes, but there was just something else. Something gnawing at me. I didn't know what it was, but whatever that itch had been caused me to sit back in the bucket sit.

"You wanna come up?" I asked, his eyes twitching wide. Believe me, no one could have been more surprised by the question. I shrugged. "I mean, to get your stuff."

He'd left his entire life behind, everything he'd come down with. I didn't recognize what he wore now and assumed he'd started over with new things.

He obviously wasn't hard up considering his choice of ride.

His jacket bunched between his fingers. "I can always come back when you guys aren't around. No big."

Kit wouldn't be around considering she had to work, and since he appeared to actually be on his best behavior now, I didn't see the harm.

"You can if you want," I said, wrestling with my hair. He made me really nervous despite myself, awkward and shy. I huffed. "Anyway, Kit's not here so…"

Feeling kind of dumb, I started to get out, but he held up a hand. Next thing I knew, he was shifting the car back into gear. He pulled us around the building, and using his fob to gain entry to the dorm's private parking, he parked, then unstrapped himself.

I did too, watching as he pocketed his keys. We got out together, then he followed me with a heavy cadence to the back entry.

Things had gotten kind of late so there wasn't much activity as my stepbrother and I strode the halls. I felt him really close behind me, nearly on me. I knew because when I stopped in front of our door he physically touched my back.

My shoulders bare I felt *everything*, hot lava and his large presence loomed over me. Rather than confuse myself with it, I opened the door, then let us both in.

"Everything's where you left it," I said, watching him close the door behind us. "We haven't messed with anything."

Not that he'd left us anything to mess with. He'd kept all his stuff in his room, his door locked.

I mean, we'd checked.

In a rage, Kit and I both wanted someone to pay for how Jax had treated me over the weekend.

His stuff was the next best thing, but he'd kept his door locked.

I was happy about that now as he circulated the place. My stepbrother seemed generous now, calm, but who knew what would happen if he'd noticed all his things violated. He eased his hands in his shorts' pockets. "Thanks. I'll just make a few trips then."

Nodding, I left him to it. I noticed him watching me as I left, but I paid no attention to it. I couldn't.

Instead, I decided to shower and wash the evening off. I still felt Lawson's *hands* on me, and I wanted to remove the sensation as soon as I could. I exited the room with my shower caddy and a change of clothes. I assumed Jax was gathering things since his door was open and light spilled out into the hall.

Moving quickly in an attempt to avoid him, I went right to it with the shower. I didn't use the communal area after the incident with him and stayed behind a private curtain. Something told me I wouldn't have a problem tonight, though.

It seemed I was right, a completely quiet and easy shower. More than nice, I relished in the heat awhile before wrapping it up. When I got back to the room, I figured Jax would be done, gone, but I noticed his light still on down the hall. I didn't hear anything so I figured he'd just left it on.

Padding lightly in my shorts and tank, I snuck a look into the room. He wasn't in there, the area completely cleaned out outside of the bedspread and a few clothes in the walk-in closet. Since he wasn't done I started to leave until I noticed the picture frame on his desk.

It had my father in it.

Well, my adoptive father. Truth be told, I hadn't seen my biological dad in years. He'd stopped paying child support at eighteen, and outside of a few "How are you doing?" texts, I didn't hear from him at all. He checked up on me, of course, from time to time, but had moved on. He'd even remarried.

I guessed like Jax's dad.

But it wasn't my mom and me in the photo with Rick Fairchild, but another family, a past.

There was a crazy beautiful woman in the photo, like crazy beautiful, and I assumed that was Jax's mom Sherry. Blond, her hair breezed in the wind of whatever beach they were on. A younger version of my adoptive father, Rick was on the other side of her. He appeared so, so happy, a smile I'd seen many times, and to the left of Sherry, I found it hard to identify the boy under her arm.

Jaxen was so young, eyes far from anger as he held the waist of his mother on the beach. He maybe looked ten in this photo, if that, and the smile on his face he wore for days. It was obnoxiously huge like he was trying to win an award for it, on the tips of his toes. It was as if the very expression attempted to pull itself out of him, so much joy on his face as he grinned directly at the sun. I really didn't recognize him, or this family. My adoptive dad held both his wife at the time and Jax, his reach that extensive. He held them both, his entire family gathered up under his arm.

It took me a moment to realize I was being watched and another to gather my wits as I'd somehow come to hold the keepsake. Jax, my Jax today, had his big body lounged up against the room's empty desk, his arms folded and ankles crossed like he'd been there for a while.

"Sorry," I said, completely flustered as I put the photo down. He pushed off the desk, coming over, and honestly, I didn't know what he'd do.

"Sorry for what?" he asked, analyzing the photo before studying me. I stood so close I could taste him, his spicy aftershave.

Overwhelmed, I looked away, and he reached to take the photo himself. I shrugged. "I was just checking to see if you were done. I saw the light on and came to turn it off. I didn't mean to get into your stuff."

The truth, but I wrestled with my hands as if I were guilty. I had kind of sort of gone through his stuff. It wasn't mine, and I had no right.

A shake of his head as Jax returned the photo to the desk.

"No big," he said, all the attention he gave to the photo. I noticed it was one of few things he'd left in this room beyond his bedspread and clothing items. Had he been intending on leaving it? He cuffed his arms. "I am almost done so… just doing one more sweep."

Nodding, I thought to leave him to it, but was curious when he passed the photo completely and started getting his clothes out of the closet. Gathering them up, he shoved them all in a box he had at the foot of the bed.

I watched him pack away, staying out of his way. I thought he'd get the photo, but all he did was close the box.

He picked it up. "I'll be 5230 E. Lakeshore Dr," he said, a subtle lift of his broad shoulder. "You know. Just in case."

In case what? In case he forgot something? Maybe even he didn't know. Because he said

217

nothing as he passed me with the box. I stopped him, grabbing the photo. "You're not going to take this?"

He looked at it again, frowning. "I have others. That's not my favorite. I look like a fucking goober in it I'm smiling so big."

I thought it was cute, smiling myself. I touched his little face. "Where did you guys go?"

"Uh, St. Clare," he said, sliding the box down and taking the photo. His gaze drifted to the ceiling in thought. "Like a summer or two before the divorce or something. One of our last family trips."

There wasn't any emotion behind what he said, and maybe it'd been so long ago there wasn't any emotion.

I lounged back, gripping his desk. "My family's was at Disney. World, not Land. It was a good time."

A great time really. We had no worries back then, no drama.

And we'd had Nathan.

He'd only been like two and would never have remembered the trip if he were alive today. I barely did, all of it fading so much.

Jax's hand slid down the photo. "You still talk to your dad?"

I nodded. "Here and there. He sends a text every once in a while. But it was like, once I turned eighteen, he just kind of was gone. He struggles a lot. Gambling. Drinking. He got so bad after…"

I nearly said his name, Nathan.

Almost instantly the sickness rose, but it didn't used to be this way. I could say his name. It'd been okay. I wasn't okay, but I'd gotten myself to a place where I was.

I guessed after last weekend, things were

really fresh.

Again, Jax's attention was on me. He completely put down the photo once more, just staring at me. He opened his mouth, as if to say something, but I realized in that moment, I think I overstayed my welcome.

Playing with my braid, I passed him, but when I clipped his shoulder, Jax angled himself in front me. He was full blown heat, height and body, and none of it, I had any idea what to do with.

"I'm sorry again for getting into your things." Instead, I chose an apology, easy and my default. My guilt had returned, guilt surrounding my lost sibling, and I thought maybe, apologizing for something else, would help. Help anything going on inside me. Giving myself always made me feel better. But no amount of volunteer or charity work ever completely removed the pain. I had an eternal debt, a sin that would always plague me.

Jax was one of them. Because no matter how much I wasn't supposed to feel attracted to him, I was. I couldn't stop the feeling of wanting to touch him, taste him, which was precisely the reason I didn't back away.

And let him get closer.

His hand on the desk, he angled his body near mine in a way our chests nearly brushed. His lips wetted, his head dipped. "Why didn't you tell me about your brother, Girl Scout?"

My heartbeat punched a hole directly through my rib cage, my eyes flashing wide at him. "How did you know about that?"

Had he always known? Had he always played me for a fool? Did he know about my brother before pretending to drown in that water? A million questions in my head, Jax wrestling with his hair.

"Rick," he said, frowning. "He said that's why… Last weekend?" Another wrestle of his hair. "I wish you would have said something."

So he *hadn't* known.

Complete silence on my end. Because what could I have said? I freaked out because my actual brother died in that same way? I freaked out because *I* felt guilty.

Because I'd basically killed him myself?

I did by neglecting him, letting him fall in that pool. My little brother's death was my fault, only mine and no one else's.

No, I wouldn't say any of those things to my stepbrother now. I wouldn't have him see me weaker than I already felt.

Hugging my arms, I started to shoulder away from him, but he grabbed me.

He grabbed me.

My hips fell into his heavy hold, his jaw worked so tight his temple pulsed, and the vein in his neck protruded. "Why would you *ever* go in that water after me?"

I had no words for him, because each word was one I didn't want to hear. That I cared about him.

That I more than cared about him.

That the concept of life and death and *fear*—I didn't think about that day. I just thought he'd been drowning.

"You were…" I started, my lips trembling. "I *thought* you were drowning."

"But why—" His lips opened and closed, his voice thick and gravelly before he gripped his jaw. "But you didn't know how to swim."

"I do," I said, clearly surprising him when his

head shot up. "I just forgot. I… I panicked."

I spoke the words weaker than I meant to, that I had panicked, seeing him. It had brought back so many horrible memories for me.

"Panicked because of your brother," he said, closing his eyes. He shook his head. "Why would you ever take that risk? That risk *on me.*"

His words had been quiet this time, and though not weak, they were laced with just as much emotion.

"Jax…"

"You know I want to fucking hate you," he started, my eyes twitching wide. "I want to, but you make it so goddamn hard."

But why? *Why* did he want to hate me? Hurt me? I started to touch him, but he backed away as if I'd burn him.

He swallowed. "But the worst part about this? Is that he wins. Every goddamn time, he wins."

"Who wins?" I rushed to him, but he just angled away again.

His expression fell. "I want to hate you. I *need* to hate you. I don't want to…"

He didn't finish. Because in the next moment, he was reaching for me.

And cradling my face.

His mouth actually trembled over my lips, light before crashing hard. He tasted my tongue, aggressive as he gripped my hair and pulled my head back. This gave him better access, his mouth completely devouring mine.

"Why do you hate me?" I gasped but for some reason, kissed him harder. I felt his ache, the force of it quaking through his lips. It surged off him like raw heat. He was Lucifer in the depths, a fallen angel.

He didn't answer me as he spun me around by the hair. Closing the door, he pressed my body up against it, his cock pillowed between my ass cheeks.

He ran himself up and down, dragging his mouth through my hair and making my nipples burn.

"Just let me have this," he retched, as if he actually needed it, *needed me.* Gathering my breasts, he pulled me to him. "I need inside you."

"Please…" My only response as I faded into vapor in his hands, every touch a scalding hot burn I actually wanted to mar me. His mark was truly needed.

And had been for so long it actually hurt.

I'd dreamed about his touch more than one night, fantasized about it. I wanted my stepbrother, my bully.

I really had come to him.

I was beyond caring at this point, Jax biting my lips from above. He undid his pants while he backed us up to his bed. He forced them down and when he picked me up, he tossed me on the sheets.

"Girl Scout," he dragged over my mouth, so hard through his boxers. Since I was only wearing sleep shorts I felt everything, his body a simmering force of want and warmth. "God, if you don't fuck with my head."

He didn't want this. He didn't *want to want* this and probably even more than myself. This was the last thing I wanted as well, to be obsessed over him, to need him.

But when he pushed his hands up my body, I not only let him but ached for him. He gathered my shirt above my breasts, nibbling the swell. I still had my sports bra on but he made quick work of that. It snapped at the front, and he released it with merely a flick of his digits.

"Fuck, have you really only been touched by me?" he asked, and as if to confirm, he laved one of my nipples. His tongue flicked, and I mewled in response, quaking beneath his hands.

"This is mine," he said, his tongue drawing circles around one of my hardened peaks. He sucked it in, releasing it with a pop. "No one touches you but me."

I couldn't disagree even if I wanted, like I could. I couldn't ever fathom anyone else doing this to me but him. I didn't want to think about anyone else, be surrounded by anyone else. Jax kissed his way down my stomach, and I thought I'd die in a puddle.

"Strip for me," he said, watching as I tugged my shirt off, then forced my shorts down. His eyes ignited at the sight of soaked panties. I went for those too, but he stopped me.

His lengthy digit parted my pussy lips, and with a pinch, he had me bucking beneath him.

"Jaxen…"

He gripped my breast as he played with me through my panties, his eyes wild and untamed. He tugged off his shirt, and his hair was a tease of tousled and unruly hotness, his body the pure golden of a local. No section took my attention over anything else, his body muscled perfection as he tossed his shirt and surrounded me with his weight. He licked me from my shoulder down to my trembling thighs, turning me on my stomach as he righted my ass in air.

He breathed heat over my sex through my panties, my body instinctively shying away from him. I'd never been kissed down there before.

"Only me," he said, his finger hooking the hem of my panties and following the line. He moved the crotch away when he got there, his thumb probing my sex. "I only get to taste you here. Play with you here."

"Jax—"

He impaled me, his tongue tunneling deep. He hooked his tongue, gathering my juices into his mouth, and I bucked, trying to nudge him away. He wouldn't let me, taking my arms and securing them behind my back.

"Jax... Jax, *please.*" I was going to come like this, all this too much. "No one's ever touched me but you. I'm going to come."

He merely pleasured me more, pleasured himself. Taking my bottom, he pressed his face right against my sex, and the heat burned fiery in my core.

I didn't fight him now, my eyes rolling back as he spread me wider and sucked my lips into his mouth. I pressed my bottom to his lips, so close, but as I burned right there, he forced me on my back.

He shoved his boxers down, his cock springing to life before he pulled me over to him by the thighs. He didn't ask about protection like he had the first time. He just went ahead and did it. He had condoms in the dorm room's end table, and after rolling one on, he gathered me by the hips.

"Mine," he said, sliding himself inside me. I stretched slow, resisting at the size. I really hadn't been with anyone else, and we hadn't been together since the beginning of term.

"You remember me," he growled, disappearing inside me. "Take me, Girl Scout."

I did, completely full as my head rolled back into his sheets. He eased me up, and on his haunches, he worked himself against me, my hair dragging across the bedding. My breasts slapped against my chest as he picked up pace, and rising, I cradled his neck, holding on for dear life. I didn't want an inch between us.

It seemed he didn't either.

He hugged me close, like my full body as his rolled with sweat and labor. He fused my body into his, ripping my hair back and kissing me.

I disappeared in his kisses, evaporated like hot rain in a thick rain forest. I couldn't breathe. I could barely see.

I sighed into his neck. "Jaxen…"

I didn't want to let go, trembling wildly. The burn in my core returned, and my muscles squeezed him so hard I thought I'd die. I literally thought I'd die with him inside me, the feeling so familiar. This was what it'd been like the first time, and though it'd been painful, I'd succumbed to it. I gratefully sunk into oblivion.

As long as he went with me.

He did, grunting as he picked up the pace. He milked me as he came down from the high himself, my body shaking around his pulsating cock. He flooded the condom between us, my body completely pooling around him. Spent, I only held him closer.

And for some reason he did too.

His fingers gripped into my hair, his breaths unsteady in my ear. We both smelled like sex, covered in sweat.

"I can feel your heartbeat," he said, light and playing with my hair. In fact, he'd spoken so softly I wasn't sure I was supposed to hear it. But since he'd said something, I felt for his too.

A hard slam hit me right back, like we were

having a boxing match in the ring. I thought he'd let go of me in response, but in the end, he merely continued to play with my hair. He did that for a long time, still inside me.

I went to sleep not knowing who let go first.

Chapter Twenty

Jax

What *am I doing?*

My first thought, my *only* thought.

I'd gotten my stepsister to sleep with me again, but what should have been a mission accomplished was me lying in a bed not wanting to let go of her. Was me *staring at her* for half the night instead of letting her go and heading back to my place like the quick fuck she should be.

Also me, waking up to the smell of her, the taste of her in my mouth. I actually kissed her awake.

What the fuck was wrong with me?

She was making me think all kinds of stupid things, like she wasn't just a pretty perfect princess. Like she wasn't just the hero and I was the villain. She was making me feel like *I* should be the hero and not the villain. Like I should be taking care of her. So quick I went to her rescue last night. Got her to *sleep with me* instead of her coming to me herself. I'd lost this game.

I'd fucking played myself.

There'd been no games last night. There'd been no challenge. Kit called me to get her, and I went like a bitch, then got even weaker when it actually seemed like she jumped in that water *for me* and not for some image she was trying to put off. Like she wasn't just the perfect doting daughter, like she was actual perfection.

Perfection...

I'd seen a lot of naked women, fucked them, but nothing was like waking up to Cleo with those curvy, lengthy limbs around me. The girl was built

227

like an Amazon, Xena Warrior Princess incarnate. I had to admit I was attracted to strong women, women who had height and stance about them. A lesser guy may want to look down at his girl, but I didn't mind standing chin to chin with her. Cleo wasn't quite my height but she was the tallest woman I'd ever been with.

I gripped her bare asscheek, making out with her. We'd been attacking each other's faces for the last hour or so, but neither one of us seemed to be trying to leave.

God, I was so fucking stupid.

For many reasons, stupid as a dumbfuck. I wanted inside her *again*, and I'd had her plenty last night. She'd ridden my dick a couple times before I had her on her back again.

"I like how you taste," she said, touching my mouth. "It's like jelly beans or something."

I eyed her, pulling back. "I highly doubt that."

Neither one of us had left this bed, but morning breath had been far out of each of our minds, I think. We'd just wanted a taste of the other.

She pushed at my chest. "I don't mean the actual taste."

"What do you mean then?" I played with her hands, again fucking stupid.

She shrugged. "I guess the way you feel... I don't know. The way *they* feel." She shook her head, looking shy. She was so good at that. Looking fucking cute. She smiled. "That probably doesn't make sense."

I hated to admit that it made more sense than anything else. More than me being in this bed with my stepsister for reasons beyond screwing my father over. I was here because I wanted to be.

And that was damn dangerous.

Her lips *also* tasted like jelly beans to me, even more dangerous. She was everything sweet to everything vile about myself. A complement to every terrible fucking thing. I should really throw this girl away.

Instead, I hugged her closer. I kissed her closer until I had her on her back.

I sunk inside her, *deep* and with no condom this time. She'd mention last night between one or two of our tryst that she was on her birth control and taking it regularly now. Normally, I would have said fuck it to that shit. I was raised by two women who really didn't want to be grandmothers when I was like fifteen and just starting to have sex, so it'd been drilled into me no matter how good going bareback felt on my dick. There was nothing better than that shit, but I only did it if I trusted the person. For whatever reason, I knew nothing about my stepsister, but not only took her bare once, but twice. I trusted her twice.

I trusted her.

I wanted everything about this girl to be a show, a lie. I wanted her *to lie to me* and give me a reason to hate her. I wanted her to play me because I could understand that. What I couldn't understand was someone being genuine to me when they both had no reason to and had also been raised by my absent father. So her being the way she'd been was fucking confusing and made my mind spin.

Just like this.

I eased Cleo's head back, popping her tits and angling them perfectly for my mouth.

I couldn't even get her jugs into my mouth, so fucking large and beautiful. I'd played with them enough times last night to own them. I did own her. She'd only been with me.

That made this girl *mine*, and I completely took ownership of that as I disappeared inside her. Grunting, I slammed my cock wildly, forcing an ache from her throat I covered with my mouth. She bit me, and I roared, biting her back.

"Cleo, you're going to be the death of me." Because she was, *on me* last night after I'd been tired.

Pulling out of her, I forced her on her chest, taking her wrists and tugging them behind her. I fucked her no holds barred, unable to physically hold back if I wanted. I came too quickly this time with this girl on her tits and her ass up. I slapped one of her cheeks, and she cried out.

I was gone.

I died, right there above her, spilling my seed like a teenager. She came pretty quick too, doing this cute little cry thing that she did every time. It was so innocent. Ridiculous.

Jax...

Internally scolding myself, I shut off all thoughts, just enjoying the fall from the high. Sliding out, I kissed Cleo's reddened ass cheek before turning her back on her side. I got her up under my arm after that, getting my cell phone off the end table. She asked for hers too so she could check it and it took me about two seconds to realize I had the wrong phone and she had mine.

Lawson: Hey. I'm sorry for leaving you last night. I was an ass. Can we talk? Tell me you made it home all right.

She really went out with a fucker named Lawson?

Smirking, I started to text back but instead,

gathered Cleo up.

She giggled. "What—"

I kissed her, right on the mouth with her naked body pressed up against me. She had all the essential bits covered. This guy wasn't getting a show. I had her tits pressed right up against my bare chest and my hand on the curve of her ass. The only thing *this guy* would see was that she was mine and I'd like him to try and do something about that.

Cleo, as cute as she was, was only there for the kiss. That's all she thought this was.

Until she heard the camera shutter.

I snapped the pic right above us, then quickly sent it to that Lawson guy through her phone.

"What are you doing?"

Text sent, I gave her back her phone before looping an arm around her. I took my phone back from her. "I think you got my phone."

In silence, she eyed me, but took the moment to studying her phone before saying something. Well, at the sight, her eyes completely widened.

Her phone buzzed right in her hands, and I studied it over her shoulder.

Lawson: Nice, Cleo. Real nice. I guess that's what I get for checking on you.

Cleo's jaw dropped open. "Jaxen?"

I feigned innocence as I looked at her, her eyes completely bulging out of her head. I shrugged. "What?"

She shoved at my chest, but I merely laughed.

I hugged her to me. "That guy was an asshole. He left you."

"So you thought sending him a naked picture of us *from my phone* was supposed to remedy that?" A squeak on the end of her voice. She actually looked panicked, like she or, I guessed, *I* did something wrong here. Her jaw clenched. "Lawson basically called me a cock tease last night. That's why he left me and now you sent him a picture that makes me look completely terrible."

I deciphered what she said in slow mo, but in that time, she worked her way out of my arms and off the bed. I was quicker, though, and crossed in front of her.

She growled. "Get out of my way."

My response was to grab her hands, both of us still naked by the way. Dropping her phone, she wriggled with her little squeak, which I thought was cute. I got her against the door, pinning her.

"Let go!"

I didn't, leaning into her. "So you're saying this asshole left you because you wouldn't put out for him? Tell me you're kidding."

This guy should hope she was kidding. Cleo fought me again, but since I was stronger than her, she didn't move an inch. Instead, she faced away from me, and maybe realizing I wasn't about to let her go, she sighed.

"It wasn't exactly like that."

"Then tell me what it was about."

Her eyes lifted. "Okay, it was exactly like that. But—"

No buts as I grabbed my shorts off the floor. I didn't know who or where this guy was, but I was going to fucking find him.

"Where are you going? Jax—where are you going?"

She got me as I went for my shirt, but shorts on and partially decent, I'd leave all that shit and go hunting as is. What I wore was nothing but common down here. I bared teeth. "I'm going to kill that fucker."

"You're not. Jax—"

I was at the door, but she wedged herself between me and the exit. Had Kit actually come home last night she may have wondered what was up. Cleo said Kit often didn't since her friend worked at a bar too in addition to a barista. She apparently sometimes went from one job to the other, then back again. I guessed the girl caught sleep in the afternoons while she could like some vampire. Cleo spread her arms, blocking my way. She was still naked as fuck so it took all I had to keep my eyes on her actual face. She huffed. "Don't. His mom and mine are friends. They know each other."

"Even more reason why this little shit needs to be exposed. People can't do shit like that and get away with it."

I started to pull her off, but she grabbed my bicep.

"Don't *please*," she pleaded and actually smiled now. "How about this? You don't kill him, and I'll forget about the fact that you sent him a raunchy picture of us through my phone."

"Not a good enough bargain, Girl Scout," I said, eyes narrowed. But then she did some stupid shit.

She unzipped my fly, pulling me out of my shorts. I froze as her hand completely fisted my cock.

"Girl Scout…"

She massaged, staring at me with pouty lips while she rubbed me off. She added my balls to the mix, and my eyes literally rolled back in my head.

"Not fair," I grunted, rocking into her. Folding my hand behind her neck, I pressed her against the wall, biting down on her shoulder while she gripped me. "And still not a good enough bargain."

Though I was well aware I made it sound like it was, growling like a beast in her hands. Lifting my head, I bit her lip. "I'm still going to kill that fucker."

But then, she fell to her knees, and I thought... hell.

Now, my stepsister couldn't have possibly ever done this before. Completely unlikely, but fuck if she didn't have me slamming my hand against the door the moment she put those perfect lips around me. She sucked me deep into her mouth, gagging a little, and helping her out, I pulled her back a little.

"Just relax your throat," I said, grunting. "Do that and it'll fit."

It took her a second to adjust, to get used to that but eventually, she did exactly what I said.

She bobbed over me, taking me deep like a pro, and both hands hit the door. I tossed my head back. "Fuck, Girl Scout. It's like you've done this shit before."

She better not have, *mine*. I never thought I'd come again this soon, but not only did I, I barely lasted. My balls tightening, I spilled my seed, starting to pull out, but Cleo dug her nails into my ass.

Fuck me.

Stars behind my fucking eyes as she took me down her throat like a complete champ. By the end, I really had questioned if she'd done this before, and pulling back, she stood while I tucked myself back into my shorts.

She looped her arms around my neck with nothing but a hellacious grin. "Was that okay? I mean..." She played with my hair. "That my first.

So…"

Well, if that was her first, she could teach any woman I'd ever been with a few things.

I didn't want to think about those other girls in the moment, though. Instead, I gripped the back of Cleo's neck.

I immediately tasted myself on her tongue, the girl sighing on my lips.

"It was perfect," I told her, picking her up and going back to bed. Too much about all this was perfect. Too much about *her* was perfect.

And so I was playing myself again.

Chapter Twenty-One

Cleo

"So let me get this straight." Kit's eyebrows jumped. "You slept with your stepbrother... again?"

Kit's words were definitely an understatement. I hadn't just slept with my stepbrother. We'd had over twelve hours of all-consuming, mind-alternating sex, which hadn't lasted the *entire* night. Obviously, we had to sleep, but what we did again and again and *again* this morning made up for those hours.

I'd feel ashamed if I didn't want to do it so badly again. Jaxen Brett Ambrose was addictive. I'd never made love before him, and needless to say, he was an excellent instructor. He knew how to do things with my body that were just *maddening* and beyond toe-curling.

I palmed my face, actually in *my* friend's face with all this. I'd come by to get coffee at the Bean Brewery mostly to see her and tell her everything that had gone down last night and this morning. I obviously hadn't gotten to last night. Besides being, erm, um, busy, Kit hadn't come home since she had two jobs. After her shift at the Brewery, she'd gone to her late night job bartending job. She was back at the Brewery until mid-morning today, which wasn't uncommon for her since she paid her own way through school. There were many weekends I didn't see her at all since she tended to do such close shifts on the bar's busy nights like yesterday. She definitely would be sleeping this afternoon when she got home so I needed to tell her all this stuff now.

Chewing my lip, I nodded, tapping my coffee

cup. "I know. Like WTF, right? I don't know what my problem is."

I did. My stepbrother was hot as hell, and I had a weakness for him. I still didn't know why.

"I need to hate you."

But he didn't, and I told Kit that too. She'd been floored, but I didn't think because the statement held truth or not. It was because Jaxen had actually admitted that fact to me. That he wanted to hate me, but didn't necessarily feel that way. It left a lot of open questions about him, and he hadn't wanted to talk about them last night.

He was too busy making my toes curl.

Kit was on her break now and had been on break for the past forty-five minutes. She said she'd combine her first break and the time they gave them for breakfast, so she wasn't too worried. Currently, she was very much not eating her scone and looking at me. She ripped down blond curls. "I don't know whether to say you're crazy or just…"

"Crazy is good, yeah," I said, chuckling. I groaned. "I don't know why I did it. I don't know why he did it."

We were both all kinds of messy and completely screwed up.

I lifted my eyes. "And he's my stepbrother."

"Newsflash, chick. Your stepbrother is hot *and* charming when he wants to be. And oh, yeah. Hot." She started to laugh, then paused. "But it's totally not like that now. I mean, I know what happened between him and me, but ugh, no. Not now. Not after you guys and all…"

I knew what she meant so I waved it off, most certainly saving her from her own misery. Her face had shot up like a million degrees in color.

She chuckled. "You got it bad for him, and clearly, he's got a thing for you as much as it grates him. I mean, he actually said he wanted to hate you?"

I nodded, and Kit tilted her head.

"Dude's obviously plagued with something. Doesn't want to be into you even though he is. But it's like, what are you supposed to do with that?"

I had no answers, silent. "The guy's a vault. Like literally. I asked, but no dice."

"Could be about your dad and all that. Like you said."

I had said, but still, we didn't know. Jaxen Ambrose was confusing as hell, confusing me.

She pressed her coffee to her lips. "You two need to hash this out."

I agreed, but my attention shifted at the buzz of a text message.

Jax: This or that?

Jax's text followed with two pictures of him sporting different blazers. The first was hunter green, dark and complemented his lightly colored eyes. The other was black and sat so smoothly on his hard body it popped every bump and swell of his muscular arms. Each option, though, hugged his stocky frame like sin as both jackets narrowed in tight at his thick waist. I started to text him back, but then my phone buzzed with a call.

It was him.

"Oh my god. He's calling me." I mean, did guys even call still anymore? Completely floored, I waved my hands. "What should I do?"

"Well, I know what *I'm* going to do," Kit said, picking up her half eaten scone and coffee. "I'm going to get my ass back to work before I'm fired, and you're going to figure this crap out with your hot-as-fuck, but crazier-than-shit stepbrother. Let me know how it goes."

No help from her. *At all*, as she chuckled off with her stuff. I watched her toss her garbage away before taking a breath, tucking back my hair, then answering my phone.

"Bummer."

I frowned. "What?"

A deep sigh into the phone. "I was hoping for your voicemail."

"Why?"

He chuckled. "Because I only kinda sorta actually needed to talk to you."

Trying to figure out if I should smile or not, I rubbed my neck. "Kinda sorta?"

Another sigh. "Yeah. I wanted your opinion on the text. Should have waited for your opinion on the text. But… I called you."

I chewed my lip a little. "Why?"

"Fuck, I don't know, Girl Scout. I wanted to talk to you. Shit. I'm regretting it now."

"Don't. Don't. I'm…" *Oh my God.* "I'm happy you called. I wanted to talk to you too."

"You do? You are?" True and honest to God shock in his voice. "About what?"

"I don't know, Brett," I joked, using his alias. "Shit. I just wanted to talk to you."

It sounded as funny coming out of my mouth as I was sure it was to him on his end. He laughed, the deep timber fading into the line. "All right. Shit."

"Shit." Okay, now I really couldn't help my smile.

Are we really doing this right now?

Because we were. He called me because he wanted to talk to me, and I answered because I wanted to talk to him.

I mean, who were we right now?

Obviously, a pack of crazy folks. I messed with my hair, still too long when my fingers got caught. I wore it down because, after I finally left Jax's bed, I got in the shower, then headed right off toward the coffeehouse. Jax had left prior to that. He'd decided to take his own shower at his new place since he wanted to get his stuff over there. Still, before he'd left, he wasn't shy about telling me we'd rain check a shower together in the immediate future.

Good God. Yes, my stepbrother and I were a couple of crazy folks.

Honestly, I didn't know what my mom or adoptive father would feel about me taking up any sort of anything with him. But for all I knew, this *wasn't* anything. Jaxen was so hot and cold.

"And you know it's not Brett," he said into the line. "Jax is fine. That's what everyone else calls me. My friends."

"What about Jaxen then?"

"My mothers... when they're mad at me."

"Jaxen it is then." I snickered. "I don't want to call you what everyone else calls you."

A growl in his voice. "I guess you can have that one, Girl Scout."

He said this, but he didn't sound angry. If anything, there was laughter in his voice.

And he called me Girl Scout again.

Really, that should get under my skin, but I was beyond caring that not only did it *not* bother me, but played with me in a way that danced in my tummy.

I drew invisible circles within the grain of the coffee table. "So what did you really want to talk to me about? Those blazers or…"

"Yeah. Right." Like he forgot too, he moved around wherever he was. "I'm trying them on, but I'm not sure which one. You're a girl so you know shit like this. I think I've gotten too used to shorts and flip-flops."

Yeah, and he looked like Hades himself had decided to walk the earth in a beautiful man suit rocking them. It was really ridiculous how pretty my stepbrother was and even worse when he did dress down to nothing but beachwear.

I thought guys in suits looked good.

Casual, or just fucked, I'd seen Jax dressed down as well as he could be. I hadn't seen him in a suit yet, but I had a feeling I'd be nowhere close to disappointed.

"What do you think?" he asked, gratefully focusing my attention. "Green or black? You need to look at the photo again?"

I didn't. I was well aware of how heavenly he looked in both, but I did, playing along. I smiled at both pictures. "What are they for?"

"Eh, uh. Royal. You remember him from the weekend?"

Um, yeah. He'd been the one giving all those intense stares. Anyone could tell the guys all looked up to him. He moved, and they did too. "I do. But for him?'

"Well, not for him. Per se. It's for me. His bachelor party is coming up so I'm trying to figure out what to wear."

Oh, yeah. December had mentioned she and Royal were engaged. I nodded, though he couldn't see. "I'd go with the black then. I like the way the green one hits your eyes, but the black is just…"

Perfect? Ridiculous hot? I scrubbed into my hair. "Better."

"Better?"

"Yes, just better." My face hot from my own thoughts, I rubbed my cheek. "Yes. Go with the black. It is better."

"Black it is then. Oh, and uh, thanks for the pretty eye compliment." Laughter on the end there, and I totally didn't say that.

Even though it was true.

I grinned, but rolled my eyes. "Whatever."

I got his chuckle in response, which I loved more than I definitely should. It literally shot goosebumps over my arms. I shook my head. "When is his bachelor party?"

"Next weekend actually. The guys are all coming back down here because, you know, Miami?" Another laugh. "It's also the only other weekend we could nail down to make the time. We could have done it last weekend, but…"

He didn't need to say anything about *that*. He and my adoptive father were supposed to be spending the time together, but things had gone sour.

Silence between the pair of us, and I was ninety percent sure Jaxen was mulling over the same thoughts. There was a lot unspoken there, a lot that needed to be said. I mean, Kit was right. We needed to talk about some stuff.

"Anyway, December's party is going to be down here too," he ended up saying, and I was grateful he'd moved the conversation on for now. Especially when he mentioned his friend since I liked her. A smile in his voice. "They're going to be separate events, but she told me to invite you too if you're free."

Floored beyond belief. Mostly because we'd gone from what we were talking about… that more than tense weekend *to this*.

He'd spoken to his friends about me. His friends that he obviously cared about. I'd seen that, how much they did care about each other, and not only had he spoken with them, he wanted me to hang with them more.

If he didn't, he wouldn't have said anything about the invite.

No words on my end, a harsh breath into the line on his.

"But no pressure, you know," he started, nerves in his deep voice I hadn't heard before. "You're probably busy so—"

"No, I'm not. I mean…" Stumbling over my words, I fought to get them back. "I mean, I'd love to go. Which day?"

"Uh, Saturday. Should be a good time. You all seemed to have gotten along."

We really had, and that'd be perfect. I smiled. "That's actually perfect timing. I'll already be home Friday for Dad's birthday and can just drive over…"

I stopped myself.

But not soon enough.

Definitely silence on the line, almost eerily. I only made it worse because I had stopped in the middle of a sentence.

Dammit.

I wasn't sure if I should mention anything about my adoptive father, let alone his birthday. They'd had some tension that weekend, a lot, and that'd been before Jax had fooled around with his near drowning. Dad had gone into the hall, and they'd been out there a long time. When he came back in, clearly my adoptive father had been heated.

Since I already had spoken the words about his birthday, though, I needed to finish the thought.

"It's, um, Friday." I cleared my throat. "His birthday. We usually do a thing."

Making this worse, Cleo.

How did I know? Because I could hear a pin drop on the other side of the line. I actually checked to see if he was still on the call.

I cleared my throat again. "It's not a huge thing, but it's Friday."

Did he know?

Did he care?

That was something I *didn't* know, and it was no news to me that he and Rick had something going on. A big something that was bothering both of them. I'd seen that in spades last weekend.

Only more questions.

I wanted to ask Jax about them, but this wasn't the time and…

He'd finally been starting to open up.

He was sharing himself, sharing with me.

"Jax?" I prompted. "You still there?"

"I am."

A grit to his voice, confirming none of this awkwardness was in my head. I didn't know what he'd do next. If he'd go off and revoke his invitation to hang with his friends or what, but I did know one thing.

I didn't want him to leave.

In more than one way, I didn't want him to return those walls that weren't down by any means but at least could finally be touched without a burn. I wanted him to stay and not run from me.

"You should go on Friday," I said, trying. "I

mean, it'll be a good time. Always is, and I want you there."

I couldn't speak for my dad, but I was sure he felt the same. I saw how he was when Jax had arrived. He wanted to be around for him.

He wanted him.

Easy to see when my adoptive father looked at him.

Jax still didn't say anything, and even though I wanted to push, I didn't. Pushing didn't seem to be good with him.

"I'll, uh... I'll consider it," he said, but it didn't sound like he would at all. A clear discomfort in his voice when he cleared his own throat. "Anyway, thanks for the advice. About the blazer. I'll do the black."

Fuck.

"So, uh, Saturday," he said. "I'll give December your number. She'll contact you."

I started to open my mouth, but he was telling me he had to go. I couldn't remember what he used as an excuse.

I was still reeling about what he didn't say.

Chapter Twenty-Two

Cleo

Jax's appearance was fleeting over the next few days. I mean, I saw him, but usually, it was only in the evenings. He'd come sneaking into my dorm room after the place was dark and both Kit and I had turned in for bed. He'd moved out, officially, but still came and went as he pleased.

It was obviously just to see me.

He'd make it into my bed, and well, there was no more talking. We didn't talk, not at all really, and outside of a few WYD text messages here and there, the only vocalizations between us were me moaning or him groaning. He didn't seem to want to talk about anything else until he was making me come. Even then, he didn't tend to stay long. He was usually gone the next morning before the house woke up, but did always send me text messages. He'd let me know where he was headed or what classes were giving him hell.

Basically, nothing personal.

I knew exactly what he was doing, avoiding me and our conversation about Dad's birthday party, and as the days ticked down and Friday came around, I didn't even bother pushing him about it. He'd expressed no interest in coming.

I sent a text anyway.

Me: About to head out of town. Head home.

I told him I'd drive down to December's bachelorette party directly from there. My parents lived close to Miami so that made sense. Their house was only a few miles away from the beach unlike the more than an hour away from Bay Cove's campus.

Jax: So I'll meet you in Miami then? I'll get a room for us. We can chill there after we're both done.

That was all I got, my answer right there. He wasn't going back with me to our parents' house. He was choosing to stay on campus, then drive separately for his friend's bash.

Me: Yup. I'll see you.

Jax: Drive safe.

So drive safe I did, heading out after my final class of the day. I called my parents before I left first just so they knew I was coming and could look out for me.

The drive was incredibly silent and completely different than how it'd been on the way down. How ironic that day and time felt so far away now.

So much had changed.

I really didn't know what was up with Jax and my adoptive dad. I'd speculated stuff in the past, but none of it could be confirmed or denied. I just knew, whatever was, had been bad enough to bother both of them at different points.

And for my stepbrother to hate me before he even knew me.

I'd assumed before that, maybe, Jax had been in the middle of a messy divorce. I mean, my biological dad's and my mom's hadn't been great. Parents separating would be hard for anyone. I, personally, had held bitterness for a long time when my dad had left our family.

Again, I didn't know, and it wasn't like Mom and Rick had ever given me any indicator that anything was wrong back then. I had just been told not to ask about Jax, that he was staying with his mom, and that was it. Thinking back, I do think Mom and my adoptive father had kept a lot from me about his previous family. I mean, I'd been in a fragile state myself considering everything with Nathan. It'd been fresh *for years* and long after my little brother had gone.

I was in the dark about virtually anything beyond my own worries.

"Oh, baby. She's here. She's here."

I laughed upon coming into the doorway of the suburban home, and my mom basically launched herself at me in the entryway.

"Honey. Hon-*ey*." She squeezed me, making me drop my bag. I laughed. She grinned. "Gah. I feel like I don't even have a daughter. You don't text me nearly enough!"

By "not enough," she must not find her updates from me only *every few days* acceptable. I always texted her back when she texted me.

"Of course, I'm exaggerating," she said, pulling away. She tugged at my braid. "Now, tell me all about your news as we finish dinner up."

Her arm slung around me as my adoptive father filled the hallway, a wide grin on his face as he wiped his hands with a kitchen towel.

"There's my peaches." He kissed the top of my head, getting my other side. "Safe drive, sweetheart?"

"Very safe. Quiet." I forced my smile. "And what is that? Smells so good."

Probably not commonplace, but as a family, we always made birthday dinners together regardless of whose birthday it was. The way my parents put it was, those types of things could always be catered. We could always go out and make a huge thing of it, but there was nothing like gathering around in the kitchen and cooking together. To catch up more than anything and that's literally what we did after I got my things put away.

As it turned out, we were making Dad's favorite, lasagna. The dish was simple, but again, that wasn't the point. With all of us being busy, spending time together was the most important thing.

I was immediately handed my apron and joined the two already at work. I definitely needed an upgrade since I still rocked *My Little Pony*. I felt pretty silly wearing it, but it was always a fun topic to poke at and not just by my parents. I got just as much fun having a laugh at it too.

Dad wore his "Kiss the Cook" apron while Mom's looked like something Julia Child would wear. It had frills and everything.

"So tell us why we haven't heard from you." Mom eyed me, pulling that lasagna out. They'd already gotten it started, so the longest part of the meal was done. In fact, other than putting together a salad and plating the sides, my parents pretty much had everything covered. I found myself grateful since I was tired from the drive.

"Just been busy," I said, thinking about *how* I'd been busy. I hoped my cheeks hadn't colored when I threw croutons on the salad. "What about you? Why haven't you texted me?"

Really, this was a running joke. I definitely talked to them every few days, and since Mom knew that, she stuck her tongue out at me.

"Leave her alone, love." Laughing, Dad hugged his arms around my mom's waist. Those two were seriously sickeningly perfect together. So dang cute. He hugged her. "Absolutely no fighting on my birthday."

"Only if my child puts her lip away." Mom winked, then patted Dad's hand. "Come on. Let's get this stuff together so we can *eat*."

She actually groaned while saying it, which made us all laugh. Mom took the majority of the plated sides while I finalized the salad and Dad took the bread rolls out of the pan. He arranged those while Mom whisked away the sides we'd already gotten together to the dining room.

"Everything okay, though, honey?" Dad asked, peering up at me. He tossed the oven mitt he'd been using away. "Your mom's joking about the updates, but she really wanted updates. Like *really* wanted. You know her. She could talk to you every hour if you or *I'd* let her."

Laughing, I did. I rolled my eyes. "Things have been swell. And I've been good."

"Yeah?" He came over, lounging a hip against the counter. "No issues with your coursework?"

"Nope."

"No, um," he started, and when he didn't finish, my lashes flickered up. He'd been moving a hand on his jaw, as if considering something. He placed his hands on the counter. "No problems?"

I stopped adding things to the salad, putting a bag of shredded carrots down. "No. I've been fine. Really."

"I just worry, you know? That weekend? With Jax?" He shook his head. "It didn't go how I planned."

We'd all been well aware of it. But maybe, it was time, I did understand his lack of candor. I knew he was my parent, but I was at the age where neither of them needed to keep stuff from me. Stuff involving the family anyway.

Jax was his family.

The doorbell rang, and Dad's eyes flickered in that direction. He started to go until Mom yelled, "I'll get it!" from somewhere in the house.

A smile before Dad pushed off the island. Putting an arm around me, he squeezed my shoulder. "Of course, you're okay. You always are."

I tried to be for the most part. I still had a lot of work to do, but things didn't have to be okay if they weren't. *He* didn't have to be okay if he wasn't. He put on such a strong face. "Dad—"

"We have a visitor, darling."

Dad and I turned to find a visitor indeed.

He held a bottle of wine.

Next to my mother, my stepbrother Jaxen towered, like literally an expansive structure and that was just his height. Shoulder to shoulder, he filled so much of the kitchen I questioned that the room was three times the size of most.

Mom stood quietly beside him, looking exceedingly happy, albeit worried. The unease wrinkled her brow just enough for me to notice. She placed a hand out in my stepbrother's direction. "Jax is here, guys."

We both saw that. Jax, with a large bottle of Merlot in his hands. Jax wearing a sweater with product in his hair like he ever did anything like that. He had the dusky locks pulled back, perfect and looking like a politician's son. His sweater cuffed tight as his biceps and shoulders, chillier today, which was why he probably brought it out. I'd actually worn a jacket on my drive over.

He looked good. No, more than good, but where I was used to smiles starting to surface when we were solely together, not an inkling of that touched his expression now. His jaw was tight, his eyes cold and narrowed. He definitely noticed my adoptive father.

He definitely noticed me *with* my adoptive father.

Something I took for heat touched Jax's eyes, something I most certainly took note of. Rick dropped his arm from around me, and Jax noticed that too. His eyes flicked to it before finding my eyes. Honestly, it had taken me aback a little bit.

I'd gotten so used to him being another way as of late.

"Hey," I said, immediately coming over. I wanted to redirect his attention, get some of that light back.

Shifting, he didn't give me much of that, though. "Hey."

"You came."

"Yeah," he said, but it took a second for him to actually *see* me. He'd been staring back at my dad. His lips parted. "That's, um, if it's still okay."

"Of course, it is." Mom had said it, Dad just standing there. I think, mostly due to shock. He hadn't moved since Jax arrived. Mom waved a hand in his direction. "Right, Rick."

"Of course, yes." Awestruck, Dad blinked for the first time since the environment had changed. He pushed a hand behind his neck. "I'm happy you came. Yes, and thank you. For coming that is."

"Happy birthday," Jax said, but parted their gazes to glance at me. He put the wine out. "I brought, um…"

Smiling, I took it. And God, did I want to kiss him. God, did I want to *thank him.* It was so good he was here.

Good for both of them.

"Thank you... son," Dad said, so awkward when, before *that* weekend, he'd never been around Jax. Dad wrestled with his hands. "We were just about to start, so perfect timing."

A nod on Jax's end, and with this exchange, Mom appeared absolutely giddy. She took the wine from me, beaming. "Well, I'll go get the bucket for this. Cleo, wine glasses?"

I could definitely do that. Quickly, I went to get them while Mom directed other duties. She had Dad go ahead and go to the dining room since he was the guest of honor.

"And if you don't mind, the rolls, Jax?" she requested, smiling at him. She had the wine and bucket at this point, raising it. "We're really happy you're here."

"Thank you."

Another smile before she winked at me. All too quickly, she skidded out of the room, and though Jax got the bread and I got the glasses, I touched his arm before we left the kitchen.

Instead of saying anything to him, I just kissed his cheek, lingering there.

I think I said all I had to say, so grateful he was here.

I just hoped this night went okay.

Chapter Twenty-Three

Cleo

I'd like to say the evening produced some miracles after that, that after more than one occurrence of tension and unsaid words, suddenly all parties involved were forthcoming. I wanted to say, around the dinner table on my adoptive father's birthday, that my stepbrother smiled and engaged. That he'd been *open* like he seemed to be finally doing with me and that he and Dad really had a moment.

But that just didn't happen.

Dinner ended up being nothing more than clanking dishes and awkward silences when my mom was trying to make the room mingle. That was just who she was, the fixer, the helper. Whenever there was tension, she handled it, and though I aided her, trying to push on those conversations, Dad and Jax still didn't directly talk to one other. Jaxen himself basically only spoke when directly addressed, and Dad, though he did probe conversation, never did so distinctly to his biological son. My adoptive father would mention open topics, ones for all, and never pushed Jax to speak.

Maybe he should have.

Maybe then the dinner wouldn't have been basically Mom and me trying to play happy family. The two were stubborn as hell, clearly, and if my family didn't think I knew something was up, they thought me stupid. People just didn't *not* talk to each other.

Not unless they had a reason anyway.

It was like Dad didn't want to make waves

and Jax wasn't trying to be the one to move them. Because of that, the pair were at a standstill, and before I knew it, dinner was over and Mom was urging me to help her with dessert in the kitchen. She'd ordered a lemon meringue pie earlier that day, I guessed, only store-bought because it was from my adoptive father's favorite bakery. I offered just to get it myself, but surprisingly, she came with. This left two people who probably shouldn't be in the same room by themselves, so the minute we got the pie plated, I rushed back to get it to them.

That was until my mom touched my hand.

"Help me with some of the dishes first, won't you, love? So there's not so many after we're all done?" she asked, out of the blue.

I thought to protest, but Mom immediately headed over to the dishwasher and started loading. I frowned with the pie plates. "Shouldn't we…"

"Give them a moment," she said, like she knew. She jerked her head over to the dishwasher. "Rick and your stepbrother just need a minute. Just a minute."

She said it like a mantra, like it was more so to herself. Though I wanted to listen to my mother—I mean, that was my mother—I wasn't sure she was right on this.

Even still, I slid the pie plates on the kitchen island uneaten. I handed her the plates we'd gathered from the table before we came into the kitchen, but I wasn't happy about it.

"Why do they need a moment?" I asked her after a beat. I was so completely tired of being left out of everything, like there was some big secret. Like everyone was on some big ride without me. "What's going on with them? Why—"

"What's going on is personal between them," she said, sighing.

"But you know?"

She stopped her hand on the washer. "I know because he's my husband."

"So because you're married I'm just, what? The kid?"

"I didn't say that."

"Well, that's what it feels like."

A head shake. "Jax and your dad have a lot of history. A history that has nothing to do with either of us. I only know because we're married."

So she did know something. I figured as much. I handed her a dish. "Well, can you tell me what happened last weekend then?"

"Last weekend?"

I eyed her. I wasn't stupid, and she needed to stop treating me like I was. I wasn't a kid anymore, and it was insulting. "Before it started, Dad was acting completely different. *Happy?*" I shook my head. "Next thing I know, you guys were whispering about stuff."

"We weren't whispering." Mom pulled a veil of hair off her brow. "We were discussing."

"Discussing what?"

"An incident that happened on the golf course. An incident that happened between *your dad* and Jax." Mom frowned. "He and Rick had some kind of disagreement. One that led to Jaxen walking off the course and leaving your father heartbroken."

"Why?"

Mom placed her hand on my arm. "Rick was under the impression Jaxen was by no means okay when Jaxen initially came down here, but was open. Well, after the golf course..." Mom sighed. "Rick picked up some very heavy animosity on Jaxen's end. Animosity toward him, and honestly, I don't blame the kid. Not after what he *thinks* happened all those…" Waving the words away, she hugged her arms. "I just wish Rick would tell him the truth. Maybe he will now that they're together."

I opened my mouth to ask what truth.

A door slam stopped the thought.

A crash of glass followed, making both Mom *and me* jump. She rushed out of the kitchen, and I followed her.

Another slam rattled the house along the way, the front door this time, as Mom and I watched it shut. We both stopped on glass in the hall, and it didn't take a scientist to realize where the glass in the hall had come from.

On the other side of the hall, the french doors to the dining room were flung open, the glass inside them completely shattered. Mom and I had closed them when we left.

And only one person was in the dining room now.

That person was my adoptive father, his hands closed into a fist. He rested his mouth against it, his expression completely crestfallen.

"Rick…" Mom's lips parted, rushing over to him. "Rick, what happened? Oh my God."

It was like he didn't see her, staring through her. She sat beside him, and he didn't even move. She touched his shoulder. "What happened? Did you…" She shook her head. "Did you tell him?"

My dad finally sat back, his head shaking. "I couldn't," he murmured, his eyes closing. "I just couldn't. I'm sorry."

An engine revving pulled me away from the

conversation, away from *everything* since it was so
familiar. Jaxen was leaving.

Why was he leaving?

I didn't know, but I was going after him, and
when Mom called my name, I didn't answer. I rushed
away, over glass and outside. It was like I had this
pure dread inside me. That if Jaxen left here today
whatever damage had been done wouldn't be able to
be undone. Like this was it.

Like there was no going back.

I got outside, and he was already behind the
wheel. I only knew because his car was running. His
windows heavily tinted, I couldn't see him and did
the only thing I could do.

I ran in front of his car.

I got right behind as he backed out, my
adrenaline pulsing, and his tires screeched so bad,
burning rubber hit the air.

"Cleo, what the fuck!"

Out of his car and on me, holding and shaking
my arms. He was pissed, his whole face three colors
of red. "What the hell is wrong with you? I could
have fucking hit you. Did you want that?"

I just… hadn't wanted him to go, hadn't
thought. It'd been like that day sailing. I just jumped
in.

I hadn't thought.

"Why are you going?" But then the tone
changed, everything *changed.* Next thing I knew, he
was letting go of me, like he remembered why he was
leaving and headed back to his car. I grabbed at his
arm, but he angled it away like I'd burn it if I touched
him. "Jax…"

Well aware of the plead in my voice, of the
emotion. I didn't know why, but it was there and the

struggled screech nearly made his name unrecognizable.

And he stopped against his car.

His hands shifted ghost white on the top, his body stiff and shoulders shaking. It was like he was about to transform into something deadly.

And I needed to get out of the way.

"You don't get to do that," he said, the words incredibly dark. The back of his head shook. "You don't get to."

"Do what?" The tremble of my voice, at this point, I couldn't control. I was scared. I just didn't know why. I wasn't afraid of him, no, but the situation. I didn't know what this was.

Jax shoved around, his face beet red. Emotion completely colored his cheeks, his eyes strained and glassed. "Isn't it enough that you have everything?" he asked, stalking closer. "That you *get* everything without having me too?"

Words choked down in my throat, my swallow hard. "What do you mean?"

A dry laugh and my fear did shift his way, his chest to my chest, his eyes to my eyes. He stared down at me, like I was beneath him.

But what he'd said made it sound like it was the other way around.

That *he thought*, for some crazy reason, he was beneath me, his hand rubbing his eyes before he shoved a finger in my face.

"Well, you don't get me too, Cleo," he said, my heart threatening to bust, to shatter. "You don't get to have that. That's the *one thing* I can control, and you don't get to have that. You don't get to have *me*."

"Jaxen—"

"Go back to your house," he said, backing away. "Go back to your perfect life because that family inside is yours and *that man* inside is not my father. Never was."

"That's not true. How could you say that?"

"I didn't, Cleo," he continued, looking at the house now. He faced me. "He basically just did."

I… I couldn't believe that, not for a second could I believe that. I knew that man.

I knew *his* father.

"Now, get away from my car," he spat, growing three sizes in front of me. He smoldered. "And back the fuck up off me."

He did enough backing away for us both, leaving everything when he dodged inside his car. He slammed the door, and I did get out of his way this time.

I wasn't sure if he'd actually stop.

He seemed gung-ho on getting the hell away from me as soon as he could, his engine wild in the air when he wheeled down the driveway and screeched into traffic. He shifted, then peeled away with nothing but a smell of charred rubber cloaking the air, but I wasn't just going to stand there and not do something.

I rushed back inside the house, looking for my adoptive father. He needed to fix this… whatever this shit was he needed to fix because something was wrong and Jaxen believed he wasn't his son. I didn't know what that meant. That made no sense.

"Where's Dad?"

Mom had been sitting in the living room, her legs crossed and staring at the wall. She uncrossed them. "His office. Why—"

I made a beeline in that direction, not even

announcing myself when I went inside. Dad was standing at the window, staring outside. He had clear view of the driveway, no doubt had seen Jax and me completely.

"Why does Jaxen feel like he isn't your son?"

"Cleo?" Mom had followed me in, reaching for me, but I moved away from her and over to my dad. He hadn't shifted, not one inch from the window, and on his side of the desk, I saw he did have a clear view of the driveway. He'd watched the whole thing play out, had to have.

My lips parted. "Why does Jaxen think that? Why would he say that? Did you hear what he said?"

A head nod, but that's all he gave me.

I shook my head. "Dad—"

"Cleo," Mom urged, coming around the desk too. "This is not the time."

"Then when is?" I whipped around in her direction. "When are you guys going to talk to me?"

Her face fell. "I told you. This is between Rick and Jaxen."

"Well, *Jaxen* doesn't feel like he has a father." I faced Dad. "Jaxen thinks he's not your son. He thinks I have it all. That you're my family and not his."

Dad's brow furrowed, his hands cuffing his arms. "I heard him," he said, finally facing me. His eyes had completely glassed. Like he was five seconds way from letting tears fall when not once had I ever seen such a thing. This man had been so strong, strong my whole life.

But this?

This was breaking him down, this was torturing him.

He frowned. "Jaxen is my son, but the fact

that he doesn't feel like he is? Well, he's not wrong."

Not... wrong?

"I didn't do right by him," he said. "I abandoned him. I left him. I apologized, but it wasn't enough. He wanted to know why, and when I couldn't tell him what he needed, he left."

My face fell. "Well, why couldn't you tell him what he needed?"

Mom touched me. "Cleo—"

"No, why couldn't you tell him what he needed? Why does he think you don't care and abandoned him?"

"Because I did abandon him, Cleo."

My lips shut. He'd said it before but...

I just didn't believe it.

It wasn't *possible* that this man that I called father could do such a thing.

It just wasn't.

I knew his character, knew him.

In my silence, Mom came over, putting her hands on his shoulders. He touched one, then stared at me. "I do care about him, but I did abandon him. That's a fact that remains unchanged."

"Well, maybe if he just sees that you do care," I said. "*Please.* He doesn't under... Can you just tell him what he needs? He thinks you're not claiming him. That you *don't* care."

He squeezed my mom's hand, his swallow hard. "If I tell him what he needs to hear from me, that's the one thing that could make things so much worse. Worse than they already are."

How was that possible? "Worse?"

He nodded. "There's only one good thing I've ever given that boy by staying away. One thing and I refuse to take that from him. I would if I gave him what he needed. This way is just easier. Easier for him. I can't hurt him anymore. I just *can't*."

But he was hurting him. He was *killing him*, and this was killing him too, clearly.

"Dad—"

His hands lifted, as if he'd washed his hands. He left the room, and Mom followed after him. I didn't get it, questioning everything I knew about him, my mom, and *this family* in that moment. We didn't do things like this, hurt people, and definitely not on purpose.

My lashes flickering away, I headed in another direction. I was going to *my* car because I wasn't doing that, what my adoptive father just did. I was going after Jaxen.

Because that's what he needed.

Chapter Twenty-Four

Jax

The weed calmed my nerves but did nothing for my anger.

I couldn't even fucking drive anymore.

I ended up pulling off the highway and onto the beach, afraid I'd completely crash my shit and end up in a ditch somewhere. I couldn't see straight, and it was by the grace of God, I didn't have any alcohol on me. I could easily down a forty, not a fuck given.

The only thing I did have was a joint so I lit up, pausing to roar into the air until I calmed down enough to actually light it. I didn't know how I thought that talk with my sperm donor was going to go today, but it ended in ways I'd only suspected. He hadn't wanted to talk, only spew bullshit. I asked him one thing, one fucking goddamn thing.

And he couldn't even answer it.

I wanted to know why he'd done what he had and why he'd left our family like a goddamn coward after it. I wanted to know why he'd ripped us apart, why he'd been so selfish, and not just once but both times. He'd cheated on my mom, the most fucked up thing, then ran like a coward after. I wanted to know if it'd been worth it.

I wanted to know the why.

He'd stumbled all over himself and actually tried to apologize for his mistakes. He'd tried to apologize *to me* like that was a Band-Aid and would make this all go away. He wanted to give me fucked up apologies instead of telling the truth. That he was a shit person who'd left his son. That he hadn't cared, and ironically enough, that's what he'd done by saying everything he couldn't say. He showed me that in spades. He hadn't wanted our family.

He hadn't wanted me.

I'd fucking *lost it* at his cowardice, ashamed that this man's blood ran through my veins. I'd given him all I had after that, called him every goddamn word in the book. I'd only come to his stupid fucking birthday because I'd wanted to talk to him.

I had wanted to try.

A lot of good it did me, my fist bruised from punching my car. I shook it off and drew off my joint again, blowing smoke into the air. Waves crashed and fell ahead of me, my headlights staining the beach. Between the joint and my car, that's all the light I had, all I needed. I didn't want the noise.

The darkness inside was more familiar.

Cleo: Where are you? Please tell me.

The sixth or seven text from Rapunzel herself, Pretty Pretty Princess acting like she cared about me too. Maybe she did, maybe she didn't. I honestly didn't care, and she wasn't my problem anymore. I'd gotten what I wanted from her and Dad had gotten what he wanted from me. I'd come down here to be a part of his sickeningly perfect family.

How fucked that he always won.

I knew that as another one of her texts pulled in, how she was worried about me and needed to see me. My heart twisted more than I wanted it to, and roaring, I threw that shit on the beach. I wanted to knock my own damn head in.

I just wanted the pain to stop.

So much pain, always goddamn pain, and it was feeling too familiar, too *normal*. I'd learned to deal with it being so far away, away from him and his faux apologies. But coming here now, being in his life…

Meeting her.

It fucking sucked. All of it had fucking sucked, and I should have listened to my boys. I should have never come down here. I knew that now because as soon as my phone buzzed again, I dug it out of the sand. More texts from Cleo, more goddamn texts.

Cleo: Please. Please.

Me: The beach off 150.

It was in these moments I was happy I didn't self harm. Because if I had a switchblade, I had no idea what I'd do in that moment.

Roaring again, I punched the air, tossing my blunt. I put it out, then waited. Waiting for what I didn't know, but the moment I heard a busted up station wagon in the distance, I knew exactly what I was waiting for.

What's wrong with me?

I told her she couldn't have that part. She had everything so why was I giving her this, me? I didn't know, but the moment a car pulled up to mine and the air filled with the scent of cherries, I no longer associated it with whore.

It was just *her*, Cleo with her hair down to her ass and explorer shorts on that made her look like a goddamn wet dream. She wore them high-waisted, tight and belted at her flat tummy. Her brown boots and tank on, she'd changed before leaving the house. Or I guessed, had taken off her sweater. She'd been wearing the same shorts and boots.

Why the fuck had I noticed?

Her hair swaying in the wind, she pressed her curvy body against the hood of my car, everything about her close enough to touch. She wore no makeup, never did, and I took inventory enough to notice before looking away.

She trembled in the wind. "Hey."

Hey.

Always so innocent, awkward and I hated that turned me the fuck on like a motherfucker.

Silent, I folded my arms, and she pushed off my car to stand in front of me. This was better, no more of her goddamn thighs burning me through my shorts.

"Jaxen, I'm…" Always with the Jaxen, always so formal and uptight. That was just her, couldn't help being herself. "I'm just so sorry."

More sorries. Sorries from everyone, now *her* like they meant anything. Was she sorry for taking everything from me? For being the replacement kid? The only good thing my dad had done for me was be completely absent from my life. I didn't have to deal with his influence, got to be raised by two amazing women. I guessed my dad had done something for me in the end.

I started to spout off some mouthy shit, to tell her exactly what I had to my dad. How I hadn't cared either, that I was glad they all had each other, that she should leave me the hell alone.

"I don't know why I keep doing these things."

But then she said that, making me look up. She had actual tears in her eyes, unable to even look at me. She really was shivering now, holding her arms. "I ruin everything. I ruin everyone's family."

I twitched, the words foreign. I had no idea what she meant.

Until, I did.

Until, it came back to me, that day when Rick

had told me something. He said she blamed herself, took responsibility for her brother's death.

She wet her lips. "I let go of his hand, you know?" she said, nodding. "My brother Nathan? I let go of his hand, and he drowned."

Drowned.

A head shake before her tears hit the beach. "I told him I hated him because he wanted to play, and I didn't want to. I mean, who does that?"

A kid, a child.

I stayed silent, watching her. At this point, she looked like she wanted to be sick, but she didn't turn away.

"My dad left after that," she said. "He left our family because of me, and now he's so busy drinking and gambling his life away. He doesn't even remember us, remember our family." She swallowed hard. "I ruined my parents' marriage. I lost my brother, and now, I've wrecked your life too."

I would have said the same thing, that she had wrecked my life by basically being me. That she'd been what my father had chosen instead of being there for me.

But in my head, it sounded just as much of a lie as what this girl had convinced herself of being true. That she'd been responsible for her little brother's death, a kid herself. It all sounded like bullshit.

It all sounded sad.

"I'm so sorry, Jaxen," she said, shrugging. She dropped her arms. "I get why you hate me. I'd hate you too."

She'd hate me too.

She should hate me, hate me for taking my rage out on her when my shit lay only with one person. It hadn't been her fault.

I'd just needed it to be.

Dropping my head, I couldn't see straight, unable to make out the beach even if I wanted to. I got lost in the individual grains of sand and sea shells, a placeholder for all the crap in my head. With a breath, Cleo started to walk away, and I knew that was it. She wanted nothing from me. She just wanted to give me her truth, no matter how fucking wrong it was. She'd wanted to offer me that peace, but wanted nothing from me in return. She thought she was sparing me.

"Why can't you just let me hate you?"

She stopped right in the sand after I spoke, then froze when I pulled her over to me.

I massaged her hips, making her tremble as she melded into my lap. My previous words radiated in the air, rupturing through me as I wrapped my arms around her waist and touched my forehead between her breast. She smelled like heaven, *my* fucking hell. "Why, Cleo?"

My fingers embedded into her thighs, fucking perfect. Gazing up, I looked at her, clouded through my eyes. She had tears herself.

"Because I," she started, her tears falling to her chest. "You don't hate me?"

"Why do *you* hate you?" I asked, a better question. "You can't possibly think… Your little brother? You know that wasn't your fault, right?"

I could see that, deep in her eyes, she did believe the lie. She let herself believe it, drowning herself in it.

Her shoulders shook as she gazed away, and she didn't get to do that. She'd look at me.

I made her as I forced her mouth on mine,

270

drowning in her sorrow. It felt better than my own. I mourned my own hate toward her, so strong before.

"I want to hate you so bad," I admitted, more than one time now. "But I can't. It'd be a lie."

This was the only truth, all I had. I cared about this girl.

I think I more than cared.

I couldn't admit any of that, though, all this needing to be enough. It was enough, for now. I needed her.

"I want you," she whispered, biting my lip and hardening my cock. "God, Jaxen. Please."

She didn't even have to beg, my eyes falling closed as I tugged her hips and tucked her between my legs. I undid her belt, then pulled it out, tossing it on the sand. After that, I ripped off my shirt and was standing before her.

Her arms weaved around my neck as I juggled her weight against the hood of my car. I was going to fuck her. Fuck her right there.

Because I wanted her too.

I wanted her so bad it ripped apart my insides. I shouldn't want her, the worst possible thing because I did think it let my dad win. He won because I couldn't hurt him the way I knew fucking with his replacement kid would. I found my needs overshadowed his in the moment.

"Girl Scout..." I dragged her lip into my mouth, making her call out. Cradling her waist, I worked my shorts down, then undid hers. I got one of her legs out, then pulled her right back on top of me, her knees on my hood. A hooked finger and I eased the side of her panties over, adjusting myself beneath her. She knew what was happening and held on, letting me angle into her center. It took little more than a touch before I slammed, making us both cry out.

Holy fuck.

I rocked with her, slapping her inner thighs as she rode me, kissed me. I had one hand on her and the other on my ride, not letting her go as I impaled her again and again.

"Jax, oh my god." She tossed her head back, her perfect tits bouncing in her tank top. Needing a taste, I forced her top up, then eased her breast out of one of the cups. I sucked a nipple in immediately, making her mewl and shiver. Her nails grated my back, and I roared, clamping down on her tit.

This wouldn't last long.

I shifted, getting her on the hood of my car. Sprawled out like this, she looked heavenly and on my fucking car, a goddess.

I drilled her, gripping one of her legs and angling it up as far as it could go. I got her so deep like this, disappearing and reappearing inside her. This girl was the stuff pornos were made of, a goddamn queen on my car.

"Jaxen, I'm going to come." Her ass slid up and down as I pounded, nearly there myself. In a breath, her walls squeezed my dick, and I spilled, coming hard like I'd never touched a woman in my goddamn life.

I completely filled her, my dick covered in cum and her sticky heat as I fell from her. I didn't let her go far, kissing her. I wasn't letting go of her.

It was like I couldn't.

Chapter Twenty-Five

Cleo

Jax and I ended up at the hotel room he'd booked for us in Miami. He obviously wasn't going back home to Mom and Dad's, and it wasn't foreign to me that the place probably didn't feel like home to him anyway.

Not that he was wrong.

My adoptive father was hiding something from him and definitely from me, which was crazy. That's just not how he was. Obviously, he didn't tell me everything about his life, nor did he have to.

But to hurt someone on purpose?

We hadn't talked about my adoptive father last night or this morning. We'd just been together, all that easy. If Jaxen had hated me before, he definitely didn't now. He'd told me, but I didn't think I needed to hear the words. He'd texted me to come to the beach.

He hadn't pushed me away.

That meant more to me than anything else. He was hanging around and didn't want to go. I played with his hand, under his arm while he texted. He finally checked his messages after we made love this morning—a lot. In fact, we screwed so many times that it'd taken several texts coming in before he finally picked up. His friends had been blowing up his phone apparently.

"Shit," he said, shooting off a final text before putting his phone down. He had a sexy, curled bedhead that made him basically smoldering, muscled man candy. I definitely didn't want to leave this bed but knew we'd have to eventually. His friends were supposed to be arriving today. He looked at me. "The guys have been at the airport for an hour."

"What?"

"Yeah." he scrubbed into his hair. He looked at me. "Probably should have checked my phone sooner. I was supposed to pick them up."

"Crap. Do you have to go?"

His response to this was covering me, like his whole big body. Hard heat surrounded me, and parting my legs, he slid himself inside.

My eyes immediately rolled back, my body humming as I rolled my hips. Dipping his head, Jaxen laved one of my nipples, and my toes curled.

"Probably," he hummed too, sucking what he could of my breast into his mouth. I'd always had big boobs and used to be a little insecure about that. Especially when I'd been younger. I found I didn't care now as Jaxen tweaked one, then bit the other. "But they'll probably be okay."

"Probably?"

Again, his response was to thrust, a heaved grunt as he smacked his hard thighs against the insides of mine. I hugged his ass, my ankles crossed behind his back. He held my feet there as he got on his knees and drilled his dick inside my sensitive core. We'd had sex a lot, so deliciously sore.

"That's it, Girl Scout," he growled. My nipple still in his mouth, he swirled his tongue around my areola. "Come for me. Feel me deep."

I did, not here with him long before my tummy warmed and heat flooded inside my core. I exploded like a rocket, Jaxen picking up until he hit his own high. His biceps flexed and his eyes closed as my breast popped out of his mouth, and he let his head fall back.

"Fuck," he gritted, his body golden and moist with sweat. We'd really had sex a lot, his body shaking like he didn't have any more in him. But he always seemed to, his cum sticky and warm as he pulled out and my walls clenched from his absence. He always cleaned me up. Even after last night on his car. He'd had napkins then, which we used like the tissue box in the room now.

It might be weird, but that was one of my favorite parts, him taking the time and caring for me. He'd been so different.

I kissed his arms before he tossed the tissue and kissed me right back. He didn't stop, making me laugh when he shifted to my neck, and I squeezed his arms. "Shouldn't you go?"

Again, he said, "Probably," making a smacking noise against my neck. He didn't stop until he had me in a fit of laughter on the sheets. It was like he couldn't until he heard it. Seemingly accomplishing his mission, he fell to his side, laying a heavy arm on me. I noticed his ring, and that's what I'd been playing with this morning. He often wore it.

"This like a class ring or something?" I asked, studying the animal. I mean, it could be a mascot or something. It was kind of violent looking though.

"Something like that," was all he said before kissing my hand. His phone buzzed again, and he rolled his eyes before shifting me and finding the device in the sheets. He studied it a second before rolling his eyes again and shooting off another text. After that, he tossed his phone again. "Yeah, I do need to go. Royal's about to lose his shit. He said the guys already got a ride share and left, but they're on their way to the tux and suit rental place and want me to come. December and the girls already headed back to the hotel in a cab."

"You're renting tuxes?"

"Buying suits and yeah. For the wedding." Picking up my hand, he played with it. "Royal's idea. He wants to get it done since we're all here. The other guys go to school all over the place too. We're all pretty much coming home for fall break but he wants to get it done '*now*.' None of us would tell his ass, but he's being a complete groomzilla already. December seems so lax about all this shit whenever she talks about the wedding, but Royal, it's like legit serious."

Laughing, I hugged his arms. "He probably just wants it to be perfect. Perfect for her."

"Maybe." He looped our fingers together. "But he's being annoying as fuck." Another buzz, which he didn't even check this time. He smiled. "And I'd rather be with you."

I'd rather be with him too, and we started to kiss again before the incessant buzz triggered and didn't stop this time. It was so obviously a call, and when he picked his phone up, he winked at me before answering.

"Yeah?"

I couldn't hear the other person on the line clearly, but he was male… and sounded pissed. A deep voice shot off like a minute long sentence before Jax was able to cut in.

"Yes, I'm fucking up. Jesus, Royal." Groaning, he rested on a bicep. "Give me two seconds to get some clothes on and eat and shit. You want me to come down there naked?"

Snickering, I watched him roll his eyes *again*. He winked. "I'm sure you'd like that, though.

Wouldn't you, big boy?"

He pulled the phone away at this point, that deep voice blasting into the line. He covered one of my ears like this was too sensitive for me to hear before kissing me and returning the phone to his head. He snugged the phone between his ear and shoulder before throwing his big thighs out of the bed. He stretched huge arms, and I already missed them wrapped around me.

"9678 W. Appleton Court. I got it. Yes, writing it down now." He frowned. "How the fuck you know I'm not writing it down?"

Smiling, I watched, a long conversation as he grabbed his shorts from the floor and put them on. He left his boxers, covering a firm ass when he got up. He snapped them from the front. "I'm on my way so let me get there. You know I won't leave you hanging. Never do."

That made me smile too and Jax as well as he let his friend go before tossing his phone on the bed. Dipping, he picked up his shirt, shrugging it on before bending over and kissing me.

"Probably better go earn my slot now," he said, pulling away. "He made LJ, Knight, *and* me his best men, and I'm not trying to be low hanging fruit. The asshole will quickly snipe my ass if I give him the chance."

"Groomzilla?" I grinned.

He snorted. "Epitome of. Anyway, you're free to do whatever. I probably won't see you again until I get in, whenever that is. Dude's actually having us go to a fucking vineyard before going to the club tonight. Even then, I'm told there won't be any strippers. All responsible and shit and get this, that was *his* idea. Vineyard and all. Sometimes I don't even know if he's my same best friend."

It just sounded like he grew up and was over it, and since Jax didn't protest *too* much, maybe he was a little bit too. Then again, that just might be wishful thinking on my part. I obviously didn't want any naked women all over him.

"I don't know what December is doing," he said, but then frowned at me. "But I really don't want to hear about you being around any strippers. You see something, you call me or just get the fuck out of there."

"I will not!"

He grabbed my hands, and before I knew it, he was on top of me. He nibbled into my neck until I wriggled, making me promise to call or text him if I saw any dick.

He grinned. "I don't need any fuckers throwing their cocks in front of you, Girl Scout."

"Okay, *okay*," I laughed, completely awkward anyway. Knowing me, if I did see a dick, I probably *would* run. My cheeks even warmed just thinking about it.

I mean, unless it was his.

That thought made my face warm too and my whole body when he stopped playing and just kissed me. Eventually, he just brushed our noses together, lacing our fingers before putting them above my head.

"You going to be all right?" he asked, the humor gone from his face. "You said some things last night, and we really didn't talk about it, but I wanted to."

We'd said honestly quite a few things. I wondered which one.

He studied me. "About your brother?"

Oh… that thing.

Yeah, that I didn't want to talk about, looking away, but he took two fingers to my chin and wouldn't let me.

"What happened wasn't your fault," he urged, so serious. "You were a kid, Girl Scout. And even if you weren't, it was an accident. You're not to blame, and I doubt any of your family feels that way either."

I knew that, been told that. But that didn't mean I felt any better. I still held that on my conscience and may forever. "It doesn't stop the fact that he's not coming back."

"No, but you don't need to carry it."

But I did, though. It still *hurt* like yesterday. I mean, my family shattered. We'd lost so much with Nathan.

"You're using too much of this," he said, touching my temple. "And believe me, that can be dangerous."

I think I saw that on his end. I *know* I saw it. I frowned. "I don't want to carry it anymore. I just don't know how."

"Start with saying the words then." He fell off of me, but didn't let go of my hand. "Say it's not your fault. That it was an accident, and maybe one day, you'll believe it."

Gratefully, he didn't make me do that in front of him. I wasn't sure if I could, at that point, anyway.

Instead, he let go, kissing my nose before picking up his phone. "I'll see you later. Okay?"

"Okay."

A smile before another wink, and he left the room. I thought his words would go with him, but I lay back, studying the ceiling.

It's not my fault, I thought, sighing. I didn't

want it to be my fault, but how could I make the truth a lie? Then again, maybe it wasn't about that.

I studied the door Jax had left through, wishing for faith. Strength. I'd seen change. I'd witnessed the cusp of healing personally. Jaxen was starting to heal.

So maybe I could too.

Chapter Twenty-Six

Jax

"And so he lives."

In their suits already, my boys situated around what appeared to be a dormant men's formal wear shop. There were literally no other people around aside from the shop attendants who cared for each of them. Knight, the one who'd spoken, currently had one of his gorilla-sized guns hanging off one of the racks, a doting shop attendant smoothing his collar and brushing lint off his sleeves. LJ wasn't far off with his own swag team doing something similar. The cake was Royal. The dude stood in front of about five goddamn body mirrors with one grown-ass man primping and fashioning him while another held a tumbler of what appeared to be bourbon on a silver platter. My buddy was extra as fuck and apparently, rented out the whole goddamn place just for the four of us. Knight smirked. "So whose legs were you between?"

"Fuck off," I gritted, letting the door snap shut behind me. Another doting attendant immediately came up and asked me my drink order. I told him beer before he bowed like a servant, and I guessed he was for the day. I clipped my aviators into my collar. "And whose legs I was between is none of your goddamn business."

Out of his wallet, LJ fashioned a thick wad of bills, grunting before slamming the cash into Knight's awaiting palm.

"Nice doing business with ya, buddy," Knight crooned, standing before fanning the cash. He grinned. "We had a little wager *that* was what hung you up."

"And here I thought better of you." LJ's string-bean-looking ass tackled me in what was easily a five-thousand-dollar suit. I knew since I had a few. I often had to wear them for events back home and, of course, whenever I appeared at one of my moms' restaurant openings. Our buddy Royal had expensive tastes, and where LJ might have cared before since he didn't always have money, he didn't now. He wasn't in the drug game anymore, but he'd been smart and invested a fair amount of it, I guessed. The dude was basically printing money these days so here was Daddy Warbucks tackling me. He used to do that a lot in high school since he was taller than like, well, everyone in the goddamn world. He wrestled my hair. "So who is she, buddy?"

Again, none of his goddamn business. I wasn't ashamed I was sleeping with my stepsister. Fuck no. But none of that shit was any of these fuckers' businesses. Growling, I turned the tides and got behind LJ, and when Knight looked like he wanted to join in too, Royal barked a throat clear.

That shit *drummed* in this empty place, and stepping off his podium like a friggin' lord, he snarled at us.

"If you're done," he stated, his eyes green fucking fire. He jerked his chin in the direction of the changing rooms. "Jax, you're set up in room four."

"Yes, Daddy," I pouted. This fucker actually grabbed my goddamn head, *faced me* in that direction and pushed me off like his kid. I laughed my ass off the whole way, and when I turned around, I noticed both LJ and Knight pretended not to find the whole shit funny as well.

Knight had shrugged, "What?" before

scampering back to the racks and pretending to look at shit. LJ dodged Royal's eyes completely, and I rolled mine before getting into the room.

Royal had me set up with a similar three-piece suit, gray with coal-black tie and matching dress shirt. He himself just wore a different cut and since my buddy always had good taste, I wasn't surprised to come out looking ready for a red carpet event.

The guys whistled like assholes when I came out, but Royal actually smiled before shaking his head and getting a look. I ragged on him for all this wedding shit, but I really did want to make him happy. We all did.

"So who was the girl?" he asked, standing behind me. Considering how we'd left things the last time we'd all seen each other, it was nice to not see him blazing daggers into the back of my head. Looking back, I realized those were deserved now, but still, I never liked the tension. We were brothers, friends since before I knew what a friend was.

I shrugged and only got a head shake behind me through the mirror. He'd find out soon enough. They all would. They'd been shocked as hell I'd entertained the idea of inviting Cleo to December's bachelorette party. Obviously, December had been the one to throw that idea out there, but I had passed on the information. That fact alone had shocked the hell out of them, and I did get questions.

I dodged them all, not wanting that pressure. I didn't know what Cleo was to me, but I didn't need folks overanalyzing it.

I did that enough for the both of us.

In any sense, the door to the shop pinged, and Royal and I both turned, I think, on instinct considering no one else was here besides us.

"Hey, guys. Sorry I'm late."

A fifth came in, a fifth I definitely recognized as the fucker's height *matched* my boy LJ's height and then some.

Ramses Mallick, a kid I knew from high school, walked up in this bitch and greeted my boys Knight and LJ like they'd been expecting him. They put their hands out to him, a shake and a back pat. I was fucking floored and even more so to see *Royal's* reaction.

Mallick sprinted his ass over to us and not only had Royal given him his hand, he cuffed Mallick's shoulder.

"Looked up the weather in Providence. Glad you were able to beat the storm out," Royal said, actually *smiling* at this dude.

What the fuck?

These guys were the epitome of rivals in school, understood as Mallick had tried to mack on Royal's girl. It got so bad at one point the two nearly killed each other.

Yet, here he was, hand in hand with Royal like they were *friends?* Nah, that was a strong word. *Civil* was a better one when Mallick shook back and slid a hand in his pocket. He was dressed for Rhode Island weather, jeans and a collared shirt, and his curly hair did look like he'd been caught in the rain at some point before it'd dried. He had it all over the place and wrestled with it.

"Yeah, delays out the ass coming away from Brown, but I made it," he said. "Sorry for being late."

"No worries. We got you set up in five if you're all set."

Royal waved him to follow him and as they

passed, Mallick noticed me. He raised a hand. "Hey, Jax."

"Hey… Mallick."

A nod and more than friendly at me. I felt like I was in the fucking Twilight Zone as my buddy walked this dude he literally couldn't stand last I checked toward the dressing rooms. Mallick trailed after him, and I moved into the center of Knight and LJ, who didn't look as shocked as I felt. I tapped Knight's bear chest. "What the fuck?"

I got a smirk from LJ and a chuckle from Knight, who propped his arm on the racks again. Knight lifted his fingers. "What? You didn't hear?"

"Hear what?"

LJ leaned in. "Mallick is, shit you not, December's man of honor."

"No fucking away."

"Way, bro." LJ tucked his hands under his arms. "Royal just told us on the plane. I couldn't believe it."

"I guess he and December kept up with each other while he was away at school." Knight shrugged. "And get this. Dude's transferring to Pembroke next semester."

"No way."

"*Way*," he said, the statement flooring me. Pembroke-U was Knight, Royal, and December's school. "Don't know why, but it's fucking weird, right?"

I'd say. I mean, who the fuck transfers from *Brown* University in the middle of their senior year? I knew I came down here for my senior year, but I didn't go to fucking Brown. I exchanged glances between the guys. "Royal's like okay with that? Okay he's the man of honor too?"

"Why shouldn't he be, bro?" Still hanging on the rack, Knight laced his fingers. He smirked. "He got the girl."

Laughing, I guessed he was right about that, and maybe that's what kept Royal's calm so cool. He came back to us looking like he had not a care in the world, Mallick not far behind after he'd changed. He was in the same suit as us, making quick work of this shit as I had.

The three of us ambled over to them, crowding. Between the five of us, we looked like something out of *GQ*, even Knight's ape-looking ass.

"Not bad if I do say so myself." This from Mallick, the dude's grin high as fuck. He had on the same ring I currently wore, the ring from our high school days at Windsor Predatory Academy. Normally, the other guys had theirs too, but they'd given them to their girls to signify their own personal steps in their varied relationships. The rings we'd all earned from being a part of a society known as the Court. That felt so far away now, a dark history connected there. But seeing us all standing here now, *getting along* with the likes of Mallick, I'd say we'd come a pretty long way. Mallick popped his collar. "I guess I don't mind you fellas looking like me."

This fucking dude. I popped my own collar. "You look like us, bro."

He smirked. "Right."

"Tell me, Mallick." I propped an arm on his shoulder. "You going to hang with us *all* day or…"

Royal elbowed me. Again, weird as fuck. He rolled his eyes. "He needs a suit too. I'm sure the guys told you he's a part of the wedding party."

"They did."

"So don't make a thing out of it." Royal lifted

his eyes. "Anyway, I think we're about done." He pointed to Mallick. "You need to check in with Em or anything? Wedding stuff?"

"Yep. She did want to go over some of the particulars since I'm in town. After, I thought I'd hang out with you guys, though. If you don't mind?" He shrugged. "December said I could tag along with her and the girls tonight, but I didn't want to cramp her style being the only guy."

LJ grinned. "You mean, eating dick cake and hanging at the strip club with a bunch of screaming women isn't your thing, Mallick?"

Royal growled. "Em and I agreed no strippers."

"Nah, man." Knight propped an arm on his shoulder. "You said *you* weren't doing strippers and *hoped* she wouldn't."

"Same thing," he said, but a noticeable heat lingered there I felt. I obviously wasn't too keen hanging out at a vineyard like some uppity-ass goober, but if that kept dongs out of Cleo's face, I didn't mind.

Yeah, this girl is totally in my head.

Might not be a bad thing, though.

"Well, you better hope that's the same thing." A darkness hit Knight's eyes. "Greer doesn't need to be seeing all that shit."

"Would you guys just trust your girls?" LJ waved his arms. "Billie told me December said there weren't going to be any strippers. We're good."

He pounded it out with us, but I noticed Mallick's ass smiling a little too much before he joined in with his nod. He may know something we didn't know. Being December's man of honor and shit, but he better hope for his ass he didn't know anything. We, *Royal*, may be civil with him now, but how the tides would turn.

Me: You heard from December about tonight?

Even still, it didn't hurt to check, and as the guys broke off to get back into their street clothes, I texted Cleo.

Cleo: Yep, all set for tonight. Sounds fun too! The girls have rented a yacht. I was kind of worried about that at first, but it sounds exciting. LOL.

How could this girl be fucking cute through a goddamn text? I wet my lips.

Me: You'll be fine, Girl Scout. Anyone goes overboard you'll save their ass *wink emoji*

Cleo: Let's hope it doesn't come to that. Haha. It does sound fun, though. I'm excited.

Me: Good. Like I said, you'll be fine. You have fun.

Cleo: You too. *heart emoji*

Me: And no strippers will be there, right?

I couldn't help myself. They may be on a yacht, but…

Cleo: Doesn't sound like it.

Me: Doesn't sound like or…

Cleo: Jax.

Me: Just check will you please?

Cleo: *eye roll emoji*

She could roll her little emoji eyes at me all she wanted as long as there weren't dicks flying in her face.

Cleo: Okay, just heard back. There will be NO strippers.

Me: Are you sure?

Cleo: Zero strippers.

Me: Okay, good. Have fun.

Cleo: You too. *kiss emoji*

Now, that I'd take. Smiling as I put my phone away. I was going to help my buddy enjoy his night, chilling at a vineyard, then the club later tonight, a nice trade-off for some peace of mind, I supposed.

Chapter Twenty-Seven

Cleo

Okay, so there were definitely strippers.

There were strippers in the suite the girls had booked. Then strippers *again* on the party bus heading away from the hotel room. The finale had been strippers once more joining us all on the party yacht, and I got to stare awkwardly through the spaces of my fingers during it all.

I honestly hadn't lied to Jaxen. December had texted me, *telling me* there would be no strippers. Apparently, they'd been a surprise because when December opened the door to the suite her friends had rented for our "pregame" drinks, a couple of officers with thighs the size of great oak trees and arms the size of *cannons* not only made her drop her drink on the carpet but fall back into her friends. She'd invited Knight and LJ's girlfriends, of course, Greer and Billie, but also her high school friends Shakira, Kiki, and Birdie. It'd been the latter to book the strippers apparently.

"Oh my *god*. Royal is going to kill me!" December'd said as they had swarmed the hotel room. She'd looked like a knockout, of course, raven-colored tresses pulled up and pinned out of her face. A few strategically placed, curled spirals fell from the front and back of her do, nothing but a bold red lip on her mouth while she rocked a "Bride to Be" sash on her deep black dress. The rest of us wore "Bride Tribe" sashes, her friends equally hot and gorgeous. For starters, her friend Kiki looked like a model and apparently, had done a lot of print work lately in South Korea. Her jet black hair fell to her butt like mine, and since all December's high school friends were tall, I actually blended in with them pretty well. I guessed they used to all play basketball in high school. Shakira and Birdie still did in college.

They'd all hugged December and kept her from fleeing, assuring her things were fine.

"Ramses has got the guys covered," they'd said, and I had definitely heard the name before since it was unique. I guessed December had chosen her guy friend as her man of honor. "We made him promise to keep the other guys busy. It's your night, girl!"

"That fucker knew about this!" she squealed, but laughed when the strippers grabbed her hands. She shook her head. "Royal is going to fucking *kill* him."

"That's if Knight doesn't first. Oh, God." This from little Greer who looked definitely just as mortified as me when large as hell dudes appeared and quickly began stripping every shred of clothing but the little piece of metallic man-panties they wore. I definitely think she was the youngest, and she hugged up against me, the pair of us an awkward fit of giggles and mess when the guys sashayed around us. Billie, LJ's girlfriend, on the other hand, didn't necessarily look comfortable when the strippers came around, but she didn't appear stiff either. She may have been around the block a few times and merely laughed, clapping the party on.

She'd nudged me at one point. "I'd hate to be this Ramses guy later. Because once LJ finds out…"

She'd whistled after that, making both Greer and I laugh. Apparently, *all the guys* were just as intense as Jaxen.

It honestly made me smile. These guys were

so hard, but seemed to love just as hard. I mean, I saw that with all three of the other girls, and I don't know. It just made me think about Jaxen. Made me think about him in a way that warmed my stomach. I wondered if he loved just as hard.

I had a feeling he did.

Anyway, after the, um, impromptu surprises, the party eventually settled down on the yacht. The strippers hadn't stayed long since they'd been with us half the night, and the girls and I settled in for a more intimate dinner of laughter and conversation. It was nice, just sitting around and hearing everyone's stories. They were all in college except for Kiki who was a working model, and Shakira and Birdie planned to go into pro ball after they graduated.

"So proud of my girls," December had said, true joy on her face the whole night. Especially when things died down and she just got to be with her girls. She was always smiling, happy, and when she wasn't talking or the topic of conversation, she played with the ring around her neck. I recognized it.

In fact, Billie and Greer had the same rings, playing with them often as well. They were like the ring that Jaxen wore. I asked Greer about that at one point. She and I had stayed pretty close in our band of awkwardness, and she said it'd been Knight's and he gave it to her.

"It means something to all of them," she said, grinning, and by the way the girls all played with their rings, I could see the symbol meant something to them now too. These guys were all so very intense, deep. They were multi-layered, and though they didn't appear to wear their hearts on their sleeves, they seemed to not need to. They showed how they felt in other ways apparently, and that almost seemed,

I don't know. Better. More special.

I considered that while I thought about Jax, thinking about him definitely more than once. I wanted to call him, like every second just to talk to him. It reminded me of when he called me that day at the coffeehouse just to talk to me.

I may be getting in a little deep here. Actually, I was probably beyond that. I had serious feelings for him, hard ones. He made my stomach just feel like it was going to explode and unravel at the same time, but only in a good way. I wanted him so deeply, wanted it to work. I knew in my heart he could love just as hard.

I just hoped it wouldn't break me.

After dinner, we were all just chilling on the yacht, having drinks and basking in the light ambience. The sun had set and the boat was docked so we all had clear views of moonlit water while a local jazz band played off shore. Funny enough, I had no anxiety about the setting where I might normally have had. I felt okay, at peace, and something I hadn't felt for a long time being around the water. My little brother's death had changed so many things.

Jax: Hey, how you doing?

I knew he had something to do with it, Jax, and he always seemed to pop in right when I was thinking about him. I smiled.

Me: Really good. How about you?

Jax: Well. You girls having fun? No issues with the water, right?

My heart warmed that he was thinking about that, about me.

I darted my gaze around. Now that things had died down, everyone just chatted on deck, nothing but smiles around. It'd been a pretty awesome night.

Me: I've been good. No issues. *smile emoji* The girls and I are having fun too. Just hanging out.

Jax: Cool, Girl Scout. Real, cool. I knew you'd be okay.

My heart danced again.

Jax: Glad you girls are having fun too.

Me: Yeah, we are. It's been great.

Jax: Great. So, uh, anything you want to tell me?

Crap.

Me: Tell you?

Jax: LOL. Yes, Girl Scout. Anything you want to tell me? Think long and hard.

Oh, no.

I didn't want to panic, though, and give both myself and everyone else away.

But still if he knew.

Too much silence passed, and Jax's text message bubbles popped up.

Jax: This isn't a trick question. Just want to know if there's something you probably should be telling me.

Me: Promise you won't get mad?

Jax: Just tell me, and I'll decide later.

Shit.

Me: Okay, so there were strippers, but I had no idea they'd be here. Really, I honestly didn't.

Okay, so I was weak. *Very weak*, but it sounded like he already knew.

Jax: Figured.

Me: You did? How?

Jax: Ramses Mallick. I'm sure you already heard, but he's December's man of honor. Anyway, he's hanging with us, and whenever the topic of you girls kept coming up, the fucker couldn't keep the grin off his face. It was sketch as hell, so I felt like something was up. Some of the other guys picked up on that too, so Knight threatened to beat it out of him while the rest of us watched.

Oh, God.

Jax: It would have come to that too had LJ not managed to get his phone. I gotta give it to that fucker Mallick. He's nothing if not loyal. Anyway, it was in his text messages back and forth with some of December's friends that the girls had hired some. It was supposed to be a surprise for her or some shit.

I face-palmed myself.

Me: Are you mad?

Jax: Nah, not really.

WTF?

Me: You're not? I mean, I'm happy you're not. But you're not?

He'd been very specific he wanted me to have nothing to do with exotic dancers of any kind.

Jax: LOL. No, Girl Scout. I'm not. After all, I call you Girl Scout for a reason.

Me: What's that supposed to mean?

Jax: It means you're innocent as hell and you probably spent half the night cringing and the other half hiding WHILE you cringed. I'm sure it was more awkward than anything else for you.

He thought he just knew me too well, didn't he?

Me: Well, I didn't hide…

Jax: And you just proved my point. LOL.

I rolled my eyes.

Jax: You're cute. You're innocent, and that's one of the things I love about you.

He loved…

Jax: So, no, I'm not mad. Frankly, I'm

having more fun watching these other bastards I call my friends lose their shit instead. The cavalry is coming by the way. Just thought I'd give you a heads up.

December popped up in her chair in the next second, flaring her arms.

"Shit, they're coming!" she exclaimed before the other women surrounded her. "Ramses said the guys found out. They're coming!"

Before everyone knew it, everyone's phones started blowing up. Greer was instantly on hers, and Billie the same. They clearly were talking to their boyfriends, judging by the looks on their faces, and December was on hers too.

"Royal," she started but wasn't getting a word in. She rolled her eyes. She covered her phone. "Guys, prepare yourselves. They're coming in hot."

She returned her phone to her ear, clearly trying to talk down the conversation. Meanwhile, Shakira and Kiki surrounded Birdie who was on her phone yelling about something.

"Dude, you were supposed to keep shit quiet," I heard Birdie say. Odds were she was speaking to Ramses herself. She groaned. "I mean, you had one fucking job to do, bro."

The whole boat in a panic, I shot off a text.

Me: Something tells me the others know.

Jax: Uh-oh. LOL. Well, anyway. I'll see you soon. Expect some fireworks. *wink emoji*

But I noticed not from him. He really seemed fine.

Like he trusted me.

I never would have ever thought we'd come to that place. But we had, somehow, someway.

I started to text him back that I was actually

looking forward to seeing him in all the chaos, but my phone buzzed first.

My face fell.

Mom: What is this?

Mom: Why was I sent this?

Mom: What's going on? Is this true?

Mom: I can't believe this…

I had no idea what my mother didn't believe was true.

My thumbs hovered to text back, but suddenly a picture buzzed through.

My stomach twisted instantly.

Jaxen… Jaxen and *me* in bed with his hand on my ass while he snapped a picture above us. He'd taken it the other day when we'd first started sleeping together again.

The night Lawson had left me on the side of the road.

But my *mother* had this.

Why did my mom have this?

Mom: Honey, your dad is very upset. Me too. What is this?

Oh my God. Dad had seen this?

Me: How did you get this?

Mom: So, it's true? Of course, it's true. I saw it. Oh, God. You slept with Jaxen, honey?

My mind whirled as her text message bubble surfaced, pure and absolute dread colliding with me. I waited for her response, but my adoptive father buzzed in.

Dad: I need an explanation for this. Tell me you guys didn't…

But we had. We did. I just didn't know why *they* had this picture. Mom said someone sent it to her, but the only person who had that picture was

Lawson and me. Jaxen sent it from my phone.

Lawson.

Had he done this? Sent this? I mean, he could have. He had my mom's number. Did through his mom since our mothers were friends.

I waited with bated breath as she drafted her text back, feeling like I was going to fall over the side of the boat.

"Where the fuck are they?"

A growl from behind as the yacht rocked and five guys the size of marines shoved their way onto the scene. The quickest had been Greer's boyfriend Knight, who made a beeline straight for her.

Her mouth parted. "Knight?"

"Where, Greer? And you better hope I find them first because Royal—"

"Is pissed the fuck off." Directly behind, Royal pushed his way onto the scene. Of course, December rushed right to him, her hands up.

"Babe—"

"Don't 'babe' me. We said no strippers."

She patted his chest. "Okay, I didn't technically say that."

"Not helping your case, Em." He was forced to stop his charge when December grabbed at his hands. "Tell me where they are. I'll be cool. Just tell me were the fuck they are."

"Well, I'm not going to be." LJ this time, stalking his way over to his girl. "Beauty queen, really? You tell me there's no strippers. I believed you. No strippers. I'm telling these guys to relax and trust our girls, and here I am looking like an asshole."

"I mean, it doesn't take much, my man." A tall guy holding a casual grin sauntered into the belly of the beast. I didn't recognize him, but his playful eyes and relaxed expression reminded me almost of Jaxen's as of late. I mean, aside from the fact this guy was probably a head taller, held far more curl in his brown hair, and sported a golden complexion that made him naturally tan where most people around here had to try for it. He leaned into LJ. "I mean, you did just rush a bachelorette party."

"You don't talk, Mallick," LJ growled. He started to go after the guy until Billie tugged him back.

She frowned. "You guys are Hulking out over nothing. Anyway, the strippers are gone. No harm done."

The twitch in LJ's eye said different and he draped an arm across Billie's shoulders like he was staking a claim. Meanwhile, both December and Greer were still trying to talk their guys down, and in the chaos, I spotted Jaxen. He watched on for a bit like I had before colliding gazes with me and after that?

Well, nothing else.

He came right toward me, a smile on his face in the sports jacket I'd helped pick out. He looked so handsome, his hair slicked back and his smile cool, and I almost forgot for a second. I forgot that my life was literally imploding. I forgot that our parents found out about us. I forgot that I cared.

Mom: The message came from your stepbrother.

Chapter Twenty-Eight

Jax

Something... happened. I knew when her expression changed.

I left my friends behind and their arguments that would be a nonissue in like an hour. These people loved each other, a harder love than most people would probably ever see. This talk of strippers and the like would be nothing in a matter of moments, which was why I found all this humorous.

But there was nothing funny about the way Cleo was looking at her phone now.

Something put her off, stiffened her up and had her covering her mouth. Something put unshed tears in her eyes.

I saw when our gazes collided.

Shock rippled through me at the sight of it, and I picked up my pace. I left everything else behind, needing to get to her.

And as soon as I did...

Slap!

My face in another direction, the burn from her hand seared heat into my flesh. It happened so quick it took me a second to gather my bearings.

And the record stopped.

No arguments behind me now, no more of my friends going on about bullshit that really would be a nonissue in an hour. I knew these people, knew them well, and this fight was a fake one at best. They couldn't stay mad at each other longer than a night. Really, it was laughable.

But whatever this was with Cleo was here and now, her hand shaking, and it was still in air. She'd actually hit me.

And she came down to do it again.

I got it this time, her wrist, and she tugged at me. "Cleo. What—"

She jerked away, her heels stumbling on the deck and her Rapunzel hair falling over her shoulders. She looked beautiful in her own quirky way, a dress with so many ruffles she drowned in them. They covered her neck like some Amish nun, completely gorgeous in the weirdest fucking way. I'd think more about it if she hadn't tried to flee away from me, and in her stumble, she hit the yacht's rails. I grabbed her.

"Let go!"

"No." I tugged her back. "What's wrong with you?"

She shoved me, shoved me so hard I might have fallen with her in my hands had I not been stable. I ensnared her wrists, pulling them down, and at this point, all the fighting behind me really had stopped.

My friends lingered on in the distance, watching us. More than one looked on the cusp of jumping in, but I held up a hand.

I shook her. "What's wrong with you!"

Out of my arms when she jerked away, cringing. "Was it always a game? A sick fucking game?"

"*What* are you talking about?"

"This, you asshole!"

She shoved her phone in my face. I took it, and she let me look only to see myself.

To see us together.

It'd been the picture of us I'd taken on her phone. I shook my head. "I don't understand."

"Oh, you don't understand." She nodded, nothing but sarcasm in the statement. She tossed her hand out. "Look who it was sent to."

I read her messages, text messages back and forth from her mom and my dad. It was a group thread.

They'd gotten the picture?

"What the fuck?" I jerked my head up. "How the fuck did they get it?"

At this point, she appeared on the cusp of slapping me again, her eyes cold, and this time, she allowed her tears to fall. They blinked down, her cheeks red. "You're so full of shit. Look at that last line."

I did, instantly twitching.

Her mom accused… *me*, but before I could say anything, Cleo grabbed her phone.

She darted around me and I pushed between Knight and LJ to get to her. They'd had their girls, crisis averted as expected. They currently hugged them against them, confusion and shock on all their faces. Knight shook his head. "Buddy?"

I didn't know. I didn't know what *any of this* fucking meant. I got the same looks from both Royal and December. They were holding hands so obviously they were good too. Royal looked on the cusp of saying something, but I had no time.

"Cleo." I got her hand, managing to twist her around before she left the boat. She couldn't leave. Not like this. "Cleo, you can't honestly think this was me. I don't even have that picture—"

She took back her hand. "Let me see your phone."

"What?"

"Let me *see* your phone, Jaxen."

I did only to prove to her this was crazy, finding it in my pocket. She was going to see this was all some big mistake. That her mom and my dad had misunderstood.

I pulled out the device in silence, well aware the entire boat was looking at us. Despite knowing I was innocent, the blood rushed to my head.

Then had to have drained from my face at what I saw.

My screen, like my entire screen, was filled with messages from my dad. He kept asking why I'd sent what I had and how I could do such a thing.

I unlocked the device to find more of the latter, more accusations on his end. He said I sent the photo to my stepmom, but that was bullshit. I didn't have this picture and I didn't even have my stepmom's number.

I scrolled away despite what I'd seen. I was innocent. I was and would find nothing.

Until I didn't find nothing, until *I did* see a message thread from a number I didn't recognize.

I opened it up with a dry mouth, text messages over and over again with confusion. They asked me why I would do such a thing? They ask me what was the meaning of this. I scrolled up to find what *this* was, a picture I'd sent.

A picture of Cleo and me.

But that didn't make sense. I didn't have this picture, and before I could make sense of it, my phone was being taken from me.

Cleo had it, studying it, and though she looked at the device like she needed to confirm, so much despair cloaked her features.

I honestly thought she'd keel over where she stood. She actually visibly paled, holding her stomach like she would be sick. She threw my phone against the deck, instantly shattering the screen.

"Cleo, I didn't do this." Panicked now, panicked despite what I knew. That I didn't do this, that this was completely fucked up. I crossed in front of her. "I don't know how your mom got sent that picture, but I didn't do it. I didn't even have that picture. I sent it to that asswipe you went out with from your phone."

"Because you didn't have ample opportunity to take it from mine. Jesus, Jaxen." She shook her head, blinking down more tears. "How many opportunities did you have? How many times had we *fucked*? You could have easily taken it while I slept."

Silence around us, again everyone watching on. At this point, I noticed some of the girls cover their mouths, and a couple of my friends looked away. The guys had accused me of being with a girl before making it out to them today.

I guessed they'd been right.

Forcing myself to ignore their response, I kept my attention where it mattered.

"But I didn't," I pleaded, trying to make her look at me. "Someone must have gotten my phone."

"Yeah, that's rich."

"No, that has to be it." I stopped her again, a hand out. "I must have put my phone down. Actually, I did. We were at the club tonight, and I didn't have it the whole time."

I had left it on the bar at one point, for actually most of the night before I'd realized.

I shook my head. "Cleo, that has to be it. I left it on the bar. I hadn't even realized it was gone until before we were about to come out here. I had to get it from the bartender *and he* had to get it from the lost and found."

The complete truth, no lie. Someone had clearly set me up here.

But my stepsister looked no closer to buying it. If anything, she only hugged her arms closer to her body. Her expression twisted. "You're trying to tell me that someone got your phone and sent that horrible photo to our parents with the sheer intent of screwing you? Screwing us?"

I knew how that sounded, but that's exactly what I was saying. My lips parted. "I know how that sounds."

"Yeah, like bullshit."

She clipped my shoulder, but she couldn't run from this. I was fucking innocent.

"Cleo, I didn't do this. Please. Just—" Another hit to my arm. Another shove to my chest. She would have gone for my face too, but I dodged. "Cleo, I'm fucking innocent!"

"Oh, you're beyond that," she said, sniffling. Staring back at my friends, she cringed. "I'm sorry I ruined your party, December. I'm just…"

As if ashamed, she fled, and I made steps to move, but I was grabbed.

"Buddy, you probably shouldn't—"

I shoved Knight off me. "Don't get in my way. I didn't do this shit she's accusing me of."

"But it looks like you're guilty, man." Royal, his arm around December. He squeezed her. "Until it doesn't, you don't have anything."

Objective, logical. He was right, of course, always right.

I fucking roared, punching the air. I didn't fucking have anything. I did look guilty.

And maybe my shit, shit *with her* was finally

coming full circle. I'd done a lot to that girl in the past.

I guessed it was just catching up with me.

Chapter Twenty-Nine

Jax

Cleo wasn't hearing me out. She wasn't hearing anything at all from me. I'd heard from everyone else, of course. My dad. Even my moms had reached out. My dad, I guessed, had called them, let them know what happened and about "my behavior." Those had actually been his words.

And so a years-long silence between all my parents was finally broken.

I'd been the one to bring their worlds together, and though I did believe that would come eventually, not in this way. I'd wanted to screw my father, ruin his world. Crazy enough, I'd accomplished that mission. I just hadn't thought about the collateral damage. I hadn't thought *about myself.*

And I definitely hadn't thought about her.

Cleo had completely ghosted me, and yeah, I knew her routine. I found her several times on campus, studying her feet as she always did. She hugged her books and did her thing, and every time I thought I should make my presence known, I always held back. I just let her be. I let her live her life. I was still looking very guilty in her eyes, and until I wasn't, I really couldn't go back to her. I couldn't talk to her.

I did have nothing.

Time headed into midterms after weeks of hell, weeks of trying to forget that night I busted shit up with Cleo and threw a bomb into *both* my friends' bachelor and bachelorette parties. Of course, both Royal and December told me it was okay, that they were only sad at how things had turned out. They had no idea about Cleo and me. None of the guys did. I'd kept it pretty quiet. They thought I'd still been trying to handle her.

Not that I'd fallen for her.

Which I had like a sick fucking puppy. I wanted that girl and was stupid *for wanting* that girl. She was nothing like me, fragile and just good. I wasn't good. I was the villain. I was the head case who still wanted to destroy my father's life, but I was in deep fucking feelings with his stepdaughter. I wanted to have my cake and eat it too. I'd destroyed that fucking cake. I put a bomb through my life. I'd gotten rid of the girl.

Only to long for her in her absence.

I decided to go home after midterms, just for the weekend because I needed a goddamn break. A break from fuck ups, a break from seeing Cleo walking campus and not being able to do anything about it. I needed to just be home so that's what I did.

I took a break.

I'd arrived to the Midwest as the seasons started to change, the end of fall upon us and the cusp of winter threatening its chill. Maywood Heights bared naked trees, multi-colored leaves breezing about the sharply cool air. There were no beaches and absolutely no golden sand. In fact, the temperature switch had been so jarring I thought my dick would snap off the moment I left the airport. Forty degrees felt like sub below after being in constant heat and I knew it'd only get colder once I did get home.

Both my moms were home this weekend. In fact, they said they would be since I told them I'd be in for the weekend. They were busy, but made time to be home with me there.

I was greeted with disappointed faces and distant hugs when I arrived, more than one conversation had before I got there. They'd let me have it for what I did to my stepsister, my biological father's portrayal of events the only side they had. I hadn't heard the conversation between them, of course, but I was under the assumption he felt I'd taken advantage of my stepsister. I doubt Cleo told him that. Because that's not how she felt.

At least, I hoped that wasn't how she felt.

Honestly, I didn't know her position. She hadn't talked to me, not answering my calls or texts. I stopped after a week or so following the parties. Again, I looked guilty and hadn't seen the point.

Both moms gave me what they had the minute I arrived through the door, but they left me alone until they called me for dinner that night. I hadn't wanted to go downstairs, hadn't seen the point. They'd said what they had to say, *what they believed*, and I had nothing else to add. I was paying for my sins, sins that had been true and ones they didn't even know about.

"Baby, would you please come down for dinner?"

Mama behind my door, Mama trying to coax me out. The peacemaker and kind-hearted spirit that kept this family together. She was our foundation here, and she wanted me to come downstairs.

So I listened.

She was probably the only one *who could get* me out. That was probably why Mom had sent her. My biological mother had barely been able to look at me after I'd gotten home.

Shooting a basket into the hoop attached to the door of my childhood room, I forced myself up and opened the door for my adoptive mother.

Mama was beautiful, a woman of a honey brown complexion with voluminous curls who appeared half her age on even the days *she said* she looked tired. Point-blank, my adoptive mother was a knock-out, was from her angelic smile to the glow of her hazel eyes, and I'd had to check more than one of my asshole friends for commenting on such over the years. The comments had started when I was about thirteen and ended that same goddamn year. This was my *mom*, and eventually, my friends respected that. She'd obviously knocked my biological mother on her ass as well. More than ten years separated the two in Mama's favor.

She held the door frame. "I was beginning to forget your eyes, sweet love."

Found that hard to believe. They no doubt appeared dead and cold once I'd arrived through that door today. At least, that's what they looked like whenever I stared in the mirror these days. I was stressed the fuck to hell lately.

And I didn't hide it.

Where Mama usually greeted me with a smile, I noticed this time it wasn't there. Her hand came out, making me move into stride with her. Somewhere along the way, I'd gotten bigger than her, looking like a beast and she the kid. She rubbed my back. "Your mom wants us all to sit together so we can talk. As a family?"

Fucking hell.

I figured they'd both said enough whenever I got here, but whatever.

Shrugging, I prepared myself for the worst, but did go downstairs with her. I was scrubbing into my hair by the time we made it into the kitchen. And though my biological mother was there, Sherry, she wasn't sitting at the table by herself.

Familiar eyes stared up at me, mostly because I'd seen them every day. We had the same goddamn eyes.

We had the same goddamn everything.

My father's heart was just as dead and cold as myself, and I growled, coming between both him and my biological mother.

"The fuck is he doing here?" I charged, but Mama pulled me back.

"Jaxen," Mama scolded, shaking her head. She put a hand on mine before tugging me back and making me take a seat between both herself and Mom. Mom was playing with her hands, staring at them.

And I swore to God she'd aged in a day.

Obviously, my mom was a little older than Mama, but she'd never appeared so tired looking. Mom had dark creases under her pale blue eyes, her blond hair tied up but bunched in a messy way. She rubbed her arms without words.

And she hadn't said anything despite me cursing.

Mom was the first to hand me my ass for that shit, always had been. It'd been Mama who never scolded. But now, the roles seemed to have reversed.

Mom opened her hands. "I asked your dad here today to talk. We need to talk. As a whole family, we need to talk."

This man wasn't my family, though, and in Florida, he'd made that all too clear. He'd chosen his own family.

Dad sat there quiet now, staring at the grains in the table. He had fingers pressed to his lips, a part of the action without being a part of it.

With them all around me, I thought, well, would you look at that? Here they *all were* to tell me about my shit. Tell me how disappointed they were in me for what had happened under Dad's watch. I'd get to hear it now for how I'd taken advantage of my stepsister straight on.

"I messed up, Jaxen."

But then *Mom* said that, Mom who couldn't seem to look at me in that moment. Jaw tight, she continued to squeeze and massage her arms. "And you're suffering for it."

So confused as I looked at her, I shook my head. "What are you talking about?"

Silence next to me, no words on her end and Mama reached behind me to squeeze her wife's shoulders.

"It's okay, honey," Mama said, sounding like she was almost coaching. "It's okay."

Mom's jaw moved, and beside her, Dad huffed.

"You don't have to do this, Sherry," he said, his expression hard. "I told you we don't have to do this."

"But we do, Rick." She faced him, her brow wrinkled. She touched a hand to the table. "You see what he's done. We're *both* hurting him."

"What are you talking about?" I asked, exchanging glances across the table. No one seemed to want to look at me. At least, not directly. "What aren't you telling me?"

Mom laced her fingers. "Rick told me about your conversations. About your hurt. But not until this whole thing with your stepsister did I realize how bad it was. Your hate for him."

My stomach fucking twisted, jostling and shit like I was on a roller coaster.

Mom swung her gaze at me. "That's what that all was about, right? What it all boiled down to?"

I said nothing, more complicated than that so I said nothing. Maybe a long time ago, I would have owned up to that shit—hell, preached it from the rafters. I'd screwed my father by literally screwing his stepdaughter. I would have been proud of it, gloating it.

That was if that fact remained true.

So many things weren't what they were anymore and I cuffed my arms.

Mom touched my arm. "Baby, I haven't been telling you the truth."

I looked at her, frowning.

Mom wet her lips. "I let you believe something that isn't true."

"We both did," Dad stated, his gaze once again averting. "And really, we don't have to do this."

"Not 'doing this' is what started all this." Mom put her hands out. "Not doing this is hurting our son, and I'm not going to make him suffer anymore. Not for things I've done. Not on my watch."

"Mom?" Emotion in my voice that surprised me. I couldn't even fucking fathom how this woman could ever possibly hurt me. Even when I was mad at her over some trivial shit, she'd never truly hurt me. Never had. She could never.

"Jaxen, your father never cheated on me," she said, her eyes so sad. "It was me, me the whole time who was unfaithful to him."

Chapter Thirty

Jax

A pin fucking dropping could have been heard, nothing in that goddamn room. I caught a look of my father in that moment.

But he looked sadder than my mom.

In fact, visibly sadder, like none of this shit should be happening. None of it *should* be.

None of it.

"What are you talking about?" I asked, gritted. "Why are you saying this?"

"I'm saying it because it's true. It was me who cheated on your dad." She pressed a hand to her chest. "Me and your father left this family because of that."

I didn't understand. What she was telling me was complete bullshit. "But I heard…"

"You heard wrong." Again, looking at me. She touched my face. "And I let you believe that because I was angry. I was angry at your father for just leaving us. For leaving you? It was the wrong thing to do on my end, and something I never should have done."

My face tugged out of her reach. "He left because of you?"

"And me, my love." Mama reached for Mom's shoulder behind me, squeezing. "He left because of us. Our affair."

"You know your mama was my sous chef," Mom said, squeezing Mama's hand. "I… I fell in love. Fell in love with her. We started an affair, and it lasted for almost a year before your father found out."

My whole body chilled, sobered. Mama had come into our lives right after Dad left.

Almost right after.

I hadn't thought about the timing then, just a hurt kid who was mourning the loss of my father. He didn't even call me.

He just fucking left.

He was here, and then he wasn't so quickly, gone for almost a year before I saw him in the courts. He dragged my mom and me through all that custody shit, talking about how he wanted me to choose him.

I couldn't breathe, my chest caving in. "Why would you do that? Why would you let me *think* that? That he didn't…"

Want me.

Because that's what I'd thought. He'd left so that's what I thought. "Why would you let me think that he abandoned me?"

"Because I did, Jax."

My father's eyes clashing with mine, his hands folded on the table.

He nodded. "I did leave you, left you by leaving the situation. Thinking back, I know it was my pride." His gaze escaped, almost shame there before it returned. "I was angry at your mom too, and it took almost a goddamn year before I got my head out of my ass enough to come back to you."

"Why didn't you just tell me the truth then!" I shot. "Why make me think that it was you who ripped this family apart this whole goddamn time—"

"Because I played a part in it, Jax!"

His words ricocheted across the room, ping-ponging with mine.

He shook his head. "I left you for a *year*. And yes, you were okay in the end. But I did that, it was on me. I couldn't deny what I did, that I ran from you and the situation. I left my son because I was angry with his mother. So when I did come back and found out she let you believe what you did, I didn't make her correct it. How could I? I was guilty myself. It'd have been completely hypocritical of me."

"But I needed you," I admitted, hating that I was admitting that. My nostrils flared. "I didn't think you fucking cared."

"I did what I did *because* I cared," he rasped, his voice so thick his throat worked. "You had a good thing going with your mom and her partner by the time I came back. You were *happy*. If I would have told you the truth, you would have resented me *and* her. The admittance would have completely imploded everything for you."

But I would have had him.

And now, I knew they were both liars.

They were both full of bullshit, even Mama. She'd been the other woman, gone along with it.

Everything I knew was completely turned on its head, all the people I loved, trusted. In the end, I only had one real thing.

I'd blown that up too.

I fucked with Cleo, and she and her mom were the two people who didn't have anything to do with this. She was the one piece of pure fucking light.

And so, I really was paying for my sins.

"We're all to blame for this, Rick," Mom stated, looking at my father. "We all imploded everything. Each of us in our own ways."

Leaning forward, I laced my fingers, no words for any of them. Mom touched me, and though I wanted to draw back, I was just so tired. I was tired of hate.

I was tired in the darkness.

I drowned in it, lost in this fucking shit just as much as my parents. I was tired of the weight of it.

I was just so tired.

"We all messed up, Jaxen," Mom said, Mama taking her hand behind her. "And we're not asking for your forgiveness. We don't expect it. We just…" She rubbed my back. "We don't want you to hurt anymore. Suffer over lies or half-truths. We don't want you to hurt yourself or others for things we all had a part in."

My eyes fell shut, knowing exactly where she was going with that. She thought I'd hurt others, more specifically, Cleo, and she didn't have to say it.

That's how they all felt.

They thought I'd hurt Cleo intentionally, and I shoved my hands into my hair.

"I wasn't trying to hurt Cleo, Mom," I said, lacing my fingers behind my neck. "I'd never want to hurt her."

They studied me as I braced my arms, a million eyes on me in that moment. I think the heaviest were on myself. I didn't want to hurt my stepsister, not on purpose and never again.

I wet my lips. "I'm in love with her."

Chapter Thirty-One

Cleo

I took out the trash pretty late that night, but it took me that long just to get the energy. I'd decided to come home for the weekend after midterms, pretty common at Bay Cove. The professors tended to schedule examinations early in the week, so Fridays, students basically blew off if the professors didn't flat out cancel classes anyway. It became customary for me to come home and Mom catered a big meal for us to eat. Dad typically was in town too, but he'd left early this morning.

He hadn't said exactly where he was going, but that it'd been important. I figured it must have been since he'd skipped out on us today. It'd been pretty out of the blue, but work did tend to take him away sometimes. It happened.

In any sense, I wasn't angry. Mom had made sure to be around, and we stuffed our faces while watching old episodes of *Friends*. We did that for hours before she let me know she was zapped and wanted to go to bed. She'd kissed me goodnight, then I decided to take the trash out before heading up to bed myself.

That's when I saw him.

Lawson Richards strolled the street in a pair of sweatpants and university hoodie, a border collie guided by a leash in his hands. He must have come home too for the weekend, his dog well-mannered as it didn't tug at the lead. I'd seen the pair of them before. After all, Lawson and I lived in the same neighborhood and went to the same schools growing up.

The guy had just never left me for dead before.

That was outside of the strike against him for attempting to put his hands on me without my consent.

The pair passing my house, I immediately stiffened, but since I was basically on the sidewalk Lawson saw me easily upon striding past.

One would have thought he'd seen a ghost.

He stiffened too, tugging back his collie who'd decided to go on the walk without him. I didn't think he'd actually say anything to me. After all, he had no right at all.

But then, he guided his dog in my direction.

"Cleo. Hey," he said, wrapping the dog's leash around his big fist. He wrestled with it. "You're home too."

Not really wanting to do this, I topped the trash can with the lid. I started to open the gate to go back inside, but he waved a hand.

"Cleo…" he started, but what else did he have to say? The guy was a complete jerk, and I couldn't believe I'd idolized him the way I had. I had a tendency of making a lot of piss-poor mistakes lately. "Come on. Can I just…"

"Can you what?" I turned, bracing my arms. "What could you possibly have to say to me?"

As it turned out, it wasn't much. He rubbed his mouth. "I guess I just want to apologize."

Physically laughing in the open air at this point, I glared. "You already did that. Your text. Remember?"

And boy, did I remember it well. It came *the next morning* to check and see if I was okay. The only reason I believed he was even standing here apologizing now was because he happened to see me.

He tapped his leg with the leash. "Not for that. I mean, yes that. But…" His jaw shifted. "For something else I did. It was completely sophomoric, and had I known that guy was your stepbrother…"

"Wait. What?" He had my attention goddamn him.

He mentioned Jaxen.

My stomach did that twisty-unraveling thing again. Except this time, it didn't feel like butterflies. *This time* I wanted to be sick where I stood.

Truth be told, neither of my parents had brought up the thing with Jaxen after I flat out refused. They'd kept coming at me with all kinds of things, wanting to know if he'd manipulated me. If he'd coerced me into sleeping with him. They wanted to know if he'd hurt me on purpose, but I hadn't wanted to talk about any of it. If I did that, I'd have to admit that my feelings for him were all one-sided and that he had played me. I'd have to admit that I had screwed up.

I'd have to admit how I felt meant absolutely zero things to him, that he'd screwed me over and I'd fallen like an idiot for someone who didn't care.

Avoidance had been easier, and though I didn't want to talk about Jaxen now either, what Lawson said put me off.

I hugged my arms. "What are you…"

He showed me something, his phone. I started to back away until I recognized the number.

It was Jaxen's.

Lawson had sent a text message to Jaxen's phone, the picture of Jaxen and me in bed. I didn't understand, and Lawson pulled the phone back.

"Honestly, I just thought I saw the guy you'd

been in bed with at the club that night," he said, cringing. "I saw a guy you fucked after you got on me for—"

I stepped up on him. "What did you do?"

"Like I said, something stupid." Scrubbing into his hair, he unraveled his dog's leash, letting the breed walk a little. "It was so petty. He and I were both at the same club. Like I said, I recognized the guy. Anyway, he put down his phone for like a second, and I didn't think. I happened to be at the bar too and saw an opportunity."

Chilled, I stared on. "Opportunity?"

Lawson's mouth worked. "I sent him the picture of you guys to his phone, then deleted the thread after saving it there. After that, it was a quick send over to your mom from his line. I wanted to embarrass you. Call you out on your holier-than-thou shit for turning me down."

I shook my head. "I'm assuming you got my mom's number from your mom."

"Yeah." He had the nerve to actually appear guilty. He moved his jaw. "As you know, they're friends. I made up some excuse about needing your line for some school stuff and asked my mom if she could send me your mother's number. Told Mom I was going to ask for your contact, and she believed me since she knows we go to school together."

Unbelievable, completely unbelievable.

"Cleo—"

A punch to his jaw and so hard, I actually thought I broke my fist.

I cursed in the air, and with his dog, Lawson asked me if I was okay. I didn't know if I was madder that he was arrogant enough to pretend to care or that I'd done no damage to his pretty face at all.

"Back the hell away from me," I seethed, on the cusp of tears. He had no idea what he'd done. *No idea.* "Do you have any clue what you've done? To my family?"

My dad was so upset, both of my parents freaking out. It'd been nothing short of talking them down to keep them from doing anything *about* Jaxen.

Jaxen.

Reality hit me like it hadn't before.

He'd been telling the truth.

Oh, God, he'd been telling the truth, and I hadn't believed him. I'd left him out to dry like my adoptive father had in the past.

I wasn't there for him.

"Cleo, I'm so sorry. That's why I said something. I overheard my mom talking to yours on the phone today about it. I had no idea *that guy* was your stepbrother. I just wanted to call you on your shit. I hadn't… I mean, your stepbrother?"

How funny this guy wanted to judge, like he had a right?

I pointed at him. "You didn't want to call me on my shit. You wanted payback—point-blank, because I wouldn't let you put your hands on me."

He said nothing, of course, and how could he? It was true.

I really was hella freaking good at picking guys. I actually thought he'd been the nice one.

And tossed the one I wanted away.

Chapter Thirty-Two

Cleo

I tried Jaxen several times that night, but his phone must have been off or dead because it went straight to voicemail every time. I ended up having to give up and go to bed, but when I woke up the next morning, same thing. I couldn't get past the voicemail option. I thought to leave him a text message, but decided on a whim, just to head back to school. Odds were, he didn't go back home for the weekend and I needed to talk to him. This couldn't wait.

I needed to apologize.

I hadn't held faith in him like I should have, so first thing, I was up and heading on the road. I told Mom everything this morning, that what happened wasn't Jaxen's fault but Lawson's. I told her this whole thing was a big misunderstanding, and she immediately contacted Lawson's mom too. Odds were, he *hadn't* told the truth to her. He was a coward, and cowards didn't tell the truth. It'd probably be best if he decided to go to another school next term because I had a feeling once Jaxen learned Lawson's place in all this, he'd be coming for him as he should. He'd screwed us both.

Mom hadn't understood my need to go until I told her that truth too, that it hadn't been just *sex* as awkward as the conversation was. I had real feelings for my stepbrother, and though she hadn't been in love with that, she hadn't stopped me from going.

"I trust you know what you're doing," she'd said and that we'd discuss everything when Dad came back home. I asked if she knew where he went and she said she didn't have too many details herself. He just said that he had to leave quickly and was supposed to check in with her this morning. I assumed he had a work obligation, usually the case and since Mom didn't seemed to be too alarmed, I wasn't either. Anyway, I didn't want to bother him with all this anyway. That wasn't priority. I needed to get back to campus and talk to Jaxen.

My hour-plus-long commute was anxiety-ridden, and not one moment of it did I think about anything else. My thoughts were completely on Jaxen and what I'd say to him. I didn't know how to handle this situation.

I'd never been in love before.

Of course, I'd loved people. I loved my mom, my adoptive father, and my biological dad. I loved my baby brother, Nathan, but this kind of love with Jaxen was completely different. It was all-consuming and so overwhelming I couldn't even easily admit it to myself. It was terrifying, but also the most beautiful thing I'd ever felt. I wanted to be surrounded by it every day, which made all of this just that much more scary. Odds were, he might not feel the same way. Topics such as this, openness and feelings, were just so much harder with him, and add to the fact I hadn't believed him about the text? I just didn't know what would happen.

Instead, I attempted to focus on driving, and though I didn't normally answer text messages on the road or even look at my phone, something compelled me to glance over to my device on my passenger seat when it buzzed.

Jaxen: I don't expect you to talk to me. You haven't been, so you probably won't, but I got to tell you something. I know you'll at least read this so that's why I'm sending it as a text instead of just calling you. I hope you'll respond.

The messages buzzed in one after the other, long and I tapped a finger to navigate to my text messages screen.

Jaxen: Something happened last night. Something big that completely fucked with my head. I basically found out everyone's been lying to me. My mothers. Rick.

Dad?

Jaxen: And this lie basically made me blow up my life. It made me try to punish Rick for something he didn't even really do. As it turns out, my biological mom had actually done the thing I thought he had. He'd been lying to me, he said, to protect me and my life as I knew it.

My thoughts traveled back to those last conversations with all of us, how my adoptive father had said he needed to keep something from Jaxen. That he couldn't take something away from him. He'd been so adamant about it. Like there was no other way.

Jaxen: I thought I'd be more angry finding all this out, but honestly, I was just tired. I was tired of hating my father. I was tired of pain. He, my moms, and I talked a lot after they all fessed up. Fuck, my mothers were losing it. Tears everywhere by the end, and Rick got emotional too. He flew all the way over to my moms' place just to hash this out, and I was glad he did. I was glad we all didn't have to do this anymore, this shit thing, and I actually got to talk a lot with Rick. Just us. It was good for us. It was good.

Oh my gosh.

Jaxen: Anyway, why this relates to you was I royally messed up. I fucked up. I was operating by a lot of false information. Things I felt Rick did to me, and I punished you for them. I wanted to hurt you, hate you for a bunch of stuff that had nothing to do with you. My issues were with my father, and I took it out on you, easier than just being a decent fucking human being, which is actually who Rick Fairchild turned out to be. It makes sense because of who you are, the kid he did end up raising, but you're more than just a decent fucking human being. You're everything.

Everything…

Jaxen: I don't have words for how good you are, Girl Scout. Not good at this shit at all. I just know you're too good for me, and I don't blame you for not believing me that night. I gave you more than one reason not to in the past, a million reasons. I'm a screwup who fucked with the only pure thing I had in my life. The only thing that wasn't pain, the only thing that wasn't lies. I thought you were playing me all this time. But really, I was the one who ended up playing myself.

My throat constricted, breathing while trying to navigate the road. I shouldn't be reading these while driving, for many reasons.

Jaxen: What I'm basically trying to say and that I'm terrible at is I'm sorry. I'm sorry for everything. I'm even more sorry that I can't, in good faith, have you. You're better than me. So much better and deserve a hell of a lot more than a shit human being with all this fucking baggage. I hate what I did to you. I hate that I destroyed your ability to trust, but what I hate the most is that I had the fucking nerve to fall in love with you. Which I did, Girl Scout. So fucking hard I can't even see straight, and it's so shitty because I'm the worst for you. I can't ask you to choose me. I'm not the one good girls choose. Not if they want to remain whole on the other side.

Tears in my eyes on this end, that he actually felt that way about himself, that he didn't feel good enough.

Jaxen: I'm not expecting anything from this. In fact, I expect nothing from you. I've already taken enough.

He had no more texts message bubbles after that, and even though I shouldn't have behind the wheel, I picked up my phone off the seat. He couldn't not know how I felt. He couldn't continue to think he wasn't good enough.

My thumbs on the screen, I texted him back.

Me: You're not taking anything from me. You never could. Jaxen, I love—

A car honked before I could send, and I jerked my gaze to the road. I'd veered into another lane, and I dropped my phone to put both hands on the wheel.

The minivan screeched beside me, dodging onto the shoulder and when I checked to see if they were okay, I failed to realize traffic had slowed in front of me.

I jerked the wheel left, which skidded me into the third lane.

The impact hit immediately.

Crunched on my side, my car in a roll as I tumbled and was impacted again from the back.

The hits continued, again and again at all sides. It was as if this was a game of pinball and my station wagon was the ball. Cars weren't able to stop in time, hitting me from all sides as the glass shattered all around me.

I think I was screaming. I think I was crying. I honestly didn't know.

I just knew when it all finally... *gratefully* went dark.

Chapter Thirty-Three

Jax

Rick and I showed up at the hospital together, coming at this thing *together*. His wife Maggie had called him early this morning.

Cleo had been in an accident.

She'd been trying to get to the hospital herself since it happened while Cleo had been driving back to school. Because of that, Maggie didn't have too many details, but the urgency in her voice told of her fear. She said the hospital hadn't told her much, but that she needed to get there asap.

Rick and I had both been on the next flight.

We'd gone together, and I hadn't asked if I could go or should. I just went. I was going to go.

We arrived there together.

Rick gratefully knew his way around the place. He'd been there a time or two through community work so new exactly where the ED was. He gave a little information to the front desk, and they told him where to go from there. We found Maggie right away, by herself with a clipboard in her hands. She'd been thumbing through about a million cards on her lap.

"Maggie!" Rick picked up the pace right away, me flanking him. He waved right at Maggie, and the woman appeared on the cusp of tears.

Oh, God.

I couldn't think upon seeing that, not letting myself. We didn't know anything, and it'd be foolish to panic. Not yet until we knew anything.

"Rick. Oh my God." Literal tears pushed through my stepmom's eyelashes. She squeezed on

Rick, trembling. "Thank God, you're here. I don't know what to do. I don't…"

"It's okay," he said, pulling back, and I had to give it to him.

He kept his shit together better than me.

Because seeing Maggie like that, in goddamn tears and fucking panicked to hell, *I* wanted to lose my shit. But for his wife, he kept cool, holding her.

"What's going on? What do they know?" he asked. Again, I was admiring the shit out of this man. I never would have thought that not even twenty-four hours ago. So much had changed, and here I stood in awe of him now. He held her face. "Just breathe. Talk to me."

She did, forcing it out through quivering lips. After a nod, she appeared to have composed herself enough to speak.

"She'd been driving back to school," she started. "Collided with several cars. She rolled and… God, Rick. I don't know. They wouldn't tell me much more than that. Just that it was bad, and they needed to do surgery. I've been filling out these papers all morning, and I…"

"That's all right." He took the clipboard from her, again completely calm aside from a wrinkle of worry between the eyes. My father no doubt had a fury going on inside him right now, but he'd checked himself. He nodded. "Let me do this. I'll go find out more information."

"Please. Dear God. My baby."

"It's going to be okay. I'm going to figure this out."

She nodded, bowing her head and letting him kiss her. After that, he grabbed me. "Can you stay with her while I…"

He probably could have asked me just shy of anything in that moment. I would do anything.

Keep your shit together.

"Of course," I said. "Yeah. Of course, fine."

Not nearly as stable as his, my voice, but it appeared to be good enough to let him go. He squeezed Maggie's hand, kissing it before moving off into the ED somewhere. The place basically had people falling out of the windows it was so busy.

"Do you need anything?" I managed to ask my stepmother, fighting to keep my voice as level as my dad's. "I can get you coffee."

They had a machine by reception. It wasn't Starbucks, but I was sure it would help.

As if in a daze, Maggie looked at me, nodding, but before I left, she touched my shoulder.

"She'd been trying to get to campus, Jaxen," she said, her eyes glistening. "She'd been trying to get to you. We know you didn't send that picture."

They did…

And she what?

Cleo was *trying* to get to me?

Maggie's lips parted. "The person who did confessed to Cleo. A local boy. Lawson Richards? Said he spotted you at a club and sent the text from your phone."

Why wasn't I surprised? Fuck.

"Anyway, Cleo told me how she felt about you," she stated, causing my heart to race. "I'm just so sorry that all this happened. So quickly, we believed that you could do such a thing to her. That you would take advantage of her?"

I had, in many ways I had. I'd given that girl enough reasons for a lifetime not to have anything to do with me.

"She told you about us?" I asked, my stepmom nodding. "What did she say?"

I couldn't believe that, that she'd been trying to get to me. It didn't make sense.

Cleo told me how she felt about you...

"Just that you mean a lot to her," she said, blinking down more tears. "The police said it'd been you she was texting when..."

I couldn't see straight. I couldn't think...

And squeezing my arm, my stepmother didn't finish. She just took her seat, on the cusp of falling apart in her hands. She hugged her arms, dropping her gaze to the floor. But in that silence, I heard the words loud and clear. Cleo had been rushing to get to me. Cleo had been texting *me*.

Cleo was in here because of me.

*

My own coffee went cold as I waited, ignoring my cracked phone as it blew up in my pocket. I'd heard from basically all my friends, my moms multiple times. Outside of telling them I'd gotten here okay, I answered none of them. I was too busy battling the war consuming my brain. That I'd been the reason my stepsister was here, that I was the reason our parents currently didn't know anything about her state and we were all left in gut-rupturing fear of the unknown. Rick had come back multiple times after turning in Cleo's paperwork. But each time, no information. He checked every hour on the hour, but eventually, decided his time was better spent with his wife.

He currently held her hand now, rubbing it with a far off look in his eyes. I was responsible for that.

I guessed I really had ruined his life.

I ruined both him and his wife, a shell of the people they'd been before I'd made it into their lives, and Cleo? God, Cleo was somewhere in this hospital now possibly fighting for her goddamn life. That was me. This one was on me.

"Mr. and Mrs. Fairchild?"

It was like their number was up, a golden ticket arriving that was both desired and unwanted when a doctor in blue scrubs with a kind smile appeared in front of my dad and Cleo's mom.

The pair stood on autopilot.

"Yes. Yes, that's us," Rick said, "Do you have an update about our daughter?"

I stood too, as if I could. As if I had the right. Despite that, I couldn't help myself. I needed to know she was okay.

I needed to know I hadn't lost her.

I did that, and I could walk away, let her live her life. She'd live a safe life, a happy life, but before, I had to have that one thing. Selfish, I knew.

"I do," the doctor said, and though her smile was kind, warm, it didn't reassure. There was no false hope there, this kind smile the best she could give us. "I'm Dr. Fieldhouse. I'm the one who performed surgery on your daughter Cleo. She's sustained some significant injuries. Do you know the details of the accident?"

"Just that she was texting." Cleo's mom leaned into my dad, the man holding her close. She'd explained that detail to him too, and though neither of them had given me grief, it was all out there. We *all* knew why Cleo was here.

Just find out if she's okay, and you can let her

go.

I had to. There really was no world in which this girl and me should be together. I knew that now, everything I'd texted to her this morning stupid. My phone had died last night, which was the only reason I waited to do it today. I realized the device was dead this morning, charged it, and odds were, all *those texts* had been what she was trying to respond to today.

God, I'm such a fucking idiot.

All this shit really was coming in full circle, my breath a heavy one as I slid my hands inside my pockets and forced myself to listen.

"She was," the doctor said, frowning. "It was a pretty bad pile up. Cleo was hit from several angles."

"But is she okay?" Rick asked, rubbing Maggie's arm. "My wife said she had to have surgery."

"She did, but there were no complications. In fact, Cleo's doing quite well despite the extent of her injuries. She had a few broken ribs, a shoulder injury, and some cranial damage. The blow to her head was the most severe, but we were able to act quickly. She had some swelling to her brain, but we were able to release the pressure."

"Oh my God." Maggie squeezed Rick's side. "My child had brain surgery?"

"She did, but the surgery was successful. We'll have to monitor her overnight, of course, but we're very hopeful she's out of the dark there."

"Can we see her?" Maggie started to go that way, but the doctor held up her hands.

"Normally, this is the point where, yes, we would say that, but there's an issue that requires urgency, and that's why I've come to speak with the family now."

"But you said you felt she was out of the dark," Rick said. "I don't understand."

"Regarding her head injury, yes." Dr. Fieldhouse nodded. "But there are some internal injuries that hold our concern. More specifically, surrounding Cleo's kidneys. She was impacted pretty severely on her left side, which has left the state of that kidney in pretty bad shape."

"How bad?" My stepmom bunched Rick's shirt.

The doctor sighed. "It's destroyed I'm afraid. It'll have to be removed."

"But she can function with one, right?" Rick asked, the first waver I'd heard in his voice. He'd kept it together, together completely through this whole thing. "People can function just fine with one."

"Again, normally."

"Normally?"

The doctor's expression shifted grave. "I was reviewing Cleo's chart, and I see she has a history of poor kidney functioning. Her right one's never been as strong as the left?"

"She has a birth defect, yes," Cleo's mom said. "She's had issues in the past, but keeps up on her doctor's appointments. We've monitored the situation her whole life, and she's never had an issue."

"That's because she's always had the left to overcompensate, but the right is having to work too hard now."

My stepmom paled. "What does that mean?"

"It means your daughter will need a transplant, Mrs. Fairchild. And sooner rather than later. I've added her to the donor list, and though we hope to hear something, your daughter's need is immediate and it is a long list."

Sickness at this point and now, my dad actually had to hold my stepmom up. She wavered in his arms.

"What can we do?" My father had completely broken the wall. The dam of his strength had been nuked, and holding onto my stepmother was his only strength. He swayed too.

Except he wasn't the only one.

I rocked behind them, my hands bunching in my pockets. I couldn't see straight again, all this shit not real.

"It's at this point we ask the family," the doctor stated. "Odds of a match are higher from a biological recipient."

"Of course." Maggie pressed her hand to Rick's chest. "I'll be tested right away. Anything she needs."

"Can only family be tested?"

I think the parents had been the only ones surprised when I opened my mouth.

Because I sure wasn't.

The doctor mentioned all this shit, and all I was thinking was what did I have to do. How could they do this shit now, this test, and get this girl anything she needed. I started to step forward, but my dad grabbed me.

"Son, you don't have to—"

"I know I don't." I faced the doctor. "If you're not family, can you be tested?"

"Of course," Dr. Fieldhouse said, her smile light. "But it is a big decision. You need to be certain."

"And it's major surgery, son." Rick put his hands on my arms. "This isn't just… It's not something that can just be undone. Something could go wrong even. *You* could need—"

"I don't care." And I didn't. I just needed this shit to happen now. "Whatever she needs."

Tears in my stepmother's eyes, not sure if they were a combination for myself, Cleo, or something else entirely. I just knew she took my hand, and suddenly, I was with her.

Suddenly, I was with both of them.

She squeezed my hand as Rick nodded as well. "I'd like to be tested as well," he said, acknowledging me in that same sentence. "My son and I aren't biologically related to Cleo, but that's what we want."

I let him know that, nodding too, and then, the doctor was away, moving on to next steps. In her absence, I found arms around me.

My stepmother.

"Thank you so much," she said, squeezing me. Pulling away, she touched my face. "Just God bless you."

I had no words, only that I didn't have to think about it. There hadn't really been another option.

At least, not in my mind.

Chapter Thirty-Four

Jax

My stepmother and father were in a frenzy after that, a round of calls back and forth. Maggie had the idea to reach out to as many family members and close friends as she could and had even contacted Cleo's dad. Unfortunately, he was ineligible. He said he'd wanted to, but his struggle with certain vices in his life wouldn't allow it. He'd even offered to fly out as soon as humanly possible. He wanted to be there, to see her.

And so that light of Cleo's brought out everyone else's, more than one person outside of this hospital wanting to help her. Maggie and my dad just needed names at this point, people willing to help. Before we all knew it, they had over half a dozen. People literally willing to donate their kidneys for this girl.

I wasn't surprised.

Those names were waiting on standby while Maggie, Rick, and I waited for the results of our own tests. And eventually, they did come in.

"Mr. Ambrose?"

My name was called, mine and not my dad's or stepmom's. Dr. Fieldhouse had come back, wanting to just talk to me.

I knew I was the one without her even telling me.

It was just the look she gave, that all-telling look, and I didn't need to be taken off into some room. I didn't want to be spoken to and stressed that I could change my mind and that I could wait for a donor to come through. Cleo might not have time.

"I want to do it," I said, probably the easiest decision I'd ever made. I didn't need to think about it. If something I had inside me kept her alive? Well, really there was no decision at all. I stepped up, ready for it.

I just needed to know where to go.

*

My own phone calls came quick after that, everyone either trying to talk me out of it or to really consider what I was doing. The worst had been my moms, of course.

"Don't you do anything until me and your mama can get down there," my mom had said.

She'd told me they were booking the first trip down to Florida, but by the time they got down here, who knew the kind of state Cleo would be in. Dr. Fieldhouse and her team had her stable, but waiting for the sake of my moms' arrival wasn't a good enough reason. Cleo needed me, needed this.

I'd been able to talk them down eventually, my friends eventually. They called in succession after I finally texted them all back.

"Jaxen Ambrose, if you die, I'm going to kill you." This from Royal's girl, December, and who was I kidding?

This girl was like a sister to me.

I loved her like I loved her own sister, Paige. Paige'd been one of my dearest friends, and we'd all lost her way too soon. She passed away when we all were in high school, and the event had brought December into our friend circle. We all loved her, our good friend.

"It'll all be fine," I said, assuring her like the

calls before. LJ and Knight had said something similar. It'd been a little more threatening if one could imagine. If I died, they'd make me suffer for it in the afterlife, a damn promise on Knight's end especially. The big guy hadn't broken down or anything, but he'd been close enough to it to have to get off the phone.

I heard it in his voice.

I'd admit hearing that had made me a little emotional too, but after getting my shit together, I called up Royal, my last call. He put me on FaceTime with himself and December, both of their mugs staring back at me from my hospital bed.

"You better be," December said, holding the phone. Her cheeks were all red, her eyes puffy. "I can't lose someone else in my life I care about."

She had lost a lot, one of the strongest people I'd ever known, male or female. I grinned. "Aww, December. I didn't know you cared."

"You know I love you, you stupid asshole," she chuckled, more emotion than I wanted to hear in her voice. I barely had the strength for any more of it. My moms had basically broken down before they finally let me go. December sniffed. "You call us as soon as you can."

"Yeah, have your dad call us even if you can't," Royal said, frowning. He was tucked in beside her on the line. "As soon as you're out of surgery, I want a call."

Rick had a list of people to both call and text, his name on there.

"He already knows," I told him, then watched as my buddy rubbed his fiancée's shoulders. She blew me a kiss before leaving the line, but Royal stayed.

"I guess all I can say is don't die," he said, one of the only people not to either try to convince me out of this or make me think longer, harder. He smiled a little. "Who am I kidding? I couldn't get rid of your ass even if I wanted to."

He was damn right about that, making me chuckle. I tilted my head. "No other final words? No 'really stop and think about this, Jax?'"

I gave my best stick-up-his-ass Royal impression, the guy always taking himself way too seriously. That was just him, our leader. He kept all us guys' heads on straight and had since school.

Royal shook his head, somewhere inside his apartment now. "I'd only be wasting my breath."

"Why?"

"Because you're in that bed right now, aren't you?" he stated, smiling wide. "And that tells me everything I need to know."

I guessed it did, this guy my first best friend.

"Love ya, guy," he said, tapping the phone with his knuckles, and I did the same.

"Love ya."

Before surgery, my dad came in one last time, checking on me and making sure everything was okay. He brought Maggie too for a time, and after she hugged me, she said a silent prayer. I'd never been much of the religious type, but in her words, Cleo definitely lingered in my head. I willed all I could for those prayers to go to her.

"Thank you so much," she said. One would think she'd be all cried out by now, but even still, she patted away more tears. Rick had given her his handkerchief, and it was a permanent staple in her hand most of the day. After she left the room, my dad came over to me.

"They haven't let you see her, have they?" I asked. As far as I knew, none of us had. Things had been moving very quickly, urgent.

Rick shook his head. "No, but the doctor says she's still stable."

"Good."

He nodded, and when he looked like he wanted to take my hand, I gave it to him. He squeezed it, reaching in and hugging me, but when he started to pull away, I found myself holding his shoulder.

I just stayed there in that moment and let myself feel it. For two seconds, I let myself be completely consumed by the fact that this was my dad.

And I was his kid.

I needed whatever this moment was from him. I just needed it.

"You come back out of this, you hear me?" he stated, fucking choking on the words. He patted my back. "I'm not going to lose you. I spent too many years without you."

I closed my eyes.

"I'll be fine," I said, gripping his shirt. I squeezed. "I'm your son, right?"

A nod before he fell away. He touched my face. "Hell yeah."

He started to pull back, but I held his hand.

"Can you give this to Cleo for me?" I asked, taking off my Court ring. I gave it to him. "Just in case she wakes up before me. I want her to have it."

I'd explain it to her once I saw her again. But I didn't know how long that'd be with me going under too.

Rick studied it. "Is this some kind of class

347

ring?"

How funny as she'd asked the same thing. I nodded. "Something like that."

I watched him pocket it. "Of course. If I see her first, of course."

"Thanks."

He shook my hand again, touching the top. "I love you, son," he said, and letting go, I knew he didn't expect any more from me. I mean, why should he? Neither of my parents expected me to forgive them. My mom had said it herself.

"You too, Dad," I returned, easy. Because I did love him, and even if we had our issues, even if he and my mom lied, I had too. I'd lied every day I said I didn't need him. I'd lied every day I convinced myself that hate would fix all the pain inside.

But what I said, what I *felt* proved a far better feeling than any hate I'd felt for this man. It was like breathing air.

It was feeling again.

A glisten to his eyes as he looked at me, but he didn't make me say anything more. He just touched my hand again.

And that's all I think was needed.

Dad walked with me as far as he could, until the elevators cut us off and I was left to the care of Dr. Fieldhouse and her team. He said he'd call my mothers and tell them I was about to go up.

"Tell them I love them too," I said, knowing I'd already said it. Of course, I had when they called. I did love them. I'd love them forever.

Dad had nodded to me, waving. After that, it was a quick ride upstairs and into the room I thought only reserved for me.

Which was why my breath caught at seeing

Cleo.

They had her lying there, in my operating room with the bed upraised. She was in a medical gown just like me, a sheet covering her waist.

And she was so bruised.

The right side of her face was completely purple, under her eyes puffy and the same. They'd cut her hair too, chopped at her shoulders and a bandage was on her head from where I guessed they'd shaved it.

My stomach clenched, my heart raced, and my need to be close to her bogged me down like a heavy weight. I wanted to rip all the leads away and take her, hold her and make her safe. I wanted to be the one in that bed.

And wished so hard that it had been me.

She'd been collateral damage in all this, and as the doctor wheeled me closer, I just stared at her.

"We figured you might want to see her," Dr. Fieldhouse said. "She's been a hell of a fighter."

I bet she had. The fact that she survived me and all the things I'd done her greatest feat. I swallowed. "Can I touch her?"

I shouldn't have asked that, had no right to ask that, but when Dr. Fieldhouse nodded, the first thing I did was reach for Cleo's hand.

It warm, soft and so beautiful like her. I didn't want to let it go.

Touching her was so dumb.

It made me want for more things, things I had no right to have. It had made me give my ring to my dad to give to her, but I didn't give that to him with intent. Fact of the matter was, no one could have that part of me after her, impossible. There was the me before.

Then there was the me with Cleo.

She'd always have that part. She'd always have that piece, and with this surgery now, it was like a symbol of that. I could go the rest of my life knowing I'd always be a part of her.

Even if, in the end, that's all it could ever be.

I fingered her wrist up to her elbow, relishing in those moments as long as I could. Eventually, Dr. Fieldhouse asked me if I was ready, and I didn't hesitate. The moment I went to sleep, Cleo would be relieved of her nightmare.

And the moment she woke up, I'd be relieved of mine.

Chapter Thirty-Five

Cleo

My limbs sagged. My body pulsed. My lashes fluttered open, and the soft light in the room shot a bolt of pain straight into my scull.

I moaned.

"Rick... Oh my God. Rick, she's awake. Go get the doctor!"

Awake?

I'd been asleep.

I knew that now, my mom's voice as she materialized in front of me. My mouth felt like someone had shoved about thirty cotton balls up in it.

"Baby. Oh my God." Mom touched my face, tears in her eyes, and I didn't understand. Soft fingers ghosted the tender flesh of my cheek. Everything throbbed. *Everything* hurt, and my head felt like someone had bashed me over my noggin, then swung back and gone for a second round.

"Mom..." My voice strained and cracked, and the mere sound caused my mom's tears to fall. The word "miracle" fell from her lips, my arm pinned to the side. I couldn't move it. I couldn't move anything. My whole body felt like a reinforced, steel weight, and a slight shift had my whole body radiating in awareness, pain. Especially my side.

I felt like someone had cut me from the inside out, and when I attempted to move again, Mom placed a hand on my shoulder.

"Don't move, baby," Mom said, but her smile was so wide one would have thought I brought her the stars. It appeared I had, her eyes glistening in those tears. "You've been in an accident."

An... accident?

I remembered it well, crashing and colliding. I even remembered when the rolling had finally stopped, and things had suddenly gone dark.

I hadn't been here, though, clearly a hospital room around me. They had me in a bed, hooked up and IV'ed to all kinds of stuff. My left arm was also secured to my side, fastened down, and I couldn't move it. My fingers and toes curling, those appeared to work, though.

"Cleo." My adoptive father appeared, so much joy on his face. He had a fist pressed to his mouth as he came over to me. "Hey, sweetheart."

"Hey, Dad." Soft words, but they proved enough to bring tears to his eyes as well. He touched my hair and I realized someone had cut it. It currently sat in a slight curl at my shoulders.

"Welcome back, Cleo."

In the door frame stood a petite woman, dark eyes, kind smile. She had a white jacket on and a stethoscope around her neck, so I assumed she was the doctor my mom had spoken about.

She smiled. "My name is Dr. Fieldhouse. How are you doing this morning?"

This morning. It'd been morning when things went dark. Was it the same day?

I forced my mouth to make words, and when they strained at my vocal chords, the doctor sent for water. Mom helped me sip through a straw, and after, I nodded my thanks. I relaxed with a sigh into the bed. "I feel like I was hit with a cement truck, but other than that? Right as rain."

The laugh was a mistake on my part as it completely radiated my insides in even more pain, but its presence brought a smile to more than one person in the room. My parents, for starters, looked like they'd melt into a literal puddle of joy. How long had I been out? Were my injuries bad?

They sure felt like it. Like everything hurt. Even my toes. Though that could have been in my head. Honestly, how was I even alive right now? I hadn't been in a head-on collision, but close enough. I'd been hit at all sides on the highway.

"Well, I'm happy to see, despite your current state, you're still in good spirits." Another warm smile on me before the woman checked me out, touching, feeling, then listening with her stethoscope. "Breathe for me."

I did and after that check, she returned the device to her neck. "Well, I'll say you really have beat some odds here. That accident you were in was quite bad. Required a few surgeries, and you've been off your feet for almost two days."

Wow.

"Do you remember what happened? Your accident, I mean."

Since I did, I nodded. I'd been stupid, trying to send a text.

Jaxen.

Immediately, my thoughts traveled to him, to his own texts that fluttered in. I hadn't gotten to answer them. He told me how he felt, and now, it looked like I had ignored him. Did he know about my accident? He wasn't here.

"Well, besides a head injury, a few broken ribs, a dislocated shoulder, and some internal damage, you are right as rain." The doctor winked, but did smile. "We've fixed all that, though. You should be just fine after you've healed up and, of course, rested."

Jesus, all that had happened to me?

I really must have had someone looking down on me. All of this was wild.

At this point, the doctor had her clipboard in her hands when a nurse gave it to her. Once in hand, the doctor appeared to be checking off and noting things on it.

"You had some swelling to your brain, but even with that, you should be able to start getting back to your old self in about four to eight weeks and, generally, the same time frame for the rest of your ailments. We will need to make sure we monitor your kidneys. Especially, the transplant. But—"

"Transplant?" I gazed up after my mom adjusted my bedding. She'd been smoothing it down and getting it arranged for me. I looked at her. "I had a kidney transplant?"

"Yes, baby," Mom said. "And it was a miracle. You did so well. Jaxen too."

My mouth dried again, as if I'd never had water.

As if I'd never *ever* had water.

"What do you mean?" I whispered, and Dad angled a hand toward me. He had something in his palm.

Something I recognized.

The chunky ring had a gorilla mouth on it, *Jaxen's* metal ring. But why did he have it?

Dad placed it in my hand, closing my fist around it. "He wanted you to have it. Said if you woke up first, he wanted you to have it."

"Well, is he awake?" I shifted and fell back in immediate pain. The room erupted in frenzy, a need to keep me laying down, to tend to me, but no one was telling me about Jaxen. "Where is he?"

"Mr. Ambrose is in his own room, resting." The doctor smiled again. "He had some issues coming out of the anesthesia, but he's being monitored."

"What kind of issues? Dad?" I faced him. "Mom?"

"He just got really sick, baby," Mom assured, absolute dread filling me. She touched my adoptive father's shoulder. "We've both seen him, though. He's resting like the doctor said."

"Well, can I see him?" Another move and an absolute *bad* idea. Forget someone hitting me with a cement truck. They basically backed up and did it two more times.

"You gotta be careful, Cleo." The doctor nodded. "Any physical movement won't be possible for you at this time. Just focus on resting. Getting yourself better."

"But what about Jaxen?" He'd donated a *kidney* for me. I just… "When can I see him?"

"The doctor said you need to rest, honey." Mom drew some of my short hair away from my eyes. "Jaxen will be okay. He just needs to rest too. Like you."

She'd said this with a smile, but it faltered a little upon looking at my adoptive father. It made me feel like they knew something.

Like they did but felt I was too fragile to tell.

*

More than three days passed with little word about Jaxen and more than enough about me. Dr. Fieldhouse and her team kept me completely informed about my current state and progress. I was even told when I'd start physical therapy, but every time I asked about Jax, all I got were canned responses. He was okay. He was resting. Both my parents had seen him often, but not once had they mentioned about him asking about me. They said every time they came in to check on him, he'd been sleeping.

And I noticed he hadn't come by.

The internet said the recovery time for a transplant was about one to three days on the donor's part. I'd made my parents give me my phone so I could check. I asked about that, his recovery time, and when he'd be able to go home, but all I got were assurances. Telling me not to worry about my Jaxen, to relax myself as stress couldn't possibly help *my* condition. I didn't care about myself or my state. I cared about Jaxen's.

I mean, he'd donated a kidney for me.

I had a part of *him* inside *me*. I was physically closer to him in more ways than I'd ever been, but still felt so far away from him. I felt like if something was seriously wrong with him, someone would tell me, but every time I asked, I just got more assurances and was told to take care of myself. It didn't seem like anyone was taking care of or worrying about him, and that pissed me off.

So many people came through this room to check on me, people from Mom and Dad's church, friends and family, and of course, Kit. She'd come after her classes one day, and after finding out who gave me my kidney, she'd been floored. She actually cried.

I had too.

I just couldn't believe it. Jaxen had said so many things to me before the accident. But even with those confessions, even with him saying he loved me, this was different. This was him making a far bigger declaration.

And then this ring.

I kept it on my thumb, too big to wear anywhere else. I had no idea what this meant or why he gave it to me. I assumed maybe good luck to get me through this, but shouldn't he have it?

I just wanted to talk to him.

I continued to worry, and my parents kept me more distracted than I liked. They also kept bringing people in to see me.

The greatest shock of all had been my biological father.

He'd looked so good, cleaned up and solid on his feet. He came all the way here to see me when I knew he lived several states over.

"Ninety days sober," he'd said to me, and so happy. I hadn't seen him in years, and though he hadn't been able to stay long, had to get back to his life and work, it'd been good to see him. He'd said he had even wanted to donate to me himself.

It'd been truly crazy.

So many people came through my room, and I appreciated them all, but they weren't the person I found myself wondering the most about. I still had few updates from my parents about Jaxen's state. Like they were keeping things from me on purpose, and I didn't like that. It'd been almost four days now and still no word.

"I want to see him," I urged to my adoptive father one day. My mom had gone out for coffee, basically here around the clock. Dad had been a frequently flier, of course, too, but had to leave a time or two for a few hours to tend to some things surrounding his work. He'd also arranged for the university to allow me to do e-learning while I was in the hospital.

Dad frowned at me. "You know you can't move yet, sweetheart. Just be patient. I'm sure once Jaxen is up and moving again, he will come see you."

But why hadn't I heard something already? Something good when the internet said he should be coming around? Obviously, a mere Google search wasn't always reliable, but something just felt wrong here and as it did, a new form of dread surfaced.

I wondered if he actually *wanted* to see me, or he changed his mind about, well, everything.

"Dad, you don't understand," I whispered, my mouth dry again. "I need to see him. He doesn't know."

My thumb played with the ring gracing my other hand. I hadn't been able to tell Jaxen my feelings, and if his had changed, I at least wanted to thank him. I needed to.

He'd saved my life.

In so many ways, and Dad touched my shoulder.

"What doesn't he know?" he asked, and I said nothing. I mean, what could I say? That I loved his son? Would he understand? Mom hadn't loved that when I told her, and though it hadn't come up again, I had no idea her feelings surrounding it. I hadn't even gotten to talk to my adoptive father about the situation.

"I just need to ask him about this," I stated, pulling the ring off. "Can you figure something out? *Please.* I need to see him."

I'd literally never asked for anything from him. I'd never needed to. Rick Fairchild had always been there and ahead of anything I'd ever asked or wanted. He'd always been my dad.

He touched my cheek, the swelling down now. He told me to give him two seconds, then he left the room. I felt like I waited all day before he came back, but once he had, he appeared with a team.

There were literally half a dozen nurses and hospital staff, and when Dr. Fieldhouse herself showed up, I was more than confused.

"You're being moved, Cleo," she said, smiling. "I hope you don't mind, but I put in a request for a better room for you."

"Better room?" I asked, looking around. Her team got my pain meds and stuff, then literally wheeled my whole bed forward.

"Yes, and I think you'll like the change. It has a view," she said, winking at my adoptive father before leaving the room. I thought he'd follow me, but he stayed at the door.

"I'm going to go find your mother and let her know about your room change," he said, his eyes creasing hard in the corners. "We might get a little lost on the way up, so don't expect us right away, all right?"

He flashed me a wink after that, so much behind it. Of course, he'd done this, the room change.

And that told me everything I needed to know about how he felt regarding who I was clearly about to see.

Chapter Thirty-Six

Cleo

Jaxen was also in a room by himself, looking like the most beautiful sleeping prince and my heart stopped at just the sight of him.

Lack of breath followed.

He didn't look like me, bruised and bandaged up. He appeared like himself, hauntingly lovely and breathtakingly gorgeous. His tawny brown curls lay wavy and messy, a more than five o'clock shadow on his face that made him look rugged, but not unkempt. He had been here for a little while, currently sleeping with a sheet over his waist and his hands positioned at his sides. His large chest rose and fell as Dr. Fieldhouse's team wheeled my bed next to his.

They left little space, pushing us right up against each other. I found that curious until Dr. Fieldhouse looked at me.

"We'll be back in a few to move you over to the other bed," she said, pointing to the one on the other side of the room. She winked. "But I figured you may want a few moments. You two seem close."

I didn't know what we were.

But I wasn't complaining since Jaxen was close enough to touch.

Which he was, right next to me. Sleeping soundly, he hadn't moved through all this, and I hadn't been surprised. He'd been a solid sleeper when we'd been together.

"Let us know if you need anything," Dr. Fieldhouse said, watching as a nurse set my call button on my bed. I nodded, then they all went away.

We were alone.

I was alone with *him*, and God, if I couldn't stop looking at him. It was like he was some kind of anomaly and hadn't existed until that moment. I'd felt that way since my parents had been so tight-lipped about him. Whenever I'd asked, they had kind of passed the question off. Jaxen was tired or resting.

But they hadn't said he was perfect.

Not a flaw to him, not even a flush to his skin. The way Mom and Dad *hadn't* said anything about him, I would have thought something was wrong, but he appeared completely normal.

I reached out, my fingers curling to touch him, but something made me hesitate and return my hand to my bed.

Instead, I fingered the ring I'd been told he wanted me to have.

"Why did you give this to me?" I asked, slipping it off. I studied the teeth of the ape and forced my nail between the grooves. I touched this thing enough to know how every space of it felt. I gazed up at Jaxen. "Was it for good luck? Just to get me through this?"

He said nothing, of course, his eyes still closed in slumber, and sighing, I breathed deeply. I placed the ring on his bed, by his thigh.

"They told me what you did," I said, my fingers so close to his leg. "What you did for me. Why did you do that?"

Mom said they could have waited for a donor. My need was urgent, yes, but Jaxen hadn't even allowed consideration of the process after he'd been tested. He'd just donated, no more talk or debate once he'd been cleared.

"You could have died," I said, knowing that people did donate every day, but also died every day

too. If something had gone wrong, if I had lost him…
I swallowed. "You would have been gone, and I
wouldn't have been able to…"

Fingers laced with mine, fingers on his bed
when he lifted and inserted our digits together.

I gazed up to find crystal green eyes staring at
me, so sleepy.

I must have woken him up.

Jaxen uttered no words, just staring at me, and
I wondered for how long.

"How long have you been looking at me?" I
asked, feeling shy now. I mean, I didn't look great.
The swelling on my face had gone down a little, but I
still appeared bruised.

I started to turn away until Jaxen lifted our
fingers. He ran a digit down my cheek, and I swear I
healed in that moment.

That was all it took.

My insides and every physical ache ceased to
throb, a different sensation, a warmer one stirring my
insides now. It was hard to see past it.

It was hard to see beyond him.

"Long enough," he said, a smile to his lips.
His lids hung heavy, and he seemed to be on just as
many pain meds as myself. His chest rose high with a
breath. "So you got them to bring you here?"

I noticed he didn't let go of my hand; if
anything, he forced them tighter together.

Distracted by them, I shifted to the side as
much as I could without hurting myself to the point
of crippling pain. A little discomfort felt worth it in
these moments, though. I smiled. "Dad worked it out.
I wanted to see you. *Thank you* for everything."

They also hadn't told me anything about him,
and I couldn't help worrying. He had donated an

organ for me. So yeah, I worried.

His smile faltered a little after what I said and faded away completely as his gaze fell to the sheet. He noticed the ring I'd taken off, his ring I'd placed by his hip. His lashes flashed up. "You don't want it?"

He actually… *wanted* me to have it? I opened my lips. "I thought…"

He picked it up, and as if instinctual, slid it right back to the place it'd been on my thumb. It was like he knew that's where I'd been wearing it, suddenly my most precious possession.

"I gave this to you," he said, studying the ring on my digit. "It's yours. I wanted you to have it."

He started to retreat, but I held him to me, gripped his big hand. "Thank you."

A nod before he let go, let *me* go, and I didn't know why. Had I said something?

"I was worried when you didn't come by," I admitted. "I see now why. You're still in bed. Are you still sick? Mom and Rick wouldn't tell me anything."

He wouldn't look at me, as if he was lost and wanted that sun through his window to take him away. After a beat, his attention shifted my way. "Over the worst. Just had a bad reaction to the anesthesia. I get to leave tomorrow, though. My moms are in town. They're going to make sure I get back to campus okay."

That made me happy they were here, that he was staying. Hopefully, despite all this we'd both still be able to finish the semester strong and graduate on time.

I nodded. "That's good. I'm glad."

"Yeah. And don't be mad at Dad and your

mom. I told them not to tell you anything. Didn't want you to worry about me."

Well, it hadn't worked.

And I noticed he called him... Dad.

I recalled his final texts that he'd sent me, the ones about my adoptive father and what had happened. Jaxen said Dad had lied to him, but they'd also worked whatever the issue was out. It seemed they really had.

There was no malice there when he spoke about him and I'd be more happy about that if I could get him to actually look at me. Jaxen was avoiding my eyes, like he couldn't keep my gaze and I didn't understand.

"Are you regretting what you did or..." I chewed my lip, shaking my head. "I mean, I'm glad you're okay. Going home? And thank you. You saved my life."

A million times over and I wouldn't be able to thank him enough. I was alive because of him.

But my words certainly didn't help the situation. If anything, it caused tension to stir. Jaxen did nothing but frown in response, his jaw tight. He worked his hair and he returned to his back.

"You're *in here* because of me, Girl Scout," he admitted, eyes suddenly sad. He faced me. "Had I not been sending you all those texts, you wouldn't even have been in this situation. They told me you'd been texting. Texting me?" He shook his head. "I never should have..."

I took his hand.

And this time I didn't let go.

A breath escaped his chest, appearing how I felt the moment I was wheeled into this room and initially saw him. Like his mere presence gave me life. Like just an ounce of his existence brought me peace.

"Me texting was my fault," I said, completely true. He hadn't done anything wrong.

He'd only done something right.

He'd told me how he felt, and that meant more to me than anything else. He'd done that believing I was still mad at him and hadn't expected anything in response. He'd just wanted me to know the truth.

I smiled. "And did they tell you what I'd said? What I'd been texting you back?"

The message hadn't gone through. I saw that when I'd gotten back my phone.

His mouth parted, his head shaking.

"What did you mean when you came in?" he asked, his swallow hard. "You said, you wouldn't have been able to tell me something."

Without words, I brought his fingers up to my mouth. I closed my eyes, just breathing him in, and when I opened them, I had tears in my eyes. I loved him so much, akin to actually breathing. I physically needed him.

And he'd almost taken that away.

"I want you like I've never wanted anything," I said, physically unable to see him through my tears. I sniffed them back. "And if you'd died, I wouldn't have been able to say that. If something had happened during that surgery, I wouldn't have been able to."

I was almost angry with him for that, that he might leave this earth without knowing the truth.

My throat constricted. "I love you, Jaxen."

My tears blinked down as he used our fingers to touch my face. I shied away again, hating how I looked. I had to look awful.

"My face," I started, but he wouldn't let me go there. He pinched my chin.

"This means you're here," he said, his finger lifting and outlining my bruise. I knew because I'd seen it, well aware that's what he traced. "It means you're alive and that *I* can tell you I love you too. Of course, I donated my kidney to you, Girl Scout. I'd give you my heart if I could. Hell, you already have it."

I rasped in his palm, letting him cradle my cheek. Both of our scars meant we were here.

"They cut my hair," I laughed, gazing up at him and I noticed he smiled too. He did through his own emotion coating his eyes, his nostrils flaring.

His thumb ghosted my lips. "And I've never seen you more beautiful. The shit I'm going to do to your ass when I'm out of this bed."

I laughed again, my whole body telling me what a bad idea that was, and when he cringed too in his laughter, I knew he had the same problem. The two of us where a mess.

A beautiful goddamn mess.

"That a promise?" I asked him.

He grinned. "It's a hell fucking yeah."

His fingers slid into my cut hair, and where I would have normally told him not to, that he'd hurt himself even more, I didn't fight him when he leaned over and covered my mouth. I needed that kiss like I needed my next breath.

And something told me he felt the same.

A moan against my mouth, his tongue dragging across mine. He started to deepen it before the ache left his lips and his body seized up.

"Fuck," he breathed, twisting my hair. "I want

you so bad."

And he'd have me, but this would have to be enough for now. I gripped his gown. "Just lay with me. Sleep?"

I didn't know how much longer we'd have together before they'd separate us, and I wanted to just lie with him for awhile.

Jaxen fingered my hair away before taking my hand with a smile. He kissed it before bringing it to his chest. "I'll watch you. I'd love that."

Nodding, I let him lace our hands together, closing my heavy eyes. I felt myself fall into a world of just him and me, our hands together as I drifted off to sleep. This guy would forever be a part of me, a connection that could never be broken for the rest of my life. He literally let me have a piece of him, and no one could take that away. It was ours.

It would be forever.

Epilogue

Jax

I watched my friends get married today.

And it was kinda fucking beautiful.

Royal had pulled out all the stops, his and December's wedding a winter fucking wonderland. It helped that it was smack-dab in the middle of winter. They'd chosen to get married during holiday break before spring semester, and the January wedding provided for snowflakes and frost-covered trees in the town of Maywood Heights.

They'd brought all this shit back home, where it had all began for many of us and brought them together. There were quite a few perks choosing to get married in the Midwestern city, one of which was holding their nuptials at Windsor House, a symbolic place to us all back in high school, and what a sight to be seen that day.

Basically a storybook castle on steroids, the location provided the means for my buddy Royal to pretty much be extra as fuck. I mean, that shit was ridiculous, faux icicles dripping from the ceilings and enough ice sculptures to make Elsa herself roll her eyes. Add to that the twinkling lights and crystal dishes, Windsor House quickly transformed from the headquarters of our youth to the damn Yule Ball out of *Harry Potter*. It was completely my buddy Royal in spades and appeared to make his blushing bride happy. December couldn't keep the grin off her face all day, and I had to say…

That shit was catching.

I'd obviously come to the wedding with Cleo, officially dating now for about three months, but still, once I got up to the front of the aisle I wasn't staring at Royal and December. I mean, they took my attention sporadically, of course. This was their day and all that. But being up front with them, Knight and LJ, and the rest of December's wedding party, I couldn't help but stare at the place reserved for our girlfriends. Cleo sat there, tucked right between Knight's girl Greer and LJ's girl Billie.

And she looked goddamn beautiful.

She'd been so self-conscious for so long after her accident. She'd walked around with her arm in a sling for months and prior to that, her face swollen for weeks. It'd been a long recovery for her, for us both after the transplant, but when the painful memories of that trauma started to subside, she transformed herself. She kept her hair short on purpose now, her dark hair cropped, which gave way to her stunning eyes. Back at the hospital, she'd actually found out they'd saved her hair, and she ended up donating it.

Such a Girl Scout.

I wouldn't take my girl any other way, her petal pink dress in frills and matching the flush on her cheeks. I couldn't keep my eyes off her the whole fucking ceremony.

"Jax?"

I had to be nudged by Knight. He, LJ, and I had done a coin toss for who'd hold the rings since we were all the best men. I'd been the one honored with the deed, but actually missed my fucking cue staring at my girl.

An exaggerated grin as I pulled that shit out of my jacket, making the whole room laugh, but I hadn't done it for them.

I winked at my girl in the first row, making

her smile shyly. She never loved the attention, but I always gave it to her. She waved me off, which got more laughter, but tabling my antics, I made sure to serious myself up and give Royal the rings.

He passed me a bit of an eye when he received them, but that fucker wasn't fooling anyone. He was deliriously happy, and watching both him and December throughout the day thus far told us all that. The pair had done their first look photos before all this even began, and being the nosy fucks we were, Knight, LJ, and I had looked on from a distance with our women.

Needless to say, our friend Royal was brought down to his knees by his bride, his entire face filled with emotion. December had come out in this dress fit for royalty, her train crazy. The photographers snapped away, and they'd have those pictures for the rest of their lives.

Just like this moment now.

"You may now kiss the bride."

Royal took hell of fucking advantage of that moment, clasping December behind the neck and pressing her body up against him. The dude put it completely on her in front of about five hundred people, and I guessed I couldn't blame him. His bride was gorgeous, and had that been my girl and me up there? Yeah, that shit would have been X-rated.

Crazy my mind even went to that place, but it did. I caught Cleo's eyes during their exchange, and my mind may not have been the only one in that place. She smiled so warmly at the pair, her fists clasped. Then, she found me, and her cheeks—well, they shot up like one hundred degrees in color. The two of us may have only been dating for a little while, may have only been directly in each other's lives for so long, but that ceased to matter after what we'd been through. We were linked for life her and me.

I had the scar on my side to prove it.

The happy couple raised their hands together after Royal finally let December go, and the room exploded in applause. Half the town had tried to fight their way into this bitch tonight, the social event of the season. Hell, it was even being televised, and Knight had had the idea to make some money off the venture. The asswipe had sold tickets to online access and had gotten away with it too before Greer busted his ass out. Royal had wanted him to give the money back, but Cleo had suggested donating it.

Gotta love my girl.

I snagged her arm when it was time for the procession to leave, refusing to do so with just Mallick again. As man of honor, he and I had to walk next to each other since I had the rings and needed to be closest to the groom.

Needless to say, he looked relieved as hell to see me grab my girl and actually made room for us to go ahead. Chuckling, he stood at attention, shaking his head before he let us go forward and followed behind. I supposed December could have done worse for her head attendant. He'd done right by her all day and even came to town early to help Royal and the rest of us go over things at Windsor House before the events took place.

I'd never tell him, but he was kind of a stand-up guy and *would never* tell him because I still hadn't forgotten about the whole stripper thing. I obviously hadn't given Cleo a hard time about it, but that didn't mean I was particularly happy about what went down.

I think the other guys kind of felt the same way, but with the joys and smiles of the day flourishing around, it seemed alliances were more sought after than divisions. Happiness was more desired than history. Today was a good day.

So why linger on about things of the past?

That happiness continued on as we all walked down the aisle to "Don't Stop Believin'" by Journey. This was our good friend Paige's favorite song, a way both Royal and December wanted to honor her. It also was fitting for all of us, a fucking bop and had aged hella well. We rocked that shit, making the whole crowd laugh.

Let the reception begin.

Champagne toasts and high spirits filled the night, first dances and stolen kisses in the air. More than one of us escaped off to the more, um, secluded areas of Windsor House with our girls. It was a house once full of secrets, and though tarnished by histories in the past, tonight it was nothing but a place of celebration. I kept Cleo close every reasonable moment I could, but couldn't keep her all night. I had to let her go when the band called for the bouquet toss, but that didn't mean I was happy about it.

"Hurry back," I made her promise, so into this boyfriend shit it wasn't even funny. My buddy LJ had been right. Once this shit happened, it just happened and there was no fighting it.

She dropped her arms around me. "Would it bother you if I caught it? The bouquet?"

We were all well aware of what it meant once a girl got the bouquet. It meant she was supposed to be next, one of us guys next.

I gave her a tap on the ass, telling her my answer. If I honestly thought the world and *our parents* wouldn't find us both fucking crazy for wanting to get married after only three months of dating, I already would have done it. The 'rents were all cool about us dating, but getting married? Probably should let them get used to this scenario a little longer first. Cleo and I both also still had a semester left of school and since we'd been able to catch up despite what had happened last term, I didn't think either of us wanted to get too distracted planning a wedding on top of schooling.

But after all that? Well, who knew, but I think we both did. This girl had one of my kidneys so she might as well just bide the time before I asked.

Like she knew my thoughts, she kissed me, saying she loved me. I returned the same before pushing her on to the group of crazy women clustering on the dance floor. Billie and Greer were already out there like a pack of hungry lionesses, and when Cleo joined, hunkering down, I had a feeling one of them was getting that bouquet.

"Finally decided to let her go, kidney boy?"

This from Knight Reed, lead asshole on the charge of my new *pet* name.

I'd gotten to hear from all the guys about that shit once I'd finally healed and they'd realized I wasn't going to die. The ragging had gone on for weeks, but honestly? I think they all were just a pack of sick fucks who were pissed I'd gotten to look like the hero when they hadn't been able to do that for their own women. Even Royal had grunted when he explained December had been going on and on about how "romantic" the gesture had been. My friends were jealous as hell, and I rubbed that shit in their faces whenever I could.

"Don't hate me because you ain't me," I said,

popping my collar.

Knight got me under his arm, but didn't do it as rough as he might have normally. I think all the guys were being a little lax about the roughhousing since I'd had surgery, but I wasn't going to complain about not getting my ass kicked. If I could get away with calling them shit and ragging on them and they didn't retaliate? That was a fucking win for me.

He relaxed his arm as the other guys fell in, all of us standing around at a couple cocktail tables. It was prime viewing for the Hunger Games across the dance floor over there and LJ had even brought us all a platter of beers.

The groom himself took back a Heineken, grinning like a fool all day. Midas himself wasn't a happier man, and all of us would be damn lucky to even have a smidgen of what he felt on what was clearly the happiest day of his life.

I had a feeling we were all in store for that, and as we watched December head to the front of the dance floor, we all laser-focused our attention. Serious as hell, I don't think LJ, Knight, or me breathed in that moment. December tossed the bouquet, and our heads all flew, even Royal's.

The four of us stood from the table as December, who apparently had A-Rod's arm, launched that thing so far it glided over the sea of screaming women and toward the person lounging casually against the wall. I hadn't seen Ramses Mallick all night.

But if that fucker didn't catch the bouquet.

He looked surprised himself, pushing off the wall with a wobbling grin. An audible groan could be heard from all the women who'd missed, but suddenly, he was the most popular guy in town when like all the girls—well, all but *our* girls—rushed over to him and started instantly chatting him up.

I had to say, the fucker was pretty hot shit when we'd been in high school, being the former mayor's kid and all that. I mean, he wasn't *us*, but he got around the block a bit.

"Well, I'll be damned," LJ said, laughing before taking a swig of his beer. He pushed it down. "Fucker ain't even show up with a date and he's drowning in pussy."

I'd say, laughing with the other guys. We clinked our beers before raising them.

"To whoever's next after Mallick, I guess," Royal said, his shoulders bumping in laughter before taking a drink. He gestured his beer toward me. "Will it be you, kidney boy? We've all noticed your ring on Cleo's thumb."

And it hadn't left since I'd given it to her, wouldn't just like their rings would leave their girls. December had even placed hers as part of her bouquet, a special one that obviously hadn't gone to Mallick's ass.

I shrugged. "I'm not opposed to it."

"You better fucking not. At least, not right now and make *us* look like assholes." Knight waved between LJ and himself. "You already donated a kidney to the girl. Why don't you let LJ or me have this one?"

"Yeah, I'd never hear the end of that shit if you got married first." LJ chuckled. "Billie would have my ass."

"Only after Greer gave me back my balls." Knight grunted. He shot a finger at me. "No proposing. Not until you ask us first."

"Aww." I batted my eyes. "I didn't know you

guys felt that way about me. But *two* handsome suitors vying for my heart?" I put my hands together dramatically. "How will I ever decide between you both?"

Okay, so *that* I wasn't getting away with. They both went for me like it was open season, and Royal watched on from the best seat of the house.

I honestly didn't think any of us would ever grow up, and I hoped we wouldn't. Growing up made you serious. Growing up made you hard, and I think, at least for me, I'd had enough of that. We were all past the places of trying to control every little thing. We wanted to be happy, *had found happiness*, and there was no going back after that.

The women in our lives made us better men, better brothers. They made us all see the world in a different way and accept that there was more to it than pain, suffering, hatred, or even revenge. But most importantly, they allowed us to see that life, at least mine, didn't have to be so hard.

As far as I was concerned, my girlfriend Cleo had given me a second chance at an actual life instead of a half one. I hadn't been living before. Not until she found me.

And she thought I saved her.

CPSIA information can be obtained
at www.ICGtesting.com
Printed in the USA
BVHW041417301122
653118BV00003B/84

9 798682 270293